Denial

Jackie Kennedy

Affinity
eBook Press
NZ

Denial
© Jackie Kennedy 2013

Affinity E-Book Press NZ Ltd.
Canterbury, New Zealand

First Edition

All rights reserved.
ISBN: 978-0-9922548-5-8

No part of this e-Book may be reproduced in any form without the express permission of the author and publisher. Please note that piracy of copyrighted materials violate the author's rights and is Illegal.

This is a work of fiction. Names, character, places, and incidents are the product of the author's imagination or are used fictitiously and any resemblance to actual persons living or dead, businesses, companies, events, or locales is entirely coincidental.

Editor: Ruth Stanley
Cover Design: Nancy Kaufman

Acknowledgments

I wrote *Denial* and put it on The Athenaeum at Xenaficton.net, which is a great source for all types of original lesbian fiction and one my favourite sites. I posted it there, not thinking—given some of the brilliant writers who post there—that it would get more than a few hits. As it turned, Denial got much more than a few hits! So much so, that Affinity came knocking and here I am about to publish my first novel...*who knew!*

I'd like to thank The Athenaeum site owners, Bardeye and WebWarrior. Cheers for starting me on this journey.

A special thank you to my editor, Ruth for helping me make *Denial* what it is today.

Dedication

To Lorna

Table of Contents

Chapter 1 1
Chapter 2 4
Chapter 3 8
Chapter 4 14
Chapter 5 20
Chapter 6 26
Chapter 7 35
Chapter 8 41
Chapter 9 51
Chapter 10 57
Chapter 11 61
Chapter 12 69
Chapter 13 79
Chapter 14 83
Chapter 15 92
Chapter 16 95
Chapter 17 105
Chapter 18 111
Chapter 19 117
Chapter 20 122
Chapter 21 129
Chapter 22 134
Chapter 23 140
Chapter 24 144
Chapter 25 151
Chapter 26 159
Chapter 27 167
Chapter 28 175
Chapter 29 180
Chapter 30 185
Chapter 31 193
Chapter 32 203
Chapter 34 218
Chapter 35 228
Chapter 36 238
Chapter 37 248
Chapter 38 256

Chapter 39..270
Chapter 40..277
Chapter 41..280
Chapter 42..285
Chapter 43..292
Chapter 44..303
Chapter 45..315
Chapter 46..321
Chapter 47..330
Chapter 48..336
Chapter 49..346
Chapter 50..353
Chapter 51..359
Chapter 52..366
Chapter 53..372
Chapter 54..383
Chapter 55..388
Epilogue...393
About the Author..402

Denial

Chapter 1

Amy pulled nervously on the hem of her loose-fitting, paint-splattered sweatshirt and watched Josh hug his sister. A few inches shorter than his six foot two, Celeste's dark hair moved around her shoulders as she hugged him tightly. Her striking hazel-green eyes blazed with happiness.

Amy had waited a long time for this meeting. Hopping from one foot to the next, she noted how similar they were in coloring and complexion. Feeling a mess, she pulled her sleeves over her hands and wished for the zillionth time that she hadn't hastily thrown the sweatshirt on this morning.

Releasing Celeste, Josh introduced her.

"Hi," Amy said, holding out her hand.

Although painting was her passion, Amy was in her final year at university, and was working on her first real architectural project at a local farmhouse. Yesterday, she had made the fatal mistake of telling the farmer that she hadn't ridden since she was tiny. Being pushy, he had her saddled up within the hour telling her it was a docile mare and not to worry. And Amy didn't until the mare left her flat on her arse halfway down the paddock.

A visit to the ER convinced Amy, as she hobbled home, that nothing short of a frontal lobotomy would force her back in the saddle. It wasn't until this morning, staring at a fat lip and a nose so swollen it could hide a pair of Manolo Blahniks, that she saw the full impact of the evil little mare's antics.

Celeste slowly took her hand.

Embarrassed, Amy realized Celeste wouldn't believe this badly dressed, frazzled, bruised creature standing before her was, in fact, her twin's fiancée.

Amy shook hands, and wished *again* that she hadn't let Josh talk her into coming with him to the airport. Celeste was a doctor, he had told her as he cajoled her out the door, one who had treated all kinds of injuries and wouldn't be fazed by a few bruises. Now would she?

Amy tried giving the brunette her most charming smile, but the swelling made it lopsided. "Nice to meet you," she said, feeling what little confidence she had left slip away.

"What truck hit you?" Celeste asked, eyeing her.

Jeez...nice to meet you too?

Not sure if Celeste was really snarking or teasing, and feeling far too fragile anyway, Amy replied, "The *truck* was a ten-year-old mare named Ginger who went completely rodeo on me."

Celeste raised her eyebrows, but didn't say anything.

Not even a twitch of a smile, Amy thought, feeling the first tendrils of dislike.

"I've really missed you, Celeste," Josh said. He beamed a huge grin at his sister.

Amy closed her eyes briefly and fought an unusual urge to whack him for sweet-talking her.

"I've missed you too," Celeste said then grinned back at him.

Oh...all soft and cuddly now, are you? Cow!

Hugging Celeste Josh whispered, "I can't believe it's taken this long for us to get together." He gripped her shoulders. "Every friggin' time I try to catch up with you you're off on another adventure. Nigeria for vaccinations; Guatemala for the hurricanes. Where's your next stop?"

"Somalia."

He let her shoulders go. "For how long?"

"It depends on how long they need me."

He frowned. "I worry about you." He touched her cheek.

Amy eyed the small scar that ran from the corner of Celeste's right eye to the tip of her cheekbone. She hadn't noticed it in the family photos. Amy chewed on her bottom lip suddenly aware that all she really knew about the brunette was that she worked for Médecins sans Frontières, was based in Paris and had that French chic look nailed.

"Josh, right now, I'm here," Celeste said gently. "Well, some part of me is here." She frowned. "It seems my luggage is on its way somewhere else."

Denial

An airline representative approached them. The woman was small, slight and looked very tired. "Ms. Cameron, it's not great news, I'm afraid," she said, looking at her watch. "Your luggage is scheduled to arrive in London in the next hour."

Celeste looked at her. "*Seriously?*"

The woman's cell phone rang. "Yes, and I'm so sorry about this," she said. "Please excuse me, I won't be a moment." She walked away to take the call.

"This is unbelievable," Celeste said. "Twice this has happened in the last two months!"

Josh shrugged. "We'll get it sorted."

"Josh, right now I don't care what happens to my luggage." Celeste looked at the official. "It's taken me thirty-six hours to get here." She eyed the exit. "I'm outta here."

Startled, Amy watched Celeste walk away. She blinked then looked at Josh.

Josh ran a hand through his hair. "Can you take care of this?"

"Eh?" Amy asked. "Take care of what?"

"Could you give the woman my contact details?"

Unable to believe Celeste had stomped off, Amy glared at Josh. "Whoa...you're joking right!" She pointed in Celeste's direction. "I know Celeste is tired but who does she think she is just walking away like that." Amy shook her head. "And what kind of comment was that about what hit me?" she asked. "Didn't you tell me she was in the caring profession?" Amy crossed her arms. "Who does that woman care for...*corpses?*"

"Honey...please," Josh said, rubbing her arms. "Look, Celeste gets really cranky when she's jet-lagged," he said as if the explanation excused his sister's behavior. "I'll take her to the car and meet you out front in a few minutes. Okay?"

Before Amy had a chance to respond he was gone.

Mortified by how shabby and how much of a bruiser she appeared a flush rose all the way up Amy's cheeks and straight to her blonde hairline. She tried to smile as the airline official approached her.

Chapter 2

One year later

"*Merde,*" Felice forced out. She tried to scream but her lungs emptied. The sound of gunfire surrounded them. She reached blindly for Celeste. "Do not let me die... Not here...not in this!"

It was raining hard. Celeste grasped Felice's wet hand. "I won't."

Eyes wide, the doctor searched Celeste's face. "I...wanted to...go with you." She struggled to get the words out. "Meet your family."

Drenched, Celeste choked back a sob. "You will." She pushed wet hair tenderly from her colleague's face. "I promise."

Felice screamed. She gripped Celeste's hand and writhed in pain. Her neck corded as she struggled to draw breath.

Freeing her hand from Felice's grip Celeste threw open her medikit and searched through it. "I think your lung's collapsed."

"I...can...feel...it!" Her face ashen, Felice sucked in air. "I...am...suffocating."

Hands shaking Celeste struggled to rip open the blood-soaked shirt. She paled when she saw the injury. It was a sucking chest wound. She fought back panic when Felice coughed up blood. Shaking, she wiped the rain from her eyes and focused. She examined the entry hole. There was no doubt a lung had collapsed.

Felice's eyelids fluttered wildly. Gasping, her mouth opened fully dragging in air. Swallowing, she gagged on her own blood.

Celeste dug through her medikit. There was no occlude dressing.

"*Fuck!*"

Celeste needed something at least three times the size of the wound to prevent the dressing from being sucked in. Her eyes fixed on the plastic wrapping tucked into the side of the medikit. She grabbed for it. Drawing in a shaky breath she pulled tape from her medikit and tried to tape the plastic around the wound.

"It hurts…like fuck!" Felice shouted, shaking violently.

"Now you swear," Celeste said. "And here I thought it was just me that liked to cuss." She tried to smile. "I knew you had it in you."

Felice whispered, "How…long…do I have?"

Celeste looked at her and saw the terror in those dark blue eyes. She opened her mouth, but nothing came out.

"Tell me!" Felice gasped.

As doctors they both knew the first hour was the golden. Survival depended on whether you could stabilize the patient during those precious sixty minutes.

Felice groaned.

Relief filled Celeste when she saw James with another field nurse running toward her. "Thank God, you're here," she yelled at him.

Celeste looked at the carnage around her. The militia had been brutal today. Celeste had been in Somalia for almost a year. Felice had been here only a few months. Their team arrived in the compound a week ago to treat what should have been routine medical problems but they had struggled with the number of gunshot wounds.

"Tell me!"

Needing to get Felice to a trauma center and onto an operating table, Celeste said, "We've got time."

James dropped to his knees into a puddle beside them. "Jesus," he said, staring at Felice.

Celeste glanced over her shoulder to the other nurse who was running to the injured young boy near her. Since the team had arrived the militia made it clear they had a shoot-to-kill policy should any internee try to leave. To her utter despair, they were enforcing the policy liberally.

"What happened?" James asked as he stared at Felice.

"We were waiting for the copter," Celeste replied. She pointed to the boy the other nurse was working on. "He ran toward us with a solider chasing him." She dug through her medikit. "The maniac was firing at him. The only reason the bastard stopped shooting was he realized his captain was with us." Rage etched her face. "By that time Felice and the boy were down." She looked upward. "Where's the copter?"

"It was shot at on its way here." Rain flew off James head when he shook it. "It's not coming."

"What?" Celeste looked at him in disbelief.

"It couldn't land," he replied.

"What are the options?"

"We can't stay. The soldiers are on a killing spree. It's no longer just about the people trying to leave the compound." He searched through the medikit and yelled over a burst of gunfire. "We have to evacuate by road. The ambulances are ready."

Celeste shouted. "How many people are down?"

"Too many." He shook his head. "We can't take them all."

Aware how poorly equipped with medical equipment the few old, battle-scarred ambulances were Celeste fought back tears. She knew James meant they should only take the people who would survive the journey. The roadblocks the militia had set up between the compound and the hospital meant it would be difficult to get there.

Hiding her fear, Celeste refocused on Felice and quickly relayed her vital stats. "She has a punctured lung. It's collapsed. I've occluded it. There's a pressure dressing on her chest wound, but I need to get a line in."

Unrolling a pressure cuff, James began working on Felice as Celeste opened an IV line. "Her pupils are sluggish," he said as he puffed up the cuff.

Working, Celeste shook her head. "I know, but we've got time."

James pressed a stethoscope on the crook of Felice's arm.

Celeste looked down at the beautiful French woman. She was struggling to stay conscious. The blood loss and lack of oxygen would soon cause her organs to fail. "Felice," she said, putting her hands on the doctor's face. "Listen to me. Keep fighting. We're going to make it. Just hang in there. Please, just...stay with us!"

"She's shocked already," James said, letting the air hiss out of the cuff.

Celeste ignored him. "Just hang in there."

Felice's eyes lost focus and fluttered closed.

"We're going to get you out of this," Celeste said desperately. She stroked Felice's face. "I promise."

James grabbed Celeste's arm. "She's unconscious. We can't stabilize her here!" He quickly stood when an ambulance careened to a stop near them. "She's taken a K6 hit," he yelled to the driver.

Standing, Celeste's hands balled into fists as the rain battered down. K6 was medical shorthand for someone being hit in a kill zone. Bile swamped her mouth. She gagged then spat, horrified that Felice had just been written off.

Chapter 3

Maggie opened the front door and heard Josh muttering from behind the large potted plant he was struggling to hold. She pushed the door wide. "Not another one!"

"Help me!" Josh said as he shuffled through the door.

Maggie grabbed the base and they made their way down the hall and took it out to the backyard. They put the pot down.

Maggie eyed the growing number of plants. "It's beginning to look like the Everglades out here."

Josh stretched his back.

"You should've never encouraged her to leave Scotland, Joshie," she said. "Cold weather means fewer plants."

"Amy should have studied landscape gardening not architecture," Josh said, looking around him.

"Yes. She should have." Maggie ruffled his hair. "Anyway, I thought you two were going to Irene's barbeque?"

"We are, but you know Amy, she wants to get things organized before the move." He eyed Maggie then said teasingly, "She takes after her mom that way."

Maggie's eyes narrowed. "Yeah, let's hope that's the only thing she takes from her."

Josh laughed. "Yet another grudge you can notch up against her mom then?"

"Too right," Maggie replied and headed for the kitchen.

"Hi," Amy said, sliding the two small plant pots she was carrying onto the work surface. "Just in?" she asked, quirking an eyebrow at her cousin.

Maggie had a fiery mop of short red hair and the most amazing green eyes. At five foot seven Amy wasn't small, but her cousin's six-foot frame easily towered over her, particularly when she wore her biker boots.

Maggie ignored her. She opened the fridge and rustled through it.

Denial

"Are you?"

Maggie dipped her head into the fridge and mumbled something.

"What was that?" Amy asked, coming closer.

Maggie pulled out some snacks. She looked at her cousin and said sheepishly, "I got caught in a storm."

"Oh...a...storm?"

"Yes!"

"Really?"

Maggie muttered under her breath.

"There wasn't a storm last night."

"Was!" Maggie said, taking an armful of food out of the fridge.

"What kind of storm?"

Exasperated Maggie sighed. "An electrical kind of storm with lightning and other thingies." She put her snacks down. "A storm that hisses then crackles then hisses again and blows a few things up." She opened a packet of cheese and put it and other things on three slices of bread. "What other types of storms are there?"

Amy smiled slowly. "Well. Let's see there's figment-of-your-imagination type of storms that stop you from coming home."

"Yeah?" Maggie sandwiched the bread together and bit into it. She chewed. "I couldn't comth home becauth there wath fog as well."

"Oh! Not just an electric storm with thingies blowing up...but fog too!" Amy said, cocking her head. "No wonder you couldn't come home."

Nodding enthusiastically, Maggie bit another large chunk from her sandwich. "Yeth...exacthly."

"I think it's right about now," Amy said, her eyes shining with humor, "that you should be telling me what you got up to last night."

Maggie defiantly bit into her sandwich.

Amy looked at her cousin and thought no matter how carefully constructed her tomboy look was there was no hiding her features. She was a stunner.

"So...where were you last night?"

"I'm the older cousin, remember?"

"Don't change the subject."

"Eh...a frat party."

"You're kidding...a *frat party!*" Amy shook her head. "Are you cradle-snatching now?"

Josh walked into the kitchen and gave his fiancé a quick kiss. "Bye, hon."

"Where are you going?" Amy asked as she reached out to smooth down his dark hair.

"To pick up Celeste?"

"What about the barbeque?"

"It's okay," he said. "We'll be there by three."

Amy frowned. "Okay."

"See you later, cradle-snatcher," Josh called out to Maggie as he made his way down the hall.

"Bye, bye Joshie boy," Maggie called after him. She finished her sandwich. "I didn't know his sister was here."

"Yeah," Amy replied her frown deepening. "She flew in a few days ago."

"You met her before you moved here didn't you?"

"Celeste came to stay in Glasgow for a few days last year when Josh was finishing his studies."

"I must have been hiking."

Amy nodded. Maggie was a keen hiker.

"Yes, I remember now," Maggie said. "You two didn't get along. There was a bit of fracas wasn't there at the airport or something?"

"Hardly a fracas, Maggie," Amy said, sounding annoyed. "We just didn't click." She raised a hand. "And before you ask, I'm going to make a real effort to get on with her this time."

"Does she still work for that organization...whatitsname?"

"Médecins sans Frontières," Amy replied. Her eyes narrowed as she recalled that first meeting with Celeste over a year ago. For most of Celeste's stay she'd made every excuse to avoid spending time with her.

Taking a carton of apple juice out of the fridge, Maggie filled two glasses and handed one to Amy.

"You're coming this afternoon, aren't you?" Amy asked, accepting the cool glass.

Maggie shrugged. "Maybe."

Amy sighed. "We already talked about this and you agreed."

Maggie made a face.

"Oh, c'mon. Maggie! Don't pull this stunt on me. Not today."

"Don't blame me...blame your mother," Maggie said, leaning against the breakfast bar. "She's always interfering."

"Maggie," Amy paused and caught her temper. Knowing this could end in an argument, she breathed in deeply. "Look, she just wants us all to get together to talk about your outfit."

"Outfit...*frilly dress*, you mean!" Maggie looked down at herself. "Look at me. I'm a biker."

"I need you there today."

Maggie ran a hand through her short red hair. "Amy, you know I haven't worn a dress since I was at school, and even then it was a struggle to get me into one. And you're letting her make me wear a stupid outfit to give you away!"

"You'll be wearing the same dress as Caitlin and Rosie."

"Exactly. They're kids! And it's just marginally acceptable to look like a bloody Oompa-Loompa when you're a kid!"

"Aw c'mon, your dress isn't that bad."

"Yes, it bloody is."

Amy eyed her cousin. "It's not."

Maggie stared back. "You wear it then."

"Okay," Amy conceded. "I guess it has a little bit of a flair to it and—"

"*A bit!*" Maggie snorted. "It has more flair than a Samba dancer."

"Please," Amy said, clasping her hands together. "Pretty please. Go on for little ol' me."

"No."

Amy widened her eyes and pouted. "You owe me."

"How?"

"*How?*" Amy replied. Her eyes widened. "Well, let's start with your DIY disaster last week."

"It wasn't a disaster. It was more like a wee technical hitch."

"A wee technical hitch was it?" Amy replied with relish.

"I was changing a bulb that's all."

"You fell off a ladder which fell through a window and smashed it," Amy said. "On your way down you grabbed the ceiling fan and ripped the whole thing off. And to top it all, you landed on a brand-new table that I'd just bought and shattered it!"

Maggie huffed. "I told you I had vertigo."

"So you did," Amy said, nodding. "And that's why I told you I would do it."

Maggie eyeballed her cousin. "It was a one off."

"Was it?" Amy said. "What about the tree you cut down?"

"What about it?"

"It took out next door's greenhouse?"

"It was an accident."

"Really?" Amy replied. "Funny, they didn't see it that way. I had to plan an extension for their daughter…*free gratis!*"

"It's a tiny extension."

"Still means you owe me."

They stared each other out.

"Okay," Maggie said eventually. "I owe you," she mumbled. "But, I still think the dress is ugly."

Amy tried to hide her smile. "And your preferred choice is better?"

Maggie grinned. "Yup."

"Really? Leather is better?"

"I'm talking snug-fitting, all-in-one black leather."

"God only knows what kind of outfit you would have me wear," Amy raised her brow. "Some hot bunny outfit for sure!"

"Now we're talking." Maggie grinned then sighed when Amy gave her that look. "Okay, cuz, I've got your back." She wiggled her eyebrows. "Me in a frock…who knew!"

"Thank you."

Denial

Maggie looked out the window to the backyard. "When are you moving the botanical gardens to your new place?"

"Soon," Amy answered.

"How's the house coming along?"

"Do you want the short or long answer?"

"Short."

Her eyes fired up. "Fantastic."

Maggie went to her cousin and hugged her. "You're unbelievable, you know that?"

"Why?" Amy hugged her back.

"Because, hon, it's *you* that should be going all bridezilla on us." She tapped Amy's nose. "Not your mother."

Amy's eyes narrowed.

Letting her go, Maggie raised her hands. "Okay…okay, I've got your back, remember!"

Chapter 4

"Come in for a swim," Josh said, treading water at the edge of the pool. It was late afternoon and they had been at Irene's house for a couple of hours.

"In a little while," Amy replied. She laughed when her six-year-old half-sister, Caitlin, ran up and jumped into the pool.

"Josh!" Caitlin squealed in delight when he grabbed her and tossed her in the air.

Rosie, at four years old, was more hesitant. Wanting to watch she reached for Amy's hand but soon let go when Josh encouraged her into the water.

"Amy," Maggie called out.

Turning, Amy watched her lanky cousin flop onto a sun lounger. She made her way over and took the one next to her.

Passing with a tray of cold drinks Irene smiled at Amy.

Smiling back at her mom Amy acknowledged that Irene really was involved with *all* the wedding arrangements. But, wasn't that the role of any devoted parent? This new devotion struck a sad note of irony with her. It had been years since she had been close to her mother. They were, in fact, strangers.

"I still think it's weird you end up settling down in a place where your mum stays," Maggie said. "What do you think the odds are of that happening?"

"Not great when my own mother gave Josh my number."

"Yeah," Maggie replied teasingly. "Like I said, she's always interfering."

Amy rolled her eyes.

"Your dad—"

Amy drew in a sharp breath.

"Sorry," Maggie said as she patted Amy's leg.

Ten years ago Irene divorced her father and moved to Sarasota with her new husband. Staying behind in Scotland, Amy hadn't had much contact with her mother after that. Sheer serendipity brought them together now. Last year her father had died suddenly from an aneurysm. As much as she loved Maggie, Amy still found it too painful to talk about him. She closed her eyes briefly to hide their bleakness. She missed him so much.

"And I'm really sorry about going on about the wedding this morning." Maggie passed Amy a beer. "It's just a pity it's not as low-key as you wanted."

"You know more than anyone that Irene's missed a huge part of my life." Amy sighed. "She just wants to be involved, that's all."

"I know," Maggie said apologetically. "And I'm not helping the situation."

"This is just her way of making up for lost time," Amy said. "I don't have the heart to tell her the wedding is getting out of hand." She fired a warning look. "And I don't want you telling her either. We're lucky she's doing it." Taking a mouthful of beer Amy swirled it around then swallowed. She stared off into the distance. "I keep telling myself it's only one day."

Maggie eyed her cousin carefully then frowned. "Yeah…that's right…it's just *one* day."

Deep in thought, Amy peeled the label off her bottle.

"She's something else isn't she?" Maggie said.

"Who?"

"Twinnie."

Amy looked over at Celeste.

"What's she doing here anyway?"

"*Celeste*," Amy said, "is here on a break…I think?" She frowned. "I got the impression she had a bit of a rough time on her last assignment."

"What happened?"

Amy shrugged. "Not sure. But she was working in Somalia and things hit the proverbial fan."

Maggie looked at her expectantly.

"I don't know the details," Amy said, holding up her hands. "You know Josh, he's vague at the best of times."

"I heard that she used to be a swimmer."

"Yes."

Maggie sighed. "I might have to move back home after all."

"Why?"

"Whaddayathink," Maggie replied, pointing at Celeste. "My pussy will shrivel up and fall off if she's the type of competition I'm up against."

"With any luck it'll shrivel up soon!" Amy said. Maggie's slut counter had hit stratospheric numbers over the last few months.

"What do you call a blonde with half a brain?"

Entering easily into their blonde and redhead banter, Amy sat up and crossing her eyes replied playfully, "Uh...dunno?"

"Gifted!" Winking, Maggie put her shades on.

Amy stuck out her tongue.

They lounged in silence for a while

"She's gorgeous, isn't she?"

"Who?"

"Celeste!"

Amy shrugged.

"She's got a great body, hasn't she?"

Amy didn't respond.

"You could take her on."

Amy glanced at Celeste. "I don't know what parallel universe you've been hitching a ride to recently, but my stats in no way match hers."

"You definitely stack a better rack," Maggie said. She scooped out some ice from the cooler and tossed it at Amy.

"Hoy!" Amy picked up the piece of ice that landed on her stomach. "Behave," she said. She sipped some beer.

Maggie laughed. "Okay. So, are we still playing golf tomorrow with Josh and Celeste?"

Amy nodded. "Yes, in the morning."

Maggie yawned. "I think I'll have a nap. I'm jiggered. Wake me up in an hour, please."

Drinking the remainder of her beer Amy listened as Maggie's breathing evened out. She eyed Celeste and thought Maggie was right, she was gorgeous.

Suddenly, Celeste turned and looked directly at Amy.

"Shit!"

Blushing furiously, Amy threw herself down and lay flat out. Throwing an arm over her eyes she bit her bottom lip and groaned, embarrassed that Celeste had caught her openly staring.

†

It was at the tail end of the evening. Josh and Celeste were playing their final set of tennis. Watching them, Amy glanced over at Maggie, who was now stretched out on a lounger, snoring after drinking beer with Sophie, Josh's younger sister, all afternoon.

Amy watched Sophie stagger toward her. Noticing, not for the first time, how extremely pale-skinned she was for living in such a hot climate.

Sophie nudged Amy up the bench. "Do you want some of my beer?" she asked, waving her bottle and trying to settle her legs under the table.

"I'm fine, thanks," Amy said, reaching out a hand to steady Sophie.

"How's the book coming along?" Amy asked. Sophie was in the process of publishing her first book. Amy had read it, and although she appreciated the writing, horror wasn't really her thing.

"Fine," Sophie slurred.

Amy looked Sophie over appreciating her distinct ingénue look—small with jet-black short hair and deep brown eyes. She was pretty...very pretty. Amy remembered when they first met she'd found Sophie difficult, but recently they clicked. And now she really liked Sophie's quirky personality.

Leaning close, Sophie said, "Did you know Celeste was married?"

Wondering where that had come from, Amy blinked. "Uhmm..."

"Did you know she was only married for one year?"

Amy resisted rolling her eyes. Sophie had caught Maggie's *'did you know'* trivia. "I don't know much about her to be honest."

"She doesn't keep in contact with him anymore," Sophie said, waving her hand.

"Who?"

Sophie hiccupped. "Nick."

Tired, Amy carefully looked at her watch before asking, "Who's Nick?"

"Her ex, of course." Sophie eyed Amy. "Did you know I had a major...*major*...crush on him?"

"Really!"

"In fact," Sophie slurred, "I would say I was in love with him." She swallowed. "You should have seen him, Amy." Her eyes lost focus. "He was absolutely gorgeous. Tall, dark, you know, the usual, but he didn't take himself too seriously." Sophie focused on the blonde. "The only thing he took seriously was her." She pointed a finger in Celeste's direction. "He was madly in love with her but my darling sister thought she'd made a mistake." Sophie hiccupped. "A pretty big goddamn friggin' mistake, if you ask me."

Sophia pushed a flop of dark hair from her face. "Anyway, he was devastated when they split and tried everything to get the marriage back on track, but it just didn't happen."

Intrigued, Amy asked, "Why did they break up?"

"All relationships end, Amy," Sophie said then shrugged.

Not sure how she should take this information since she would be marrying Josh soon, Amy resisted the urge to open up the conversation. Tonight, she didn't want to get involved in one of Sophie's philosophical discussions.

"Ultimately," Sophie said. "He changed, I guess. I think it all came down to the fact that he struggled at med school and when he flunked, he couldn't handle her success."

Just then, the Cameron family's Labrador, Bud, decided to interrupt. Barking, he padded over. Looking for attention, he gently pawed Sophie's leg.

Denial

"You want something to eat, baby?" Sophie asked. Swaying precariously, she tried to get up from the table. "Don't worry Buddy boy, I'll take care of you... Oh..."

Keeling over, Sophie took Amy with her.

Chapter 5

"I wish I'd remembered my hat," Amy said, pulling strands of hair from her mouth. "I think I've managed to eat half the hair on my head this morning." Breathing in deeply, she looked around. "But it's worth it. What a beautiful morning."

"It's a shame Josh had to work," Maggie said, dropping her golf bag at her feet.

"His boss called looking for information that couldn't wait until Monday."

"Too bad we're out here and he's cooped up."

Amy nodded. Since moving to Sarasota Josh's work was beginning to seriously encroach on their personal life.

"Do you know we've hardly played any golf since we got here?"

"I know."

"Do you know why that is?"

Amy shook her head.

"Men," Maggie whispered teasingly. "You're rolling over too easy for them. Well, one in particular."

"*Me!*" Amy replied loudly. Aware Maggie had not stopped shagging since she got here, she replied indignantly, "What about you!"

"Shhh," Maggie said. "Celeste's trying to play her shot."

Suddenly aware of Maggie's ploy, Amy blushed furiously. She looked over at the brunette and smiled apologetically. Maggie was a good golfer, and because Amy had a similar handicap, they often teased each other. It was routine for them to try anything to get an advantage.

Celeste smiled then prepared to take her shot.

"That's some killer smile she's got."

Amy nodded and watched Celeste take the shot.

"She's good," Maggie said, watching the ball travel down the fairway. "You sure Joshie was right when he said she hadn't played in a while?"

"I don't know." Amy shrugged. "You asked him."

"Hmmm, I expected this round to be easy," Maggie whispered. "I bet Josh a hundred bucks I'd take her."

"Well, there's your answer," Amy whispered back then grinned. "Josh would never look a big fat gift horse in the mouth."

Maggie glared at her then reached into her bag, removed her driver, and strode off.

Amused, Amy watched her cousin take a few practice swings. She smiled at Celeste when she approached and stood next to her. Since Celeste's return home Amy hadn't spent any time with her. If she were honest, she hadn't gone out of her way to be around her.

Feeling awkward, Amy watched Maggie prepare for her shot while surreptitiously eyeing the brunette.

Aware she hadn't said anything to Celeste and knowing she should make some sort of effort, Amy asked, "Are you going to lunch at your folks after this?"

Celeste shook her head. "No, I've got plans."

"Oh," Amy replied. Not able to think of anything else to say she watched Maggie tee off.

"Uchhhh," Maggie cried out when her shot landed in the rough. "Ya bugger!" Throwing her club down, she stormed past them muttering she needed to pee and was going to find a bush...*somewhere!*

Celeste eyed Amy. "Is she always so sweet-natured?"

Relieved she could see the humor in the situation, Amy nodded. "Yes, especially, when losing—"

"Money to Josh," Celeste interrupted.

"Yes," Amy said in surprise. "How did you know?"

"I used to play a lot of golf."

"Did he tell you Maggie expected to win?"

"Yes." Celeste smiled slowly.

"Oh?" Amy replied. She suddenly realized Josh and Celeste had set her cousin up. "Does he always get a return on his bets?"

"Mostly."

Surprised at being teased, Amy eyed Celeste.

"Are you settling in okay?"

"Yes," Amy replied. "I'm still missing home, but I'm getting used to it now."

"Missing anything in particular?"

"Yeah. Fish and chips." Amy grinned. "I miss that the most."

"Really?" Celeste said in surprise then laughed warmly. "Fish and chips, huh…who knew?"

"What do you miss when you're not in Paris?"

Celeste looked thoughtful. "Lots of things, but mostly movies. The French take their movies very seriously."

"Really?"

Celeste nodded.

"Sorry folks," Maggie said, striding toward them.

Knowing she didn't have the heart to tell Maggie she was being royally swindled, Amy just nodded and tried to hide her amusement behind a comforting smile.

†

After losing badly to Celeste, Amy and Maggie headed to Josh's parents for lunch as arranged.

After lunch, Maggie left as she had plans for the afternoon.

While Amy was waiting for Josh, Camille, Josh's mother, insisted she relax by the pool, which she did and promptly fell asleep.

When Amy opened her eyes some time later, Celeste was making her way over to her. Surprised, she sat up.

"Oh, hi," Amy said. She looked at her watch then raised her hand to shade the sun. "I thought you had a lunch date?"

"A change of plan," Celeste replied. "Something came up and Alex couldn't make it." She removed her sarong. "Have you met Alex?"

Eyes widening, Amy nodded. She watched Celeste reveal a black bikini. She couldn't help but agree with Maggie that she had an amazing body. Celeste still had the build of a swimmer.

Her dark hair was off her face. Her olive skin offset the clarity of her hazel-green eyes. Amy eyed her appraisingly. Her eyes drifted down and lingered on her tanned chest and full breasts before moving to follow the outline of her defined stomach. She stopped at the small tattoo around her belly button. Intrigued, she studied its detail.

Celeste cleared her throat.

Amy looked up.

Clearly amused, Celeste lifted her brow inquisitively.

"Uhmm..." Amy uttered. Dismayed she was caught staring her cheeks flared. "Yes," she said, turning pink. "Yes. I've met Alex. He's...he's a really nice guy."

Feeling exposed Amy hurriedly stood. Looking for a distraction, she picked up her T-shirt, and slipped it on before tightening her ponytail.

Moving closer, Celeste whispered in her ear, "Your label's sticking out."

Amy almost choked on her tongue when Celeste's fingers lightly brushed the back of her neck as she tucked the label away. In complete surprise, she looked at Celeste. Tingling coursed through her. Her blush deepened. "Thank you."

Celeste smiled.

Needing a distraction Amy asked, "Would you like a beer?"

Celeste nodded.

Amy reached into the cooler and opened a beer. She passed it to the brunette. Trying to shake off her sudden nervousness she said, "Your mom insisted I relax with a few beers." She looked into the cooler. "Camille must think I drink like a fish, there's a stack in here."

Laughing, Celeste settled on the lounger next to Amy's. Lying back, she drank some beer then sighed heavily. She placed the bottle on her tanned stomach then looked up at her. "Join me?"

"Oh…Okay," Amy replied. Slowly, she sat down on her lounger then stretched out.

Celeste closed her eyes. "This is lovely," she said almost wearily. "I miss being home."

Amy nodded. "Yes, I know what you mean."

Celeste looked at her.

Feeling a sudden twinge of homesickness, Amy peeled the label from her bottle. "You must have found it difficult being away from home."

"Yes." Celeste watched Amy's fingers. "I didn't intend for it to be so long, but my work makes it…difficult." She clicked her tongue. "I haven't really stopped in the last year."

Aware something had happened in Somalia, Amy wanted to ask her if she was okay but instinctively knew the question would not be welcomed. "You'll be glad your home now," she said lamely.

"I…" Celeste shook her head. Her face darkened.

"What?" Amy asked gently.

"It's…complicated," Celeste said then half-smiled.

Aware Celeste's thoughts weren't in a good place Amy changed the subject. "I don't know if Josh has mentioned to you, but I'm throwing a bachelorette party." She paused then asked, "Would you like to come?"

"Yeah, Josh mentioned it," Celeste said. She looked at Amy. "He said you're having some friends over from Scotland."

"Yes," Amy replied, shredding the label. "They're coming to Sarasota first. So, I thought it would be a good idea to have another one here as well. You know…for the friends I've made here."

"I know the Scots have a bit of a reputation when it comes to those kinds of parties," Celeste said her eyes sparkling with humor.

"True." Amy grinned. "But, don't worry. Generally only the bride-to-be is targeted for complete humiliation."

Celeste laughed.

Camille called out hurrying toward them.

"Hi, Mom," Celeste said, shading her eyes.

Denial

Leaning down, Camille kissed her daughter on both cheeks and took her hand, tugged on it. "Come, I have something to show you."

Standing, Celeste smiled at Amy apologetically.

Amy sat up and watched them disappear. She rubbed her neck, surprised it still tingled where Celeste had touched it.

Chapter 6

That evening Amy stretched out on the sofa and smiled at Josh when he entered the living room carrying two glasses of orange juice, and a large pack of sweets.

Accepting the glass, Amy put it down on the polished floor.

Josh sat down. He took a long drink before placing his glass and sweets within easy reach.

Amy put her feet on his lap.

Taking her right foot Josh began massaging it.

Amy groaned with pleasure and lifting her arms covered her eyes. She loved it when he massaged her feet. Enjoying his skilled manipulation, she murmured approvingly.

As he worked on her foot, Amy thought about how this time last year marrying Josh was the furthest thing from her mind. She realized how dramatically her life had changed in the last twelve months.

When they began dating two years ago neither had expected the relationship to turn serious. Back then, Josh had come to Scotland to finish his doctorate in software and electronics, and his temporary status was half the appeal. She liked the idea that it wouldn't be long-term, but somehow their relationship went from casual to serious and last year and Josh made it clear that he wanted more. He wanted to make it permanent.

When he proposed Amy had refused, explaining that at only twenty-four she wasn't ready. That had changed with her father's death. It had devastated her so much that permanency suddenly appealed.

"How's Maggie settling at the hospital?"

"She loves working with kids," Amy replied. "I don't how she does it, being a nurse and working with sick kids must be one of the most difficult jobs there is. Don't you think?"

"Totally," Josh said, focusing on her foot. "Do you think this whole situation about her not wanting to wear the dress is about getting at your mom?"

"Since my parents' divorce," Amy said, lifting her arms from her eyes, "Maggie's never had time for Irene. In fact, I think she's hell-bent on pissing her off as much as she can."

Josh smiled. "I know it's not the wedding you want. But we can't really let Maggie turn up in some crazy outfit." He rubbed her foot soothingly. "And we know that she's more than capable of it." He looked at her. "Do you want me to talk to her?"

"No," Amy replied. She smiled at him appreciatively. "We've already talked." She wiggled her toes. "And, I'll have a good chat with her when we're in Barbados celebrating my last days of freedom."

"With your friends from Scotland?" Josh said, visibly relaxing. "I doubt you'll have any time for a heart to heart given how crazy those chicks are."

"Josh," Amy said and laughed. "Crazy is allowed. It's a celebration."

"Talking about celebration," he said. "Thanks for including Sophie and Celeste. I really appreciate it."

"Well, just following instructions," Amy teased. "You were the one who asked me to have a night here so I could invite your sisters."

"I know, and like I said, I really appreciate it," Josh replied. "Anyway, I hope your night doesn't get too crazy. You're flying out the next day, remember," he said, squeezing her foot. "The good thing is that Sophie is actually going and it'll be good for her. She does nothing but hunch over her laptop." He lovingly rubbed up her leg. "This trip will mean a change of scenery, and an opportunity to get out of the routine she's gotten into lately. And, it'll give you and Celeste a chance to get along better."

Amy looked at him in surprise.

"I'm not that dumb you know," he said. "I know you haven't really hit it off with her since the time she came to visit me last year." He looked at Amy. "I'm not making excuses but she was exhausted from the flight. You know there was a series of delays. And," he added, frowning, "I'm worried about her."

"Why?" Amy asked suddenly intrigued.

"Celeste still hasn't told me what happened to her in Somalia, and I know it's serious." He rubbed the weekend growth on his face then sighed. "She'll talk when she's ready, I suppose."

"You're right, it's time Celeste and I got over that hurdle," Amy said reassuringly. A note of humor crept in. "But, I still haven't forgiven you for dumping me at the airport."

"Honey, we're talking over a year ago," he replied. "I thought it was ancient history." He leaned over, grabbed her hand, and kissed it. "Didn't I make it up to you that night?"

"Ah. So that poor, pathetic performance...was you making up!" she teased.

"Hmmm. Poor performance was it!" Josh said. Reaching over he tickled her sides.

Amy squealed.

Smirking, Josh stopped then picked up the remote control.

The blue screen flickered.

Amy thought about her conversation with Sophie. Unable to resist finding out more about his twin, she asked, "Sophie was telling me about Celeste's marriage."

"Hmmm."

Wanting attention, Amy flopped her feet back onto Josh's lap.

"Uggghhh."

"You've never really told me much about that," Amy said. She pushed a foot into his hands. "Or that her ex-husband was a nut?"

Josh sighed.

Typical bloke tells you nothing. "What's the story?" Amy prodded him. "What happened?"

"Look," Josh said, pressing the pause button. "There's not much to tell. She married young, and the guy was too possessive, end of story."

Amy wiggled her toes.

Denial

Josh grabbed a foot and massaged a familiar tension knot with both thumbs.

Amy groaned.

"I didn't really know the guy. She met him at med school. When they broke up, he was weird." Josh worked the knot out. "I think she broke up because eventually she couldn't go anywhere. At her graduation, he put a guy in hospital for giving her too much attention."

"Why would he do that?"

"C'mon. You've seen her?" Josh said, releasing her foot. He picked up his orange juice. "Nick couldn't accept she got attention. And, boy, does Celeste get attention."

Amy nodded. "I know what you mean, Maggie thinks she's beautiful."

"Just Maggie?" he queried. "Not you?"

"Okay," she said reluctantly. "I guess me too."

Josh raised his eyebrows. "She's got some kind of allure."

"Allure?" Amy said. "What? Like a Venus flytrap kind of allure?"

Josh laughed. "Get those claws in, tiger."

Amy grinned.

"All I know is that when we were in high school, I was plagued with horny teenagers wanting to ask her out. Celeste had the pick of the bunch, but she really only had time for her homo friend Alex."

"Josh!" Amy said, surprised at the uncharacteristic attitude. "C'mon, you know better than that. Alex is a great guy."

Amy had met Alex several times over the last few months. She was aware he was a childhood friend of Celeste's, and she had gotten to know him as he regularly visited the Cameron household.

"Just teasing," Josh said. He stifled a yawn. "Let's see…when Nick came along they were inseparable." He thought for a moment. "At first I didn't notice his jealous streak because they were so close, but after a while they drifted apart. I used to wonder if Nick would have been so heavily involved in Celeste's life if her swimming hadn't ended when it did." He drank some juice then smacked his lips. "Celeste was a swimmer on her collegiate team. Back then, she didn't have much time for anything but swimming and studying." He looked at Amy. "Time's in short supply when you compete."

Amy watched with interest as sadness filled his eyes.

"Her swimming career ended when she was kayaking with some friends and it overturned and busted her shoulder pretty badly. It was a tough time for her." He lightly ran his finger down his right cheekbone. "And she was left with the scar as a reminder." He raised his brow. "I think Nick was nothing more than a distraction." He paused. "Celeste's not the only gorgeous one in the family." He lowered his voice. "The ladies find me irresistible."

"Oh," Amy replied, eyes twinkling. "Don't you mean irritating as hell?"

"Do you want me to show you how irresistible I am?" Josh said. He picked up her foot and began kissing it.

Knowing where it would lead and wanting the conversation to continue, Amy sat up.

Miffed, Josh stretched his arms then sighed heavily. "I'm glad Maggie is out tonight. I want you to myself."

"Don't change the subject on me. I'm interested in finding out about your sister."

"Oh c'mon, is it too much for a guy to ask to be alone with his hot, soon-to-be-wife?"

"Tell me."

Josh sighed. "Okay, I guess I'm going to have to tell you something or you'll be at me all night like some old cackling witch."

"Oh, honey," Amy said, fluttering her eyelashes. "You're such a sweet-talker!" She pressed a hand to her heart. "Tell me or else."

"Else what?"

"Or else no conjugals tonight…big boy!"

"She hates anyone drawing attention to the fact we're twins," Josh said quickly.

Amy laughed.

Josh winked. "And when she went to med school, she didn't tell anyone because of the attention it would bring."

"Why?"

"Why are you so interested in her now?" he asked. "You weren't last year."

Amy stuck out her tongue. "C'mon, answer the question."

"People have a thing about twins," Josh said. He leaned over the arm of the sofa and put his empty glass down then picked up the family-sized pack of sweets he'd brought in earlier. "Can we watch the movie now?"

"No, I want to talk."

"Oh c'mon," he said. "I know you'll like it."

Amy ran her hand up his thigh. "Is she like you?"

Josh groaned when Amy stroked him.

"Down boy." Amy patted his crotch gently then moved away. "That's just a little taste of what's to come if you play ball."

"If you play with my balls again," Josh said. "There'll be no later!"

Plucking the pack of sweets from him, Amy opened them then popped some into her mouth. "You didn't answer my question," she said, chewing. "Is Celeste like you?"

Josh reached in and grabbed a handful of sweets. "Maybe we fit the classic stereotype." He threw some into his mouth. "You know, one outgoing, one shy," he said, chomping. "Even when we were kids she hated attention. Celeste liked being in the background. When her swimming career was over, she didn't make a big deal about it." He paused, as if realizing that for the first time, then shrugged. "She just took up other sports and even married Nick on the quiet." He laughed. "My folks were really pissed when she told them."

Amy asked inquisitively. "So, Celeste marries Nick without anyone knowing and then when things go down the tubes, joins MSF." She reached into the pack for more sweets. "Why?"

"Amy...I don't know," Josh said. "Unlike what your crazy cousin thinks, we're not psychically connected."

Amy laughed. Only Maggie would try to convince the most logical guy on the planet that being a twin meant there had to be some psychic connection.

"Maggie really needs this examined," he said, tapping his head.

"Well," Amy replied wryly, "I'm afraid that's not the area being poked at every other week."

Josh laughed then shook his head. "Who's she's got on the slab now?"

"Who knows," Amy said. "I only ever meet them on their way out the door."

Josh frowned. "I really don't like her bringing strangers back here."

Amy nodded, knowing no matter how much he nagged Maggie she'd ignore him. "I'll talk to her."

"Promise?"

"Yes. Now let's get back to Celeste." Amy pushed her blond hair behind her ears, and leaning close, focused on him.

"God," Josh said, looking at her intently. "You have the most beautiful blue eyes. Do you know that?"

"So you keep telling me," Amy said then smiled. "Did Celeste join MSF to get away from Nick?"

Josh stared at Amy appreciatively then licked his lips. "God, you really are beautiful."

Amy clicked her fingers. "Stay with me, Josh."

"I can't wait to marry you," he said. Pulling her close, he kissed her.

"Josh," Amy muffled against his lips when he tried to deepen the kiss. "Spill the beans," she said pulling away.

"She didn't join MSF right away," Josh answered. "She worked in Paris first. And no, before you ask, I don't think my sister would run away from anything, particularly Nick." He picked up the remote. "Look, it's simple, Mom being French and Dad being Scottish meant we always had to split our time between both countries whenever we visited family over there." He ruffled her hair. "Celeste has an affinity with France, and I've got more of a liking for Scotland because that's where gorgeous blond lassies hang out."

Amy grinned. "More."

"When we were young," he continued, indulging her, "Dad used to take us to visit Mom's family in Paris then his in Scotland, but when we got older, Celeste wanted to spend all her time in Paris. She loved my old battle-ax of a grand-mère."

"Didn't you like her?" Amy asked in surprise.

"She was okay," he answered, frowning. "But, she didn't like Dad." He looked at her. "She thought Mom had married beneath her."

Amy looked at him in surprise. This was the first time he had ever shared this with her.

"You know…working-class, upper-class stuff. The shit the older generation likes to cling to." Josh shook his head. "No matter how hard Dad tried, she couldn't overlook where he came from."

Amy smiled and thought it romantic the way his parents had met. She remembered Camille telling her that when she was young she had danced with the Royal Ballet and Josh's father worked construction. They fell in love, and had been together since. They moved to Sarasota when his father got an opportunity to set up his own construction company with an uncle who lived there.

"My grand-mère had money, and when she died, she left a big chunk of it to Celeste, including a house in France."

"She didn't leave you anything?"

Sadness flickered over his eyes. "Nope. Apparently, I reminded her too much of Dad." He shrugged. "She was a character." He looked at Amy. "My sis was the apple of her eye." His finger hovered over the play button. "Enough yet?"

"Why did Celeste join MSF?"

Josh sighed then moved his finger away from the play button. "I don't think it's anything overly complicated, Amy," he replied. "I think she joined because she has a strong sense of obligation. I mean you have to care to go where she goes, right?" He threw more sweets into his mouth.

Amy nodded. "But it's an international organization. She didn't have to be based in France."

"Yeah, well. Whatever."

"You've never asked have you?" Amy said, looking at him with disbelief. "You've never asked your sister why she stays so far away."

"Amy," Josh replied with forced patience. "Like I said, we spent a lot of our time over there. It didn't seem a big deal that she would want to live there. The same way it wasn't a big deal that I wanted to finish my studies in Scotland."

"Oh," Amy said, realizing the logic.

Josh quirked an eyebrow then pressed the play button. When the film started, he pulled her close.

Amy snuggled into him. Her mind drifted and her thoughts turned to Celeste. Color stained her cheeks when she remembered how long the nape of her neck had tingled after she had tucked in her label.

Chapter 7

Irene, the designated driver for the evening, stopped her car outside Amy's apartment block. Amy opened the car's back door and, after a few moments, staggered out, followed by Celeste.

"Thanks for driving us back," Celeste said as she leaned into the open window at the passenger side.

Amy pushed her head into the car window beside Celeste and slurred, "Shanks for the lift, Irene." She hiccupped. "Are you sure you don't want to come in for a wee drink?"

Celeste watched Irene's eyes narrow. At the barbeque last week, she noticed Irene flinched whenever Amy used her first name. She wondered if this appellation was something new.

"No sweetheart," Irene replied. "You better get to bed. You've got an early start in the morning." She hesitated then put the car in park, got out, and made her way around to hug Amy goodnight.

Irene and Bruce had been friends with Celeste's parents for years, but until Josh started dating Amy Celeste had no idea that Irene had an older daughter. When she queried her mother about Irene's relationship with Amy she was told it was too painful for Irene to discuss. Apparently, the divorce was so acrimonious that Amy's father tried everything to keep Irene out of her daughter's life.

Celeste watched them. She had always liked Irene. In many ways she reminded her of her father, both carried the Scottish trait of speaking their mind, and both were industrious and hard working.

Looking at them, Celeste thought it was hard to believe there was enough of an age gap. Irene didn't look old enough to have a twenty-four-year-old daughter.

Celeste eyed Amy. She knew only too well her brother had an eye for pretty girls. He had chosen well. She still regretted their first meeting, and hoped her being here tonight helped heal the rift. Last year, at the airport, she had simply been stressed and overtired. Unfortunately, they hadn't clicked since. Hopefully, after tonight, they would draw a line through their initial meeting.

Amy's blond hair caught Celeste's attention, and her thoughts turned sharply to Felice. She still found it hard to believe only a few weeks ago Felice had been happy and alive. Aware her mood was darkening, Celeste focused on Amy. To say she was surprised when her brother said he was getting hitched would be an understatement. Josh was a player, and never one for deep, meaningful relationships. Watching Amy, she easily saw the appeal.

Amy pulled out of her mother's arms. "Okeydokey," she said with a sloppy smile.

Irene looked at Celeste. "I'm glad you're here tonight," she said. She added in a teasing tone, "Did you see the amount of booze her friends put away?"

Celeste's eyebrow quirked, but she said nothing.

"What a rowdy bunch your pals are," Irene said, tucking a strand of blond hair behind Amy's ear. "They weren't like that at your graduation in Glasgow, were they?"

"They were." Amy swayed. "You left before the party really got started and didn't get to see them at their best."

Eyeing her daughter, Irene said, "It looks like the good doctor will need to keep an eye on you. I saw you drinking shots with your little helpers."

Amy shook her head and protested, "I've only had a few—"

"A few too many," Irene interrupted, filling the role of an overprotective mother nicely.

Amy frowned and began working out with her fingers how many drinks she'd had.

Irene raised her brow when Amy's tongue peeked out.

"It's a pity Sophie pulled out of the arrangement tonight," Irene said to Celeste. She watched Amy's tongue stick out further when she moved to the other hand.

Denial

Not wanting to elaborate that Sophie pulled out of the arrangement once she realized it would be a crowd of heckling girls, Celeste nodded and smiled at Irene.

Amy held eight fingers up. "Six!" she exclaimed triumphantly then hiccupped.

Celeste tried not to laugh.

"Where is that overbearing cousin of yours when you need her?" Irene asked, eyeing her daughter.

Amy dropped her hands. Looking down, she shuffled her feet.

Irene moved closer. Lifting Amy's chin she said gently, "Nowhere to be seen that's where."

Amy pulled her chin away. Straightening her shoulders, she looked defiantly at her mother. "I wish you two would sort this feud out."

Pain flashed across Irene's eyes. "Remember to give me a call before you catch your flight tomorrow," she said, hugging Amy again. "I know you're only going for a week, but you know the girls will be peeved if they miss saying goodbye to their big sister." She released Amy then tenderly smoothed the hair and took her face in her hands. "Because they adore and love you very much."

Nodding her head vigorously Amy said, "I'll call them."

"Promise?" Irene replied, fixing the dress strap that had fallen loose from Amy's tanned shoulders.

"I promise," Amy replied then grinned. "What's the mating call of a blonde?"

"What?" Irene said in confusion.

"What's the mating call of a blonde?" Amy repeated.

"Eh…I don't know," Irene answered, staring at her daughter.

"I'm sooo drunk!" Amy said then laughed heartily. She stopped suddenly when she realized she was the only laughing. "Don't you get it?" she asked incredulously.

"Of course, sweetie," Irene said soothingly. Covertly, she winked at Celeste.

Amy looked at Celeste. "What's a redhead's mating call?"

Celeste tilted her head, "I don't know," she said with confused amusement.

"Has the blonde gone yet?" Amy said then grinned.

Charmed by Amy's lame jokes and easy humor, Celeste laughed.

"Maggie is going to love that one," Amy said, eyes twinkling.

Rubbing her daughter's bare arms, Irene reminded Amy, "You have a lot to do before you start your break tomorrow." To herself she muttered, "Let's hope that cousin of yours makes it home tonight, and doesn't cause you to miss your flight." Irene turned to Celeste. "Please make sure she gets to bed soon," she said. "When she was a wee girl, I could never get her to sleep when something exciting was planned."

Irene kissed Amy's cheek then made her way to the car.

"Goodnight Celeste," Irene said, opening the car door. Deep love filled her face as she looked at Amy. "Goodnight, jellybean."

†

Amy rolled her eyes as her mother drove away. Sometimes, Irene completely exasperated her. Unlike Josh's mother, Irene insisted on joining them. She realized it shouldn't have been a surprise since she always liked being kept in the loop. When Amy told her that friends were visiting, she wanted to know every last detail about each of the girls.

"Jellybean?" Celeste asked teasingly.

Amy swayed a little.

"Why jellybean?"

Amy ran her fingers through her loose hair, ruffled it and tried to remember. She pouted then grinned. "It was my favorite sweetie as a kid."

Celeste smiled. Turning toward the apartment block, she asked, "Ready?"

Amy nodded and together they walked the short distance.

Outside the door, Amy dug into her shoulder bag and rummaged for her keys.

Searching, her mind wandered. She'd forgotten how much her girlfriends partied. Amy knew even though they were flying tomorrow her friends would be out to the very last second.

Thankfully, with a lot of persuasion, Amy managed to cut the night short explaining she had to check-in with a client before leaving, which meant a six o'clock rise. Stifling a yawn, she rummaged more. Feeling a lump of steel in her hand, she energetically pulled it out. "Eureka!"

Waving a metallic hair clasp, Amy staggered then veered to her left.

Celeste grabbed her.

Pleased that Celeste hadn't changed her plans when Sophie pulled out, Amy fought the urge to hug her and, instead, gave her a big sloppy smile.

Celeste smiled back.

Hiccupping, Amy took a moment to look Celeste over. With so much going on tonight she hadn't really had a chance to focus on anything other than her friends. Amy openly appraised her, liking the tight black sleeveless silk top and how it formed itself to her. Eyes widening, she noticed the matching black silk trousers.

God, how does she always manage to look so damn amazing!

Amy took in the silver necklace resting against Celeste's tanned throat then the other few pieces of jewelry, all expensive and equally understated.

Oblivious that Celeste was aware of her open appraisal, Amy's gaze fell to her dark hair, and she studied the way it fell around her shoulders. Slowly, she focused on Celeste's lips and noticed not for the first time her full mouth. Finally, she gazed into very amused eyes.

Damn!

Sobering, Amy tried to cover her embarrassment by handing Celeste her shoulder bag. "Could you look for the key, I'm not having much luck."

Celeste retrieved the key quickly. She unlocked the door and stood aside for Amy to enter.

Amy entered the apartment she and Maggie shared and switched the lights on. It still surprised her Josh hadn't wanted to move in. Instead, he suggested they wait until they were married. She found it amusing that although he liked a good time—a very good time according to some of his friends—he was, at heart, a traditionalist.

Amy moved through the apartment, kicking off her shoes. She loved this place. It was airy and spacious. If they hadn't been building a home of their own Amy would have convinced Josh to live here. Walking into the living room she asked Celeste if she would like a drink.

"Tequila with ice."

Heading for the kitchen, Amy called out. "Make yourself at home."

Chapter 8

Celeste settled on the sofa. She stretched out her long legs, crossed one ankle over the other, and let the tiredness seep into her bones. She only roused when Amy handed her a chilled glass. Sipping her drink, she watched Amy settle at the other end of the sofa.

Amy held up a glass. "I'm on orange juice," she said, sobering. "I have an early start tomorrow morning."

Silence fell between them. Tonight at the bar while she talked to Irene, Celeste had watched Maggie, to the loud cheer of friends, pull Amy onto the stage. She hadn't known what to expect as she watched them tune borrowed guitars. After a few songs, she was astounded by the sweetness of Amy's husky voice.

"You have a great voice, Amy," Celeste said. "I was blown away when I heard you sing. I had no idea you and Maggie played." She smiled when Amy blushed and asked, "Did you organize the acoustic set you played tonight?"

Tucking her feet underneath her, Amy responded shyly. "No. It was just chance."

Celeste smiled. "It was great. I really enjoyed it."

Amy sipped at her juice. "So, did Maggie bore you with her story?" she asked. "Did she talk about her band days?"

Hesitating, Celeste smiled. "She did get animated after you'd played."

"It wasn't much of a band." Amy chuckled. "Maggie used it to pull guys. She loved the idea of performing."

Celeste's attention was caught when Amy put her glass on the floor, then sitting back, ran her fingers through her blond hair. Raising her eyebrows appreciatively, she asked, "And what about you?"

"I started off as her number one groupie," Amy replied. "I'd tag behind Maggie wherever she went. She couldn't shake me off."

Instinctively, Celeste's eyes appraised Amy. She wore a thin-strapped black dress with a deep V-neck. The dress, she noticed, showed Amy's shape—in particular—her breasts beautifully.

"I hounded Maggie night and day to play in her band." Amy laid her head back against the cushioned sofa and continued to reminisce. "And since I was tagging along with them, the boys eventually talked her into it. So, she let me play guitar." She smiled. "At sixteen, it meant the world to me. Back then I had little to work with. I wore braces and looked like a stick insect."

Celeste's eyes fell to Amy's breasts, and she fought the urge to tell her she didn't have that problem now. "You're painting a really attractive picture here," she teased.

Amy laughed. "By the time I was eighteen the braces were gone." She looked down and added playfully, "My boobs grew. Thank God! But, eventually, Maggie gave me short shrift. I was getting far too much attention for her liking. She told me my studies needed to come first."

Amused, Celeste smiled. Enjoying Amy's intimacy, she asked, "So you never wanted to pursue a music career?"

Amy stretched and Celeste's eyes fell involuntarily to her breasts.

"Yes, for a wee while," Amy responded. "Who doesn't carry dreams of making it big at that age?"

Celeste smiled. She liked the Scottish burr and huskiness of Amy's voice.

"I played in a band at university but the chemistry was never right," Amy continued. "I guess I'd been spoiled. I loved being in Maggie's band. The boys were like brothers to me. It was all about having fun, a laugh, nothing more. But I lost interest. They took themselves far too seriously."

†

Denial

Sometime later, Amy looked at her watch, and was shocked that it was so late. A twinge of regret shot through her that she was going to have to end their chat. She really had enjoyed Celeste's company but, if she was going to get up early to meet her client, she really needed to go to bed now.

"Celeste, I hate to cut it short, but I really need to get some sleep."

Looking disappointed, Celeste nodded. "You've got an early start." She tapped her glass. "I'll finish my drink and follow."

Amy said goodnight and headed for her bedroom. On her way up the stairs she decided to detour by her studio to quickly tidy it up. It would only take a few minutes and experience had taught her that she loathed coming home to a mess. She headed for her studio, but stopped when the phone rang.

God, it's so late, Amy thought and toyed with the idea of ignoring it, but curiosity got the better of her. Running down the hallway, she entered her bedroom and answered it. It was Josh. Sitting on the bed, she shared the highlights of the evening with him.

When Amy hung up she toyed with the idea of leaving her studio until she returned from Barbados, but she pushed herself off the bed instead knowing she wouldn't be happy leaving it a mess. Padding barefoot down the hallway to her studio, Amy was startled to see Celeste standing there when she opened the door. Shocked, she asked abruptly, "What are you doing in here?"

"Maggie showed me this room when I got here, but I never got a chance to look." Celeste picked up a paintbrush. "I've heard how talented an artist you are. Maggie said it would be okay to look around. I hope you don't mind?"

Yes, I do bloody mind!

Putting the paintbrush down Celeste motioned for Amy to come into the room.

This room was Amy's inner sanctuary, and usually Maggie respected her space. Biting back, she entered and closed the door. Resting against it, she watched Celeste move around the room.

Celeste examined a model build of the new house and other projects Amy was working on.

"You're a busy woman," she finally commented as she peered through a window on the miniature new build.

Color rising in Amy's cheeks she watched Celeste continue to touch her things. When she stopped at a painting, Amy cringed.

Celeste tilted her head to view it.

Embarrassed, Amy slowly approached the brunette and noticed she was barefoot.

"When did you do this?" Celeste asked, staring at the painting.

"Uhmmm…a few weeks ago," Amy replied. "The day of the barbeque at Irene's actually."

That day she had been unable to resist the urge to sketch Celeste. Since meeting her she had mused at the similarities and differences between the twins, and in the afternoon an opportunity arose when everyone was watching the football game and she found Celeste alone at the edge of the pool, deep in thought.

Impulsively, Amy had retrieved crayons and a sketchpad from the children's room and quickly sketched her.

Watching Celeste look at the painting, Amy studied her profile. She remembered wanting to find out which was stronger between Josh and Celeste, their similarities or differences in looks and gestures. Instead, she had captured something else, an essence that radiated from Celeste, something that surprised her—melancholy.

Turning her head, Celeste looked at Amy curiously. "I'm flattered."

To Amy's complete astonishment, Celeste, as if needing the closeness, hugged her.

Startled by the physical contact and unsure how to react Amy placed her arms awkwardly around Celeste and squeezed her gently. "You're welcome."

"I've never had my portrait done before," Celeste said, her arms around Amy.

"It was a pleasure," Amy responded. Feeling awkward and uncomfortable she tried to fight the urge to pull away. Aware she

Denial

didn't want to overreact to an instinctive moment, she forced herself to relax.

"You caught me thinking of someone," Celeste said eventually.

Amy noted the rawness in her voice.

"I lost someone very special to me," she said, her hold on Amy tightening.

Surprised, Amy listened as Celeste inhaled deeply.

"Her name was Felice," Celeste whispered.

Unsure how to react but sensing Celeste needed to talk, Amy waited for a moment, "What happened?"

Celeste hesitated, her hold loosened. She looked at Amy. "I probably don't need to tell you about the war in Somalia?"

Amy nodded. "I know what's going on."

Celeste shut her eyes. "A few weeks ago my team was sent to a camp." She wearily opened them. "The camp was a compound, surrounded by militia, and we needed to treat the people inside." She paused then sucked in some air. "I'm sorry, Amy," she said, pulling away. "I don't mean to…burden you."

Sensing this need to talk was uncharacteristic, Amy quietly pleaded, "Stay. Tell me. I want to hear." She hugged Celeste, encouragingly. Celeste lowered her long, dark lashes.

Amy shuddered unable to imagine the kind of violence Celeste must have witnessed over the years.

Celeste pulled out of Amy's arms. "It was agreed that we wouldn't be harmed, and we were sent there to provide medical assistance."

Amy held her breath, registering for the first time Celeste was probably often in situations where she could be killed.

Celeste folded her arms. "We were told that thousands of displaced people were in the camp, but when we got there," her voice lowered as she recounted the moment, "many had been slaughtered." She frowned deeply. "The militia suddenly decided the camp was a sanctuary for their enemies."

Amy could barely imagine the fear she must have experienced about the fate of those people.

Celeste swallowed. "We couldn't find anyone. The place was littered with belongings, but it wasn't until we moved deep into the camp that we found them." She closed her eyes briefly. "Thousands of terrified people herded together." She looked at Amy. "Like sheep. All huddled along a ridgeline that ran through the camp."

Celeste held Amy's gaze. "We worked for days. The casualties were never-ending. I had never seen anything like it. The injuries were horrific." She broke eye contact and shook her head. "We were only equipped for basic problems—dysentery, infectious bites, malaria, things like that. Anything more, the hospital in the city would treat." She bit her bottom lip. "The militia made it a rule that anyone caught trying to leave the camp would be shot." Her eyes closed. "But, people were terrified. Even knowing how dangerous it was some people still tried to escape." She frowned. "We were completely powerless to stop them from being hunted down and killed." Her eyes darkened. "The soldiers weren't good marksmen. Even close, they could still miss. And if they managed to wound someone, they wouldn't waste bullets they'd just bayonet them to death."

Amy had seen news footage. Although appalled by what she saw, she realized there was no way she would ever comprehend what it was like to witness carnage like that firsthand. She looked at Celeste with new eyes. It must have been soul destroying watching the lives of people she was trying to save be so easily snuffed out.

"After a few days the militia went on a killing spree." Celeste shook her head. "The day Felice was...killed, people were being shot all over the camp." Anger flickered across her eyes. "It was a hopeless situation. We weren't equipped to treat gunshot wounds. All we could do was gather up the casualties and have them flown to the hospital. Celeste's eyes widened. "We were waiting for the helicopter to arrive, this young boy," she shook her head, "couldn't have been more than eight years old, ran toward us screaming for help. A soldier was chasing him. He was firing at him." Celeste's face tightened. "The boy ran toward Felice, ran straight into her arms, screaming for her to help him. It was only when the soldier saw an officer with us that he stopped." Pain tinged Celeste's tone. "But Felice and the boy were hit."

Tears stung Amy's eyes as images of this unknown woman, horrifically shot down, flooded her mind.

"The helicopter had been shot at earlier and couldn't land." Celeste swallowed. "Felice was in serious condition and we couldn't treat her at the compound. We needed to get her to the hospital. But the roadblocks the militia had in place were a nightmare to negotiate. An army officer tried to get us through checkpoint after checkpoint. And I couldn't do anything. I was in the back of the ambulance with Felice and the others." A look of desolation crossed her face. "I did what I could but we weren't equipped." She closed her eyes. "When we eventually got through, it was too late." Her voice cracked. "We lost her." Her voice broke. "Amy…she fought so hard."

Amy pulled Celeste into her arms and hugged her.

Celeste held Amy tightly.

Feeling her pain, Amy shuddered at the horror of such an impossible situation. She understood loss—her father's death had devastated her—but losing someone like that. She could not comprehend what it must have felt like to watch someone you cared for die before your eyes. Feeling a wealth of compassion for Celeste, Amy cupped her face and looked at her intently. "You're safe here," she whispered. "It's okay to let go."

Leaning her brow against Amy's, Celeste caught her breath.

Aware she was probably one of a few people to see Celeste this vulnerable, Amy watched transfixed as tears slid down Celeste's face. Unable to resist, she caught one with her thumb, and rubbed it between her fingers.

Celeste leaned into Amy and wept. After a few minutes, she opened her eyes.

Grabbing a nearby rag, Amy gently dabbed Celeste's cheeks. She kissed her cheek tenderly. "Release is good."

Nodding, Celeste said, "It was…unexpected."

Amy whispered, "I know."

They looked at each other.

Celeste cleared her throat. "Thank you." She looked at the painting and changed the subject. "You can see my scar."

Amy glanced over her shoulder. "Yes."

Aware that Celeste was vulnerable, Amy decided not to break contact. Turning in Celeste's arms, she added, "Its good…your scar. I like it."

Her arms hanging loosely around Amy, Celeste frowned.

Immediately embarrassed by how stupid the remark sounded, Amy added quickly, "I mean…I really like your scar because," she tried to justify, "it…it adds depth."

It was true, Amy did like Celeste's scar. When she had sketched Celeste's face, her hazel-green eyes were initially the dominant feature followed by her lips and cheekbones, but the small scar somehow, inadvertently, held center stage. Looking at the painting Amy contemplated why she liked it. After a moment, she realized it was because it robbed Celeste's face of perfection and somehow that pleased her, as her artistic eye always found imperfection more appealing.

Arms tightening around Amy Celeste whispered, "But, still, you've made me look so…so…" she seemed to struggle for words as she looked at the painting, "beautiful."

Surprised Celeste would think anything less, Amy took a breath. "That's because you are beautiful." She turned her head to look at Celeste. "Very beautiful."

Their eyes locked.

Amy thought about how good it felt being in this woman's arms and blushed.

"Thank you. It's a wonderful surprise," Celeste said then kissed the top of Amy's head.

Amy wanted to let Celeste know that it was good what they had just shared. "I'm glad you trusted me."

Celeste nodded slowly.

Watching Celeste, Amy focused on her generous mouth and full lips, then finally her eyes. Her lips parted slightly in surprise when Celeste bent her head and kissed her cheek then her mouth. It was a gentle kiss, warm and sweet. One meant to communicate more affection than desire. One never designed to ignite the full-body hormone rush that exploded through Amy.

Eyes wide, lips tingling, Amy stared at Celeste. Completely overwhelmed by the unexpected intensity of her physical response, she whispered, "Did you feel that?"

Celeste nodded slowly. She sucked in air. "Yes," she answered huskily. "I did." Moaning lightly, she pulled Amy to her.

Heat rose within Amy. Her senses exploded when Celeste encouraged a full-blown, open-mouthed kiss. Pressing her against the workbench, their mouths hot and demanding, Celeste's hands moved urgently up Amy's rib cage. Kissing her deeply, she lowered the straps of Amy's dress.

Dress falling to her waist, Amy moaned when Celeste cupped then caressed her bare breasts. Unable to focus on anything but Celeste's mouth and the incredible sensations exploding within her Amy could do nothing but completely surrender.

Celeste let Amy's mouth go. Sucking gently, she bit down the length of her neck. Leaving a trail of moisture, she nibbled her way down then back up.

"Oh God," Amy whispered, her hair falling to the side as she allowed Celeste access. She gasped when a deep growl escaped Celeste as she sucked on her neck.

Amy's groin clenched when Celeste's hands worked on her very sensitive nipples. The more she caressed the more Amy responded. Soon, her hips were undulating.

Moaning, Celeste pulled Amy's dress up above her thighs. Pulling the silky briefs aside she rubbed her fingers over Amy's soaking clit.

Wrapping her arms around Celeste's neck, Amy moved against her hand, groaning deeply.

Hissing out her breath, Celeste slid her fingers deep inside Amy as her mouth kissed a moist trail down Amy's throat. Biting down on her neck, Celeste thrust into her.

The combination of the sharp pain and the feel of Celeste drove Amy's hips forward. Crying out, her entire body flushed as she came.

The pleasure coursing through Amy faded. Coming down, she opened her eyes and looked at Celeste.

Slowly the brunette pulled away from her.

The cold air cutting across Amy's nipples focused her mind. Looking down, her brain scrambled. Dazedly, she pushed herself away from the workbench.

Breathing hard, Celeste leaned against the wall.

Unnerved, body shaking, Amy fled the room.

Chapter 9

Rushing to her bedroom Amy threw the door open and hurried in. Shaken to her core and feeling bewildered, she stopped in the middle of the room and looked around. She shook her hands to relieve the growing panic.

"*Ohmygod, ohmygod, ohmyfuckinggod!*"

Amy looked at the door and realizing it was still open rushed to it. Closing it, she leaned her full weight against it and felt for the key. Alarmed, she remembered it was on her dresser. Eyes widening, she realized she had never used the key before.

Quickly retrieving the key, Amy tried to put it into the lock but her hands were shaking violently and she dropped it several times before succeeding. Sighing heavily, she leaned against the locked door. Fixing her dress, the full force of what had happened hit her. Shame filled her and tears started to fall as she sobbed in disbelief.

"Amy, are you okay?"

Amy could hear the worry in Celeste's voice.

Celeste repeated, "Amy, are you okay?"

Amy stood frozen.

Celeste knocked on the door. "Amy, please answer me."

Amy wiped tears away. "No, I'm not okay, Celeste. What happened is not okay!" She clenched her fists. "Okay!"

"Amy, I think we should talk. I—"

"I think it's best you go," Amy interrupted, wringing her hands together. "I don't think any amount of talking can explain what just happened."

Celeste tried to turn the door handle.

Amy yelled, "For God's sake, didn't you hear me?"

"Amy, I want you to try and stay calm and take deep breaths."

Amy paced the room. She was angry and confused. She needed time alone to think.

"Amy?"

"How am I supposed to stay calm when I've never done anything," Amy stopped pacing and faced the door, "I mean absolutely anything like that before!"

A vivid replay of what had taken place ran through Amy's mind. Clasping her cheeks, she tried to absorb the enormity of the situation.

"I know it's a shock, Amy." The door creaked as Celeste pressed against it. "It's a shock for us both." She paused. "But I'm sure if we talk we can sort this out."

Beginning to hyperventilate, Amy drew out her words. "We just had...*sex*, Celeste! I don't think anything you say can talk us out of that!" She stared at the door. "I can't deal with this...you...right now!"

"Amy, open the door."

Trying to regulate her breathing, Amy leaned against the wall closest to the door. "I don't...want...you here. Okay? There's...nothing...to say...right now. I can't—" Amy's breath came in short gasps, cutting off her words.

Standing outside Amy's room, Celeste listened helplessly.

"Amy. Listen to me, take deep breaths." Aware that Amy was going into shock, Celeste injected authority into her voice. "I'm happy not to talk just now." She tried being persuasive. "But I don't want to leave you like this. It's clear you're having an anxiety attack, and I have no idea if you have a history of this or if you have respiratory problems." Her tone precise, she added, "Amy, I need to know you are not on any type of medication or suffer from any problems like asthma?"

No response.

Celeste swallowed. Her own anxiety increasing she tried again. "If you want me to go, I'll leave. But only once I know you're going to be okay."

No response.

Her face pained and voice tight, Celeste leaned further into the door. "Amy, please. I need to know you're going to be okay when I leave."

Denial

After a long silence, Amy responded. "No...I don't have a problem." Still struggling, she forced out. "I know what to do. I'll get a bag and breathe into it." Celeste heard her suck air in deeply. "I'll be fine...as soon as you leave."

Relief washed over Celeste. Leaning her head against the door, she responded gratefully, "Okay. I'm going downstairs to get my things, and then I'll go." She stroked the door. "It'll take me just a few minutes, I promise."

"Just go...please."

Pushing off the door, Celeste made her way to the room she would have slept in. In the bedroom, she sat on the edge of the bed holding her head, wondering why the hell she hadn't seen this coming.

Rubbing her temples, she exhaled slowly and remembered the golf day with Amy. She thought about how aware she was of her and that *something* that passed between them when she tucked Amy's label away.

Celeste looked at her fingers aware on that day they had tingled for a long time afterward. Shaking her head, she blinked several times understanding she wouldn't have seen it coming because since Felice's death she hadn't been thinking clearly.

Standing, she looked at her watch, she didn't want to leave Amy but medical experience told her it was best. Picking up her hair band from the bedside cabinet, she caught her hair and tied it back. Realizing she was barefoot she picked up her overnight bag and hurriedly stuffed in items she had removed earlier. She threw it over her shoulder and quickly made her way to the living room to retrieve her shoes.

On the street, Celeste called a cab. Not wanting Amy to look out the window and see her hanging around, she gave an address two blocks down. Walking, her thoughts turned for the first time to Josh.

"Josh!"

Celeste's hands covered her mouth. Stricken to the core her heart thudded hard against her rib cage. Tonight's events would directly impact her twin. The adrenaline coursing through her veins forced her to speed up. *Oh my God!* Her stomach churned.

"Jesus, Josh," she whispered. Her stomach lurched. "Sweet, beautiful, adorable Josh," she muttered. Her stomach heaved. "How could I hurt him like this?" Her vision blurred when an image of her brother flashed through her mind.

Halting, Celeste placed a trembling hand against the nearest wall and, unable to control her physical reaction, threw up.

†

Amy could hear a noise in the distance. It took a while, but finally she realized a phone was ringing. Stirring, she looked at her watch but couldn't see it properly. Groaning, she squinted at the blurred numbers, which eventually came into a hazy focus and read seven thirty. She sat bolt upright, lurched forward, and frantically reached for the ringing phone.

"Hullo," a gruff voice said at the other end.

"Hello, Mr. Dreyfuss," Amy said, trying to hold back the panic in her voice as she realized that she had stood up her client. She ran a hand through her hair and pulled the bedsheets around her then profusely apologized. She explained it was her bachelorette party the night before and it hadn't ended as quickly as she hoped.

To Amy's relief, her client showed some sympathy and was happy to discuss the salient points of the project.

After the call ended, Amy stared blearily at the phone before slowly placing it back on its cradle. Sinking into the bed, she pulled the covers over her head and groaned. Throughout the entire conversation she was bombarded with flashbacks from the night before. To her utter humiliation, during the call she knew for sure she had tutted in the all the wrong places. She was even sure she had said 'shit' once.

Oh God, Amy thought, he probably thinks I have Tourette's. She groaned in despair. Covering her eyes with her arms, she whispered, "What have I done?"

The sun pouring in through her bedroom window, and in need of some air, Amy threw back the bedsheets and absorbed some of the sun's energy. After a few minutes, she checked the time then forced herself out of bed. Heading for the shower, she hoped Maggie was back and organized for their trip.

In the shower, Amy leaned against the tiled wall and let the water rain down on her.

Unable to believe she had let last night happen, Amy groaned. That she had cheated on Josh was unbelievable. With a woman—her future sister-in-law—was incomprehensible. She groaned. She could not have been more shocked if someone was to tell her that her brain had been missing for the past twenty-four years.

Feeling sick, Amy leaned her head against the wall. The now familiar feeling of panic welled up inside as she asked herself for the hundredth time, "How could you have let that happen?"

Unable to answer the question, Amy finally accepted that she didn't have an answer. Turning off the shower, she got out, toweled herself dry then quickly dressed. Brushing her hair, Amy froze when she heard a knock on the door. Her heart pounded when the door handle turned.

"Amy?"

It was Maggie.

Sighing with relief, Amy quickly unlocked the door. Glad to see her cousin and needing some comfort, she pulled Maggie into her arms and hugged her tightly. "You look like hell," she said, releasing her.

"Thanks, I love you too."

"What time did you get in?"

Apparently too hung over to ask why the door was locked, Maggie looked at her watch. "Errrmm, about now," she said sheepishly. Groaning, she moved toward Amy's bed. Lying back, she croaked, "What an awesome night!"

"Are you organized?" Amy asked briskly, approaching her.

Maggie peered through one eye and muttered, "I'm ready whenever you are, jellybean."

"I did all my packing yesterday."

Maggie sighed. "I thought I was to meet you at the airport?"

Amy's pulse quickened. "Aye, well change of plan." Pulling Maggie up off the bed, she added, "Let's get the hell out of here."

Amy groaned when she entered Maggie's room. Her cousin was anything but organized. The room was chaos.

Maggie flopped onto her bed.

"Where is it?"

"What?" Maggie's muffled voice asked from under her pillow.

"Your suitcase!"

"Under the bed."

Finding it, Amy opened a couple of drawers and threw whatever she could find into it. Aware the redhead was particular about what she wore, Amy knew Maggie was in for a shock when they got to Barbados.

While helping Maggie get organized, Josh then Irene called. Amy struggled to speak. She kept each conversation brief, hoping they would think she was too excited about the trip to chat for long.

"Are you ready?" Amy asked when the taxi arrived.

Maggie nodded wearily.

"Let's go."

Soon they were at the airport. To Amy's relief, when they arrived, her friends were all nursing serious hangovers, which meant they were too tired to give her much attention. It wasn't until they were boarding the plane that Maggie finally remembered about Celeste staying over.

"Did you get a chance to chat with twinnie last night?"

Amy tensed. The color drained from her face.

Frowning, Maggie looked at her. "I hope everything was all right? I know you've found her a wee bit awkward."

Amy looked down and muttered, "Everything was fine."

Maggie persisted. "Where was she this morning then?"

Wanting to end the conversation, Amy replied, "She left early." Leaving no room for Maggie to ask further questions, she called to her friend, Islay, who was preparing to sit in the seat across from her, and asked, much to her cousin's confusion, if she would like to sit next to her.

Chapter 10

About to leave her room, the phone rang. Hesitating at the door, Amy let it ring a few times before picking it up. "Hello?" she answered cautiously.

"Hi, honey."

Amy rubbed her forehead, relieved it was Josh. Closing her eyes, she exhaled slowly. Since that night last week, Celeste had haunted her thoughts. On the one hand, she was relieved she was here in the Caribbean and out of reach, but on the other she desperately wanted to resolve it—whatever 'it' was with Celeste—and get back to her life. So far, there had been no communication.

"Hi, Josh," Amy replied, trying to clear her mind of images of Celeste.

They briefly chatted about some issues Irene was having with the wedding arrangements then Amy said her goodbyes. Each time they spoke, guilt filled her and left her throat as dry as a bone. Thankfully, her friends thought her distraction was just a bout of pre-wedding jitters, but Maggie was a different matter. She had picked up that something was wrong. Amy's stomach lurched. Suddenly nauseous, she headed to the bathroom. When she eventually came out, Maggie was there.

"That's the third morning this week you've thrown up, isn't it?"

Wiping her mouth with a tissue, Amy nodded weakly.

Maggie hugged her. "C'mon," she said with a note of concern. "I think you should go for a wee nap."

Amy nodded, and headed for her bed.

☦

"Wake up, jellybean."

Amy blearily opened her eyes.

Maggie looked down at her.

"What time is it?" Amy asked, sitting up and rubbing her eyes.

Maggie looked away at the alarm clock. "It's let's find out time." Producing a package from her pocket, she rattled it.

Amy squinted at the package. "What's that?"

Nudging Amy over, Maggie sat beside her. "A pregnancy test kit."

Color drained from Amy's face. Groaning, she lay back down. Covering her eyes with her arms, she whispered, "Impossible. I'm always careful."

"Amy, you know you recently changed to a new pill because your body reacted badly to it," Maggie said, gently removing Amy's arms from her face.

Amy's voice grew huskier than normal. "I can't be?"

"Jellybean," Maggie said softly, "you've been off the pill for two months." Trying to make a joke of it she added, "I know you're blonde, but is that really an excuse?"

Tears welled in Amy's eyes. "I'm just about to start my career. Having a baby right now is not part of the plan."

"Men," Maggie said, stroking Amy's hair. "Didn't you tell him you like your eggs unfertilized?" She shook her head. "If Josh didn't want to use protection you should have put a staple through his nob." She smiled. "He'd have got the message pretty quick that you weren't ready for the pitter-patter of tiny feet."

"Look, Maggie," Amy protested. "Do you think I'm daft or something? Believe me," she said indignantly, "we used protection!"

Maggie rattled the package. "Let's see if it was effective then." Raising her eyebrows, she said gently, "Don't be scared."

Amy sniffed.

"Jellybean," Maggie said standing, "if you used protection then it's highly unlikely you're pregnant." She held out her hands. "But, we need to be sure."

Amy threw the bedsheets back and took her cousin's hands. "Maggie," she said, standing on shaky legs. "I'm ninety-nine point nine percent sure I'm not!"

"Then, it'll do no harm to round it up to a hundred, will it."

Amy lowered her dark blond eyelashes.

"Jellybean, one way or another you'll find out. And it's better now rather than later." Handing Amy the pregnancy kit Maggie shooed her into the bathroom. Pulling the door closed, she leaned against it. "I'm here if you need me."

After a few minutes, Amy opened the door. Taking her hand, Maggie led her into the kitchen.

"Well?"

"I didn't look," Amy replied shakily. "Can we have a cup of tea first?"

Nodding, Maggie sat Amy down at the breakfast bar before putting the kettle on.

After her third cup, Maggie said, "You should go and check."

Amy nodded but didn't move. "I just remembered something."

"What?"

"A couple of weeks ago," Amy replied, eyes downcast. "We were out with friends, and Josh was up for celebrating…" Her voice trailed off.

"And?"

"And, we ordered champagne."

"How much did you have?"

"I don't know," Amy shrugged. "There were four of us."

"And?"

"And, I can't really remember. But, I could've sworn that we used protection." Amy rubbed her forehead. "But now, I'm not so sure."

"Hmmm." Maggie looked at her cousin then nodded toward the bathroom.

Amy didn't move. The thought of being pregnant terrified her.

Maggie nodded toward the bathroom again.

Amy sighed. "Will you go?"

Maggie looked at the blonde for a long moment then headed for the bathroom to retrieve the results. Returning, she gave Amy a sad little smile.

Covering her mouth, Amy burst into tears.

"Aww, c'mere," Maggie said, holding out her arms. "It'll be all right, jellybean."

Chapter 11

"Mike, it's Friday afternoon and I'm at the house. Just wondering where you are. Give me a call when you get this message." Hanging up, Amy looked around and noted with a detailed eye the work still to be done. She shook her head, unable to believe that after all the hard work the contractor was now slacking off just when the house was in the final stage of the build.

Amy wondered what to do and decided to look the house over thoroughly. She wandered around the interior and thought about how tough this, her first real project, had been. The project was over budget, and six weeks late, but given all of that she thought, taking an appreciative look at her designs, it was worth it.

The blonde smiled when she heard a car coming up the drive. Thinking Mike hadn't taken the afternoon off after all, she made her way out of the house and onto the front porch. When Amy got there she froze and her heart almost leapt into her mouth when she recognized Celeste's car.

On her return from the Caribbean a few weeks ago, Amy had mentally prepared herself, even psyched herself up, for some sort of showdown, but to her surprise there was no contact whatsoever from the elusive Doctor Cameron. All she knew was what she had gleaned from Josh's increasing complaints that Celeste was never around.

As the weeks passed, with no word, Amy eventually rationalized her bizarre encounter with Celeste. Although she couldn't fully explain why it happened, she had read somewhere a woman's hormones tended to be all over the place when pregnant which led to erratic behavior and mood swings. With some relief, Amy decided her encounter with Celeste was nothing more than a hormonal blip.

Drawing in a breath, Amy watched Celeste get out of the car and look around. Accepting that a conversation with the brunette was long overdue, she unconsciously firmed her chin then squared her shoulders before making her way down the stairs.

Approaching Celeste, Amy couldn't help but admire her outfit. She wore a tight-fitting white shirt, which showed off her tanned complexion, and sleek black trousers. She's so incredibly beautiful, Amy thought. Since their first meeting, she had admired Celeste's style, particularly the way she used a rich color palette to bring together fabric and textured clothing. No synthetics for this girl, Amy thought. Stopping in front of the brunette, she noticed her hair had been restyled. Normally longer, it was layered and a few inches above her shoulders. Overall, Amy thought, she definitely has that French chic look nailed.

†

Closing the car door, Celeste was surprised by the rush of desire that swept through her when Amy stopped in front of her. "Hi, Amy."

Amy frowned. "Hi. What brings you here?"

Taking off her shades, Celeste looked at the blonde. She liked her style, and fully appreciated the sexiness of her look. Amy's white T-shirt accentuated her full breasts and her boots and her jeans showed her shapely legs off to their maximum. Ignoring the suddenly charged air between them, and fighting the urge to touch her, Celeste looked away. She took a moment before meeting Amy's intense gaze. Slipping her shades on top of her head, she replied, "I know it's…unexpected, but I spoke to Josh on the phone this afternoon and he mentioned you were here, and since I was in the neighborhood he suggested that I stop by and see the house." She looked toward the house. "This is quite spectacular, how about a tour?"

Amy eyed Celeste. "Okay."

Celeste walked toward the house. At the top of the stairs, she stopped and looked back in surprise, Amy hadn't moved more than a few steps. She gestured with her hand for her to follow.

†

Amy didn't move when Celeste made her way toward the house. Instead, she watched her. She had always known Celeste was an exceptionally beautiful woman, but now she wasn't just admiring the way she looked. Now, she realized, stomach knotting, she was responding to it.

When Celeste looked back at her inquiringly, Amy smiled briefly. Swallowing hard, she followed.

Amy showed Celeste around. Initially, she found it difficult to focus on anything other than the physical proximity of the brunette and how her body was reacting to her closeness, but as the tour continued her enthusiasm, and Celeste's easy manner, eased her tension.

With a little coaxing, Amy showed Celeste the design plans for the house, explaining her inspirations, and detailing what was still to happen.

Coming close to Amy, Celeste looked at the plans. "Josh mentioned the house was being put forward for some sort of award for green homes in Florida."

Amy nodded. "A lot of that's due to your dad, Celeste," she replied. "I owe him big-time. I would never have managed without his help. He gave me a crew, and he was the one that negotiated this acre of infill redevelopment."

"Yeah, he's a generous guy," Celeste said. "Tell me about the green aspects of the house."

"Well," Amy began. "Most of the house is built from materials from the local area. We've recycled construction waste on-site to create our own mulch. We've saved and transplanted trees, including live oaks and magnolias, and where possible used engineered lumber made from shredded wood or junk trees." Amy looked at Celeste and, catching her eyes, blushed. "I'm sorry, I could go on forever."

"I want to hear more," Celeste replied, leaning against the kitchen counter. "I'm impressed. This place is something else."

Amy watched Celeste's shirt pull against her breasts as she rested her hands on the counter. "There's a whole-house vacuum and there's automatic faucets."

Suddenly aware that she was staring at Celeste's chest, Amy focused quickly on the floor. Embarrassed, she cleared her throat. "Uhmm, and the bamboo flooring is renewable, maturing in five years rather than the typical thirty for traditional wood."

"Sustainability, I like it," Celeste said staring intently at Amy.

Amy locked eyes with Celeste.

"Tell me more."

"Ermm, there's also cork flooring throughout, which is harvested without harming the plant. The lighting," Amy added, feeling flustered as she flicked a switch on and off, "uses less energy, generates less heat, and lasts longer than normal lighting." She pointed upward. "There's high-efficiency air-conditioning."

"It's wonderful," Celeste responded quietly.

Amy's pulse picked up. Needing to put some distance between them, she said, "Let me show you some more." Quickly, she led the way through the house. "The pool uses natural salt for purification, taking away the need for chlorine. The photovoltaic heater will warm the pool with solar energy."

Aware she sounded like some sort of energy-saving zealot Amy said, as they walked back to the kitchen, "You get the gist; living in this type of house is really all about using resources and energy wisely."

"I didn't realize you were such a green ambassador."

"This place means a lot to me," Amy replied, genuinely delighted that Celeste liked it. "I wanted the house to blend with its natural habitat, but I also wanted it to be sensitive… environmentally." Amy blushed. "My father," she said, looking at Celeste and wondering fleetingly if they would have got on, "was a keen environmentalist and many of the green elements I've incorporated," she pointed to several areas on the plans, "would be constructs that would have met with his approval."

Denial

Celeste moved closer to Amy. "I'm sure your father would be as amazed as I am," she said gently. "I love this house. It seems to reflect a lot of your personality, and probably his too." She touched Amy's arm reassuringly. "There is no doubt you have a real talent. That's evident in your art, and in the design of this house."

Aware of the searing heat of Celeste's hand on her bare skin, Amy took a deep breath.

"Do you find it completely different from what you would have built in Scotland?"

Eyes wide, Amy nodded. Aware of nothing but Celeste's touch, she swallowed. "In some ways it's very different, and in some ways not," she said, her voice sounding weird to her ears. "Here, everything tends to be big in scale in terms of the size of property. But, in reality, the homes here are notorious for having small garages and limited storage space."

"How so," Celeste asked, her hand still burning Amy's skin.

"Uhmm," Amy said, fighting the strong urge to pull her arm away from the intense heat. "Builders are sneaky and save on construction costs by making closets, attics, and garages smaller. With not very many basements because of the sandy soil and wet conditions you get huge houses with no storage."

Celeste smiled. "Is there more?"

Suddenly aware that Celeste was engaging her but keeping conversation away from anything too personal, Amy pulled away. "Loads and loads more," she replied. "But I won't bore you."

They looked at each other for a long moment.

Celeste moved closer. "Amy, I want to—"

Amy jumped when her cell phone burst into life. She looked at Celeste and tried to communicate her regret as she answered it. "Hello," she said her eyes on Celeste.

"Hi, Amy, it's Mike. Look, I'm sorry I wasn't there, but—"

"Mike," Amy interrupted, watching Celeste pick up her car keys. "Look, don't worry about it," she said hastily. "We'll talk about it tomorrow. I'll call you. Bye." She hung up.

"Amy, I have to go," Celeste said. Frowning, she looked at her watch. "I'm meeting Alex at three." She motioned to her car. "Walk with me?"

Amy lifted her eyebrows in surprise at the sharp sense of loss. Nodding, she murmured, "Sure."

They walked to the car in silence.

"I also need to finish packing," Celeste told her, stopping at her car. "I'm leaving for Zaire tomorrow morning."

Amy's jaw slackened and a wave of concern washed over her. Only this morning she had listened, in shock, to a news broadcast about the violence in eastern Zaire. She wanted to reach out to Celeste and tell her not to go. To her surprise, she had to physically hold back and bite her tongue to keep from saying the words, "Don't go." Instead, she stared at Celeste. God, how can she do it? The news reports said over a million refugees were caught up in the violence. I should stop her. What if I never see her again?

Amy's eyes searched Celeste's face and her mind worked frantically. Suddenly aware she was staring she looked away and focused her gaze on the house.

Celeste watched her.

Amy knew when Celeste had come home she had confided in Josh that she was taking time out, even contemplating leaving MSF as her last field trip had been traumatic. Josh didn't know the details, as Amy did, but he was delighted Celeste intended to settle in Sarasota. Closing her eyes for a brief moment, Amy thought how devastated he and his family would be at the news. Opening them she turned her head to Celeste and asked huskily, "I thought you had finished with MSF?"

Smiling poignantly, Celeste whispered, "So did I."

"When did you get the call to go?"

"A few days ago."

Amy felt strange. All sorts of emotions were running through her. She was having difficulty fighting off the need to slip her arms around Celeste's slim waist and hug her tight. Instead, she wrapped her arms around herself and fought the desire to tell her to stay. She even tried to joke. "Helluva way to get out of a wedding invitation."

Celeste half-smiled. "Perhaps."

"I take it you won't be coming back," Amy paused, "for the wedding, I mean?"

Celeste moved forward slightly.

Amy could see she was struggling to say something.

Celeste raised her hand as if to touch Amy's face, hesitated, then dropped it. "No. I'm sorry. I won't be back for the wedding."

Turning from Amy, Celeste opened the car door and got in. She rolled down the window. "I hear congratulations are in order."

Not grasping what she meant, Amy looked at Celeste quizzically then briefly closed her eyes. Unlike her, Josh was completely thrilled by their unexpected pregnancy. The thought of being a parent blew him away and he wanted to tell the world. With a lot of effort, Amy had reined him in and asked him not to tell anyone until she passed the three months stage. *Why Josh? Why did you have to tell her, for Chrissake? Why did you have to tell Celeste of all people?*

Amy stepped closer to the car, and placed both hands on the car door. "When did Josh tell you?"

Starting the engine, Celeste looked at Amy. "A few days ago."

"When will you be back?"

"I really don't know." Her eyes lingered on Amy's lips. "But it's unlikely I'll be back anytime soon."

"How long?" Amy asked, frowning.

Searching Amy's face, Celeste replied, "It's a promoted post and the first year's mostly fieldwork. The overall assignment's for three years, possibly more."

Amy flinched. "You took an assignment for three years!" She bit down on her bottom lip to stop from saying anything more. Acutely aware that she didn't want Celeste to leave, Amy's pulse began throbbing in her neck. An unexpected wave of fear washed over her. Where Celeste was going was dangerous, what if something happened to her?

Amy cut off any further thoughts. Get a grip, she told herself. This is for the best, her internal voice rationalized; she's doing the right thing. The reason for her leaving might be unsaid, but you both know why. That night should never have happened. This way, both of you can have distance.

Amy sighed. Even though she understood the logic, her thudding heart was telling her something else. She looked into Celeste's eyes. Unintentionally, she leaned closer, and thought how easy it would be to kiss her.

Celeste brought her face closer just as Amy's inner voice told her to back away. *Remember, Josh? The man you're about to marry? Her brother, for God's sake!*

The reality of the situation hit home and Amy stepped back from the car.

Celeste's eyes searched Amy's face intently. Eventually, she nodded as if in acceptance then put her shades on and drove off.

Amy watched Celeste's car disappear. *We should have talked. We should have talked about what happened and together tried to put some rationale to it. Maybe then she wouldn't have had to leave.*

Feeling empty, Amy walked back into the house and collected the drawings, putting them away. She left the house, got into her car and drove home, no longer in the mood to talk to anyone.

Chapter 12

Four years later

"George, it's going to be fine," Amy said. Cradling the phone on her shoulder she tried to tie her hair up. It was seven thirty in the morning and already her boss wanted reassurance that an important meeting this morning would go without a hitch.

"You shouldn't have let Maggie go home," he said petulantly.

"Oh, c'mon George, play nice and stop being a big baby," Amy replied. "She's my cousin not an indentured servant. She can take as much time off as she wants."

That morning, George had almost passed out when Amy told him Maggie wasn't back and Josh was unavailable.

"When is she due back?"

"At the end of the week."

Two weeks ago Maggie had left to visit family and the mornings had been nothing but a complete nightmare. Since having the twins, a small army was required to mobilize getting them out the door.

Thankfully, Maggie offered to help them when the boys were born, supposedly taking a leave of absence from her nursing job until they found a suitable nanny, which Amy realized three years in wasn't going to happen anytime soon.

"Couldn't you have talked her into coming back earlier?"

"Look, George, I've already explained this to you. Maggie has decided to stay a little longer. Okay?" she said, annoyed that he seemed convinced she wouldn't manage to get the boys out the door this morning.

"Yes. Okay, but you know this meeting is very, very important for the firm. If we clinch this deal we're on the map."

Smiling sweetly at her children, Amy watched them eat their breakfast while she explained to George once again that nothing, absolutely nothing, would make her late for the meeting at nine o'clock sharp.

While she placated her boss, Amy watched Ryan, the more precocious of the twins, pick up a piece of toast dip it into his egg and chew on it. She abruptly stopped talking when the said piece of toast flew through the air and hit her white silk shirt dead center.

Amy's mouth dropped open. Transfixed, she watched the toast slide down the front of her shirt, halt briefly, then flop onto the tiled kitchen floor. Stunned, she dropped the phone. Mouth hanging open, she looked down at the mess. Exasperated, she shook her fist in frustration at her son. "Ryan, you little shit," she wanted to yell but managed to hold back.

Ryan and Christopher giggled.

Controlling her temper, she fumed. "Right, that's it!"

About to march out into the hallway and along to Josh's office, Amy paused when she heard a small voice. Realizing that George was still on the line, she scrambled for the phone mumbled something then hung up.

Looking at the boys, Amy repeated. "Right, that's it!" Turning, she strode toward Josh's office.

Josh had organized an early morning conference call to finalize the arrangements for an upcoming software release. For the last few years he had been working for a software company. He often tried to explain to Amy what he did, but she couldn't help but glaze over whenever he fell into technical jargon. She understood that he worked in software development and knew it had something to do with robotics, but the dynamics of what he was doing seemed to change constantly. Often he was working on several prototypes. She did try to show interest, but his work just didn't do it for her. Although she used design software for work, the thought of sitting day after day staring at a computer screen filled her with dread. She needed air and lots of activity.

Storming down the hall, Amy looked at her watch. "Bloody hell," she said, realizing if she didn't get out of the house soon George would serve her up on a platter. As she approached, Josh's office, Amy noted the door was closed. Normally it was

Denial

left ajar for the boys to have access, but a few weeks ago they had brought home two golden retriever puppies, Mac and Flynn, as a surprise for the boys. Josh now kept the office door closed to keep the pups out.

At the end of her rope, Amy burst in regardless. "Josh, will you help me?" she cried out. "Not only do I now need to change my shirt, but every single morning since the pups arrived it's been a complete nightmare getting the boys away from them and into the Jeep and out to nursery school. Normally, it wouldn't be a problem because you're always there, but this morning," she bellowed, "it's a different matter!"

Josh sprang out of his chair, a look of bewilderment crossing his face. Looking at his wife, he spoke briskly to his team, "Let's take a twenty-minute break guys." He hit a button and ended the call.

Josh quickly followed Amy as she marched down the hallway. They stopped in their tracks at the kitchen door. Amy gaped in horror. Ryan and Christopher were rolling around on the kitchen floor playing with the puppies. The clean outfits she had just put them into were covered in breakfast and puppy slurp.

Throwing her hands in the air, Amy looked at Josh in exasperation. "Look at them!" Looking down at herself, she gulped. "Look at me!"

"Amy, why didn't you put the dogs out in the yard?" Josh asked, rallying the pups and putting them out into the newly fenced portion of the backyard.

Amy tutted. "I was about to," she replied, "but the phone rang."

Josh slid the glass panel closed then clapped his hands. "Right boys, move it!"

Amy left the kitchen and hurried upstairs toward their bedroom. Sliding back the doors to her wardrobe, she remembered George's astonished gasp when she hung up on him. He was terrified something would go wrong this morning. "So far, he's right!" she muttered, shaking her head in disbelief. "Everything is going tits up!"

Reaching for a clean shirt, Amy cursed Maggie for leaving and Josh for having his meeting this morning. Pulling a shirt from its hanger, she cursed the alien children that had arrived since those puppies had come. Hurriedly, she put on a white cotton shirt and tried to button it. Having difficulty, she gave up when she glanced at her watch. Quickly, she made her way downstairs.

Amy paused outside the kitchen. Raising her eyes to the ceiling, she begged, "Please. Don't let this day get any worse!"

Squaring her shoulders and firming her chin, Amy headed back into the war zone. Once in the kitchen, she looked around her and smiled delighted that, at last, there was some semblance of order.

Pleased that most of the remains of the boys' breakfast had been removed from their outfits, Amy knelt down to straighten their hair. She kissed them, and for the first time that morning, the knot in her stomach loosened.

Josh pointed the two boys toward the door and tried to lead them out. Wanting to say a final goodbye to the pups the boys clambered between Josh's legs, trying to get to the back door.

Josh sighed and gave up trying to walk the boys out. Instead, he hoisted Ryan over his left shoulder then picked Christopher up and tucked him under his right arm. He turned to Amy. Puffing his chest, he warbled Tarzan's jungle cry.

Startled, the twins fell silent then broke into fits of laughter.

Amy chuckled then called out as she tried to button her shirt, "My hero."

Josh laughed. Turning toward the door, he announced, "Celeste was supposed to be here this morning to help you out with the boys because I knew I would be tied up." He frowned. "It's not like her to be late."

Abruptly, Amy stopped buttoning her shirt. Unsure if she had heard him right she said, "What?" Heart suddenly thudding, she waited, watching Josh struggle to hold the boys.

Getting a better grip, he replied teasingly, "Remember, my twin? She's coming over this morning."

Denial

Trying to absorb the news, Amy blinked a few times, and confirmed slowly, "Your sister is coming over here? This morning?"

Josh answered just as slowly, "Yes. That's right. My sister, Celeste, is coming here."

Still blinking, Amy said, "She's home?"

Losing his hold on the wriggling boys, Josh replied distractedly, "Yup."

Alarmed, Amy's eyes widened in shock. *Celeste is coming here? She can't be!* Sucking in air, she squeezed out, "What do you mean Celeste is on her way over? I didn't even know she was home!"

Grabbing the countertop, Amy breathed in deeply. *This can't be happening, not today.*

Smiling, Josh tightened his grip on the boys then looked at his wife. His smile faded when he saw Amy struggle for breath. He let the boys slide down him then quickly made his way to her.

"Honey?" Josh said, grasping Amy's shoulders. "Amy?" His grip tightened. "Calm down," he instructed. "Take a few deep breaths."

Amy inhaled deeply then exhaled slowly.

"That's it," he said. "Nice and slow."

Sensing an opportunity to play with the pups, the twins slid the glass panel back and slipped out into the backyard to find them.

Light-headed, Amy closed her eyes. Even after all these years, the mention of Celeste's name generally gripped her. Never mind the thought of actually seeing her. She looked at Josh. He couldn't have just arranged for her to come over like it was something she did all the time.

"Why the hell didn't you tell me she was on her way over this morning?"

"Celeste is here to spend time with the family," Josh replied, taking Amy into his arms. "She intends to stay with my folks for the next few months."

Amy stared up at him. "Why didn't you tell me? I could have prepared something!"

"What?" Josh frowned. "What would you need to prepare?"

"I…" Amy tried to think. "I don't know." Her eyes searched the room looking for a clue. "Something!" she added. "There's always something to prepare."

Confusion flickered across Josh's eyes at Amy's logic. "Look, honey, what's going on? I've only ever seen you like this once before, and that was on our wedding day when I thought you were going to run out on me." He kissed the top of her head comfortingly. "I didn't know she was coming home until a few days ago, and I didn't tell you because I thought it would be a good surprise. Listen, it's not a bad thing. We really do need help with the Terrible Two. It'll be a nice surprise for the kids."

"Josh, how can it be a surprise when they don't even know her." Amy pushed out of his arms, and made her way to the large open glass panel leading to the backyard. Huh, she thought, if you knew what happened between us then for sure that would be one helluva surprise.

Shouting to the boys to hurry up, Amy turned to Josh. "Why didn't you tell me?"

Shrugging, Josh threw his hands out questioningly. "What's the big deal, Amy?" he asked, frowning. "I thought you would be glad to see her. She's only visited once since we had the boys, and you didn't see her then because you were visiting family with Maggie."

Amy's aunt, Maggie's mother, had died suddenly a few years ago, and when Amy called home after the funeral, she was told Celeste had made an 'impromptu' visit to see the boys. An impromptu visit, my arse, Amy thought at the time. From that moment on, she decided to reciprocate by deliberately avoiding anything that would involve taking an interest in Celeste. Up until now, that arrangement had suited her just fine.

Obviously surprised by Amy's reaction, Josh continued to appease. "She's only coming this morning because I asked her to help me with the kids. I thought I would mention to her, after discussing it with you, of course," he mollified, "about staying here for a few weeks instead of at my folks. It would mean having an extra pair of hands here while Maggie's away, and a little female company amongst all these guys. I mean even the goddamn pups are male."

When Amy didn't respond Josh added, "To be honest, honey, I really miss her and want her around."

Amy knew he was right. Although she hadn't seen her, Josh had, several times. His job increasingly took him abroad and whenever he could he met up with his sister.

Embarrassed at her overreaction, Amy ran her fingers through her hair. Keep it together, she thought. There's too much else going on this morning.

Trying to calm her rapidly beating heart, Amy breathed in slowly then distractedly shouted again for the boys to hurry up. She focused on Josh. "Of course it's okay to have your sister around," she said, removing her hair band from her wrist and this time efficiently tying her hair back. "I know how important Celeste is to you, but…well…it's not like you to make arrangements and not let me know."

Puzzled, Josh looked at her. "Amy, she's my sister," he said, frowning. "I didn't think it would be a problem."

Ashamed that he had no clue why she was upset, Amy blushed and, feeling guilty, assured him, "It's not."

His voice softened. "Look, honey, it makes sense. Maggie isn't here and everyone else is on vacation, your folks, my folks." He smiled. "No one else is around. Even Sophie cleared out, frightened we might ask her to help." Shrugging, he held out his hands. "Celeste's here and, for now, has plenty of time on her hands." Clearly unsure why Amy was so resistant to his sister helping out, Josh's frown deepened. "And until Maggie gets back she'll be a great help around here." His frown cleared. "You know it makes perfect sense."

Unable to explain her reticence, Amy conceded. Nodding, she smiled at Josh.

Grinning, Josh moved toward Amy just as she lurched forward, thrown completely off balance by the force of two strong puppies hurtling past her.

Josh grabbed Amy, steadying her.

Amy gasped as the pups, with lolling tongues, clambered up her legs looking for attention. Her jaw dropped and she watched in horror as they slapped morning dew mixed with mud all over the cream skirt of her brand-new designer suit.

Unable to believe the number of things that were going wrong this morning, Amy gritted her teeth and grabbed her suit jacket and workbag. "I need to get to work. Could you please get the boys organized and into the Jeep before I lose it completely!"

Moving out of the house quickly, Amy threw her stuff into the passenger seat. Pulling baby wipes from the Jeep she frantically tried to remove the muddy paw prints. For better advantage, she unzipped her skirt and tried to remove the marks of a disastrous morning.

Josh successfully managed to get the boys out of the house, and into the Jeep.

Working at getting the marks out, Amy listened to Josh chat to the boys as he fastened them into their seats. Her lips twitched then she grinned when she heard the boys' laugher as Josh tickled them senseless.

Not happy with the results, but desperate to escape before Celeste arrived, Amy stopped wiping down her skirt. Thank God, she thought, there's a spare suit at the office.

Amy held her breath when tires crunched their way up the driveway. "Shit," she muttered.

Holding her loose skirt in one hand and baby wipe in the other, Amy felt a tingle on the nape of her neck. She turned around slowly and watched Celeste get out of her car. The brunette was dressed casually in jeans and a black T-shirt with her hair in a ponytail. Still as beautiful as ever, Amy thought.

Their eyes locked.

"Hey, Cel," Josh said. Sweeping his sister up in his arms, he hugged her tight.

Unable to break eye contact, Celeste gazed at Amy over Josh's shoulder and wondered what was going on behind those amazing turquoise-blue eyes. Her heart twisted when a cautious look crossed the blonde's face

Denial

"It's great to see you," Josh said, letting Celeste go. He looked at Amy. "Believe it or not, I've worked very hard to get her here."

Celeste smiled. "I'm glad to be here."

Over the last few years, Celeste's job had been more than demanding with little time to visit home. But, if she was honest, it had taken her a long time to accept what had happened between her and Amy. The betrayal factor alone had kept her away; so much so she had only come home once in the last few years, and only when she found out Amy was out of the country.

Looking at Amy, Celeste was forced to admit that back then she wasn't comfortable with the idea of meeting up with her sister-in-law. But now, four years on, she was home for a couple of reasons, one of which was to bury the past with Amy.

Breaking out of Josh's embrace, Celeste approached Amy. Her voice full of warmth, she whispered, "Hi."

Lifting her chin, her voice guarded, Amy replied, "Hi."

"It's good to see you," Celeste said. Stepping closer, she took Amy's hand and squeezed it.

A look of surprise flitted over Amy's face and she quickly pulled her hand back. "I am so late," she said. "Josh, there's no way I can drop the boys off and get to my meeting on time."

Sensing the panic in the air, Celeste offered, "If it helps, why don't I take them?"

Josh and Amy looked at her. With relief, Josh replied, "Great idea, sis."

Amy zipped her skirt. Hurriedly, she thanked Celeste before fetching her workbag from the Jeep. Quickly, she said goodbye to the boys and got in her car. As she pulled out of the garage she rolled down the window.

"See you later, hon," Josh said. Reaching in through the open window, he kissed Amy lightly on the lips.

Celeste looked on amused when Amy blushed heavily.

"Thanks for your help, Celeste."

With humor, Celeste looked into the blonde's vivid blue eyes and nodded. "You're welcome, but Amy, you should know…" She moved her hand up and down the front of her body.

Looking confused, Amy frowned.

"You're…" Celeste pointed at Amy's breasts.

Amy looked down; her wrongly buttoned shirt was gaping open at the cleavage. She turned bright red. "I'll sort it later," she said. Smiling awkwardly, she revved the engine and drove off.

Waving goodbye, Celeste wondered why Josh hadn't told Amy her shirt was wrongly buttoned. She watched him wave goodbye then smiled knowing full well her brother was mischievous enough to let his wife go to work without telling her that her shirt was undone.

After Amy's car disappeared from view, Josh turned to Celeste. "Let me reintroduce you to the Terrible Two." Pointing both hands at the Jeep, he spoke as if narrating for an old western movie. "You might have served in battle-torn countries, dodged bullets, survived hurricanes and saved countless lives. But," his voice timbered as he took her hand and pulled her gently toward the Jeep, "I'll be amazed if you last a week with these two."

Enjoying the playful glint in Josh's eyes, Celeste winked at her brother and laughed freely when he dropped her hand, and beating his chest, roared. She grinned when she heard gleeful giggles coming from the Jeep.

Chapter 13

"It's great to be home," Amy said, smiling widely at Celeste.

Celeste glanced at her watch. It was nine o'clock. "Here, have this." She handed Amy a glass of red wine and smiled warmly at her.

Celeste picked up her own wine and took a seat across from Amy. For the last two weeks Amy had worked late most evenings, and for the last few days was locked up in business meetings with a bunch of solicitors in New York finalizing, according to Josh, a lucrative, long-term contract.

Celeste watched Amy as she sat contentedly on the sofa with Christopher in her arm, gently rocking him to sleep. Ryan was already sound asleep with his head on Amy's lap. As it was Friday, the boys were allowed to stay up later than usual to welcome their mom home.

Celeste smiled as she watched Christopher fight to keep his eyes open.

Taking a seat on the sofa beside his family, Josh asked, "Are you hungry, honey?"

Smiling, Amy shook her head. "No, thanks, I ate earlier." She sipped her wine. "Has Maggie called? I haven't managed to get hold of her in the last few days."

Josh chuckled. "Every friggin' day." He raised his eyebrows. "Hasn't she tried to call you?"

"Yes," Amy replied, her husky Scottish burr lilting in Celeste's ears. "But because of the length of time the meetings went on, I kept missing her." Amy looked at Celeste, and included her in the conversation. "Apparently, some old friends from New Zealand have paid a surprise visit, and because Uncle Jim's feeling better, she's taken off into the hills with them, but it's practically impossible to get a signal there."

Josh nodded. "She talked to Celeste recently."

"We spoke yesterday," Celeste said, making eye contact with Amy. "She knows you're due back this evening, but she wasn't sure if she would catch you tonight as she's off to bag her last Munro."

Celeste's eyes widened with pleasure when Amy smiled at her. She held her breath when Amy bent her head and brushed her lips over Christopher's forehead.

"Maggie is a keen hiker and has bagged all but a few of the Munro Mountains in Scotland," Amy explained. "Munros are climbed by hikers with near-religious fanaticism, and Maggie's dedicated. I'll give her that." Looking at Celeste, she added with a touch of humor, "She bags those things with the same kind of dedication that wee, spotty adolescent comic collectors have."

Celeste smiled at Amy's description of Maggie. Sipping her wine, she listened as Josh questioned Amy about her trip. Unobserved, she allowed her expression to become open. Exhaling slowly, she carefully appraised Amy, liking her professional look. She looked great in her white, long-sleeved cotton shirt with onyx cufflinks, and smart tailored black trousers with heeled shoes. Celeste looked at Amy's suit jacket. She liked the way the blonde had thrown it over the sofa when she arrived home.

Taking a sip from her wineglass, Celeste watched her brother and his family. Six months ago, having a family was the last thing on Celeste's mind, but while working in Sierra Leone a four-year-old boy, Daniel, had come to her attention when treating his mother, who was dying of AIDS. His grandparents were old and, given the crisis, wouldn't be alive much longer. This meant that Daniel and his four-month-old baby sister were vulnerable.

Years of experience made Celeste fully aware of how bleak their future was without a family to protect them. She had seen it before, been exposed to similar types of situations over the years, but this time it affected her. Normally there was some sort of network of extended family for the children, but not in this case. There were no relatives. The orphanages were their only hope, and life there was nearly always grim.

Daniel was extremely bright. Something about the boy and his vulnerable baby sister touched Celeste. When she made the decision to plan for a future that included them she was surprised at how certain she felt she was doing the right thing. She thought of Felice, who had told her often it was only a matter of time before a child would reach in and touch her heart. She smiled ruefully. Felice was right.

Focusing on Amy, Celeste's fingers tingled when Amy laughed at something Josh said. Her pulse quickened when he reached out and loosened Amy's dark blond hair from its hair band. Celeste's eyes widened appreciatively when Amy's hair fell around her shoulders. She focused on Josh and watched him look adoringly at his wife. Her eyes narrowed and her stomach twisted as new feelings of jealousy swamped her.

Surprised and frightened by the intense emotions running through her, Celeste stood, put her glass down and excused herself, uttering as she left the room that she had an early start.

Startled, Amy watched Celeste leave. Concerned, she queried Josh, "Is she okay?"

Josh squeezed Amy's shoulder. "Nothing's wrong with her."

Amy smiled up at Josh then sipped her wine.

Over the last two weeks, Amy had noticed that Celeste singularly sought out Josh's company. It warmed her heart they were so comfortable and good fun around each other. The boys too, Amy admitted, adored their aunt. Her lips quirked, knowing that the reason was mostly due to Celeste giving in to the boys' every whim.

To Amy's surprise, Celeste was a fabulous cook and was happy to prepare meals for them most evenings. To her further surprise, Amy realized she liked having the brunette around; she was easy company.

Josh stroked Amy's cheek lightly. "There's been a change of plan."

Surprised, Amy looked at him. "What?"

"I won't be able to come with you to my folks tomorrow."

Seeing the disappointment in her eyes, Josh explained there was a problem with the software due for release.

Amy sighed then listened patiently as Josh explained the situation, telling her it would take a maximum of two to three days to sort out. This week they had planned a break as Fraser and Camille were returning from their tour of Australia.

Amy really liked Josh's parents and over the last few years had developed a strong relationship with them. She loved that they doted on the children. Recently, the couple had chosen to retire and move to Jacksonville; a few hours' drive away. Fraser preferred north Florida, as the climate was different—the winter months tended to be chilly—and there was easy access to places like Atlanta. The attraction, he told Amy when she queried, was being able to escape to the Georgia mountains in August when tourism got heavy. The couple promised that it wouldn't impact on time with the children, and to date it hadn't. All it meant was the kids tended to spend entire weekends at their grandparents.

"Thank God, Celeste has been here over the last two weeks," Josh said, rubbing his forehead. "Given the pressures you've been under and the problems with the software release, we would've really struggled if she hadn't been." He stood then picked Ryan up. "Why don't we turn in?" He looked at Amy. "Let's put the boys to bed and," his tone suggested something, "have an early night."

Amy nodded then stood. She thought he was right, overall, Celeste had turned out to be a great help. But, she reflected as she hugged Christopher to her, although Celeste was friendly enough, there was a definite distance between them. Celeste only seemed to relax fully when her brother and the children were around.

Amy resolved that what happened between them, if not forgotten, was now very much a part of the past. Celeste, she concluded thankfully, was only here to strengthen her relationship with her brother and build a relationship with the twins.

Amy felt for the first time since Celeste's arrival, a great sense of relief. She began to hope their 'encounter' was behind them, and hoped with a little work a friendship could be encouraged.

Chapter 14

"Josh, please make sure it's no more than two days," Amy said, hugging him.

"I promise." He kissed Amy then headed for his car.

Amy waved goodbye and wondered absentmindedly if that was all Josh did—sort software glitches. She was sure the company he worked for would never release this software as there always seemed to be a problem with it. When she told him that grumpily this morning, he laughed and told her the business he worked in meant that even when it was released they would still have problems.

Closing the door, Amy frowned. She didn't understand how his company could spend so much time and money sorting something that probably would need to be sorted again when released anyway. In her business, when you built something, you tried to ensure it was built right the first time.

Amy smiled at the ruffled sight of Celeste and the two boys coming down the stairs. Moving toward the kitchen, she called over her shoulder, "Let's have a decent breakfast before we head out this morning."

Eventually, after a few false starts and lots of running around, Amy and Celeste managed to pack the Jeep with the boys, the puppies, and their accoutrements, and get going. Amy laughed at Celeste's incredulity over the amount of stuff they needed to pack.

During the drive, the excited noise from the boys about seeing their grandparents encouraged the pups to bark. Within the hour, Celeste asked Amy if she had any headache tablets.

On arrival, Celeste asked, "How do you cope?"

The boys asleep, Amy started to unload things from the Jeep quietly. She looked at Celeste in surprise then teased, "Ask my therapist."

Laughing, Celeste said, "You're a Scot, Amy. The Protestant work ethic surely doesn't allow time for a little therapy."

"Okay, you got me there. Only therapy I get is retail, and that's usually in the boys' department."

Celeste helped Amy unload the Jeep. "This is good. I need the practice. Motherhood is seriously tough."

Amy looked at her quizzically. "You want to share something?"

Celeste shook her head. "No jumping to conclusions, Amy. It's not what you think." Her eyes twinkled. "Forget the twenty-six miler," she said, heaving a bag out the back of the Jeep. "There should be an Olympic award for endurance with motherhood, don't you think?"

"You're not kidding," Amy replied. She smiled. "Especially with my two ragamuffins."

"Are you planning any more?"

"*What!*" Amy exclaimed. "You have met my kids, haven't you? She laughed. "Don't you know what motherhood does to a woman?"

Celeste smiled. "You want to tell me the horror stories?"

Amy grinned. "Just remember at the thousandth story you asked first, okay?"

"Remind you at the thousandth story, got it."

"Where do I start?" Amy said, scratching her head. "Oh yeah. A couple of weeks ago, Josh and the boys met up with me after I was finished at a hair salon I use. We'd made plans to take the boys somewhere that afternoon. When I went to pay, Ryan decided just at that moment to release some pent-up energy and run amok. Josh gave chase, of course, and I got so distracted that instead of asking how much it was for a shampoo and blow-dry, I asked how much it was for a shampoo and a blow job."

Celeste grinned.

"*A blow job!*" Amy turned beet-red. "I asked my hairdresser how much for a blow job."

"Wasn't on special that day I take it?"

"Blow jobs aren't a service they offer apparently."

Celeste laughed. "Okay, point taken. Note to self, Amy would rather hit her head until unconscious than have any more kids."

"You've got it." Amy looked toward the house. "You sure your folks said they wouldn't be long at store when you spoke to them? They haven't decided to run out on us since the last time they had the kids?"

"Nope, from what I've heard Mom's over insisting Ryan eat his vegetables."

"He puked you know."

Celeste smiled. "I know." She tried not to laugh. "He puked in a restaurant, right in her lap."

Amy nodded. "He had the cheek to insist he told her carrots made him sick."

"They're here," Celeste said as her parents' car pulled into the drive. "If you want them to hang around, don't ask for a blow job anytime soon."

Amy smiled. "It's a deal, but only if we both make an effort to check the oven for teddy bears, next time your dad volunteers to make brownies."

"Who was it?"

"Chris. He thought the teddy would help his Papa with the cooking."

Celeste grinned. "Insurance job?"

Amy nodded.

"You gotta deal."

Getting out the car, Camille called out to them.

Amy smiled. "You get the boys, I'll get my in-laws."

Once they unloaded the Jeep and settled in the house, Fraser had gifts for the boys.

"I've brought some kites back for the boys," he said, showing Amy kites from large to small.

"They look great," Amy replied, pleased and grateful that Josh's parents were such a thoughtful couple. Wherever they went they always returned with wonderful gifts for their grandsons.

"Kite flying was a childhood hobby of mine," Fraser said, unraveling the string from a small kite. "I know these days kids are into everything hi-tech, but nothing can beat feeling the wind at your back and flying a kite high. What do you say boys, wanna go fly a kite?"

As Ryan and Christopher whooped with excitement, Fraser encouraged everyone onto the beach.

The afternoon was fun and passed quickly. Amy didn't quite master kite flying, but enjoyed it anyway. Eventually, they decided to quit when the boys began squabbling, and the pups more than once brought them all crashing down.

Back at the house, Amy was preparing the boys for a nap when Celeste mentioned to Camille she was going for a swim. Camille looked at Amy. "Why do you not go too?" she asked. "I will put the boys to bed."

Amy looked at Camille. "I thought you were cooking?" She raised her eyebrows teasingly. "Don't tell me Fraser is cooking now?"

Camille laughed. "Yes," she replied. "We have now agreed on a barbecue, and Fraser can't go wrong flipping a burger."

"I'm not so sure, Mom," Celeste teased.

"Go…now…both of you," Camille said, smiling.

Amy shrugged her shoulders and turning to Celeste asked, "Is that okay?"

Celeste nodded.

"Can we try the kites again?" Amy asked enthusiastically. "Let's take the big kite. I'd like to give it another go."

Celeste smiled and picked up the kite that Amy had difficulty with earlier. Together they strolled onto the beach.

Removing her shorts, Celeste challenged. "First to swim to the buoy can forget eating Dad's burgers and have takeout."

"You're on," Amy replied. Stripping off furiously, she raced after Celeste.

After their swim, which Celeste won by a mile, she flew the kite demonstrating to Amy how easy it was.

For the last two weeks, Celeste had worn her hair in a ponytail. Today was the first time she had worn it down. Amy

Denial

noted she had pulled back the top and sides into a braid; the rest hung below her shoulders. It was much longer than she remembered, but the shine was still as deep.

"So, do I really have to eat your dad's home cooking?" Amy asked. Stretching out on the sand, she propped herself up on her elbows.

The kite flying high, Celeste pulled the cords together, "Yup," she replied. "Unless you have a talent you can show me."

Amy blinked. "Like what?"

"You know, useless talents like whistling through a curled tongue, wiggling your ears, standing on your head, juggling with your feet, that kind of thing."

"I don't think I can do any those," Amy said then laughed. "How about vacuuming and using a Dustbuster at the same time?"

"Maybe," Celeste replied, grinning.

"What can you do?"

"I can do the alphabet backward and forward."

"Oh...I see," Amy replied, enjoying the challenge. "Uhmm..." She raised her eyebrows. "Okay, I carry a huge cache of commercial jingles in my head, particularly ones aimed at kids under five."

"Wow." Celeste laughed. "Now that is useless." She squared her shoulders. "Okay, I can contract my eye muscles and make them shake."

Amy clapped her hands. "No way."

Celeste nodded. "Yes way."

Amy grinned. "Show me."

Celeste fluttered her eyelashes then demonstrated.

Amy laughed hard. "Okay, you win."

Celeste smiled. "Good, because wiggling my ears is something I only do as the last resort."

"No way."

"Yes way."

"You can wiggle your ears?"

"You betcha."

"Your dad always burns everything." Amy pouted. "I'm going to have to eat his food, aren't I?"

"Aww, poor baby," Celeste teased. "Don't forget there is a doctor in the house if things get serious."

Amy stuck out her tongue.

Celeste laughed.

After a few moments, Amy pointed to the kite. "You're good at this."

A brisk wind pushed Celeste, who struggled but kept her balance. "Dad loved taking us kite flying as kids," she said, gaining control.

"Did you ever try it with one of those bike things?" Amy asked. "You know the ones the kite pulls along."

"Nope," Celeste replied, maneuvering the kite.

Amy's eyebrows rose delicately when she noticed that certain movements forced Celeste's black bikini top to push her breasts up and forward.

"But, now he's bought these, I reckon it won't be long before Dad will have one." Celeste yanked her left hand down forcing the kite to come back to her.

Standing, Amy moved close to Celeste. "You're probably right," she said, enjoying the easy banter between them. "Now that he's retired, your mum's going to have one helluva time trying to stop him filling the house with unnecessary objects."

"You're not kidding," Celeste replied. Clenching her teeth, she tried to stop a gust of wind from pulling her several feet.

An unexpected pleasure filled Amy. Her stomach tightened as she watched Celeste gain control.

"You want to try?"

"Had enough?" Amy asked challengingly.

"Maybe," Celeste said. She tilted her head then grinned.

Disarmed by Celeste's killer smile, Amy blushed furiously.

"The wind's getting up," Celeste said, looking around her. "If you don't want to be dragged across state, you'd better hurry."

"I'm ready to take the reins, Captain."

"How confident are you?"

Denial

"So-so," Amy answered. "It probably would help if you showed me."

"Okay," Celeste replied, opening her arms. "Come here."

Not hesitating, Amy moved into Celeste's arms. Encased, she looked at the brunette expectantly.

"Amy you need to turn around," Celeste said playfully.

"Uh…okay," Amy replied, cringing.

Celeste positioned herself behind Amy. Close enough for Amy to feel the warmth emanate from her body, but not enough to touch.

"If you can manage, place your hands under mine," Celeste encouraged.

Amy squeezed her hands into the space Celeste made on the handlebars. Celeste rested her hands lightly on Amy's fingers.

Breathing in deeply, Amy caught the musky scent of Celeste's perfume. Color heightening, she waited for her next instruction.

"Ready?" Celeste whispered into Amy's ear.

Neck tingling, Amy replied in an odd sort of breathless voice. "Yes."

"It's all yours," Celeste said, pulling away.

Enchanted, Celeste sat cross-legged on the sand and watched Amy fly the kite. After a few nosedives Amy's hesitation quickly faded. Celeste smiled, pleased that Amy was enjoying herself.

Celeste looked Amy's bikini-clad body over. She noted her blond hair was richer with color than she remembered. She could see the changes in Amy's body from having the twins; her breasts were fuller and her hips carried a roundness that hadn't been there before. She realized Amy was skinny before, but now the new curves really brought out her beauty. She was stunning.

A sudden gust of wind grabbed the kite. Soaring up, it pulled for release. Celeste watched Amy hang on as it dragged her on its path to freedom. Quick to her feet, she chased after Amy and grabbing her, successfully brought her and the kite down.

Laughing they collapsed alongside each other.

Turning on her side, Celeste watched Amy. She smiled, adoring the husky sound of the blonde's laughter.

Eventually, Amy controlled her mirth. "Thanks," she said then smiled. "If only we had done this after we'd eaten your dad's barbecue."

Arching an eyebrow, Celeste looked at her. "Why?"

"Given his cooking, a hurricane wouldn't have lifted me off my feet."

Propping her head on her palm, Celeste said with some amusement, "Believe it or not, Mom has repeatedly tried to teach him the basics, but I think he kind of likes the reputation."

"What reputation?" Amy asked, untangling her hands from the cords of the kite.

"He's the bad boy of cooking."

"What?" Amy replied. "You mean instead of a life of notoriety through bar brawling, booze, and broads," she teased, "he's built his reputation on being lethal around…kitchen utensils?"

Celeste laughed. "Give him a frying pan," she said as she watched Amy, "he'll cause havoc wherever he goes."

Blowing a strand of hair from her face, Amy looked up at Celeste and with big blue eyes and pleaded, "Help me, Celeste!"

Celeste grinned. "I thought you'd never ask." She reached down and quickly helped untangle the cords.

Once loose, Amy sighed and rubbed her hands together in relief.

Celeste brushed strands of hair from Amy's face. Her fingers lingered on Amy's cheek.

Their eyes locked. Stomach knotting, Celeste whispered, "Amy."

Gripped by a powerful need to touch her, Celeste slowly rested her forehead on Amy's. It would be so easy, she thought wanting to devour her. So easy, just one kiss.

Eyes wide and barely breathing, Amy lay perfectly still as Celeste's forehead touched hers. A barrage of emotions and excitement swept through her. This feels good, Amy thought through a haze, so good.

Lifting her head, Celeste whispered, "I want to kiss you." She swallowed. "I need to kiss you."

Denial

The raw want in Celeste's voice brought Amy thudding back to reality. She tensed. Oh God, she thought, remembering the only other time in her life she felt this terrified, or this aroused, was with this woman, she whispered, "We can't." Her stomach churned with desire. "We can't do this. Not again."

"I know." Celeste groaned. "God, don't I know it!" She pushed away from Amy. Sitting, she hugged her knees.

"Celeste, I—"

"Go, Amy."

Sitting, Amy looked bleakly at her. "Celeste, I want—"

"Please, Amy."

"I—"

"Go!"

Lost, Amy moved closer, and touched Celeste's arm.

Celeste stood. "I'll go before we do something we'll regret a second time."

Stricken, Amy watched her walk away.

Chapter 15

An hour after Amy's return, Fraser Cameron watched his daughter come off the beach, smile at him briefly, then go directly to her room.

After ten minutes and no appearance Fraser knocked on her bedroom door. He was unsure why she hadn't come back with Amy, and felt slightly uneasy that something had happened between them. Amy had been exceptionally quiet since her return.

When Celeste opened the door, he noticed she had changed into a pair of denim shorts and a black V-neck tank top. Even though she looked tense, his heart swelled with pride that he had created such a beauty. He reached out to embrace her and whispered in her ear as he rubbed her head. "All right, pumpkin?"

"Enough, Dad," Celeste said affectionately. "I'm not a kid, you know?"

"I know," he replied, smiling. Even though Celeste was thirty-three, he often forgot himself and treated her as if she were still nine years old. He chuckled and picking her up, swung her around.

She smiled when he put her down. Pleased the tension had left her face, Fraser took his daughter's hand and led her out to the patio toward the still smoking grill where he showed her a plate piled high with burnt food. "I've saved some for you."

Celeste looked at the plate and lifting her eyebrows looked at her father. "Dad," she said teasingly. "It's a grill. You know the simplest method of cooking since humans harnessed fire. How do you still manage to do this?" she asked, pointing at the plate.

"Okay," he answered. "I know it's bad. But you're the one with the passion for cooking, not me."

Denial

Wrapping her arms around him, Celeste whispered affectionately, "I love you, Dad, but I think it's better if I eat out. In fact, I think you should fight the urge to cook in future."

Fraser smiled. Unable to read her expression, he watched her look over at Amy, whose full attention was on the boys. Ruffling his dark gray hair, she said restlessly, "I'm going to go out." She gave him a brief smile before turning to go.

"Okay, pumpkin," he replied, watching her leave. He picked up a burnt burger and chewed on it. Out of all his children Celeste was the one he worried about most. She was the most complex.

There was no doubt Fraser was proud of his daughter. When she told them she wanted to be a doctor, he was delighted. When she volunteered to work in such extreme conditions, he was devastated.

Fraser blamed a lot of her need to get away on her ex, Nick. He shook his head ruing the day she ever met that boy. He hadn't been a good match for her.

Clearing the grill, Fraser knew what she needed. She needed to find what Josh had. She needed someone who could see the inner not just the outer beauty. She needed to fall head over heels in love, he decided.

Fraser closed off the grill. He admired what Celeste did. Over the years with Camille he had traveled many times to where she was based and had seen firsthand how vital her services were. Although he had nothing but the utmost respect for her, he couldn't deny he wanted her here. He wanted his little girl home, close to her family. He wanted her back where she belonged. He wanted her to love someone and be loved.

Fraser smiled and thought comfortingly that at least he and Camille did as much as they could to support her. Over the last six years they worked hard at fundraising for wherever Celeste was. He raised his eyebrows and stopped chewing. Six years. Is that how long it's been? He shook his head and frowned when he looked over at his wife, acknowledging that although Camille said little she worried terribly that something might happen to Celeste.

Bud, the family dog, padded over, breaking his concentration.

Fraser lowered the plate in his hand. The dog sniffed it then promptly turned up his nose.

Chapter 16

Celeste was aware her sister was finding it increasingly difficult to hide the fact that the boys and the pups were getting on her nerves. By midweek the entire family was exhausted with trying to engage Sophie, who was in the throes of completing her fifth novel and only seemed to lift her head from her laptop to complain about the boys or the dogs.

Somehow, the boys seemed to sense her animosity and instinctively tried hard to annoy her.

At twenty-seven, Sophie still lived at home. She told Celeste she didn't see the need to move out as she had 24-7 service from their folks. Their mother, Celeste realized, did everything for Sophie, and her sister good-naturedly milked it to the fullest.

Sophie was definitely a nocturnal creature. It was, according to Sophie, more conducive to support two of her favorite habits—booze and cigarettes. Since she could only get Camille to agree to one part of the day when she could indulge in both wholeheartedly, evenings it seemed suited them both.

Celeste knew their mother was relieved that it was more cigarettes than booze, but it didn't stop her worrying about Sophie's lifestyle.

That night when everyone retired, Sophie encouraged her sister to a nightcap on the beach. Celeste took a bottle of tequila, and Sophie took a pack of cigarettes along with a notepad in case an inspirational moment should strike.

Bud trailed along with them.

They settled on the sand, lit their cigarettes, and took a few slugs of tequila in silence.

Sophie poured some into her hand and gave it to Bud. "I thought you didn't smoke?"

The dog slurped enthusiastically.

"I just like the occasional one," Celeste replied. She reached for the tequila bottle and drank some. "I thought you hated tequila and why are you giving it to Bud?"

Sophie smirked. "He likes it."

Looking at her sister, Celeste laughed heartily. "God, I've missed your wackiness," she said, laying back.

Sophie lay back too and they watched the night sky.

After a while Sophie asked, "What's going on with you and Amy?"

Surprised, Celeste lifted her head and looked at her sister. Realizing the tension between them was probably obvious she replied, "Well. You know. We're just not getting along right now."

Sophie sat up. "No," she said, taking the tequila bottle and slugging some back. "I'm talking about the sexual tension thing."

Celeste sat bolt upright. "*What?*"

"Well," Sophie replied as if stating the obvious, "I've seen the way you look at her, and it *isn't* with sisterly love that's for damn sure."

"Sophie, what planet are you on?" Celeste retorted. She took the bottle and swallowed some tequila. "Somehow, you're confusing real life with those goddamn seriously warped books you write."

"They're horror, Cel," Sophie replied. She picked at the black polish on her fingernails. "Good old-fashioned, bloodcurdling horror books." Lighting a cigarette, she added, reaching for the tequila bottle, "Healthy as hell if you ask me."

Sophie drank as Bud hit her leg with his paw.

Celeste lay back down. Lifting her head, she watched Sophie pour tequila into her palm. Bud slurped it before settling down next to her. "This is crazy," she said. She let her head fall back and laughed.

"I've just finished reading a book on incest," Sophie said, drawing a heart in the sand.

Celeste sat up. She looked at her sister in disbelief. "It isn't incest."

"Ah," Sophie exclaimed as if unearthing the culprit in a murder mystery. "So, you admit that it's not purely platonic?"

Irritated, Celeste frowned. "No!"

Sophie smirked with satisfaction then explained her deduction. "There is a palpable tension between you and Amy, and over the last few days she has done her best to ignore you. In recognition of her remoteness, you've removed yourself from the situation by spending most of your time exploring the beach a few miles off."

"Ergo, Inspector Clouseau, there's sexual tension in the air?" Celeste responded, her lips twitching.

Sophie eyed her sister for a moment as if deciding something. Then dragging heavily on her cigarette, said in her best Garboesque voice, "No, dahling, because I saw you both romp on the beach the other day."

Groaning, Celeste lay back and covering her eyes uttered, "Sophie, what has gotten into you? Lifting her hands from her eyes, she asked defensively, "Why are you spying on people?"

Ignoring Celeste's accusation, Sophie responded, "No, Cel. What has gotten into *you*?" She ran an arrow through the heart shape. It pointed straight at Celeste. "This is Josh's wife you're messing with!"

Sitting up, Celeste watched Sophie inscribe her own and someone else's initials in the heart shape.

"I've been having an affair," Sophie confided.

Relieved that her sister had changed the subject, Celeste teased, "You must still be in therapy to reveal that?"

Sophie laughed. "Yes actually, I am, and guess what?" She leaned forward. "I'm having an affair with my therapist!"

Celeste's mouth slackened. She stared at her sister. "*You're kidding?*"

"There's real chemistry."

"Seriously, you're kidding?" Celeste said then grimaced.

Sophie shook her head. "I'm serious."

"I can't believe it!"

Sophie threw up her arms. "Why?"

"*Why?*" Celeste stared at her sister then shivered. "Because banging old ladies is gross. Jesus, Sophie, isn't she in her seventies?"

Sophie looked at her sister wickedly. "It's not a she, it's a he. A very young, fit he."

Celeste chuckled. "What happened with the woman?"

"She dumped me."

"Why?"

Sophie grinned. "For consistently setting low personal standards and failing to achieve them."

Feeling the tequila kick in, Celeste burst out laughing, Sophie followed. It was a few minutes before either caught their breath.

Celeste lit the cigarette that Sophie passed her.

Sophie slurped from the bottle then wiped her hand over her mouth and asked, "When did you become a rug muncher?"

Shocked, Celeste gagged on the smoke she was inhaling and coughed furiously.

Sophie slapped Celeste hard on the back while holding the bottle to her mouth instructing her to swig.

Eventually, Celeste got her breath back. But, it took a few moments before her face returned to its normal color.

"I was only joking," Sophie said. "I want you to tell me." She leaned in earnestly. "I really want to know what's happening between you and Amy."

Red-eyed, Celeste looked at her sister and said hoarsely, "I thought your crystal ball would have told you that already?"

"No crystal ball needed. You just need to watch the way you look at her."

Celeste slugged tequila and coughed slightly. For a moment, she thought about denying everything, but her sister was like a dog with a bone so she decided to be vague. "Something happened a while back, before they got married." She waved a hand in the air. "It was…" her heart tightened. "It doesn't matter." Wanting to change the subject she passed the bottle. "Your latest book is pretty horrific."

Evidently pleased, Sophie chuckled. "Thanks."

Propping herself on her elbows, Celeste fell into familiar territory. She teased her sister. "Is your shrink treating you because you're a natural candidate for de-selection?"

Sophie smiled sweetly. "Nope. It's because I'm fuckable and tax returnable," she said. "We agreed I was only billable for one of the two sessions a week. He says it makes the accounts look better or something." She wrinkled her nose. "But I go along with it because I get a thrill knowing we go," she bracketed her fingers, "'dutch.' You know women's lib and all that."

Celeste frowned. "Is it serious?"

Sophie half-smiled and shrugged.

"It's okay, Sophie," Celeste said gently.

"I've been here before." Sophie dragged on her cigarette. She frowned and rubbed out the heart shape in the sand. Sticking out her chin she added with a note of defiance, "It won't be long before he dumps me. Once it becomes too ordinary, or once he thinks he's sorted out my many neuroses." She looked at Celeste. "You know, he's a man of integrity. He likes to think he's on the job when he's doing the job." She winked. "If you know what I mean!"

"Are you okay with that?"

Sophie looked at Celeste. "It'll end somehow." She shrugged. "These things never work. He likes being married with a family. He gets his kicks out of fucking his patients." She passed the tequila. "Back to you. So, when did you get the hots for Amy?"

"Sophie," Celeste replied in exasperation. "There is nothing between Amy and me!"

"You bet your half-French froggie ass of there is!"

"No there isn't," Celeste retorted.

Sophie leaned back on her elbows. "Well, if that's true, why have you kept your distance for so long? Why were you two practically making out on the beach like two teenagers in love?"

Looking hard at her sister, Celeste decided there was no point in denying it. "Doesn't the idea of me being attracted to Josh's wife freak you out a little, Sophie?"

Sophie shrugged and said a touch philosophically, "Everyone's on a journey, Cel. Yours just might be a little more convoluted than most!" She looked thoughtfully at her sister. "What do you think Amy will do?"

"Why Amy?" Celeste asked, raising her eyebrows. "Why not what I want to do?"

Sophie laughed then drawled, "I already know what you want to do, sugar!"

Impatiently, Celeste ran her fingers through her hair. "It doesn't matter."

Sophie said quietly, "I'm here for you."

"Okay. I admit it," Celeste said then sighed heavily. "The reason I stayed away is because of Josh and Amy. Because," she hesitated, "of who she is." She rested her chin on her knees. "How do they explain things away in the movies: a moment's indiscretion, it finished before it began?"

Sophie lilted, "If all that we get, we just borrow. If all we make is just sorrow. *C'est la vie.*" Sophie smiled. "Listen," she said comfortingly. "I see that it isn't all one way."

Celeste gave her an inquisitive look.

"I've been watching her. It's clear to me she's attracted to you."

"So, what are you telling me?" Her head getting fuzzy, Celeste squinted slightly. "That it's all right to make a move on Josh's wife?"

Sophie spread out her hands. "*No!*" she replied. "No! Of course not! C'mon, Celeste, giving you permission, even for me, would be a little weird! But there's a connection between you and Amy."

Celeste shook her head.

Sophie shrugged. "Maybe you and I are destined to share the same fate, loving someone else's man." She arched her eyebrow, "Or woman in your case?"

Feeling the rawness of Sophie's words, Celeste responded haughtily, "I'm not in love with her." The tequila kicking in fully, she added wryly, "Just seriously attracted to her!" Leaning forward, Celeste looked at her sister. "A few years ago, I met someone."

"Boy or girl?"

"Girl."

"Pre- or post-Nick?"

"Post."

"Did you two get it on?" Sophie asked eagerly.

Celeste eyed her little sister. "Get back to your bridge, you evil troll. Your powers don't work here."

Sophie laughed. "Sorry. Blame the voices. I just do whatever they tell me."

Celeste grinned.

"Was it love?"

Celeste's grin slipped away. "Maybe," she replied. "It's difficult to say, it was all so new."

"New in terms of being with a woman?"

"Yes." Celeste pushed her hands through her hair. She sighed. "I guess at college I flirted with the idea, but with Felice..." her voice trailed off.

"What happened?"

"She was killed."

Sophie caught her breath. She looked at Celeste with surprise then honest regret. "I'm sorry."

Celeste nodded slowly. "Me too."

"Why have you never told me this?"

"I couldn't." Celeste looked at her sister. "It was too painful."

Sophie eyed Celeste for a while. "Amy, where does she fit in?"

"I don't know," Celeste replied. "All I know is that I meet my brother's bride-to-be and, you're right, I get the hots for her!" She shook her head. "What the hell is all that about? I must be fucked up."

"Rebound?"

Celeste shook her head. She smiled sadly. "Maybe I need an appointment with your therapist?"

"Nope," Sophie said, looking her sister up and down. "Don't you get it yet, sis. Nobody can resist you, not even Amy." She shook her head. "It wouldn't be long before he'd be offering you three maybe five weekly sessions!"

"Garbage!"

"Garbage my ass," Sophie replied. She clicked her tongue. "You're oblivious, aren't you?" She sighed. "That's what makes you so attractive, Cel." She threw out her arms. "The fact that you're beautiful and you don't give a shit about it."

"Give it a rest, Sophie. Not you too."

Sophie laughed. "Fortunately, you're my sister. She shrugged. "So, as always, I'm prepared to forgive you for not giving a shit, for some fucking reason."

"You're drunk."

"I know."

Celeste swigged some tequila. "I don't like it."

"I know."

"Why am I attracted to her?"

"She's hot," Sophie replied. "You're a dyke. The stars shine at night. It's the way things are." She shrugged again. "Accept it."

Celeste shook her head.

"Maybe it's a lot to do with your work."

Confused, Celeste looked at her sister. "What do you mean?"

"It makes you see things differently."

"What?"

Lighting the last cigarette, Sophie mumbled something.

"What are you saying?" Celeste asked as Sophie inhaled deeply.

"You see all sides of humanity."

Confused, Celeste shrugged.

"With your job you see extremes of human nature, right?"

"Maybe"

"There's no maybe about it." Sophie looked at Celeste. "You go to places where there's war and famine and all sorts of shit like that."

Denial

Knowing her sister was more than capable of going off on a tangent, Celeste frowned and tried to figure out what Sophie was telling her. She raised her eyebrows. "And?"

"And, I guess, in some ways, it's a privilege to get to see all sides of humanity."

Now completely confused, Celeste asked, "What are you getting at, Sophie?"

"What I'm getting at Celeste," Sophie replied, "is that where you've been gives you clarity. What you've seen means you don't care about the things that someone like me or most people I know care about."

Confused, Celeste replied slowly, "Okay."

"I mean, you don't give a shit about the rat race or things like material gain or what people think."

Still confused, Celeste looked at Sophie.

"Few of us will leave a legacy," Sophie said, looking at Celeste intently. "In a hundred years who'll care about what we did, what car we drove, what house we lived in, how we worked, what principles we had? Who'll know or even care about what or who we were. A hundred years from now, no one will care."

"This is all very profound, Sophie, but—"

Sophie interrupted. "But because of what you do. It makes you understand what's important. Makes you understand your own mortality, Celeste. Makes you understand that in reality rules don't mean shit."

"What's your point, Sophie?"

"The point," Sophie replied, scrunching the empty cigarette pack. "Is that it makes you less frightened to pursue what you want."

Suddenly curious, Celeste tilted her head.

"Conforming isn't what you do anymore. You might have taken your time to come back home, but I know you. I know you play down what you feel for Amy. And I can see you're fighting it." Sophie drew in her breath then exhaled slowly. "You want to go after her. You want—"

"Enough!" Celeste said, raising her hand. Beginning to feel more than a little queasy, she swallowed hard.

Sophie looked at her sister then stood. "I'm going for more cigarettes. Do you want anything?"

Celeste shook her head. She watched Sophie walk away. She looked up at the night sky and soon fell asleep.

Drops of light rain fell on Celeste's face. Sitting up, she groaned and held her head. Feeling woozy, she tried to organize her thoughts but the rain began to fall heavily. Standing, she ran to the summerhouse. Once inside, she loosened her wet clothes and rummaged around for a towel. Finding one, she threw it over her head and began drying her hair.

Chapter 17

As a mother of two normally Amy would be asleep before her head hit the pillow, but unable to forget the incident with Celeste she had found it almost impossible to sleep, tossing and turning each night. Tonight, too restless to even try, she decided she needed a late night walk to tire her out, only to get caught in the sudden downpour.

Stumbling through the door to the summerhouse, soaking wet, Amy grinned, enjoying that unique sense of exhilaration that only rain can bring. She closed the door and ran her fingers through her hair, immediately feeling her mood lighten. Turning, she jumped in shock when she saw Celeste, bent over loosening a lace on one of her sneakers.

Startled, Celeste looked up at Amy. Trying to stand, her watchstrap caught her lace. Shaking her arm, she tried to release it but lost her balance.

Transfixed, Amy watched Celeste teeter and fall, all tangled up, Celeste spread across the rug.

Rushing to her rescue, Amy asked, "Are you okay?"

"What do you think?"

Amy tried not to laugh. Seeing the normally cool, calm Celeste thrash around the room and fall flat on her arse was priceless.

Celeste glared up at Amy. "It isn't funny!"

Helping her untangle her watch from her shoelace, Amy replied soothingly, "I know. It was just so…unexpected."

Once free, Celeste shot up. The speed of her action caused Amy to stagger back and fall against the wall. The air rushed from her lungs when Celeste's full weight fell against her.

Celeste took advantage of her position. Leaning back, only slightly, she positioned her hands on either side of Amy's head, trapping her. She looked Amy over carefully then fixed her with a gaze. Hiccupping, she pouted her bottom lip.

Amy struggled to stop the laughter that was bubbling out of her. Eventually gaining some control, she looked directly into Celeste's frowning face. Clearing her throat, she tried to look serious. She inspected the light swelling where Celeste had hit her head. It was evident from the reddening on her temple that she would have a mark tomorrow. Gently, as if talking to one of her sons, Amy said, "You'll have a wee mark tomorrow, but nothing to worry about."

Celeste gave Amy a lazy smile. "What are you doing here?"

Suddenly aware of how close they were, Amy straightened and, placing her hands against Celeste's shoulders, tried to push her away. Instead of moving, Celeste astonished her by pressing her gently against the wall.

Looking into troubled blue eyes, Celeste grasped Amy's right hip.

Surprised, Amy exhaled sharply then sucked in air when Celeste ran her hand down the side of her wet denim cutoffs.

Looking intently at her Celeste whispered, "Do you remember that night in your apartment?"

Speechless, Amy stared into Celeste's eyes.

Celeste leaned in. Amy felt her hot breath on her ear. "I do."

The hairs on the back of Amy's neck stood.

Hesitating briefly, Celeste let her fingers trail down Amy's bare thigh, then slowly back up, stopping only when she reached the hem of Amy's cutoffs. Making eye contact, her hand slid further up her thigh. "In fact, I've never managed to get it out of my mind."

Amy closed her eyes and swallowed hard. Her eyes flew open and widened in shock when Celeste's fingers began an exploratory journey up and down the length of her thigh, climbing higher each time.

"When I look at you," Celeste whispered, "I want to see my brother's wife, but I don't. All I see is someone I want."

Amy caught her ragged breath; Celeste was stroking the top of her inner thigh.

Breathing heavily, Celeste leaned her head gently on Amy's. "I know it's selfish," she said, lifting her head when her hand reached its target. "I know who you are and I shouldn't touch you like this, but I'm finding it harder to fight this."

Groaning, Amy involuntarily pushed her hips forward. Dismayed by her body's betrayal and attempting to fight her growing desire, she pleaded, "Celeste. I'm begging you—"

"Begging me to what?" Celeste asked, studying Amy intently. "To stop?" She lowered her dark lashes. "It doesn't feel like you want me to stop."

Ashamed by the extent of her arousal, Amy's face suffused with color.

Celeste started the slow trail again. Looking deeply into Amy's eyes, she brushed her lips over her mouth. "I know that tomorrow we'll want to deny this ever happened," she said throatily. "But not tonight, Amy," she whispered.

Lifting Amy's T-shirt, Celeste stroked her stomach.

Amy's nipples stiffened in response. Closing her eyes briefly, she shivered with pleasure.

Celeste brushed her lips over Amy's mouth again then asked with a note of vulnerability, "Do you want me?"

Amy's stomach flipped, her insides tightened, a bolt of desire shot down her spine, but she said nothing. A shock of electricity ran through her when Celeste kissed her. She swallowed visibly when the brunette slowly withdrew her hands and pulled away.

Fire swept through her veins. Unable to hold back any longer, Amy surrendered. Shaking heavily, she ran her tongue over her lips before hungrily reaching for Celeste. "Do I want you," she replied huskily as she gripped Celeste's arms and pulled her close. "I want you so badly." She swallowed. "I want you more than *anything!*"

Never breaking eye contact and wanting to rip away anything that was between them, Celeste quickly undid the top button of Amy's cutoffs. Loosening the rest, she pushed the denim over her hips and down her thighs. They dropped to the floor.

Impatiently, Celeste kicked the shorts out of the way. Placing a hand against the wall, she slipped the other between Amy's thighs, urgently seeking her warmth.

Amy groaned and arched into Celeste. "Oh God."

Celeste moaned loudly, Amy was so wet. She wanted nothing more than to consume her. Her desire for Amy was so overwhelming that Celeste recognized she needed this like she needed to breathe.

Her thigh muscles shaking, Amy's breath was coming in short bursts. *Celeste, Celeste, Celeste.* Her mind could form no other words.

Celeste stroked Amy in small circles.

"Yes!" Amy croaked. She placed her hands on Celeste's shoulders and rocked her hips to relieve the increasing pressure. "More!" she groaned, spreading her legs. "Inside," she begged. "Please. Go inside me."

Celeste slowly pushed inside her. She caught her breath when Amy's lips brushed over her neck.

A groan left Celeste's throat. She pressed against Amy's clit and increased speed. Placing her lips gently at the base of Amy's neck, she bit.

Amy's hips surged forward and she cried out, "Yessssss!"

Celeste closed her eyes and worked Amy until her hips surged forward one final time.

A deep groan left Celeste's mouth. On fire, she instinctively took Amy's hand and placed it between her thighs. Holding it tight, and still inside Amy, she moved against her. Already driven over the edge with Amy's repeated moans, within seconds, she came.

Breathing heavily, Amy tried to move, but Celeste, catching her own breath, pushed Amy's shoulder firmly against the wall. Shaking her head, she made it clear that they weren't going anywhere. Celeste faced the truth: her desire for this woman was beyond anything she had ever experienced.

"Celeste, I—"

"Shhh," she whispered, kissing Amy's neck.

Denial

Celeste wondered what the connection was between them. Like Amy, she didn't want this. She had plans that involved her staying here, being close to her family, but she couldn't go on like this. She couldn't continue to feel this intense yearning. They needed to do something.

Celeste finally accepted that the only thing to do was to burn this attraction out. Slowly she removed her fingers and half-smiled when Amy let out a sigh of relief.

When Amy tried to straighten, Celeste pushed her fingers back inside then out and over Amy's clit. She watched with pleasure as Amy's eyes widened with surprise, narrowed with protest and finally filled with need.

Amy whimpered and her head dropped to rest on Celeste's shoulder as she pushed into her.

Celeste knew by Amy's response that it wouldn't be long. Her own desire was also building quickly. She closed her eyes, and tried to find the strength to stop. She desperately needed to leave Amy hungry for more.

Amy pushed her face into Celeste's neck, and moaned as she worked toward orgasm.

Celeste slowed.

"Don't stop," Amy said, her voice muffled. "Oh God, I can't believe what you do to me. I need you. Don't stop. Please."

Celeste stopped and pushed away.

Amy's arms reached out, but Celeste moved out of reach.

Straightening, Amy leaned against the wall and looked at Celeste in confusion.

Celeste watched Amy struggle to regain some composure. She waited until she had her full attention then moved toward her. Raising her left hand, she looked at the glistening wetness on her fingers. "I wonder what you taste like?" she asked, running her wet fingers along Amy's lips.

Wiping her mouth with the back of her hand, Amy stared at Celeste in shocked surprise.

Stepping back, Celeste smiled at her. She placed all three fingers into her mouth and sucked on them.

Turning, Celeste left the summerhouse with the glorious image of Amy's jaw gaping open and raw desire pooling in her eyes.

Walking toward the house Celeste was fully aware that she had unleashed something in them. She only hoped it would be quickly satisfied—for both their sakes.

Chapter 18

Josh followed his sons as they ran along the hallway to wake their mother. His heart swelled when he put his head around the bedroom door and caught sight of his beautiful wife.

Amy woke with a start when the boys jumped on her bed. They shouted excitedly. "Daddy's here, Daddy's here."

"Wowwhhh," Amy said. Sitting, she hugged the boys to her. Teasing them, she kissed their faces all over and at the same time tried to stop Christopher's hands from pulling on her hair. She didn't succeed.

Josh smiled and watched, fascinated, as Amy carefully unraveled her hair from Christopher's small, pudgy hands. She reached into the bedside cabinet and retrieved a hair clasp. The action caused the bedsheet to fall away and reveal her firm, full breasts.

Surprised she was nude, Josh's heart jackhammered. He watched her straighten up, pull the bedsheets around her, pile her honeydew hair up, and clasp it.

Josh smiled when Amy lovingly lifted Christopher up and cuddled him to her. He grinned when she rubbed her nose with his. Looking at his boys felt proud that they were a good mix of their parents. They had his dark hair and complexion, but Amy's fine features, and their green eyes were a mixture of theirs.

Wanting Amy up, Ryan jumped up and down on the bed. "Mommy," he said, "Daddy's here…Daddy's here!"

Amy reached out a hand to stop Ryan.

Josh entered the room and made his way to the bed. Grabbing both boys, he ruffled their dark hair playfully.

"Jossssh," Amy said in frustration as he messed their hair.

The boys yelled, "Mom!" as she tried to sort their unruly mops. They wriggled away, rolled off the bed, and began play fighting on the floor.

Squinting, Amy looked at the clock. Her eyes widened in surprise, it was ten in the morning. She looked at the boys; they were fully dressed. Camille must have decided to let her sleep in this morning.

Amy tensed when Josh sat beside her. Her stomach tightened as last night's encounter flooded her mind.

Josh reclined against the headboard. He ran his hand down Amy's bare back, resting it lightly at the base of her spine.

Unable to stop herself, Amy stiffened when his hand moved around her waist and up toward her breast. Turning to face him, she whispered, "Not now."

"I know, honey," he said, stroking the side of her breast lightly. "I can take them downstairs?"

"No…it…it would be too obvious."

"When?" he asked, removing his hand.

Amy visibly relaxed. "Soon," she replied, then swallowed. Turning, she hugged him tightly. "I'm so happy to see you."

Josh wrapped his arms around her.

She snuggled into him. "Is everything sorted?"

"Yeah," he said, pulling Amy closer. "I…" his words were lost as he nuzzled into her neck.

Amy pulled away and turned to look out the window. "Look how beautiful the morning is," she said, wanting to get up. "Let's get ready for the beach. We'll have some time together tonight."

"Okay," Josh said. He herded the boys out of the room so Amy could get ready.

Amy watched them leave. Her heart sank. For the first time since knowing Josh she dreaded the thought of spending time alone with him. Not wanting to think anymore, she threw the duvet back and headed for the shower. Opening the glass panel, she stepped inside and turned on the spray.

Letting the warm water hit her, Amy tried to block out the memories but couldn't. She bit her bottom lip hard as her mind movie reeled the encounter. Unable to stop the vivid replay of the most intense orgasm of her life, Amy groaned and rested her head against the tiled wall. Last night she knew she hadn't been aware

Denial

of anything. Not who she was or what she was doing. She was only aware of Celeste.

Closing her eyes, Amy pressed her head hard against the tiles. Wrapping her arms tightly around herself she tried to block out of the image of being with Celeste and instead focused on making sense of what had happened.

Anger flared up inside Amy as she realized that she was completely powerless around the brunette. She grappled with the new knowledge that Celeste, if she decided, could break down any barrier she put up. Tears blurred Amy's eyes at the thought of telling Josh, as she had intended on her wedding day. Tears spilled over as she remembered that all she succeeded in doing that day was seriously hyperventilating.

Minutes passed as Amy cried. Loneliness overwhelmed her as she finally accepted that she could never tell Josh. Divorce would be inevitable. Josh would never live with such a betrayal. *Who could?* Straightening, she thought about what her father went through. Turning off the shower, Amy swore resolutely to herself that no matter what nothing would ever happen with Celeste again. She and Josh would never become a divorce statistic.

Not wanting to think any more than necessary, Amy dried off then threw on a pair of jeans and a T-shirt. Tying her hair back, she straightened her shoulders and headed downstairs.

Entering the kitchen, she was filled with dread at the thought of seeing Celeste. Eyes focused on the steaming coffeepot, Amy headed straight for it and poured a cup.

Camille entered the kitchen. "*Bonjour, mon chéri,*" she said brightly. Coming up to Amy, she kissed her lightly on both cheeks. "Are you hungry?" she asked affectionately.

Amy's stomach turned. She shook her head.

"Feeling slightly the worse for wear, no?"

Blushing, Amy stared into her coffee mug.

"*Qui?*" Camille teased moving toward the coffeepot.

Amy watched Camille take a china cup from the cupboard and pour a small cup of coffee.

"Celeste mentioned that you stayed up very late last night."

Amy choked on her coffee. *Ohmyfuckinggod!*

Camille looked at Amy. "Are you all right?"

Amy gulped. "I'm fine. The coffee is…stronger than I expected."

Camille carefully placed two sugar cubes in her cup. "Celeste said you needed to sleep this morning," she said, stirring her coffee. "Do you know she left early?"

Terrified to look at Camille in case her face revealed something, Amy shook her head, and gave her coffee cup her full attention. *She's gone. Thank God!*

"Oh," Camille replied with a note of disappointment. She leaned against the kitchen counter. "She did mention something about going to see Alex."

Color rising, Amy eventually looked at Camille but didn't say anything. *Please, Camille. Would you stop banging on about Celeste!*

Camille held her cup in both hands. "I asked her what could be so urgent that she must leave so soon." She raised the cup to her mouth. "She didn't say." Camille looked at Amy for a moment before sipping her coffee. "I do not understand why she is so secretive. Do you?"

Desperate to give nothing away, Amy shook her head.

Camille took another sip of coffee then grumbled, "I mean, what is it that she is making her mind up to do?"

Amy shrugged her shoulders.

"Keep a baby, because she is pregnant?"

Amy gulped. *Pregnant?*

Gesturing grandly, Camille continued, "Is she making her mind up to bring not a boyfriend or fiancée, but a husband home to meet her parents, like she did with Nick?"

Amy's eyes widened. *A husband?*

Camille put down her cup. "I don't know what is going on?"

Realizing that everything Camille had said was conjecture, Amy blinked a few times.

"Merde," Camille sighed. *"Je ne le comprends pas?"* Nodding her head, she arched an eyebrow and looked at the door.

"Zzzooommm," she said with some annoyance. "She was out of the door before I could ask her."

Amy shivered slightly. Camille's mannerisms reminded her so much of Celeste.

Looking at Amy, a hint of pain showed in Camille's eyes. "I cannot understand what Celeste wants!"

Amy swallowed hard. *You and me both!*

Camille sighed. "I worry for her." She lowered her head. "She has an honorable profession, and I am so proud of her. But it is all-consuming, and that worries me."

Amy held her breath. It was unusual for Camille to confide in her.

"I do not expect anything. But I hope," she looked at Amy, "I only hope that she will find someone special." Camille moved closer to her. "I want her to be happy like you." She smiled. "I want her to settle down and have children. I mean," she clicked her tongue, "she is in her thirties now." Camille shook her head. "But when I ask her she is always so…vague." She gently rubbed Amy's cheek. "It is a mother's instinct to want her children to settle down and be happy. You know that, now that you are a mother." She lifted her eyebrows and looked at Amy. "I think she trusts you. I know she is fond of you."

Amy visibly swallowed. Unable to keep eye contact, she bent her head.

Placing a hand under Amy's chin, Camille lifted it and regarded her. "I know she confides in Josh," she said quietly, "but he is as closemouthed as she is. Will you at least talk to Celeste about what her future plans are?"

Desperately uncomfortable, Amy quickly nodded, then pulled away from Camille. For something to do, she refilled her cup and attempted to change the subject. "Where's Sophie?" she asked. *Oh, sweet Jesus. That was a big mistake!*

"*Mon Dieu!*" Camille uttered. She went off on a tangent about how Sophie probably wouldn't surface until noon and that *she*, too, needed to find herself someone to love. Camille concluded, "If they were only a little more like you, Amy, then I would be a happy woman!"

Blushing, Amy bowed her head in shame. *If only you knew, Camille. If only you knew.*

Amy listened to Camille's chatter for a while before looking out through the patio doors. She watched Josh play with the boys. They're your priority, she told herself.

Watching her husband play with their children, Amy's world slowly righted itself.

To Camille's evident surprise, Amy hugged her then kissed her cheek. She whispered, "*Merci.*"

Sounding slightly confused, Camille replied as she hugged Amy back. "You're welcome, *mon chéri.*" She stood back. "You must eat, darling." She looked her daughter-in-law over. "You have always had a lovely figure, but you will get scrawny if you do not eat."

Amy shook her head. "I'm fine."

"Mmmm, I know what you working mothers are like—busy, busy, busy. All work and no play, huh!" Camille rolled her eyes disapprovingly then clicked her tongue. "But listen to me, you need to eat." She opened the fridge. "Now, let's see what we can get you for breakfast."

Chapter 19

Celeste glanced at Alex's smiling face.

It was early Friday morning and they were driving to the Keys to spend the weekend with some friends.

Bemused, Celeste watched Alex carefully unwrap a sandwich from his well-stocked picnic basket. She shook her head when he offered it to her. Food, she thought swallowing a bitter taste in her mouth, was the last thing on her mind.

Celeste watched Alex bite into his sandwich. He groaned loudly with satisfaction and she laughed softly. She adored Alex. Ever since they were at grade school they had been close. Now, he taught English literature at their old high school.

Alex ate his sandwich and chatted while Celeste half listened. Normally she would have enjoyed this journey, but today too much was on her mind. She couldn't go on like this, she realized. Not after the summerhouse a few nights ago. She needed Alex to help her rationalize what was happening. Deciding to confide in him, she said quietly, "Alex…"

Alex stopped chattering, content that Celeste was now relaxed enough to talk. Since she had arrived a few days ago it was clear that she was completely preoccupied.

"Yes."

Celeste gave him a quick smile, drew in a breath and proceeded to tell him everything.

Amy! Alex was in shock. *My God, she's into Amy!*

"I should have realized something was wrong when you took off before the wedding."

Celeste glanced at Alex. "What else could I do?" Her hands gripped the wheel. "When I found out Amy was pregnant…well," she sighed, "there was no other option. We couldn't take it any further." She looked at him. "If I'm honest, I wasn't ready to explore any more than a one-time event. Felice had just been killed, and emotionally, I was a mess."

"Tell me more about Felice," Alex asked.

"Not much to tell," Celeste said. She frowned. "We didn't get much of a chance to explore it fully."

Alex nodded. "And Amy, you're sure, is more than a one-time event?"

"Yes. It's…different," Celeste replied.

Alex wondered how it would have been if Amy hadn't been pregnant. Maybe they would have gotten together. He realized it didn't matter now, his job, as her friend, was to stop her from making this mess any bigger than it already was.

Celeste glanced at Alex before focusing on the road. "Are you going to say anything?"

"Celeste, no matter how you look at it she's your brother's wife, your sister-in-law. That alone should set off major leave-well-enough-alone warning bells in your head!"

"Jesus, of course it does!" Celeste said. "But I've explained to you what happened."

Alex knew that in the last few years Celeste had barely been in a country where defining her sexuality was important. Getting on with saving lives was the important thing. "I know that we never really discuss it," Alex said. "Tell me, have you been with a few women? I mean more than Felice," he hesitated, "and Amy?"

Celeste nodded.

Pleased, Alex smiled. It was reassuring that she'd been with other women. Less chance of fixating, he thought.

"Good, then let me make it easy. This weekend you can have whatever and whoever you want." He smiled broadly. "Let me tell you, sweetie. You can have your pick." He shook his head when Celeste opened her mouth. "Except, you *know* who!" He clapped his hands. "Anyway, you've told me how you feel, but what about Amy? What does she feel? I mean surely she must be confused?"

Celeste didn't respond.

"What's Amy's take on all of this?"

Celeste gave him a vulnerable look.

Alex sighed. He was going to have to be gentle with her. "Okay. Do you want the long or short version of what I think?"

"The short."

Alex decided to be brutally honest. He ran a finger down his palm. "Let's have a look through the moral code chart." He tapped his palm. "Coveting your brother's wife. Now where would that be? Yup, found it." He looked pensive. "It's right up there on the priority list," he said, showing Celeste his empty palm. "Catch 'em and hang 'em, it says here."

Celeste shook her head.

"If I know Amy this will be tearing her apart." Alex frowned. "I'm assuming you know the baggage between Amy and her mother?"

Celeste sighed heavily.

Knowing his words were hurting her, but knowing she needed to hear the truth, Alex continued, "According to Maggie, Amy has never forgiven Irene," he bracketed his fingers, *'for having an affair.'* The very same *affair* that caused her father to fall apart, leaving Amy to pick up the pieces. Hence, the reason she has never forgiven Irene. Ergo, any psychologist will tell you she is an A-one classic type. That's the type that place serious, and I mean serious, emotional trappings on being in a monogamous relationship."

Alex drew breath and waited for a moment. "I really am being serious. I know you've been away, and I know what I'm saying might hurt you, but you've still been on the same planet, right?" He looked to Celeste. She nodded. "So you do know about the issues she has with Irene?"

"Yes."

"Then you must know that the only thing you've truly been fucking is her mind?"

Celeste winced. Her shoulders stiffened. "Is that what you think? That I'm playing a game?"

Alex shrugged. "Well, what else can it be? Look at you." He opened his hands. "You're gorgeous. You could literally have anyone you wanted." He shook his head. "Don't you think that it's more than a little fucked up that you chose to ignore all the unattached, solvent, solid in the head, good lesbian citizens of the world, and go for what should be the most unobtainable woman on the planet to you?"

Celeste breathed in deeply. "It's not like that," she responded. "In all honesty, Alex, I have never been so attracted to anyone the way I am to her." She glanced at him. "And I know exactly who she is." She shook her head. "I know that it is completely inappropriate for this...*it*...whatever *it* is between us to happen." Her grip tightened on the wheel. "But, goddamit, I want her."

"*Want?*" Alex said, waving a hand in the air. "So what, Celeste? There isn't a day goes by that I don't want Mr. Richmond, our old sports teacher. But that doesn't mean I'm going to hunt him down and break up his marriage!" Although, Alex thought dreamily, with those thighs, I might if I thought I had a chance. "It's a crush, Celeste," he added dismissively. "Nothing more. You'll get over it."

Celeste, staring ahead, replied firmly, "It's more than that."

Alex bowed his head. She was right, of course. It had to be much more than that. This kind of thing was definitely not her style. This is some serious shit and the repercussions could be horrific.

Alex loved the Cameron family like his own, and the last thing he wanted was a meteoric rift if the family found out and he knew for sure that they would find out if Celeste didn't stop this. Whatever else, he decided that she needed a reality check. He said quietly, "What about Josh?"

Celeste visibly paled.

Alex hammered home. "It would destroy him if he ever found out!"

Celeste nodded. "I know."

Alex meant to whisper dramatically, but instead hissed, "Are *you* prepared to take the risk?" He raised his eyebrows but Celeste completely ignored his dramatic flair.

Celeste exhaled deeply. "I want to say no." She glanced at him. "But I don't know anymore." She focused on the road. "I honestly don't know what to do."

Alex touched her arm. *Jeez, she has it bad.* "Darlin', it's simple. You need to find a new playmate. I only wish that you had told me all this a few years ago. Then, you wouldn't have had to deal with it on your own. I would have introduced you to a few bombshells, and let me tell you, one touch of their *buzzzzoms*," he put his hands out about a foot in front of his chest to emphasize his point, "would wipe your hard drive clean of any memory of Amy."

Celeste laughed. "Alex," she said, shaking her head. "Are you sure you're an English teacher? You're beginning to sound more like the wayward kids you teach at high school."

He smirked. "You gotta move with the times, baby."

Alex watched Celeste shrug a few times, obviously trying to relax.

"Alex, I'm not trying to fuck with her mind," Celeste said. She shook her head. "I can't explain it."

"I know," Alex said. He reached into the picnic basket at his feet and brought out a bottle of champagne. "Let's just try to enjoy our trip."

Chapter 20

"Let's not leave it so long next time," Marie said to Celeste.

"That's a deal," Celeste replied, smiling warmly.

"And next time you see your brother," Charlie, Marie's husband, said as he hugged Celeste. "Tell him I'll be in town in a few weeks and I'll be calling him for a round of golf."

"Good night, guys," Alex said. Impatiently, he pulled on Celeste's arm. "I'll see you both when I'm next down. And remember," he huffed as Celeste resisted, "give little Charlie a kiss goodnight from me when you get home."

That evening Alex had, after their meal, wanted to go to a gay bar and now he wanted to go to a club. Their old school friends, Marie and Charlie, made their excuses, needing to get home to let the babysitter go.

"Okay, Alex," Marie said warmly. "I'm sorry we can't go to a club. But, hey, having a kid means you forfeit that after-midnight pass."

"Don't worry," Celeste said, holding her ground as Alex playfully pulled at her. "You're not going to miss anything other than Alex doing his ugly sister act if he doesn't get his way."

Alex laughed. "Whatever, Cinderella! The night is young, and I'm out to find my Prince Charming."

Celeste and Alex kissed the couple good night, promising to call them soon.

Walking away, Alex excitedly explained that he had arranged to hook up with a dark-haired sports teacher he had met earlier in the bar.

Once in the club, Celeste settled on a sofa and let Alex fight his way to the bar. She looked out to the dance floor and felt the buzz from the wine at dinner and the tequila shots at the bar. Letting the warm, fuzzy, alcoholic haze wash over her, she leaned back, stretched her long legs out and closed her eyes. No sooner had she closed them than Alex roused her. Handing her a drink, he budged her up the sofa.

Full of energy, Alex tapped her leg. "Let's hope he's here," he said loudly in her ear, before scanning the whole area.

Smiling, Celeste closed her eyes again.

Alex shook her and began a conversation that would get her attention. "Okay, I accept that you are very, *very* physically attracted to Amy. I can see why. She's hot." He looked at her. "There is no doubt that she is one seriously gorgeous girl."

Amused, Celeste looked at him.

Pleased that he had her attention, Alex began ticking off his fingers. "She has bone structure that I would mortgage my home for." He looked at Celeste. "She's blond, a natural one at that. She's got those amazing blue eyes." He rubbed his forehead. "How would you describe the color?"

"Turquoise blue," Celeste responded. "Turquoise is the word you're looking for."

"Yes," Alex said. His eyes twinkled mischievously. "She has great tits. I mean really, *really* great tits." He smiled wickedly. "Have you noticed that?"

Celeste raised an eyebrow and fought hard not to grin but she couldn't resist. "They should be asset tagged."

Alex laughed. "Yeah," he said, slapping his thigh. "They'll be well up on your register." He wagged a finger. "But, look around you, honey, there's a lot of candy in the store tonight."

Celeste sat up, yawned and then stretched. She wondered if she could excuse herself soon and asked absentmindedly, "Is that a challenge, Mr. Forrester?"

"Uh-huh," Alex replied, then waved to someone at the bar.

Celeste looked over to where Alex was waving and watched a dark-haired woman make her way over.

Once she got closer, Alex budged Celeste up and motioned for the woman to join them. Seated between them, Alex looked at Celeste and smiled. "I would like to introduce you to an old friend of mine, Robin Fernandez."

†

A phone was ringing. Celeste, lying on her stomach, pulled her hand out from under the pillow and reached for it. Unable to find it, she lifted her head only to let it flop down when a blinding pain shot through her temple. "Uurrgghh."

Lifting her hand, Celeste tried again. Eyes closed, feeling tentatively around, she patted the air. Eventually, remembering she was in a hotel room, she unwillingly opened one eye blearily. She found what she was looking for and croaked into the receiver, "What?"

Alex cooed at the other end, "Morning, sweetie. Thought I would give you a wake-up call since you were so, so, sooo tight last night."

Celeste tried to make out the time on the nightstand, but couldn't focus. Her other eye refused to open. She managed to squeeze another sound out of her voice box. "What time is it?"

"It's time to tell you what happened last night, sweetie."

Celeste's mind drew a blank. She vaguely remembered going to a club and drinking lots of tequila. She groaned and tried not to think any more as her head hurt. She murmured, "Where are you, Alex?" Remembering, she asked, "Did you find your teacher?"

"I'm next door. And no, honey, I didn't find him, but I didn't go home empty-handed." He laughed then added wickedly, "And neither did you!"

Just as Celeste was about to ask him what the hell he was talking about a hand snaked across her back and rested on her shoulder. Stunned, she froze.

Like a sinister voice-over in a horror film, Alex whispered into the phone, "Yes, Celeste. Eventually, I managed to pry that gorgeous hot-blooded Latina off you long enough to get us all into a cab."

Shocked, Celeste didn't move or say a word. Lying prostrate, she felt light kisses feather their way down her back. She gulped when the full weight of a body pressed into her and a female voice moaned in her ear, "Good morning, Celeste. Do you have any idea how wonderful you were last night?"

Denial

Celeste stiffened further when hips pressed into hers and started to move.

Alex knew from the moment that Celeste picked up the phone that she didn't have a clue that she was sharing her bed because she didn't cuss him out. He heard her sharp intake of breath. *But you know now. Don't you, honey!* "Where's Robin?" he asked mischievously.

Celeste didn't say a word.

Alex couldn't help but find the whole situation highly amusing. He asked teasingly, "Is she next to you?"

Celeste replied slowly, "Uh-huh."

"Where?"

Celeste didn't reply.

Not thinking that she really was, Alex asked, "Is she on top of you?"

Celeste whispered, "Uh-huh."

Putting his hand over the receiver, Alex laughed hard. He could only imagine what Robin was up to. He removed his hand and whispered, "Celeste, let me tell you a little about the woman that's on top of you." He dragged out the words 'on top of you,' taking real pleasure in them. "Her name is Robin Fernandez and she's very beautiful."

Alex paused for a moment when he heard Robin moan. He grinned before continuing with her résumé. "She's twenty-nine years old and a Gemini. So *never* let her get pissed at you. She's a lawyer, a very successful one at that, and she comes from old money. She is very solvent, very stunning, a very sharp dresser, and sharp talker. She's very particular about who she wants. And she very, very, much wants you." He coughed lightly. "As I'm sure you realize."

"Je ne le crois pas!"

Alex chuckled, "You better believe it, sweetie."

"Comment est-ce c'est arrivé?"

"Well, it happened because there was wine, song, and serenade. Need I say more?"

"Je ne me souviens de rien."

"I'm not surprised you can't remember a thing. We were all pretty drunk—"

"—*Raccroche le téléphone, Celeste.*"

Celeste exhaled sharply. "Fuck."

Alex sniggered when he heard Celeste cuss.

Robin murmured, *"Hier soir était stupéfiant."*

Listening, Alex thought that if their night was that good he should definitely hang up the phone, but feeling a twinge of guilt that he had been more than a little involved in orchestrating the events of the evening, including getting Celeste tight, he lingered. Then about to hang up, he heard Celeste whisper, "Alex!"

Hearing the panic in her voice Alex felt a wave of guilt, knowing when he called Robin yesterday afternoon that the moment she saw Celeste she wouldn't be able to keep her hot Latina hands off his friend. He pressed the phone to his ear, listened then smiled. It was obvious that Robin was having a good time but he couldn't be sure about Celeste. Deciding to put her out of her misery and come to her rescue, he whispered heroically, "I'll be there in two ticks."

†

Celeste put the phone down slowly, unable to believe some stranger was on top of her grinding. She squeezed her eyes tight and tried to recall what happened after they left the club. Everything was too hazy; she opened her eyes, and sucked in air.

Robin murmured sensuously in her ear.

Smooth, Celeste thought. At any other time being told that she was the most beautiful woman ever would be a huge compliment. Particularly given that it was first thing in the morning when she was bleary-eyed and her breath could knock out a rhino.

Robin kissed the nape of Celeste's neck.

Celeste tensed.

Robin was making her way down Celeste's back when the door rattled.

Denial

Jumping out of bed, Celeste grabbed for something to cover herself. Quickly, she headed for the door and threw it open to a grinning Alex.

"Good morning," Alex said. He squeaked when Celeste roughly grabbed him by the collar and yanked him into the room.

In the bathroom, getting dressed, Celeste wanted to throttle Alex when she heard him ask Robin to join them for breakfast.

During breakfast, Robin asked if they would like to go sailing with her that afternoon. Alex immediately jumped at the offer, and because they had nothing planned, and short of being rude, Celeste accepted her invitation.

The afternoon was a strange experience. Robin's touch was intimate throughout the day but Celeste was having difficulty remembering the night before only recalling snippets of Robin literally ripping her clothes off.

It had been years since Celeste had been that tight. Head still aching, she recalled a clear memory of Alex toasting her return. She frowned, remembering many celebratory toasts. Realizing there was a constant supply of tequila, she looked at Alex, aware now that it was deliberate.

Alex smiled at her sweetly.

Celeste smiled back, but not so sweetly.

Surprisingly, the afternoon wasn't a complete disaster. Celeste was actually enjoying Robin's company, and the fifty-foot Catalina that her family owned was nothing short of spectacular. Celeste loved sailing. It had been too long since she had felt the thrill of the waves.

As the afternoon progressed, Alex, to Celeste's annoyance, got more irritating. He couldn't understand why she wasn't salivating over Robin and, at every opportunity, he urged her to give Robin attention, as if expecting that somehow her attraction would flit from Amy to his friend.

Whenever Alex got the opportunity he whispered background information on Robin, telling her that there was no way she could turn down someone like Robin.

To placate him, Celeste would oblige and focus on her, half-hoping as he did, that something would be set alight.

When they docked, Robin asked if they would join her for dinner. Not wanting a repeat of last night Celeste quickly declined. True to form, before they parted, Alex utilized his matchmaking skills and invited Robin to Sarasota for a weekend.

Driving home, Celeste glanced at Alex in the passenger seat. She smiled when he snuffled, then snored. Looking at the road ahead she focused on the journey home, and her thoughts turned to Robin. Alex was right, of course. Robin was beautiful, and extremely entertaining, but, unfortunately, she did nothing for Celeste. If anything, being with Robin only made her want Amy more.

Celeste began to formulate a plan.

Chapter 21

"You just take this wine and relax on the sofa, honey," Josh said soothingly. "I'll take care of the boys tonight."

"Okay," Amy replied, taking the glass of wine Josh offered. She stretched out on the sofa and smiled. It had been a long week at work full of late nights and added responsibilities. She was delighted it was finally over.

Amy listened to Josh and the boys move around upstairs. He was running their bath while the boys ran the length of the hallway. The familiarity of the routine soothed her overworked mind. Wiggling her toes, she luxuriated in the warmth of the sofa and let her thoughts turn to Maggie. Her heavy work schedule had made Amy late getting home, again, and disrupted Maggie's plans. Amy hoped she wasn't too peeved with her for ruining her date tonight. Amy had never seen Maggie take a relationship this seriously. Maggie claimed she was far too much of a free spirit to settle down but this new guy appeared to be different. So different that next weekend, Maggie was bringing him around for the family seal of approval.

Laying her head against the arm of the sofa Amy's thoughts turned to how much of a struggle the last week had been for her. She was thankful that work was demanding as she was still reeling from her experience with Celeste. The lack of contact had left her fretting. So much so that over the last week she had broken her fair share of dishes, dropped things, and tripped over almost everything that wasn't nailed to the floor.

Amy thought pensively about how Josh and Maggie had picked up that something was wrong and had begun to ask probing questions. So far, she thought with relief, she had managed to throw them off the scent by putting everything down to pressure at work with the new contract.

Amy sighed and sipped her wine. She smiled when she heard Josh chase the boys out of the bathroom and into their bedroom.

She listened to the familiar shrieks of protest then thought for the thousandth time about Josh and tried to fight the guilt. She closed her eyes, understanding that Josh considered fidelity key to a successful relationship.

Amy knew with near certainty that he had never been with another woman since they gotten together. She remembered back when she first met Josh. A few months into dating he had refused to see anyone else, even casually. At the time, she had found it endearing. He was so attractive that at the beginning even her friends batted their eyelashes at him. Even now, when Josh turned on the charm, he could still make a die-hard like Maggie weak at the knees.

Amy jumped slightly when Josh touched her shoulder.

"The boys are in bed."

Amy smiled up at him.

He reached for his glass of wine and moving to the opposite end of the sofa, lifted her feet. Sitting down, he settled them on his lap. "Thank God it's the weekend," he said, raising his glass to his mouth.

Amy nodded, enjoying the sense of familiarity as they often sat like this in the evening.

"I'm glad you managed to get home at a reasonable hour tonight."

Amy smiled. "I'm glad too. This won't be for too long."

"I hope so. Are you hungry?"

"No." In truth, Amy hadn't felt hungry for days. "I'll get something later."

He rubbed her foot. "Are you sure you're okay, honey? You just don't seem your normal self."

"Yeah," Amy replied, bristling. "I'm fine."

"Okay, but you'd tell me if it was more than just work, wouldn't you?"

Tensing, Amy held her breath and nodded slowly. "Uh-huh." She sipped some wine.

"I'm concerned, Amy. I haven't ever seen you this preoccupied." He smiled, then added teasingly, "Or go through so much crockery."

"Oh, Josh, don't worry," Amy said. Forcing down her growing panic, she breathed in slowly. "I'm fine. It's nothing I can't handle."

"Are you sure?"

"Yes," she replied, relieved that he accepted her answer. "I promise, everything is going to be fine."

For the next few hours, they relaxed and caught up on the week's events.

Josh poured the last of the wine into their glasses. Feeling sleepy, Amy said, "I promised Maggie that I would help her paint her apartment on Sunday."

"Sunday?" Josh said in surprise. "But you've hardly had a break."

Amy sighed. "I know."

"Why the sudden urge to decorate now?"

"I'm not sure. But it may be something to do with the new guy in her life."

Moving up the sofa, Josh said in a low voice, "I was hoping that we would have a quiet weekend, just you, me, and the boys."

Before Josh reached her, Amy quickly threw her legs off the sofa. "Tomorrow will be quiet," she replied, standing. "Next weekend is the busy time. Remember, your dad will be through next Saturday to take the boys back with him. And he's booked a game of golf in the morning with you."

"What's he taking the boys for?"

"Josh," Amy replied in frustration. "Don't you ever listen to a word I say?"

Josh shrugged.

"So we can have a quiet night with Maggie and her new man."

Josh stood and smiled when Amy went through a list of things they had to do. As she talked, he took her hand and led her to their bedroom.

In the bedroom, Amy decided not to do to her usual ministrations. Instead, she quickly undressed, slipped on a T-shirt and pajama bottoms and tucked herself under the bedsheets. It had been almost a week since they had returned from Josh's folks and she had managed to hold Josh off by telling him she was exhausted.

Feeling anxious, Amy curled up into a ball. She knew she couldn't keep making excuses. It wouldn't be long before he suspected something was seriously wrong. She shivered. Right now, making love to him was the last thing she needed; Celeste was too fresh in her mind.

Tonight, Amy had bitten back several times from asking directly about Celeste. Josh was so full of the software problems that the chat was taken up by his work.

Amy was nervous about making love with him. She could count on one hand the number of sexual encounters she'd had before Josh. Although she had to admit their lovemaking had become routine, until now she hadn't really given it a second thought. She still found Josh very attractive, and although he might not be the most adventurous in bed, neither was she, or so she had thought.

Amy thought about Maggie and how different she was. Maggie was sexually adventurous and loved nothing better than to share her sexual exploits with her. From Maggie's complaints Amy had decided that she and Josh were faring well. But now, everything had changed. Celeste had opened a need and Amy was afraid this time she wouldn't be able to put it back in the box.

Four years ago, Amy had experienced the same kind of thing, but back then she was sure that it was a fluke, all to do with her hormones. She had put it down to everything other than an actual attraction and, after a while, it faded into a memory. But, now there was no denying it, she was sexually explosive around Celeste. If she was honest, it left her confused and quite terrified.

Amy listened as Josh cleaned his teeth and considerately shaved his stubble. Knowing what was to come she buried her head into the pillow and sighed heavily.

Josh put out the bathroom light and quickly got between the sheets. He snuggled into her back and placing his hand on her breast, groaned. Amy felt him harden. Biting her bottom lip

Denial

nervously, she lay still and listened to him whisper how much he loved her. As he nuzzled his face into her hair she could feel his erection grow and press into her back.

In a way, Amy was relieved. Realizing she wanted everything to return to as it was she turned to face Josh and whispered, "I love you too, baby."

Chapter 22

Amy stood outside Maggie's apartment in South Venice in a pair of old ripped jeans and a grayed out T-shirt. For the third time she rang the doorbell, hoping Maggie would hear her through the din of music she was playing. She had brought breakfast—two coffees, buttered croissants filled with cheese and ham, two slices of apple pie and two slices of rhubarb tart. Although Maggie was like a stick insect, she had an extremely sweet tooth.

Maggie opened the front door. Standing barefoot in crumpled shorts and a T-shirt, she gave Amy her most beautiful smile. "Come in, jellybean," she said, standing aside.

During breakfast, Maggie detailed all the things she wanted done.

Amy looked at her cousin and wondered what had come over her. "You really want to gut this place, don't you?"

Maggie looked at her. "Uh-huh, courtesy of a sweet cousin who knows all the right people and who can get all the right materials on the cheap!" She raised her eyebrows expectantly.

The thought hit Amy that Maggie might actually be seriously considering settling down. Although Maggie gave her all to everything she did, there was no getting around it—she liked the idea of a temporary status and deliberately avoided responsibility in case the notion took her to leave. If she wanted to take off right now, she could.

When Amy was a teenager, at the spur of the moment, Maggie took off traveling. It was two years before she saw her again. Even though they had kept in regular contact, she had gone through her parents' split without her. Although she played it down, Amy desperately missed her and knew that Maggie had sensed this. Since that time, the redhead had stayed close to her.

Maggie wanted to start by freshening up the living room with a lick of paint. After breakfast she handed Amy a paintbrush and they got to work. Maggie talked animatedly about her new guy, insisting he wasn't her usual type. Describing him as quite small, sprightly, sporty with no beard, muscles or anything like that.

Amy noticed with amusement that her cousin was becoming quite flushed as she talked.

"You know," Maggie said, looking at her. "He's nothing special to look at but he just has that *zing* thing. You know that extra edge that no one else has had for me in years." Maggie stopped painting. She put her brush down and came close to Amy. "The sex is terrific. I mean he might be a wee bloke, but he more than makes up for that somewhere else." She winked. "You should see the tadger on him!" She held out her hands then stretched them to about a foot.

Amy's eyes widened. "No way."

"Aye, okay," Maggie replied. Shrugging, she brought her hands a fraction closer. "Maybe that's a wee bit of an exaggeration."

Amy laughed. "You're a dirty minx, Maggie Forsythe," she said teasingly. "Do you know that?" Shaking her head, she added, "I swear to God, you're obsessed with sex. You're like a pig snorting around for it all the time!"

Amy moved around the room snorting.

Maggie laughed. "Hey," she said playfully. "Don't knock the animal world. Did you know a pig's orgasm can last for thirty minutes? And lions can mate over fifty times a day when the lioness is in heat." She contemplated this. "I'd still want to be a pig in my next life though, quality over quantity always counts wouldn't you say?"

Amy shrugged.

Maggie asked teasingly, "What about you, quality or quantity?"

The redhead was always ribbing Amy and trying to find out about her sex life. To tease her cousin Amy always resisted telling her anything. She avoided the question. "Maggie, if it gets serious, do you expect the sex to stay that good over the years?"

Maggie grinned. "Jesus, I hope so. What else are men good for?" She looked at Amy. "You know, to be honest, I've only ever felt this once in my teens, but never since." She waved her paintbrush. "I'm in my thirties and everybody keeps saying the right one will come along. But to be honest, I was beginning to think it was never going to happen!" She laughed excitedly. "All those years and not even a teeny-weeny snifter of love, and, as you know, I've had my fair share of blokes, and some I've seriously fancied."

"Shouldn't you have fancied them all?" Amy asked, raising her eyebrows.

Maggie grinned. "Well, maybe," she conceded. "The point is I've had great sex, some very bad sex, and some very weird sex." She scratched her head. "Or was it sex with weird people?" She looked at Amy. "Anyhow, to be honest, I just thought the love thing wasn't for me. That I had grown cynical or something." She smiled. "What I'm saying is I think it's rare to meet somebody who you really connect with in every sense, who knows what you're feeling, and can almost read your mind." She smiled. "That's how I feel about Sean. I mean he's wee." She threw up her hands, oblivious to the paint splattering everywhere. "And God knows he's puny. He has just about all the physical attributes I wouldn't normally go for."

Watching her cousin, Amy realized that most of their time today would be spent cleaning up spillage if Maggie kept throwing her arms out.

"I mean the shocker for me," Maggie continued, "is that I actually fancy somebody with red hair! But this wee bloke just presses my buttons. I mean we really have something hot. And even though he's the polar opposite of what I'm normally attracted to, the chemistry is amazing between us. I mean I just want to jump on his bones every time I see him. And his personality, well, I just love it. We share the same sense of humor and the same interests. He's an expert on the *Guinness Book of Records,* you know. He knows every wildest and weirdest achievement in history. And there is loads I've still to find out about him."

Denial

Amy groaned inwardly. *Oh my God. What a pairing!* She looked at Maggie's smiling face. "Sounds like you're really serious about this guy."

Maggie looked at Amy shyly. "I think he's the one."

Amy dropped her paintbrush into the pot and went to her cousin. Delighted, she swept Maggie around. They laughed and hugged. Both excited at the thought of Maggie being in love.

Eventually they got back to work but Amy still wanted Maggie to answer whether she expected that kind of passion to last. After their lovemaking last night she had lain stiffly in Josh's arms listening as he whispered how much he loved her. Shame washed over her. During their lovemaking, Celeste had been the only thing on her mind.

Amy needed to know how quickly sexual passion like that dies. She waited a few minutes then asked again, "Do you expect it to last?"

"What?" Maggie asked, painting enthusiastically.

Amy stopped painting and turned to look at her cousin. "The zing," she replied. "The sex being great, the need to jump on his bones every time you see him. Do you expect that to last?"

Maggie looked at Amy and laughed. "No. Not forever," she replied. "But it's a bloody good start."

For the first time ever, Amy let a crack show. "Josh and I have never had that..." she started to wave her hands then remembering the paintbrush dropped it into the pot, "passion."

Maggie stopped painting.

Just tell her! Amy thought. But she froze, knowing there was no way, even if Maggie threw her on a torture rack, she would ever say that she had experienced that *zing* with someone else.

"The passion?" Maggie replied, looking at her cousin curiously. "What do you mean?"

Amy sighed knowing she couldn't let it drop, she desperately needed to speak to Maggie, somehow. "Well, I don't think Josh and I," she hesitated, "I don't think we've ever shared what you're talking about." Amy rubbed her forehead, unaware that she was smearing paint across it. "You know that zing thing." Suddenly feeling exposed, she justified quickly, "I mean, I fancy him, who wouldn't. He's gorgeous. And the sex…has always been…good." Or so you thought, her inner voice quipped.

Amy couldn't hold back from exploring further. "But it lacks something."

Suddenly aware that she had her full attention Amy looked at Maggie. She struggled for words and eventually muttered, "It lacks something and I don't know if that *something* is easy to have, or if it needs some work, or that we can't have it because it's never been there and never will?"

Go on, tell her. Tell her it's because you've experienced what she described with someone else, and you desperately want it to be with Josh.

Maggie put down her paintbrush. Going to her cousin, she hugged her then held her at arm's length. "Jellybean, are you all right?" she asked with concern. "You've never mentioned this before?"

Amy shrugged. "I know, but everyone assumes that Josh and I are idyllically happy, and we are," she reassured when Maggie frowned. "We are a happy couple, but we have our problems. You know, like everyone else."

Maggie smiled. "Jellybean, now listen to me." She cupped Amy's face. "Do you have any idea how difficult it is to find a man who is kind, sensitive, fun, and very good looking?"

Amy shook her head.

"Well, it's practically impossible. And when you do, they usually spend way more time in front of the mirror and read more gossip column inches than you do. If you know what I mean!"

Amy's lips twitched.

"What you and Josh have is brilliant. He adores you," Maggie said reassuringly. "And let me tell you, passion isn't everything, I've road tested enough models to know the fun is only in the first few spins. Once you pop the bonnet, there's always something you need to sort out, and I expect the same with Sean. Whereas Josh, he's a brilliant bloke. There's nothing that needs changing with him. He'd give you anything, and you both live for each other."

Denial

Maggie hugged Amy tightly, then looked at her and admitted, "I want what you've got, Amy. Sex, like everything else, gets ordinary, but what you've got is *real!* Do you know how many women would chew off their right arm to have what you've got?" She looked at her cousin. "Do you think all couples are banging away, having great sex all the time?"

Amy looked at her questioningly.

"The reality is that, for most, it's all about cleaning up after the kids, doing the dishes, cleaning the house. Fighting for the remote control for the telly is about the only action that most couples get. That's real life, Amy," Maggie said reassuringly. "Relationships, like anything else in life, are hard work, and like everything else, they have their peaks and troughs." She rubbed her hands up and down Amy's arms, then hugged her and finished philosophically, "Everything gets ordinary eventually, jellybean."

Suddenly feeling much better, Amy smiled and laughed. "Aye," she replied. Pulling out of the embrace, she pinched Maggie's cheek. "You're right…let's get back to work and crack on." Her eyebrows rose. "I'm looking forward to meeting Superman next week."

Maggie laughed. "Well. You'll be meeting a wee, skinny red-headed version of Superman." Turning shy, she added, "But he's my Superman."

Chapter 23

"Mac," Amy shouted as she fought the pup for her shoe. "Give it back you little runt. *Now!*"

With an expensive one-off designer shoe firmly in his mouth, Mac scampered out of her bedroom. Nails scraping, he scurried across the wooden floor and fled down the hall into the guest bedroom.

Amy gave chase. Running into the guest bedroom, she frantically looked around. Dropping to her knees, she crawled toward the bed. "Why aren't you like movie dogs; cute and compliable?" she mumbled. She peered under the bed and gasped, Mac was making a meal of her shoe.

Amy made a swipe for him. "Mac, get your wee bony arse out of there!"

Since the teething puppies arrived, Amy had picked up and put out of reach every chewable item. But several sneakers, two remote controls, and several dog training classes later proved they were a long way from getting the boisterous pups fully under control. To make matters worse, recently, and for no apparent reason, Flynn had taken to peeing on the floor whenever the doorbell rang.

Growling, Amy lunged. "Mac, give it back!" She flailed her arm around and touched the edge of the slavered shoe. "Uggghhh!" She pulled back; her fingers were dripping. "Yuck!"

Amy grabbed for the first thing she could find to wipe her fingers clean. "Mac," she said, eyeing him, "I'm at rock bottom with you, buddy, and I'm starting to dig!"

Growling, Mac shuffled to the far corner then shot out from underneath the bed. Whooshing past, Amy made a grab for him and missed.

Panting, Mac stopped at the bedroom door and eyed her.

On her haunches, Amy glared at him.

Mac eyed her triumphantly.

Denial

"Mac," Amy yelled as the brown butt sauntered out the door. "Get back here!"

Pulling herself up, Amy gave chase. Running out of the room, she reeled back when her foot slammed against the corner of the doorframe.

The doorbell rang.

"Fuc—Umph!" Amy slapped both hands over her mouth. The pain excruciating, tears filled her eyes.

"Oh Flynn, what the hell has gotten into you, peeing everywhere, man!" Amy heard Josh call out from the hallway.

Holding her foot, Amy hopped around. After several whispered expletives, she tentatively placed her stubbed toe on the floor. Hobbling to her shoe rack she picked out a pair that would accommodate her now very swollen big toe.

It was Saturday evening, and finally, Amy was about to meet Sean.

Amy saw Josh quickly clean up Flynn's mess as she hurried downstairs.

Opening the front door, Amy welcomed both Maggie and Sean into the house. She hugged Maggie, then shook Sean's hand and kissed him on the cheek.

"Welcome," Josh said, shaking Sean's hand.

Amy took their gifts of flowers and wine, and Josh led them into the living room.

After drinks were organized, they settled into a comfortable chat. Josh directed most of his conversation to Sean. Soon, they got onto the topic of motorbikes and bike racing.

Josh winked his approval at Maggie.

Maggie beamed with pride.

The rest of the evening slipped away easily with only a few embarrassing stories regaled by Amy and Josh about Maggie.

"I'm just setting the record straight," Amy said finally when Maggie took a playful swipe at her.

Once Josh discovered Sean was a poker player the cards came out and the stakes were set.

"I suppose we'll be staying?" Maggie said to Sean.

Sean gave Maggie a slight shrug and a huge grin in response.

Amy could easily see the appeal. He's cute, she thought.

Amy and Maggie played for a while and then they both went all-in and lost. Yawning, Maggie stood, saying she was ready for bed.

"Me too," Amy responded, standing.

Josh looked up at them. "We'll just finish the game." He winked at Sean.

"Josh, your head will be loosened from your shoulders if you keep my man up too late."

Sean beamed a smile at Maggie.

Amy and Maggie left the boys chewing on cigars.

Amy said in a hushed voice as she closed the door, "Josh is trying to play with the big boys. He doesn't even like cigars."

Making their way up the stairs, Maggie grabbed Amy's hand. "Sean *loves* me," she sang quietly. "He can't get *enough* of me."

"What? He loves you!" Amy teased. "Even though you refuse to separate those eyebrows?"

Maggie snickered. "Have I told you being a crabby bitch is part of your charm?"

Amy grinned.

"He loves me because," she wiggled her eyebrows, "I have tapped into a source of power that most women don't even know exists!"

"What?"

"Pussy power!"

"Unbelievable!" Amy said, pointing a finger at Maggie's crotch. "That old ginger minge of yours actually has power?"

Maggie laughed. "Absolutely."

Both sniggered. "When are the boys being dropped off?" Maggie asked.

"Probably, late morning."

"So, does that mean we get a wee extra hour in bed then?"

Amy chuckled and hugged her cousin goodnight. "That," she said conspiratorially, "can easily be arranged."

Maggie grinned. "With his big willy and my magic minge, we'll probably need an extra hour and a half."

"You're something else."

"Horny and can't get enough of it, I think is the correct response."

"See you in the morning," Amy said. She turned and walked down the hallway.

"Not too early," Maggie said as Amy opened her bedroom door.

Amy smiled sweetly. "Not too early, I promise."

Chapter 24

It was late in the morning when Amy decided to get up; it wasn't often she got to sleep in. She decided to let Josh sleep on, as he wasn't used to late nights. Much to her amusement, it had been the early hours of the morning before he appeared. Grumbling, he snuggled into her, telling her peevishly that he was only a few hundred dollars lighter.

After her shower, Amy made her way downstairs to prepare breakfast. Heading for the kitchen she realized how quiet the house was without the boys. The doorbell rang just as she picked up the phone to dial her in-laws to check what time they would be arriving.

Amy opened the door and her eyes widened. Celeste and the boys were standing there. Her heart jackhammered.

Celeste smiled. "Are we in time for breakfast?"

Amy's jaw slackened at the sight of the unexpected visitor. Unprepared, she lurched backward when the boys launched themselves at her.

Celeste quickly reached for Amy and steadied her.

Instinctively, Amy pushed her away. Bending down she wrapped her arms around the boys, almost protectively. She hugged and kissed them, then fixed their hair, enjoying the sense of relief that her sons were back in her arms.

Not wanting to let the boys go, Amy straightened and held their hands. Unwilling to make eye contact with Celeste, she looked down at her boys and asked, "Are you two hungry?"

Celeste smiled. "Last night," she said, looking at the boys with affection, "we baked cakes." She lifted her gaze to Amy. "Well, they were cupcakes designed for precocious three-year-olds. And, no matter how careful we were," she teased as she looked down at them, "we still somehow managed to get covered in egg yolk and flour. But," she produced a tub from her bag, "we've saved some for Mom and Dad, haven't we guys?"

Denial

Amy couldn't help but laugh with Celeste when the boys told her, with their chests puffed out, how great they were at baking.

Celeste raised an eyebrow smiled and explained that they had started out with eight cupcakes this morning, but now they were down to two. "Which," she said, putting on a stern voice, "had to be rescued from these two little misfits."

"Morning," Josh said sleepily as he pulled open the front door.

Amy looked at him and realized with surprise that she must have stepped out rather than inviting Celeste in.

The boys squealed at the sight of their dad and hurled themselves at him.

Enjoying their display of affection, Josh laughed and, gathering them easily in his arms, swung them around.

Amy tried not to think about Celeste standing so close and instead focused on her husband and children. But, with the tension quickly building inside her she decided she needed to get away from Celeste. She excused herself and made her way to the kitchen.

Busying herself with breakfast, Amy heard Maggie before she appeared. She smiled happily when Maggie let out a raucous laugh.

"Morning," Amy said as the couple entered the kitchen.

Sean grinned. "Morning," he said, sitting at the breakfast bar.

Maggie winked at Amy as she sat next to Sean.

Josh and Celeste had taken the boys and the pups around to the back of the house. The glass panel was open. Distractedly, Amy poured juice into the jug and watched the adult twins play with her boys and the pups. Holding the carton, she thought how similar Josh and Celeste were and blushed when she realized how intimately she knew them.

Amy watched Celeste hold Ryan as Josh ran around them with Christopher on his back. They looked the picture of happiness.

"Amy," Maggie said, "you're spilling the juice everywhere!"

Startled, Amy looked at Maggie, blinking in confusion. She looked at the spillage. "Bloody hell!" she said and quickly cleaned up the mess.

Sean looked at Maggie. "That's Josh's sister, right?"

Maggie's attention focused sharply on her boyfriend. Obviously picking up something in his voice that she didn't like, she said, "Used to be his brother until the op. He, sorry she's, making the change quite successfully, wouldn't you say Amy?"

Maggie's eyes never left Sean's.

Unsure what to think, Sean looked at Amy for confirmation.

Unable to resist, Amy nodded, then put her finger to her mouth and said in hushed tones, "It's a sensitive subject, though. We're not to talk about it until the stitches come out."

Maggie pointed to Sean's groin and then sliced her hand through the air. "Imagine your pride and joy…gone!"

Sean shuddered.

"Apparently," Maggie added with a note of regret as she continued to stare at Sean. "He had a big one too."

Sean looked wide-eyed at Maggie. "No way," he said then looked at Amy.

Amy nodded.

A look of absolute horror crossed Sean's face. Reflexively, he placed a hand between his legs.

Maggie was the first to laugh. Amy followed.

"Duh…isn't it obvious that she's his sister? If I said she had a third leg you'd believe me." Maggie reached for a glass of juice. "Why do you want to know?"

Sean looked at Maggie, then Amy, and said, half-jokingly, "Because she's…a…a looker. She must have guys crawling all over her."

At that they all turned to look at Celeste. He's right, Amy thought. She looks stunning. Celeste was pushing Ryan in his swing. She was dressed simply, all in black: black jeans and T-shirt, her hair pulled back into a ponytail. She was fresh-faced, full of smiles and her eyes sparkled. Amy dragged her eyes from Celeste's mouth.

Denial

Annoyed that Sean was paying Celeste attention, Maggie's eyes narrowed. If they could Amy was sure her ears would have flattened.

"How bad-mannered can you get!" Maggie said. "Wasn't it just this morning that you only had eyes for me?"

Sean smiled. "True." Obviously feeling he could win some ground he added, "That's because you're beautiful and smart."

Maggie looked at Amy. "Just as well opposites attract!"

Bewildered, Sean held out his hands. "What have I done?"

Maggie stared at him.

"C'mon, baby," Sean said, taking Maggie's hand. "I'm a man and she's a beautiful woman. What do you expect?" He stroked Maggie's hand. "What else do you want me to do?"

"Admitting you're an asshole would be a good first step," Maggie replied. Getting off the stool she flounced out of the kitchen.

"Jesus," Sean said. "Ain't she a ray of sunshine?" He looked at Amy. "What happened there?"

"Hurricane Redhead happened."

Sean grinned. "I like it. Hurricane Redhead she certainly is." He shook his head. "Women!" he said. "Can't live with them and..." he laughed. "Yeah, I guess that's it," he said, going after Maggie.

Amy smiled, suddenly feeling confident that Sean was more than capable of handling Maggie.

Making breakfast, Amy heard her children whoop with laughter. A wave of panic hit her. Her chest tightened. A sense of helplessness filled her. She thought about how she should be able to enjoy her family being together, but she couldn't. Tears filled her eyes.

Amy lifted her head and inhaled deeply. For the next half hour Josh, Celeste, and the children played outside. Although she could hear them, she never once looked in their direction.

Eventually, Maggie and Sean returned. Amy lifted her eyebrows when Maggie grinned at her. She looked at Maggie's hair. It was clear by how disheveled it was that she was more than appeased.

"Happy now?" Amy asked, handing Maggie plates to put on the kitchen table.

Maggie purred.

Sean winked at Amy.

During breakfast the chat around the table was amiable. They discussed the following Saturday, when they would be celebrating the boys' birthday at Josh's parents.

The phone rang and Josh answered it. "Dad says he's organized a round of golf next Sunday morning and wants to know if you would be interested?"

Sean nodded eagerly, obviously enjoying being included.

Josh winked at Amy. Putting his hand over the receiver, he said to Maggie, "Dad must think its love."

Maggie looked at Sean.

Sean went bright red but he didn't break eye contact with Maggie.

Maggie smiled at him. "Can you tell your dad that Sean's arriving a little late, he's picking up his new bike." She looked at Amy. "Why don't we have a round on Sunday as well?" She looked at Celeste. "You're welcome to come too, if you're free."

Celeste smiled. "Thanks," she replied appreciatively. "I might just take you up on that."

Before finishing the conversation, Josh asked his dad to organize a round for all of them. When he sat down he looked at his sister. "Talking about being free," he said, reaching for another slice of toast. "What are you up to these days?"

Celeste explained she would be starting a new job, a short-term contract at Sarasota's local Memorial Hospital, in the acute emergency ward. She told them she had just signed for a rented apartment.

On hearing Celeste's plans to stay, Amy sucked in her breath. Unable to believe it, she briefly closed her eyes.

Josh was full of smiles. "Well done, sis," he said. "It's great news that you're planning to stick around."

Josh asked her what she was planning to do with her house on Lido Beach, then explained to the table that Celeste had

Denial

bought the house with her ex-husband, Nick, when they first got married and that she now had it as part of her divorce settlement.

"But back then, Celeste was too restless to enjoy it," Josh finished. "She needed to get out and explore the world."

Amy watched Celeste's eyes narrow slightly as Josh discussed her freely.

"What's happening with the tenants in Lido Beach?" he asked, pouring coffee into his cup.

"They have another year to go," Celeste replied, holding out her coffee cup for a refill.

"Do you intend to move in once they leave?" Josh asked before slurping his coffee.

"Yes," Celeste replied. "But in the meantime, I've rented an apartment close to the hospital, but it needs some work done to it."

Josh grinned and threw in. "I'm sure Amy can help you out there. She's helping Maggie decorate her apartment."

Amy sighed inwardly. Since sitting down she hadn't said a word and had successfully managing to avoid direct eye contact with Celeste.

Annoyed that Josh had volunteered her services, Amy focused on her husband and said sharply, "Josh, I'm not an interior designer." She looked at Celeste and finally made eye contact. "If it's decorating tips you're after then you should speak to a decorator." She paused then added, "If it's more than that, then Celeste I'm sorry, but you should really speak to your landlord."

Surprised at Amy's response, everyone stared at her.

After a moment, Josh retorted, "Amy, I think it would be good to give Celeste a little help. You're the architect in the family and it would be nice if you could at least have a look around."

A moment of awkwardness fell around the table. Even the boys were quiet.

Aware that everyone was staring at her, Amy gripped the sides of her chair. She knew she should back down and agree to help Celeste out or questions would be asked. Causing a scene or bringing attention to either of them was the last thing she needed, but Amy couldn't help herself. She looked directly at Celeste and inhaled. "I'm sorry, but I think you should look elsewhere. There's nothing I can do for you."

Still holding the piece of toast to his mouth, Josh sat back and gave his wife an incredulous look, clearly unable to believe she was refusing to help his sister.

Amy pushed her chair back, then stood. "If you'll all excuse me, I've got plans to look over for work."

Without a murmur, everyone watched Amy leave the kitchen.

Chapter 25

Amy's stomach grumbled. She had missed breakfast this morning. She wondered what Wendy, the office PA and her friend, was doing for lunch and decided she would entice her out for something hot and spicy—Thai perhaps.

Amy grinned when the office door opened and Wendy poked her head around. "Just in time," she said, gripping the armrests of her chair. "I'm starving. Do you fancy going out for lunch to that new Thai restaurant around the corner?"

Still holding the door, Wendy smiled and said lyrically, "Nope, I don't *think* so."

Wendy never refused food, especially hot, spicy food. "What?" Amy replied amazed. "Even if it's my treat?"

"Thanks for the offer, but I might have to take a rain check." Wendy moved into the room. "You have a visitor."

Often Maggie brought the twins to the office for a surprise visit.

Amy looked expectantly toward the door but, to her astonishment, Celeste appeared, smiling at her.

Amy's jaw dropped and she stared at Celeste. She blushed. She hadn't seen Celeste since she left shortly after breakfast yesterday morning. Afterward, a very upset Josh confronted her about her behavior. Eventually, she won him over by saying that with the pressures of work she didn't need additional work. She further placated him by promising that she would speak to Celeste and sort things out.

"C...C...Celeste!" Amy stuttered.

Celeste nodded in response. "Amy."

"It's...it's good to see you," Amy said then swallowed.

Wendy asked Celeste if she would care for any refreshment.

Celeste shook her head. "No. Thanks." Looking at Amy, she said inquiringly, "Hopefully, I have a lunch date."

Amy's color increased. She tried to speak but dried up.

"I'm happy to take a rain check on lunch, Amy," Wendy said, glancing at her then Celeste. "I've got too much to work on now anyway."

Amy looked at Wendy. Acutely aware that she was picking up on the tension, she forced a smile.

Celeste smiled. "That's settled then." She looked at her watch, then at Amy. "I took a chance and booked a table."

Amy didn't move.

Amy visibly swallowed before clearing her throat. "Yes. Of course," she croaked. "Lunch shouldn't be a problem." She looked down at her desk. "Can you give me a few minutes to get organized?"

"Yes," Celeste replied courteously. Looking at Wendy, she asked, "Can I use the restroom?"

Wendy nodded, then left the room with Celeste.

Knees weak, Amy slumped in her chair unable to believe that Celeste had shown up *here*, at her office. Heart thudding at the thought of spending the next hour or two alone with her she picked up her pen and chewed on it.

Amy thought about pushing Wendy to come with them but that idea made her uncomfortable. Celeste was too unpredictable and Wendy was a natural inquisitor. A few cleverly placed questions and it wouldn't take her long to figure out what was going on. Anyway, she resolved as she threw down the mangled pen, she and Celeste needed to talk. It was time to find some closure.

Her body, though, had other ideas. Amy's eyes widened when she recognized the now familiar signals her body sent her whenever Celeste was around. She shifted uncomfortably.

Amy wondered with embarrassment if she was turning into some kind of sex maniac. Frustrated and not wanting to think too hard, she closed her eyes. But within seconds she was out of the chair.

Her pulse throbbing painfully, the ache in her groin growing, Amy moved toward the window. Taking deep breaths, she tried to ignore the strong arousal. Looking out, arms folded, she anxiously observed the view, but the ache grew as images invaded her mind of that night in the summerhouse.

Wanting to run for the hills, Amy leaned her forehead against the window and, in quiet desperation, groaned.

"Wow," Wendy said, entering the room. "Doctor Cameron, I presume?"

Nodding, Amy's head squeaked as it moved up and down the window.

"I thought so." Wendy replied, nodding satisfactorily. "You can see the resemblance to Josh." Holding her hands in front of her, she panted like an eager pup. "Woof. Woof. Woof."

Lifting her head off the glass, Amy looked at her friend.

"Bet all the guys get a jumbo-sized hard-on when they see her in her whites," Wendy said enviously. "Out there saving lives in war-torn and dangerous situations." She spun around. "Here comes Doctor Cameron to the rescue!"

"Wendy," Amy cut in. "Don't be daft."

Wendy's twenty-a-day habit made her wheeze as she motioned a few karate moves with arms then feet. "C'mon, Amy, she's an all-action hero."

Amy pursed her lips. Looking at the door, she whispered, "Wendy! Get a grip."

Wendy did another karate chop and a high kick, which wasn't high given her chubby thighs. Yelping, she clutched her backside. "I think I've pulled something."

Grimacing in pain, Wendy teetered dangerously on her heels.

Impatiently, Amy reached out and grabbed her just as she was about to fall over.

Flushed, Wendy straightened. Holding her left buttock she put a hand on Amy's shoulder. "I'm sorry," she said, trying to catch her breath. "You know how much I love all that crap," she shook her head, "saving lives, fighting against the odds."

Smiling briefly, Amy gave her friend a conciliatory nod.

Letting go, Wendy put her hands on her hips and whispered as she eyed the door, "So, what the hell is going on between you two?"

Amy groaned, wishing not for the first time that Wendy was as attentive to her work as she was regarding other peoples' business.

"Nothing," Amy muttered.

"C'mon," Wendy said impatiently, Then turning her head to look at the door, she whispered, "It's evident that you're seriously pissed at her." She rubbed her buttock. "A brief teeny-weeny summary will do."

"Look. We just don't get on, that's all," Amy said. "There's no major drama. No need to call CNN."

A hurt expression crossed Wendy's face.

Amy lowered her eyes and offered, "I just happen not to get on with all of my in-laws."

Wendy sighed. "Tell me about it, babes," she said, sounding appeased.

Amy half-smiled. Wendy hugged her then let her go.

"They—husband and in-laws—come as a package, unfortunately," Wendy said. "They should also tell you that behind every great man there is a whiny-in-your-face-never-to-let-up friggin' mother-in-law." She looked at her friend sympathetically and patted her shoulder. "That's why I'm divorced." She held up two pudgy fingers. *"Twice!"*

Not wanting a discussion, Amy nodded.

"Is she single?"

Amy blinked. Color crept into her cheeks. "Why do you ask?"

"Well," Wendy replied, "if she is single and you two kiss and make up," Amy felt her color deepen, "she'll no doubt come to our monthly girls-only nights out. Which, as you know," Wendy said with some pride, "Maggie and I have a one hundred percent record of scoring." Her mouth turned down. "Well, not so much Maggie anymore. But," she looked at the door, "if sizzle sister comes along, there'll be no guarantees."

Amy stuck out her tongue just as Celeste entered the room.

Embarrassed, Amy went to her desk picked up her bag and said rather too cheerfully, "Ready?"

Denial

†

Seated in an Italian bistro a few blocks from her office, Amy felt the tension turn up a notch in her body. The thought of eating made her stomach turn.

"Wendy's quite a character."

"Yeah, we're good friends," Amy replied. "But when Maggie and Wendy get together, it can be quite the double act."

Celeste nodded, then looked at Amy. "Thanks for taking the time."

"You're welcome," Amy replied. Her voice slightly high, she cleared her throat. The waiter appeared at their table. She ordered by rote, paying little attention to the menu that she normally enjoyed perusing as this was one of her favorite places to eat.

Celeste ordered her food and a bottle of red wine.

Once they ordered, silence.

Damn it. Isn't Celeste going to speak!

To break the silence and to keep the conversation light, Amy asked, "Are you coming to the boys' birthday party at your folks this weekend?"

Camille had insisted they throw a party for the boys' birthday and had spent the last few weeks organizing a fun-packed day.

Celeste's eyebrow rose. "Are you asking me, Amy?"

Amy's eyes narrowed. "No, Celeste. I'm simply inquiring."

"Yes, I'll be there."

Silence.

Eventually, Amy was forced to ask, "Why are you here?"

Just as Celeste was about to answer the waiter appeared with their bottle of wine. Amy silently tapped her foot and waited impatiently as he carried out the usual ministrations of pouring wine. He waited for Celeste's approval before filling their wineglasses.

When the waiter left, Celeste spoke. "I'm here because there is a strong attraction between us, Amy. And we need to," she paused, "address it."

Blindsided, Amy blinked several times.

Celeste picked up her glass and sipped from it. "I've thought of nothing else but what to do since that night in the summerhouse." She smoothed the white linen around her glass. "I can't continue to stay away. My family is here and already I've stayed away too long." Looking at Amy she arched an elegant eyebrow. "We've tried to ignore it. But that," she said, tilting her head, "doesn't work."

Amy blushed. Unconsciously, she ran her hand up and down the stem of her glass of wine and listened nervously.

"The only viable option," Celeste said, watching Amy's hand, "rhat I can see is that we burn this attraction out. With a little discretion we can dissipate it safely and no one need ever know."

Stunned, Amy looked at Celeste in disbelief. "Are you crazy?" she eventually asked in astonishment. "You're talking as if this is some kind of science project." Her color deepened. "Discretion...*dissipate*." She shook her head. "You talk as if having an affair is the answer." She swallowed hard. "And what do you mean, no one need know? *I'll know!*" Amy leaned forward, jaw clenched, blue eyes darkening, she added, "Do you really have any idea what you're asking?"

Suddenly aware of her surroundings, Amy picked up her glass and sipped from it slowly. Carefully she looked around. It was a popular place with busy lunchtime traffic. Thankfully, no one was paying them any attention. Trying to rein in her growing anger, she put her glass down and leaned in. "I don't want this to go any further." She looked at Celeste. "You must know I love Josh. That I'm happily married."

Celeste's features didn't move. "Let me clarify, Amy," she said with an edge to her voice. "I don't intend that we destroy your marriage." Her voice softened. "Whether you like it or not, something has happened between us. I wanted to believe that it was no more than a fluke, that it was arbitrary." Leaning in, she held Amy's gaze. "It's definitely not a fluke." Her voice grew intimate. "I'm attracted to you. And I can't stop it." She reached over the table and stroked Amy's hand. "Or ignore it."

Denial

Amy jerked her hand away. Her heart raced. Aware that her temper was building she took a moment. "You don't seem to get what I'm actually saying to you, Celeste." Her shoulders stiffened. "I don't care what you can't hide. I love the life I have and a...fling with you is not part of it." She couldn't help but look around before fixing her eyes on Celeste. "There is no way that I'm going to risk everything I have to satisfy a basic biological itch." She looked into Celeste's eyes and wondered why this woman affected her so. "Why Celeste?" she asked. "Why me when you can have anyone?"

"Don't you think, I've asked myself that same question a thousand times already?" Celeste looked at Amy intently. "All I know for sure, Amy, is I've been left hanging since that first night in your apartment. I need to feel right again. I...we...need this to happen."

"I can't believe you want to have an affair!" Amy said in disbelief. "Do you know what you're asking?" Amy placed both hands on the table. "What about morals and integrity and caring about family. What about all those things that are supposed to matter?"

Celeste frowned. "They've been compromised already, Amy."

Amy shook her head and leaned back. Feeling suddenly exhausted and overwhelmed, she said, "I just don't understand it."

"The last thing I want to do is tear our family apart and we won't, if we're careful. This...attraction...is strong, too strong to keep fighting it." For the first time, Amy heard a note of vulnerability in Celeste's voice. "I've stayed away for years because of it. How else can we move past it?"

With those words, Amy realized they were both trapped, caught in this strange world of desire. A thought crossed her mind; that maybe had they met first things might have been different. But, aware that there was no going back, she quickly closed the door on that thought.

Deciding she'd had enough, Amy said, "No matter how we rationalize it, it's wrong. I couldn't live with myself. To deliberately do this to Josh would be unforgivable. I'm sorry." Pushing back her chair, she picked up her purse. "But I can't."

Celeste stood, and grabbed Amy's hand.

A surge of electricity shot up Amy's arm. Her eyes widened in surprise.

Celeste looked into Amy's eyes. She gently stroked her thumb across the back of her hand. "Do you feel that?" she asked as her other hand slid around the nape of Amy's neck and pulled her close.

Celeste's warm breath caressed the side of her face. She whispered into Amy's ear almost hungrily, "This can't be ignored, Amy. If we don't do something about it, it will only intensify."

The ache between Amy's legs grew. She pulled away but the hairs on the back of her neck crackled. Realizing how much she wanted this woman she looked at Celeste and, unable to hide her vulnerability, asked, "And when it's over?" Her voice broke. "When you've finished with me? Who will pick up the pieces then?"

Celeste's hazel-green eyes gazed back but she didn't answer.

Amy strode out of the restaurant.

Chapter 26

Amy tapped her foot and looked at her watch. For the last few minutes she had been standing outside Celeste's apartment door with a finger hovering over the buzzer. "I can't do this," she muttered. "I can't talk to her, not right now!"

When she got back to the office after their disastrous lunch, Josh had called to ask if she had met with Celeste. He queried whether his sister had taken her to the Italian restaurant that Amy liked, and most importantly, he wanted to know that they had sorted things out.

Unable to tell him the truth Amy cut the call short, telling him that she had a meeting to attend and would talk to him tonight. After she hung up she realized that this was no way to handle things. Knowing that she couldn't continue to be on red alert every time Celeste was around, she recognized that things would go from bad to worse if they didn't find a resolution.

Unable to concentrate on her work Amy stared out the window. She knew for sure that they couldn't go on like this. Particularly now that Josh had a heightened awareness of the situation. If the tension continued between them, it wouldn't be long before everyone noticed it and began drawing their own conclusions. Accepting that they needed to speak and find some sort of closure she decided to call Celeste and ask if they could meet to discuss the situation.

On the phone, Celeste readily agreed to meet but asked if Amy would come to her apartment as she was cooking for friends that evening. Amy hesitated about the location but reasoned that they weren't animals; surely they could rise above this?

Amy agreed. When she hung up she felt confident that all that was needed was some common ground, which they would surely find if they talked.

But now, standing outside Celeste's apartment, talking things through didn't seem such a good idea after all. Amy was losing her nerve. Her cell phone rang.

Quickly, Amy rummaged through her shoulder bag and retrieved it. Maybe, she thought, it's a client and I'll have to go. Smiling hopefully, she answered, "Hello?"

Celeste's apartment door opened.

Smiling, Celeste spoke into her phone. "Hello," she said, hanging up. "When I dialed your number, I heard a phone ring. Glad you could make it."

Celeste motioned for Amy to come in.

Amy slowly entered. Closing the door she followed Celeste into the kitchen. She stopped at the kitchen entrance.

"Would you like to see the place?" Celeste asked.

Amy shook her head. "No." Her nostrils flared when the exotic smells coming from the marinating meat on the counter filled them.

Celeste removed a bottle of red wine from the rack.

"What are you cooking?"

"Vietnamese," Celeste replied, uncorking the wine.

"Oh…nice."

Celeste removed two glasses from the shelf and placed them on the counter. "I spent a few months touring Southeast Asia a few years ago," she said, pouring wine into a glass. "I fell in love with the place and the food."

"You like cooking, don't you?" Amy asked, recalling the meals that Celeste had prepared for them during her stay.

"Very much," Celeste replied. "If you don't want to look around maybe you'll join me?" She held out a glass of wine.

Amy shook her head. "No," she replied. "I've got the car."

"One glass, Amy," Celeste countered dryly. "Not the bottle."

Amy's face reddened.

Celeste held the glass of wine in her hand and raised an eyebrow. "It might help relax you."

Annoyed, Amy retorted, "I am relaxed."

"Look, take the glass. Then it's up to you whether you drink it or not. Okay?"

Amy nodded and took the glass.

Celeste poured wine into the other glass then brushed past Amy and made her way into the lounge.

Amy had no choice but to follow.

Standing barefoot, Celeste looked out the large window.

Amy stood behind her.

As the moments ticked by, Celeste continued to look out the window.

Amy, feeling increasingly awkward, took a gulp of wine, then another before carefully placing the glass, her cell phone, and car keys on the coffee table. Putting her shoulder bag down, she braced herself. "Celeste, we need to talk," she said. Taking the bull by the horns she added, "I've tried to explain to you that I can't embark on…on…" she paused. "I can't do what you suggested at lunch today." She hesitated when Celeste turned around and looked at her. Deciding the best tactic was honesty she dropped her eyes and said, "Regardless of what the reason is or how… attracted I am to you, I simply can't."

Waiting for a response, Amy lifted her eyes and looked at Celeste.

Celeste held Amy's gaze. "Amy, do you want it to continue for years?" she asked, putting her wineglass down. "Whether you like it or not, this *thing* between us is not going to go away."

Amy countered, "This is just chemistry we're talking about, right?"

Celeste didn't respond.

Amy carried on, "We don't need to behave like animals. Surely, we can control our basic biological urges?"

"Is that right, Amy?" Celeste responded quietly, dangerously. She stared at Amy with a look of smoldering desire; a look that made it clear exactly what she wanted. "Then let's put it to the test."

Celeste moved quickly into Amy's space. The look on her face was one of intense hunger. Taking Amy's left hand, she placed it directly on her breast.

Amy tried to pull her hand away but Celeste held it. She laced her fingers through it then manipulated both their hands.

Amy felt the full weight of Celeste's breast. Surprised by the sensual feel and softness, her heart tried to beat its way out of her chest when, nipple hardening, Celeste groaned.

Immediately, all the fight left Amy.

While Celeste worked their fingers over her breast, her other hand unbuttoned her top.

Amy's head spun. She drew in a deep breath. She was scared. What Celeste was able to stir in her was frightening. Who this woman was should have stopped her dead in her tracks, but it didn't. Eyes wide, she watched the final button pop open.

Celeste lifted their entwined hands and slowly ran them down her throat, past her cleavage and all the way down her stomach. Stopping at the belt around her black jeans, she slowly moved their hands back up.

Amy's eyelids fluttered closed.

"Look at me," Celeste demanded, her voice thick.

Amy opened her eyes wide. She was mesmerized.

Celeste dropped her own hand.

An intense wave of desire filled Amy. Instinctively, she cupped Celeste's breast. Feeling its weight rest in her hand, she ran a thumb lightly over the nipple and watched it stiffen.

Celeste gasped.

Enthralled, Amy fondled Celeste's breast and watched her reaction.

Groaning, Celeste's dark hair wisped over her bare, tanned shoulders as she slid off her top.

"You're breathtaking," Amy whispered.

To Amy's surprise, Celeste blushed. "Thank you."

Their eyes locked. A moment of intimacy passed between them. Amy dropped her eyes to Celeste's breasts. The urge to take Celeste's nipple into her mouth too strong she placed her hands on Celeste's hips and lowered her mouth. Taking the nipple between her teeth she felt the areola pucker. She bit gently before sucking.

Celeste gasped. Her body arched then shuddered. Amy smiled faintly. The move was obviously unexpected.

Denial

Celeste loosened Amy's hair and ran her fingers through it. She rested her hand on the back of Amy's head and pressed her closer.

Captured, Amy listened to Celeste's labored breathing, taking intense delight in hearing small gasps whenever she ran her tongue around her nipple. Confidence growing, she sucked in as much of Celeste's breast as possible, her tongue loving the weight of it as she worked it around the nipple.

Celeste slipped her thigh between Amy's legs and Amy began to grind.

Amy felt strong, demanding fingers tug her shirt from her trousers. With a sense of urgency Celeste unbuttoned some of the shirt then impatiently ripped the rest open. Running her hands up Amy's stomach, she cupped her breasts.

A bolt of electricity hit between Amy's thighs forcing her to press down hard on Celeste's thigh. "Uggghhh."

Removing her leg from between Amy's thighs, Celeste whispered, "Slow down."

Amy almost dropped to her knees at the loss. She removed her mouth from Celeste's breast and whispered throatily, "But I'm almost there!"

"I know," Celeste said, stroking Amy's hair. "But I want you to touch me."

Celeste quickly unbuckled her belt then unbuttoned her jeans, pushing them and her black satin briefs over her hips.

Amy watched Celeste undress.

Standing naked, Celeste slid her arm around Amy's waist. With her other hand, she took Amy's wrist and guided her hand. "Touch me."

A jolt of reality hit Amy and she tried to pull her hand away but Celeste held her wrist. Firming her grip, she parted her thighs further, giving full access.

"I don't know if I can do this, Celeste," Amy whispered.

"I need to feel you touch me, like this, now, Amy," Celeste said urgently. "I have waited so long. I can't wait any longer."

Breathing heavily, Amy tried to pull her hand away but Celeste pushed her wrist further between her thighs.

Their eyes locked. Amy sucked in her breath. She tensed when a film of wetness formed over her fingers. She rubbed her thumb over her fingers, and let out her breath. To her surprise, Celeste's wetness felt sensual.

Celeste, looking vulnerable and shaking slightly, pleaded, "Please, Amy. I can't wait."

Amy's knees weakened as she slid her fingers in.

Celeste groaned. She pressed her head against the side of Amy's and wrapping her arms around her murmured, "I need this. I need you." She caught the tip of Amy's earlobe with her mouth and sucked it. "I've thought of nothing else." She nuzzled Amy's neck. "You're the only thing on my mind."

Rocking her hips, Celeste moaned as Amy's fingers worked her clit.

Shuddering with pleasure, Amy was lost to the sounds of Celeste and the feel of her. Heart pounding, she watched Celeste build to orgasm. The sensations running through her were overwhelming. They were… Buzz…buzzz….buzzzzzzz…

Breathing hard, it took Amy a moment to realize that the buzzing noise was her cell phone. "Oh God!"

"Ignore it," Celeste said, grinding desperately. "Keep going. Amy, don't stop!"

Amy tried to pull away.

"Amy, don't!" Celeste cried out.

Amy forcibly pulled away.

"Fuck!"

Moving quickly to the coffee table Amy snatched up her phone. Wanting to stop the ringing and not thinking clearly, she answered it. Turning, she saw Celeste press her hands between her legs trying to stop the loss of her orgasm.

Clearly too late, Celeste growled loudly in anger.

"Hi…Amy?" Josh said.

Placing a shaking hand over her eyes, Amy couldn't believe it. Why did she answer the phone? Feeling dizzy, her pulse beat loudly in her ears.

"Amy?" Josh said, sounding troubled at the silence.

Amy tried to control her breathing. She looked at Celeste bent over and turned her back. "Hi…Josh?" she meant to say, but the sound coming out was more of a strangled squeak.

"Amy, are you okay?" Josh asked quickly.

Swallowing hard, Amy replied, "Yes." She cleared her throat. "Yes. I'm fine."

"Okay," Josh said with a note of relief. "Honey, I'm calling to let you know that I'll be working late tonight."

Cradling the phone and trying to button her shirt, Amy mumbled distractedly, "Oh. Okay then."

There was a moment of silence. Josh obviously expected her to ask why he would be working late. "Where are you, honey?" Not waiting for an answer he quickly followed, "I tried you at home, but Maggie said that you were putting in an extra hour so I called your office, but Wendy said you'd gone already."

Amy stiffened, shocked that Josh was phoning around looking for her. She stopped fumbling; her hands were too shaky and buttons were missing anyway.

Taking the phone off her shoulder, Amy held it with both hands. "I'm just on my way…I was…uhmm…I got caught up and…uhmm…." She couldn't think. "Oh, Josh, you know what Mondays can be like…they can be so…unpredictable…I thought I had to work late, but then…I didn't…uh…you know, have to work late," she finished weakly. She cleared her throat and pressed the phone tightly to her ear. "I'm just on my way home right now."

A voice in the background called to Josh, telling him that the meeting was about to start.

"Okay," Josh called back. "Amy, honey, I've got to go," he said hurriedly. "We've hit a problem so I don't know how long I'll be but kiss the boys goodnight for me, okay? Love you."

Amy exhaled. "Love you too."

The line went dead.

Standing with her back to Celeste a wave of crippling guilt passed over Amy. Josh thought she was on her way home to their boys.

Spinning around to face Celeste a flush of arousal gripped Amy at the sight of her naked. *Down girl!* She told herself when her flush deepened. She scrambled to pick up her things from the coffee table. "Gotta go." She hurried toward the door.

"Amy," Celeste called as she followed her. "Amy."

The blood pumping so hard through her veins she was sure that her head was about to explode, Amy threw the front door open.

"Wait!"

Not turning around until she was over the threshold, Amy replied, "What?"

"Your buttons," Celeste said, pointing to the misaligned buttons on Amy's blouse.

Looking down, Amy pulled her suit jacket closed.

Celeste's hands reached out.

"I can manage," Amy said, pushing Celeste's hands away. She eyed Celeste and tried not to look at her nakedness. "Don't you feel ashamed?"

Celeste smiled painfully and whispered, "More than you'll ever know, Amy." She shook her head and repeated. "More than you'll ever know."

Not sure what to believe Amy spun around and quickly made her way to the elevator. Too impatient to wait and desperately needing to escape she took the stairs.

Chapter 27

Amy and Camille waved to the last of the parents and their children as they pulled out of the driveway. It had been a very long day and Amy felt nothing but relief that the boys' birthday party was over.

Following the path around the side of the house with Camille Amy half-smiled, pleasantly surprised by the number of kids who showed up.

When Camille mentioned having the party at their house, Amy was reticent. Back home no one would dream of traveling for a few hours to get to a kid's birthday party. An hour would be stretching it, but Camille had argued that long journeys were the norm here and that the boys had as many friends in their grandparents' neighborhood as their own. So, Amy organized it and the kids and parents came, thankfully.

Amy breathed in deeply and for the first time that day felt her tension wane a little. This morning, when she woke, she desperately wished she hadn't arranged to spend the weekend at her in-laws or agreed to have the birthday party there. Lying in bed she had wished that it was just her and Josh celebrating the boys' birthday on their own.

Drawing alongside the pool Amy smiled at Maggie, who was lying on a lounger. The redhead called out to her to join her. But needing to put some cream on Ryan's increasingly red ears, Amy pointed to her son then picked up a bottle of sunscreen.

Ever since Amy's outburst with Celeste last Sunday, Maggie had pestered her, asking her what was wrong. Keen to avoid any personal chat Amy had been vague, blaming her behavior on pressure at work, but she knew it was obvious to her cousin that she was having problems.

Amy felt a pang of guilt that Maggie was confused then felt instant relief that she had been savvy enough to ask Wendy not to mention Celeste turning up at the office. Unfortunately, and to her amusement, the request didn't sway Wendy's need to gossip, but a blatant bribe of dinner at an expensive restaurant of her choice had her capitulate immediately.

Picking up Ryan, Amy took him into the shade. He squirmed trying to get out of her hands, but she held him tight. Maggie approached as Amy applied sunscreen on his ears. Sitting down beside them she began telling Ryan that today he and his brother were sharing their birthday with at least nine million other people in the world.

"Why are you telling him that?" Amy snapped. "This is his day. Who cares if nine million other people share it?" She stood. "Anyway, how do you expect him to understand that?"

Maggie looked at her cousin in surprise. "Well," she replied, "you'd be surprised how clever kids are. Did you know—"

"For God's sake, that's enough!" Amy interrupted, her voice low.

Maggie's brow furrowed deeply, but she said nothing.

Without another word Amy walked away from Maggie, took Ryan over to the side of the pool and put him into the arms of his father.

Josh asked her to join them but Amy made an excuse, telling him that she needed something from the kitchen.

Feeling annoyed, Amy marched into the kitchen, yanked open the fridge door and reached for a carton of juice. Closing it, she strode over to a cupboard, flung it open, reached for a glass and slammed it on the counter. Wanting to vent, she banged the carton down and looked around for something else that she could attack.

Amy stopped. Breathing in deeply she filled the glass and held it to her head. She closed her eyes and let the coolness bring her temper down. She sighed in frustration. Since her visit to Celeste's apartment on Monday she'd been an emotional wreck.

Opening her eyes, Amy watched Maggie through the window playing with the kids in the water. Immediately she felt guilty. She knew Maggie would be upset. She shouldn't have barked at her like that, but this whole thing with Celeste was driving her crazy. She sipped her juice. Unbidden, her eyes trailed over to Celeste, who was sitting on her lounger talking to Sophie.

A few days ago, Amy received a package. Thankfully, it was clearly marked private and confidential and sealed. Otherwise, Wendy would have had her sticky little mitts on it. When Amy opened it she found a key to Celeste's apartment with a note attached to it; a quote from the poet William Blake: *'Those who restrain desire do so because theirs is weak enough to be restrained.'*

Amy's blood had boiled. She immediately ripped it up and threw it in the trashcan along with the key.

Rubbing the glass down her cheek, Amy looked Celeste over. Immediately she felt a strong tug of desire. Ashamed, she turned her back on the window. Putting down her glass, she tightened her ponytail and thought about the trip here this morning.

†

When they arrived Josh got out and let the boys and pups out of the Jeep. Amy fought the urge to get into the driver's seat and drive like a bat out of hell to get out of there. Reluctantly she got out when Fraser and Camille rushed out of the house calling out their welcome.

To Amy's surprise, Sophie approached and gave her a hug.

Hugging her back, Amy saw Celeste's bare feet first. Her eyes slowly moved up to her cutoffs and widened when the slinky red bikini top came into view. Her heart raced and raw desire tugged at her. *Why, does she have to look so hot, dammit?*

Amy pulled out of Sophie's arms, terrified that her sister-in-law would feel her heart thudding.

Celeste smiled warmly. "Hi, Amy," she said casually. She gave Josh a hug then picked up Christopher and tickled his stomach.

Christopher squealed with delight.

Amy's eyes narrowed.

When Alex came out of the house Amy smiled. Over the last few years, she had gotten to know him and really enjoyed his company.

Alex hugged her tightly.

Pleased, Amy hugged him back then caught her breath as it suddenly hit her that Alex knew. Withdrawing slowly from the hug she looked at him apprehensively and tried to read him. She couldn't. Instead, trusting her instinct, she whispered, "I'm glad you're here."

Alex smiled and taking her hand, squeezed it reassuringly.

Once they unpacked and were settled Celeste asked if the boys wanted to go for a swim. They squealed and instinctively looked at Amy to make sure it was all right. She laughed at how excited they were. "Okay, let's go and get you both changed." She looked at Celeste and warily told her, "They'll be two minutes."

Amy took the boys to their room to change them.

Ryan wasn't happy.

"Mom," he protested. "No! Don't want to!" He pulled at an inflatable armband that Amy was putting on.

"You know, Ryan," Amy said patiently, "I don't think your aunt Celeste will take you swimming without them." She began to slide the armband off. "But if you don't want to wear them, I can just tell her that you'll go swimming another time."

Ryan's face fell. He quickly conceded, "Okay."

Amy smiled knowing that there would have been a battle of wills if she had insisted, but at the mere mention of his aunt Celeste, he gave in. She stopped smiling, suddenly reminded that Celeste's influence wasn't just with the boys.

†

"Are you okay, Amy?" Camille asked, interrupting Amy's thoughts.

Amy looked at her mother-in-law in surprise. "Yes, I'm fine."

Denial

"Good," Camille replied as she removed a bottle of chardonnay from the fridge.

Amy watched her take two glasses from the shelf.

"It is just that you seem a little on edge," Camille said, pouring wine. "I noticed that you have not been able to settle at all today."

"Oh…yes, I suppose I have been a little preoccupied." Amy tried to think of an excuse. "It's hectic at work and sometimes it's hard to unwind if you've had a busy week. By tomorrow I'll be fine."

Camille held out a glass. "Here, have this. It will help you unwind, no?"

Smiling, Amy accepted the glass.

"If there is anything that you want to discuss, please talk to me," Camille said softly. "I am concerned that you can't unwind because of problems at work. Sometimes it helps to unburden oneself."

"Oh, Camille," Amy replied reassuringly. "It's nothing, you know." She sipped her wine. "I'm sorry if I've worried you. I didn't intend to spoil your day."

Camille reached out and touched Amy's cheek. "No, my darling, you do the opposite. You bring happiness here always." She smiled. "That is why I noticed that you are not your normal self. Just take care. There must always be a balance, hmmm?"

Amy nodded. "I'll try."

Amy went outside and started clearing up.

"*Chéri,* you have done enough," Camille said, following her.

Amy, needing time to breathe, insisted she clear up.

Camille took hold of the twins' hands. "Right boys, your mama needs some quiet time so let us get you into the bath and to bed."

"Oh no, *grand-mère*. No!" The boys cried out in unison.

"Let me give you a hand," Alex said, picking up some glasses.

Amy smiled, happy to accept his offer.

Halfway through tidying up the sound of a motorbike filtered through. Sean must have arrived. Amy decided to give Maggie and Sean a little time together before going out to welcome him.

Amy smiled when she heard Camille shout for her boys to come back. She laughed, not surprised that the little toe-rags had escaped the clutches of their *grand-mère*. Since discovering that Sean owned a motorbike store the boys adored him.

Amy stopped laughing when Celeste entered the kitchen. Her heart started to pound.

Celeste opened the fridge door and took some beers out.

Trying to ignore her, Amy filled the dishwasher then set the cycle.

"Do you need a hand," Celeste asked, closing the fridge door.

Taken aback by the suggestiveness in her voice, Amy looked at Celeste then at Alex to see if he had noticed. She saw Alex give Celeste a withering look. Amy bowed her head. It was evident that he knew exactly what was going on.

Celeste repeated her question but Amy didn't respond. Instead, about to make her excuses and leave she hesitated when Sophie entered the kitchen. Sighing with relief, she leaned on the worktop and asked Sophie how her book was coming along.

Sophie grimaced as she fished out a cigarette from her pack. "Everything is fine, but I've hit a problem with some of the characters. I've used all my favorite methods of killing in my previous books." Placing the cigarette in her mouth, she patted her jacket pockets. "Normally, my characters die horrifically, one by one."

Amy watched the cigarette bounce up and down as Sophie spoke.

"I need to decide whether or not to wipe out an entire family," Sophie said, chewing the end of the cigarette.

Amy paled when Sophie explained some of the ways that her characters might die. Listening, she wondered if Sophie's therapy sessions were actually doing her any good.

Celeste interrupted. "Do you need a hand, Amy?"

Denial

Amy shook her head and asked Sophie, "Have you met Maggie's boyfriend yet?"

Amy froze when Celeste put both hands on her waist and, leaning forward, allowed the whole of her upper body to press into her. Her mouth touched her ear. "Do you mind moving so that I can get the bottle opener from the drawer?"

Stunned, Amy moved away quickly. "No, of course not."

Embarrassed, and trying to hide her anger, Amy quickly muttered that she was going to greet Sean before hastily retreating from the kitchen.

After Amy left, Sophie looked at her sister for a long moment. "Cel, can you check to see if there is a lighter in the drawer?"

Celeste found a box of matches and gave them to Sophie, who headed through the patio doors.

"Oh, my God!"

"Don't start, Alex."

"What do you think you were doing there?"

Celeste didn't answer.

"For Chrissake, Celeste, that was a bit suggestive!" He shook his head. "Why did you do that in front of Sophie and me?"

Opening the beers, Celeste passed Alex one. She took a mouthful. Swallowing, she looked at Alex. "Because Sophie knows that I'm interested in Amy."

Alex spat out his beer. Wiping his hand over his mouth, he stared at Celeste. "Good God, the plot thickens." He shook his head. "Hon, one thing I can guarantee; if you keep it up, she won't be the only one!"

Celeste swallowed some more beer.

Sighing, Alex took a cloth and cleaned up his mess. "Seriously, Celeste, what has happened to you?"

"Look, Alex," Celeste replied, sounding tired. "If this were an impulsive notion, of course I would fight it. If this were something I could ignore, then of course I would ignore it. I'm neither impulsive nor blasé about what is happening here."

"But you're still prepared to take a huge risk?" Alex asked sounding confused.

"Alex, it is more of a risk if we do nothing about it," Celeste replied with frustration. "Amy feels this…attraction…as much as I do. It has been there for years. I—" Abruptly, she stopped talking and looked at him.

To his astonishment a look of utter helplessness crossed his friend's face.

"Yes," Celeste finished. "The answer is yes." She added bleakly, "Yes, I'm prepared to take the risk."

Startled by the aching pain in Celeste's eyes, Alex blinked a few times. He groaned inwardly, finally accepting what he had known all along. *Shit! She's not smitten; she's over the cliff in love.*

Alex pulled Celeste into his arms and hugged her. He started to speak wanting to tell Celeste that this was wrong, that she needed to stop this, but he stopped. He had watched Amy for much of the day and whenever she thought Celeste wasn't looking, she watched her. After today, he knew the feelings weren't one way.

"I know it's hard, sweetie. But you're right, she's definitely attracted to you." Alex held her shoulders and looked at her. "I can see it in her eyes, in the way she watches you." He whispered, "But be careful, Celeste. For God's sake, be careful."

Camille popped her head through the patio doors. "Come, you two. We have a guest."

Taking Celeste's hand, Alex led the way out to the driveway.

After the introductions Alex watched Josh slip his arms around Amy's waist and hug her tightly as he spoke to Sean. He noted, not for the first time, that they were an exceptionally good-looking couple.

Alex hated this. Over the years he had come to really like Amy. *God knows what she's going through right now.* He looked at Josh. He had always had a soft spot for him. More than a soft spot when he was a teenager, he admitted. He watched them, aware that they looked every inch the perfect couple. He looked at Celeste. His heart sank. Her face was darkening at the sight of Josh and Amy in a loving embrace. *What a fucking mess!*

Chapter 28

The next morning, Amy and Maggie headed off to the golf course. They teed off a half hour after the boys and Celeste. The boys had asked Celeste to join them to make it a foursome.

This morning Amy had gotten up early, keen to get away and be with Maggie for a couple of hours. She still felt bad for her emotional outburst yesterday. Maggie meant the world to her, and although she couldn't bring herself to tell her the truth, she was going to do her damndest to make sure that she didn't pull her cousin into this emotional roller-coaster ride. She was going to do her best to resolve this...*thing*...with Celeste.

Maggie was about to take her shot and trying to distract her, Amy teased, "Are you sure Sean's tadger is as big as you say?"

"Shhh," Maggie replied as she lined up to take her shot.

Amy breathed air deeply into her lungs. It was a beautiful Sunday morning. She smiled remembering how Maggie, during the first four holes, had tried to find out what was going on with her and what was wrong with her yesterday. Thankfully, she tenaciously stuck to her mood being down to nothing more than having too much work.

Once Amy allayed Maggie's fears they chatted easily. At every opportunity, when she wasn't teasing Maggie, Amy encouraged her to talk about Sean, which wasn't difficult given that he was her current pet subject.

As the round progressed, Amy felt the tension leave her for the first time in weeks. She loved being with Maggie and, more than anything, loved the sense of balance her cousin brought to her world.

†

That afternoon Maggie decided to ride back to Sarasota with Sean on his new bike. They sneaked away during the boys' afternoon nap.

When the couple said they were leaving, Amy, restless, itched to go too. She was desperate for this weekend to end. Already she had packed everything into the Jeep in readiness for their journey home, but she was forced to wait until Josh's parents returned from their afternoon walk with the dogs.

Finishing her second cup of coffee, Amy looked out to the patio. For forty minutes Josh and Celeste had been playing the same game of chess. When Celeste stayed with them for those few weeks she and Josh played chess regularly. Amy smiled faintly as she watched Alex. He was sitting close to Celeste, flicking through a magazine. She could see that he was completely bored but still he waited patiently for the game to finish.

Amy looked at Josh then at her watch then tapped her foot lightly. "C'mon," she said under her breath. It had been at least five minutes, she noted, as she looked at her watch, since Josh had made his move. "C'mon," she whispered. "Hurry up and make your move, Celeste."

Desperately wanting Camille and Fraser to return to allow them go home, Amy moved through the open patio doors and approached her husband. "Josh, I think we should call your—"

"Shhh," Josh said. "This is a crucial move."

Silenced, Amy stood beside him.

Josh smiled up at her and, pulling her close, put his arm around her waist. Amy stiffened.

Celeste looked at Josh, then at Amy. "I have to be in New York next weekend," she said. "I'm giving a lecture on feeding centers that MSF run in Darfur." She lifted her eyebrows. "And I noticed that there is an art exhibition by Julie Shelton Smith." She smiled at Amy. "Josh told me some time ago that she's one of your favorite artists. I thought you might like to join me?"

The unexpected invitation left Amy struggling for something to say.

Denial

Josh piped up, "That sounds like a great idea, Celeste. It's only recently that she's been spending more time in her studio." He looked up at Amy. "Maybe it'll give you a little inspiration!" He added enthusiastically, "I think it's a great idea, honey. How about you?"

Amy hesitated. Annoyed that Josh was unwittingly being duped she struggled for a reason not to go. She looked at Josh then Celeste. "I'd like to think about it." With no intention of accepting, she added, "I'll need to look at my schedule."

"Oh come on, Amy." Josh tightened his hold on Amy's waist. "You'll really enjoy it, and I can manage the boys for a weekend."

Josh surprised Amy by placing a light kiss on her T-shirted stomach.

Amy watched Celeste frown.

"Surely, Amy, you wouldn't want to miss an opportunity to see your favorite artist?" Celeste said.

"Maybe next time," Amy replied, eyeing her coldly.

"No, I insist," Josh said. "A weekend break is exactly what you need. You've been working far too hard over the last few weeks." Sounding concerned, he added, "You need some time out. You need some retail therapy. You can go shopping. Let your hair down. Catch up on girl chat."

Amy was aware that Josh couldn't understand why there was tension between her and Celeste. Wanting some form of reconciliation between them he would see the trip as an ideal opportunity for them to spend some time together and get to know each other 'properly.'

Josh beamed a bright smile. "Who would make better company than my beautiful sister?" he said. "She'll happily look after you."

Ashamed, Amy blushed. *That's exactly right, Josh. Your sister wants to look after me, just not quite in the way you think!*

Mistaking Amy's silence, Josh smiled. "Great." He looked at Celeste. "She's going, sis."

Celeste smiled sweetly. "Good." She made her move.

Even though Josh had her in check, Celeste took his white queen with her black knight, her own queen and bishop already positioned to ensure that he had no place to move his king.

"Checkmate," Josh said good-naturedly, then toppled his king. Laughing, he pulled Amy onto his lap and kissed her.

Annoyed at Celeste's obvious game-playing and at Josh for being so easily duped, Amy pushed against him and accidentally knocked over the glass chessboard. The board shattered when it hit the ground.

Upset at her clumsiness, Amy shot off Josh's lap and bent down to pick up the glass.

Celeste reached down quickly, grabbed Amy's wrist and said harshly, "No, Amy. Leave it!"

Confused, Amy looked at her. "Why?"

Loosening her grip but keeping a hold on Amy's wrist, Celeste looked up. "Josh, can you get something to clear this up?"

"Sure," Josh replied and moved quickly toward the kitchen.

Alex, obviously sensing a storm brewing, decided to follow him.

Her eyebrows raised, Amy repeated, "Why?"

"It's broken glass, for God's sake!" Celeste looked down. "Lots of broken glass." Her brow furrowed. "You're only going to hurt yourself if you try to pick it up with your hands."

Pulling her wrist free, Amy replied angrily, "Hurt myself!" She lowered her voice. "Don't you think manipulating Josh is exactly what is going to hurt me?"

"We need time to talk, Amy."

Amy stood and Celeste followed. "Fuck, you mean?"

Celeste reached out, and tucked a loose strand of hair behind Amy's ear. "No," she answered, her eyes troubled. "I mean talk."

"Why don't you go away like you did last time?"

"I'm staying, Amy."

"You don't care, do you?" Amy spat out. "You don't care about the damage?"

"I do care, Amy," Celeste replied, running her fingers lightly over Amy's jawbone.

Amy shook her head. "You don't."

"Believe me, I care." Celeste dropped her hand. "I care very, very much."

Celeste looked vulnerable.

Amazingly, Amy's anger disappeared. Memories of their last encounter flooded in. Her stomach tightened and her pulse picked up speed as she gazed at Celeste. Her eyes hungrily focused on her full mouth. Unconsciously, she took a step closer.

"We need time to figure this out," Celeste said, watching Amy carefully.

Always fascinated by the fullness of Celeste's mouth Amy's fingers ached to touch her. She reached out and brushed them over her succulent lips.

Celeste groaned lightly. Without hesitation she captured the tip of Amy's index finger in her mouth and sucked it.

Mesmerized, her mouth parted, Amy leaned in to…

She jolted back when Josh's laughter broke through her haze. Shaking, she pulled her hand away.

Josh appeared through the patio doors chatting to Alex about the weekend football scores.

Stunned at what she had been about to do Amy backed away from Celeste. She turned toward Josh. Stiffly, she listened to their conversation. At any other time she would have found their chat seriously amusing as Alex didn't know one end of a football from the other.

Alex had made it known to Amy that he had no interest in sports at school. Amateur dramatics was his thing, but recently, since dating a sports teacher, he embraced all things 'athletic' with relish.

"Are you okay, honey?" Josh asked, rubbing Amy's arms.

"Yes," Amy replied unsteadily.

"Are you sure?"

"Yes," Amy said, clearing her throat. "Yes, I'm fine."

"Good," Josh replied. He looked at the ground. "Let's get this mess cleared up."

Chapter 29

Amy eyed the buttons to her left. After a few seconds thrumming her fingers she decided to press one. She laughed in surprise when the swirl changed into jettisons of water.

Sitting in the hotel bathtub, Amy pressed all the buttons several times over, completely tickled by the change in the swirl of the water. Eventually she sank back into the froth of suds and relaxed into the gentle swirl. Exhaling slowly she decided that it was about time they upgraded the bathtub at home.

Picking up the soap an image of Celeste dropped in her mind and she blushed. Amy still couldn't believe that she almost kissed Celeste last Sunday. Soaping her breasts she accepted that it was now riskier to keep Celeste at arm's length than to try to sort out what was happening between them. Pooling some bubbles in her hand she reassured herself that she had done the right thing by coming to New York with Celeste. Although they hadn't discussed anything yet, this trip was all about sorting things out.

Blowing bubbles out of her hand Amy thought about their arrival this morning. She squirmed as she recalled the relief she felt when the clerk handed them separate keys. Bringing her toes to the surface she wiggled them, then sunk further into the tub, embarrassed that she hadn't fully trusted Celeste when she said she wanted this weekend to talk.

Pressing a button for more hot water Amy reflected on her day. After checking in, they went shopping. They found an art store and Celeste waited patiently as Amy thumbed her way through the stock before leaving with a bag of supplies.

Celeste, she discovered, knew a lot about art. Given the amount of traveling she'd done over the years that seemed natural. After the art store they stopped for coffee. Probably for the first time, Amy realized, she was getting to know who Celeste was and she was intriguing.

When they returned to the hotel after six Amy stood outside her room door and smiled at Celeste's light teasing that they

Denial

needed to be ready at seven sharp. They were seeing a show, then going for something eat.

Amy slipped off her shoes and entered the bathroom. She smiled; the bathtub was huge. She couldn't remember the last time she'd opted for a bath instead of a shower. Reaching for the shower knob she decided that she didn't have time now, but then she hesitated. The urge to soak was too strong. Impulsively, she pressed the stopper down and ran the hot water.

Humming, Amy undressed. Eying the various bath salts as the tub filled, she tied her hair up. Stepping into it she groaned as she luxuriated in the enormous tub. Sinking in, she inhaled the smell of the herbal-scented suds.

Relaxing, Amy closed her eyes and laid her head back and thought just a few minutes.

Amy's eyes flew open. Sitting bolt upright she looked around. Dazed, it took a few moments for her brain to register where she was, and a few more for her to figure out what the noise was that woke her.

Brrr...brrr...Brrr...brrr.

"Shit...the phone!"

Amy shot out of the tub. Soaking wet she skidded as she hurried toward the phone. Just as she picked it up a side door opened.

Amy's eyes almost popped out of her head when Celeste walked into the room.

"I heard the phone ring," Celeste said, looking Amy over. "I thought that you must have fallen asleep."

Unaware there was a connecting door, Amy flushed all over. It took a moment for her to figure out where the distant voice was coming from. Remembering that someone was on the line, she quickly put the phone to her ear.

"Hello?" Amy squeaked.

"Hi, Amy?"

Realizing she was naked, Amy's face burned bright red. "Hi...Josh!"

Frantically, Amy scanned the room for something to cover herself. She eyed her weekend bag at the far end of her room. There was nothing.

"Everything okay, honey?"

If you consider standing naked and dripping wet in front of your always-amorous sister okay, then I'm definitely not okay.

Amy tugged hard on the bedspread. "Yes…" she said, grunting. "Yes. Everything's okay."

"I couldn't reach you on your cell."

Tucked firmly under the mattress, the bedspread refused to budge. "It's…in my purse… so I didn't…hear it. How's…things…with…you?" Amy puffed.

Celeste moved toward the bathroom.

"Fine," Josh replied then asked, "Honey, have you been running?"

"No," Amy wheezed. "I'm…just…trying…to…get…ready."

"We're missing you," Josh said, sounding confused that his wife was panting. "Here I'll let you speak to Chris."

Approaching Amy, Celeste stood in front of her with a bath towel.

Amy grabbed the towel then stepped back. She let out a silent yelp when the bedside cabinet jabbed her leg. Clutching the towel, she mumbled her thanks and unintentionally looked Celeste over. Her dress sense was impeccable. Usually, she wore her hair in a ponytail, but tonight, it was down. Its length made it curl slightly as it fell around her shoulders.

Amy caught her bottom lip. Celeste's expensive white linen trouser suit and camisole top looked stunning. *God, she, really does have an incredible body—lean, sleek, full-breasted.* Amy gulped. Her eyes widened when she saw the camisole Celeste was wearing was almost sheer. Pulse rising, she swallowed. Aware that there was no way she would get through the evening with that as a distraction, she held the towel tightly and said, "Shouldn't…you…button that?"

Celeste looked down and smiled. "Yes," she replied. "I was about to when the phone rang."

Denial

Relieved, Amy forced herself to focus when she heard her son's voice.

"Hi, Mommy," Christopher said. His voice trembled. "Mac bwit me!"

Wondering why Josh hadn't mentioned this earlier, Amy frowned. "Are you all right, baby?"

Celeste motioned to her watch.

Tensing, Amy ignored her.

"Yesth," Christopher replied, his lispy voice sounding brave. "But it 'urts."

Concerned, Amy reassured. "It's okay, baby. When Mommy gets back, she'll kiss it all better. Okay?"

Christopher sniffled, but didn't reply.

"Sweetheart, is Daddy there?" Amy asked. She could hear slight rustling as he nodded. She imagined him standing there with a little pouted lip, miffed that his mommy wasn't there to soothe him. She asked again, "Chris, can you pass the phone to Daddy?"

Christopher said nothing.

Aware that Christopher didn't want to give up the phone, Amy said tenderly, "Chris, can I speak to Daddy? Just for a moment, then I'll come right back to you, baby, I promise. I just need to speak to him quickly."

Christopher sniffed. "Okay, Mommy."

"Amy, honey, it's nothing," Josh said reassuringly. "Mac nipped him because Chris," he said sternly, obviously directing his next words to their son, "would not stop pulling on his tail! Even though he was told to stop." Josh added softly, "Amy, don't worry about it. The reason I didn't mention it was because there wasn't a mark and he didn't even make a peep. This is the first I've heard out of him all day about it." He chuckled. "Chris is looking for sympathy, honey, and he knows right where to get it."

Immediately, the tension left Amy. She smiled at Celeste's frowning face reassuringly. "Okay, that's a relief," she replied. "Can I speak to him again?"

Waiting for Josh to pass the phone back to Christopher, Amy knew that she needed to distract her son from focusing on her being away. "Hi, Chris, Mommy needs you to be a brave boy, just like you always are, and look after Daddy. Do you think you can manage that? It's a big responsibility, but I know you can do it."

Amy smiled confidently at Celeste and waited for his response. Christopher loved nothing better than being told he was a brave boy.

"Okay, Mommy," Christopher replied quickly.

When she heard the tinge of pride in his voice at being given the task, Amy winked at Celeste.

Celeste raised an eyebrow then tilted her head inquiringly.

Completely disarmed that such a small movement was so charming. Amy felt lost when her body responded hotly.

Celeste lifted her hand, and tapping her watch, showed Amy that it was six forty-five. Amy nodded, then put her head down to stop any further distraction. She spoke to her son. A few moments later, she lifted her head when the connecting door closed.

Amy chatted with Christopher, then Ryan briefly, and said goodbye to Josh. Quickly dressing, she applied some light makeup then let her hair fall around her shoulders. Her black, thinly strapped dress hung just below the knee and accentuated the fullness of her breasts. It hugged the curves of her hips and showed off her shapely tanned legs, which were enhanced by three-inch heels.

Looking in the mirror, Amy gave herself a once-over. Not bad for a mother of two, she thought, as the door clicked shut behind her.

Chapter 30

Returning to their rooms, Amy stood in the elevator with Celeste and two strangers. Leaning against the back wall, she closed her eyes and thought how easy being with Celeste truly was. Tonight, they had seen a Broadway production. Amy smiled. She had enjoyed the musical, a rework of an opera she had seen with her dad a few years ago.

Amy's smile broadened as she remembered seeing the opera in London. She recalled leaving the theater with her dad, so choked with emotion she couldn't speak through the twenty-minute taxi ride back to their hotel.

Warmed by the memory, Amy dropped her head slightly. Biting lightly on her bottom lip, she thought back to dinner.

The restaurant that Celeste chose, on Fifty-Fourth Street, was a blend of Southeast Asian and French food. The dining area was large and noisy. Amy was secretly pleased when Celeste arranged for a recessed booth, which muted the noise.

They talked easily about the types of food and wine they enjoyed. Amy wasn't surprised that Celeste had an eclectic taste, given her passion for cooking. When they ordered she went with Celeste's recommendation and chose the restaurant's signature dish.

Amy thought back to their conversation at the restaurant. She remembered how explorative Celeste was with her, drawing her out throughout the evening into conversation. She recalled Celeste's subtle compliments about her outfit, her hair, her eyes, even her perfume. She wanted to return them, but couldn't. She was too shy and unused to receiving such sincere compliments from another woman.

To Amy's surprise, during the meal she had confided in Celeste that her dad planned that they would travel extensively, visiting every continent and many countries when Amy finished university.

†

"Vietnam," Amy told Celeste wistfully, "was one of the countries my dad wanted to visit."

"You must miss him very much," Celeste said, lifting her glass of white wine.

Holding the fork to her mouth, Amy looked at her sharply.

Celeste returned her gaze as she sipped her wine.

Amy was unsure if Celeste could ever understand such a loss, then she remembered Felice and realized that Celeste's own life experience, her work as a doctor with MSF, positioned her perfectly to understand.

"Yes," Amy replied. Losing her appetite for what had been a delicious dish of lobster with Thai herbs, she put her fork down and pushed the plate away. "Every day," she added with a note of longing, "I miss him every day."

Amy wiped her mouth with her napkin.

Celeste put her glass down. Leaning in, she brushed Amy's cheek lightly with her fingers and said in a low voice, "Tell me about him."

Amy shrugged. "There is so much to tell."

Leaning back, Celeste encouraged, "Tell me why he wanted to visit Vietnam?"

Amy hesitated. She looked at Celeste. For the first time in a long time she wanted to talk about her father. "He loved Vietnamese architecture," she replied.

"Why?"

Amy shrugged. "I think, for him, it expressed a combination of natural balance and harmony."

"I love Vietnamese architecture," Celeste said softly. Looking into Amy's eyes, she added, "Did he plan to see the Giac Lam Pagoda in Ho Chi Minh City?"

"Yes," Amy answered her eyes bright. "That was the one he intended visiting on our trip to Vietnam."

"It's wonderful, Amy," Celeste said softly. "It's considered to be the city's oldest pagoda."

Celeste's eyes carried a depth of warmth that lulled Amy. "I had no idea until today that you were into architecture or art."

"Yes," Celeste replied.

"Tell me about your trip to Vietnam."

Amy's appetite returned when Celeste talked about her travels. She listened and was surprised at not only Celeste's knowledge of Vietnamese architecture, but also the breadth of her knowledge of some of the most treasured architectural sights on the planet.

Amy lost herself when they discussed the treasures they would like to see, from the lavish Meenakshi Temple in India to the obscure Solovki Monastery in Russia.

Eventually, when there was a lull in the conversation, Celeste said softly, "If we are to do this, Amy, I think we need some conditions."

Lifting her coffee cup Amy hesitated before asking, "What do you mean?"

"I mean," Celeste replied, spooning sugar into her cup, "that we both agree on a time limit."

"Time limit?" Befuddled, Amy slowly put her cup down.

Holding Amy's gaze, Celeste said patiently, "It must end, Amy. That's the whole point of this exercise."

Swallowing, Amy repeated, "Exercise."

"Affair, Amy," Celeste replied, as if clearing up a mystery.

Amy shook her head. "But it hasn't even started—"

"—It has," Celeste said, her eyes shining. She added, almost soothingly, "Amy, it started a long time ago."

Amy watched the steam rise from her coffee cup and tried to absorb Celeste's words. Eventually, she looked at her and asked openly, "You really believe we should do this, don't you?"

Holding her gaze, Celeste answered, "Yes."

Amy exhaled. She was in conflict. She was seeing different sides to Celeste and there was no doubt, as this weekend was proving, that she was a complex and multilayered person.

"Why does someone like you," Amy asked, "who has experienced so much, and who understands the types of adversities that life throws at people—"

"Amy," Celeste interrupted. "What I do is a job, that's all."

Amy shook her head and said firmly, "Oh, I think it's much more than that, Doctor Cameron."

Evidently amused by the use of her formal address, Celeste's lips twitched. "I have the same weaknesses as the next person."

Looking at Celeste, Amy went for what she hoped was her Achilles heel. She raised her eyebrows and asked, "What about Josh. Do you care about him?"

Celeste's eyes narrowed. She leaned in. "Of course I care about him."

"Then, for his sake, don't you think we should stop this?"

Leaning back, Celeste answered almost wearily, "Do you think we can?" She held Amy's gaze. "Do you want to have years of this?" she asked. "Do you want it to be knotted in our stomachs whenever we see each other?" Her eyes sparked. "To be there in every look we exchange, in every accidental touch—" She stopped when Amy lifted her hand to show her wedding ring.

"Regardless," Amy replied. Leaning forward, she lowered her voice. "I'm married."

"Do you think that's enough?"

"I believe in monogamy."

Celeste arched an eyebrow. "Your beliefs haven't stopped you so far."

Amy's heart thudded. The lines of the poem flashed through her mind, *'Those who restrain desire do so because theirs is weak enough to be restrained.'*

"In most parts of the world, Amy, sexual desire is a fact of life," Celeste said, lifting her cup. "In some cultures, people aren't expected to suppress their needs. Desire is an acceptable part of being alive. In societies where power tends to pass through women, women sleep with whomever they want. However, in more developed cultures, especially when it comes to property, the rules become more one-sided."

Listening, Amy unconsciously fixed a dress strap that had slid down a shoulder.

Celeste paused for several seconds. "Property is generally passed through the male lineage, and because it's important to know who the father of a child is, from a property perspective, men tend to continue being promiscuous and women tend to be guarded...sexually."

"Look, Celeste, I understand that you might have a different perspective on things given your exposure to different cultures, but whatever you say still doesn't normalize it for me." Amy frowned. "We're living in the twenty-first century, and I buy into monogamy."

Looking closely at Amy, Celeste said vulnerably, "All I want is for this ache to stop."

Surprised, Amy blushed.

"I want it to stop. It's draining me, Amy." She leaned back. "I can't think straight. It has to change, because the real truth is, I don't want years of this."

They stared at each other.

Amy took a drink. "Given time, it will die."

Celeste shook her head. "This type of attraction doesn't die." She looked at Amy. "Emotions are complex. People can take to their grave feelings for their unrequited first crush."

"Shucks, I'm your first crush?"

Celeste smiled. "No, but consider it a metaphor for the unrequited."

Amy held Celeste's gaze for a long time, then surprised herself by asking, "How can we make it stop?"

Celeste closed her eyes briefly. "Have you heard of the fantasy theory?"

Amy shook her head.

"For a fantasy to exist, desire needs absent objects. Desire can only support itself with fantasies."

"Meaning what?" Amy asked, intrigued. "That the moment you get something you normally can't have, you don't want it anymore?"

Celeste nodded.

Amy thought back to something that she had read somewhere about people only being truly happy when thinking about their future happiness. *How bizarre life really is?*

"So, what you're saying is that if we were to do this, we would turn desire into reality and lose interest?"

"Yes," Celeste responded.

Amy exhaled. She caught her bottom lip. Her common sense screamed indignantly, *No way!* Her baser instincts yelled out hungrily, *yes! Say yes!*

Celeste took Amy's hand. Holding it, she gently stroked the back of it.

Be strong, Amy told herself. You came with her this weekend to end it. So end it. Gazing into Celeste's eyes, Amy couldn't. Her skin tingled and her stomach fluttered. *Why can't you?* Her inner voice answered readily. *You want it to happen as much as she does. You want her. Accept it...you want her bad.*

Amy immediately thought of her mother. *It won't make you like that*, her inner voice appeased. *She left her family. If you keep the arrangement simple, it will be over before you know it and you won't have years of this. You'll be able to put it behind you, just like you did last time with her.*

Looking down, Amy watched Celeste's thumb stroke the back of her hand. The complete sensuality of her touch ricocheted through her brain.

"I want no emotional involvement," Amy said. "I don't want to discuss my relationship with Josh." Leaning in, she added protectively, "I want it understood there is no future for us." She swallowed. "Four months, no more."

Celeste leaned in, and searched her face intently. "Okay," she replied. "Let's go."

†

The elevator silently slid to a halt. Amy pulled herself away from the wall. When the doors opened, Celeste held out her hand. Aware of the stranger still in the elevator but unable to resist, Amy took it. She walked with Celeste along the corridor.

Standing behind her, Celeste waited patiently as Amy searched her small purse for her key card.

Denial

Placing the card in the door lock Amy stood hesitantly when the door unlocked.

Sensing that Amy was wrestling with her conscience, Celeste placed her hands on Amy's hips and pushed her forward gently.

Immediately, Amy's pulse sped up. Letting go of her doubt, she entered her room.

Still feeling the effects of the wine from dinner but needing a little courage, Amy decided a nightcap was justified. Turning to Celeste she asked if she would like a drink.

Celeste nodded. "Tequila," she replied, removing her shoes.

Pouring their drinks Amy wondered if Celeste was nervous and decided no, the cool, calm doctor never got her feathers ruffled. She took a large swig from her glass. Reflexively, she spluttered and gasped for air.

Moving to the minibar quickly Celeste pulled out a small bottle of mineral water, opened it, and handed it to Amy.

After a few gulps of water Amy smiled ruefully. "Thanks." She coughed. "Whisky," she rasped. "I'd forgotten it has a real kick."

Celeste raised an eyebrow then drank slowly from her glass.

Sipping water from the bottle Amy watched Celeste drink and wondered, not for the first time, what it would be like to taste her mouth again.

At one point this evening, when they were dining, Amy had found it hard to believe that, given their encounters, they had never kissed since that first night. She remembered noticing her full mouth when they first met. Although Josh had a similar mouth, somehow, Celeste's seemed much more provocative. Amy suddenly realized that everything she found attractive about Josh, Celeste seemed to amplify, and not the other way around.

Putting her glass down Celeste approached Amy. Removing the bottle from her hand, she brushed hers lips over Amy's before whispering, "I really enjoyed this evening." She added throatily, "All night, I have wanted to kiss you."

Groaning, Amy placed her hands at the nape of Celeste's neck and kissed her teasing mouth hungrily, then deeply.

Opening her mouth fully, Celeste ran her tongue along Amy's lips before slipping it into her mouth. She moaned when Amy pressed into her and kissed her intently.

After a few moments, Celeste broke the kiss and leaning her brow against Amy's whispered, "I don't think I can wait any longer."

Impatiently, Amy moved her head, seeking Celeste's lips. She tangled her fingers in her loose hair and kissed her hard.

Celeste pulled away and murmured, "I need you, Amy." Taking her hand, she led her to the bed.

Chapter 31

Entranced, Amy watched Celeste undress. Yearning raced through her forcing her to reach out for the bedpost. Her legs weakened at the sight of Celeste naked and unabashed. *What if, after this ends, I'm never satisfied again?* she thought. *What about you, Celeste, who will you want after me?*

Surprised by the jealous streak, Amy's jaw clenched. Looking at Celeste, she gave into her craving and moved to stand in front of her. With her three-inch heels and Celeste barefoot, they were at eye level. Leaning into her, Amy kissed the hollows of her shoulders before finding her mouth.

Celeste slowly pulled her mouth away. Evidently pleased at Amy's newfound enthusiasm, she murmured, "The way you make me feel is incredible." Amy slowly placed her hands on Celeste's breasts. Groaning, she closed her eyes and allowed her senses to focus on the pleasure of touching this woman, this way. She frowned slightly when a strange feeling of needing this intimacy washed over her. "I love touching your breasts," she whispered, opening her eyes.

Inches apart, Amy watched a gamut of emotions cross Celeste's face. Something deep inside her had begun to grow when Celeste had returned home and it had shaped into a need that she couldn't contain. She would combust if she didn't taste her.

Amy's lips grazed Celeste's breast, softly she sucked on a nipple. The rush to every nerve ending in her body was exquisite.

In response, Celeste's lungs emptied. Her dark eyelashes fluttered closed. She sucked in air then moaned as she gripped Amy's shoulders tightly.

Celeste made noises of deep pleasure as Amy sucked. Eventually, she whispered, "Touch me…Amy…please."

Goose bumps formed all over Amy's body. Breathing shallowly, she straightened and gazed at Celeste. Dizzy with just the notion of it, she swallowed. Slowly she moved her hands over Celeste, rested them on hips then slid one between her thighs and stroked her clit.

Arching, Celeste rapidly moved her hips back and forth. "Yes...Amy."

Instinctively, Amy followed Celeste's rhythm. Her throat tightened.

Celeste's head snapped back. Groaning deeply, she let out a long cry and climaxed.

Hot tears filled Amy's eyes.

Stilling, Celeste held the blonde tightly, then slowly kissed the tears away.

"I want you so much," Amy said.

"I know."

After a moment, Celeste whispered as she unzipped Amy's dress, "I want to see you."

Slipping the thin straps off Amy's shoulders, Celeste kissed the length of each shoulder before pulling the straps fully down. Letting the dress fall to her waist, she looked openly at her.

Breathing heavily, Amy could see that already the brunette was hungry for more.

"You are so beautiful," Celeste whispered as her hands moved to Amy's breasts.

Amy gasped when her breasts filled Celeste's palms.

"I've wanted to touch you like this all day," Celeste admitted, planting small kisses on Amy's face. "I've relived that first night in your apartment over and over," she murmured. "Relived the feel of you. You would have thought it would have faded by now," she confessed. "But, for the last four years it has driven me crazy."

A surge of exhilaration shot through Amy. She closed her eyes and smiled at the idea of Celeste being driven crazy by thoughts of her. Her eyes popped open when Celeste ducked her head capturing one nipple then the other, greedily sucking them to hard peaks.

Amy groaned loudly.

Denial

Dropping to her knees, Celeste pushed Amy's dress down further, exposing her stomach and hips.

When the cold air hit the wetness around her nipples, Amy was suddenly and acutely aware of their sensitivity as they stiffened in need of attention.

Hungrily, Celeste trailed kisses along Amy's stomach then prodded her tongue into her belly button.

Unable to resist any longer, Amy touched her own breasts. "Mmmm," she uttered, head falling back in deep gratification.

Celeste lowered Amy's dress over her hips dropping it to the floor. Lacing her fingers along the inside of her black briefs, she moved them down. Once past her hips, eyes half-closed, she leaned in and caught Amy's scent. A low growl escaped her. Quickly, she pulled Amy's briefs the rest of the way down.

Realizing what Celeste was about to do uncertainty swept through Amy. She stiffened.

"I want to taste you," Celeste said, looking up at Amy.

"Celeste! I...I...don't know if I want this...I don't know if I'm ready for this," Amy stuttered.

"Amy," Celeste said with a hint of impatience. "Do we have to fight every time?" Resting her forehead between Amy's thighs, she nuzzled her face into her and whispered seductively, "You smell ready."

Groaning, Amy's world ground to a halt. Embarrassed, she covered her face with her hands.

Celeste pressed further into Amy, loving her softness, and kissed around her thighs. She inhaled deeply and tried to fight the animalistic need that filled her.

Amy dropped her hands to her side. "Celeste," she said earnestly. "I mean it...I don't like it...this."

Celeste stopped nuzzling, and resting on her knees, she stroked up and down the length of Amy's thighs. Looking up, her chest constricted at the sight of the blonde standing fully erect, breasts full, nipples hardened, face flushed with excitement. The beauty of this woman overwhelmed her.

Feeling her control break, Celeste groaned. Gripping Amy's thighs, she said in exasperation, "Amy, do you want me to beg?

Tell you that I can't stop thinking about you? That I can't eat. I can't sleep?" Her grip tightened. "Tell you that I can't think straight since that night in the summerhouse?" She stopped and, bending her head, exhaled heavily before looking up. "Amy," she added vulnerably, "do you want me to tell you how much I need this? How much I need to...to touch you, to taste you?"

Looking down at Celeste, Amy's hands fluttered as she tried to find the words. Unable to find them she shook her head and insisted, "I'm sorry. I'm just...I'm not ready."

Celeste placed her fingers between Amy's thighs and touched her. Lifting glistening fingers, she replied softly, "I think you are."

Amy gasped. "I—"

Celeste touched her again.

Holding her breath, Amy closed her eyes briefly. Then looking at Celeste, nodded her consent.

Celeste gently lifted each of Amy's feet and slipped her briefs off. Looking up at her, her breath caught again at the glorious sight of this woman, naked. Deeply moved by how exposed she seemed she watched Amy's hands protectively cover her breasts.

For a moment, Celeste considered taking Amy to bed, but even that slight delay was too much. With her hands she put pressure on Amy's thighs to part.

As her thighs opened Amy's body tensed. Celeste looked at her and moaned; her clit was wet and glistening.

Her need to taste Amy overwhelming her, Celeste hungrily leaned in to catch drops of her. Driving her tongue between her lips she ran it back and forth, down and up the length of her. Repeatedly, letting the taste of Amy drive her wild, until eventually she took her clit fully in her mouth and sucked on it, nibbling and flicking it over and over with her tongue, continually swallowing with pleasure as Amy's hips rocked back and forth.

"OhmyGod...Celeste!" Amy uttered.

Celeste's excitement went into overdrive. Enthralled by the taste of Amy, the intimacy of her actions, and unable to contain her own excitement she touched herself as she slipped a hand between Amy's thighs.

Amy almost choked when Celeste's fingers entered her.

Celeste winced when Amy's full weight bore down on her and her nails dug into her shoulders. She tried to stay on the edge until Amy climaxed, but the sound of her moaning and the feel of being inside her drove her frantic.

Amy's hands moved to Celeste's head. "Celeste. Oh God. I…I—"

Celeste bit down then sucked on the hard bead against her tongue.

Amy's words stalled. Leaning in, she rose erect on her toes. Her body arching, she convulsed in orgasm.

Celeste almost withdrew in surprise when her mouth filled with fluid, but the force of Amy's orgasm pushed her on.

Amy's head fell back. She rocked her hips and pressed down harder, begging Celeste to keep going until finally she slowed.

Leaning her head into the softness of Amy's thighs, the unstoppable welling up of her own deep climax overtook Celeste.

†

Panting, Amy pulled away from Celeste. Trying to catch her breath, her chest heaving, unable to believe the way this woman made her feel, she made her way to the bed. In the beginning, Josh had tried going down on her often, but eventually she discouraged it. She tended to labor to reach orgasm and it always felt awkward. Never, ever, *ever*, had it felt anything like that!

Amy looked at Celeste and frowned when she saw her mouth and chin dripping. Confused, she sat. Her frown deepened as she watched small drops glisten as they ran down Celeste's throat, trail past her breasts and slide down her stomach. Suddenly aware of how wet the insides of her own thighs were she gave Celeste a worried look.

"Oh God," Amy uttered, eyes widening. "What have I done?"

"It's not what you think," Celeste replied softly, wiping her mouth.

Amy visibly paled. "What then?"

Looking amused, Celeste explained gently, "Some women, when they climax, release a little," she looked down at herself, "or a lot, of fluid."

"Huh?" Confused, Amy stood, then sat, then stood again.

"That's all it is, Amy," Celeste said reassuringly.

Cheeks stained with embarrassment, a sense of amazement filled Amy at how truly alien her body was to her. Unsure how to feel she sat and looked down at the floor.

"Amy."

"Yes," Amy responded, dazed.

"I take it you've never experienced that before?"

"What?"

"That type of physical response when you've climaxed?"

Befuddled, Amy looked at Celeste. "Are you sure it's what you say, and that I didn't," she closed her eyes, "you know…" She struggled for the words.

"Yes, I'm sure," Celeste replied. Trying to hide her amusement, she kept a straight face. "Are you sure this has never happened to you before?"

Amy opened one eye and peered at Celeste. "What are you doing to me?"

Celeste smiled and then, growling, seductively moved toward Amy on all fours.

Feeling exhausted, and uncomfortable with what had just happened, Amy quickly pulled the sheets from the bed and slipped under them.

Celeste stood. She smiled. "Okay, maybe a shower is a better idea."

Worried that Celeste might suggest they shower together, Amy tucked the sheet around her and, shaking her head, said, "No…honestly, I'm fine."

Celeste looked tenderly at Amy then headed for the bathroom.

Denial

When she heard the shower run Amy exhaled in relief and closed her eyes.

Amy's eyes flew open a few minutes later when Celeste, still naked, approached her with a damp cloth and a towel. Standing over her she indicated that Amy remove the sheet.

Amy clutched the sheet. She looked up. "Celeste, thank you. But honestly, I…I can manage."

Placing the cloth and towel on the bedside cabinet, Celeste gently tried to remove the sheet from Amy's grasp. "Trust me," she said with a glimmer of humor as Amy held on tight. "I have an excellent bedside manner."

Amy groaned. *Why didn't I just have a shower?* In no position to argue after what just happened she let Celeste pull the sheet down.

Sitting midway down the bed, Celeste reached for the cloth and tenderly washed Amy.

Entranced by the intimacy of Celeste's actions, Amy watched her use the cloth.

"Did you mean it?"

"What?" Amy asked, slowly relaxing under Celeste's ministrations.

"That you have never come like that?" Celeste asked, gently toweling Amy dry.

Amy tensed. "I…umm…" Blushing heavily, she struggled to find an answer. How could she explain that although she was a married, twenty-eight-year-old mother of two, she had never experienced *anything* like that before? "Don't think so," she finished quickly.

"I think you would have noticed. Don't you?" Celeste asked. Finishing, she stood and returned to the bathroom.

Unable to cope with all the strange emotions coursing through her, Amy pulled the sheet up and curled into a fetal position.

Celeste returned and, sitting on the bed, stroked Amy's hair and asked softly, "Why do you think you've never experienced it before?"

Sighing, Amy closed her eyes. "I don't know," she answered after a while.

"Did it frighten you?"

Eyes wide, Amy confessed, "I don't know what's happening to me."

Celeste's eyes filled with warmth. "Don't be scared, Amy," she said gently. "It's perfectly okay."

Amy closed her eyes and sighed. "Why do all doctors say that?"

"What?"

Amy rolled onto her stomach. Burying her head into her pillow, she mumbled.

Celeste laughed. "I don't have a clue what you just said."

Amy lifted her head and, looking over her shoulder, said, "Why is it that all doctors say that it's going to be perfectly okay." Feeling less unnerved, she teased. "Why does every person in the medical profession have sentences with the word 'perfect' in it? She mimicked, "Oh, Mrs. Cameron, don't worry, although you have two overgrown gremlins stuffed up inside you, it's fine to be overdue. It's all perfectly normal."

Celeste laughed lightly. "Cesarean wasn't an option then?"

Amy shook her head. "And a big fat bribe didn't work either." She smiled. "Mrs. Cameron, you might have been in labor for more than your body can take, but it's all perfectly fine. And no, we can't give you more drugs, no matter how much you beg or try to bribe us."

Celeste grinned. "The boys didn't want to come out."

Amy smiled. "Nope. They hung in there until the final hour, and then some." Yawning, she rubbed her shoulder. "I'm tired."

Celeste moved closer. "Are your shoulders stiff?"

Amy nodded.

"Let me take care of that."

Going to the bathroom, Celeste returned with a bottle of lotion. She positioned herself over Amy then pulled the bedsheet down. Straddling her hips, she poured cream down the length of Amy's spine.

Surprised, Amy yelped at the sudden coldness.

"Feel good?" Celeste asked, running her hands over Amy's back.

Amy groaned in pleasure.

Celeste smiled as she massaged Amy's shoulders. She worked the knots at the base of her neck before running her thumbs up and down her spine.

"When was the last time you had a back massage?"

Amy mumbled, "To long to remember."

"You should make it a priority. You have great posture but your back is full of tension knots."

Amy groaned as the tension seeped out of her. "Is that an order, doc," she asked, then groaned loudly when Celeste worked the knots out from under her right shoulder blade.

"Yes," Celeste replied, then frowned. "Your muscles are really tight. You need to find time for this."

Amy winced when Celeste worked at a particular knot. "In case you haven't noticed," she said, "I'm a working mum with two little monsters, two hairy dogs, a husband, a cousin who I hardly see because she's in love, an overworked and overwrought, boss. And, just now, for a while," she threw a look over her shoulder, "a very demanding you."

"Shhh," Celeste responded. She moved Amy's head to center position then ran her thumbs down her spine again, stretching it. "To enjoy this thoroughly, we need quiet."

"Expert, are you?" Amy mumbled.

"Mmmm," Celeste murmured. "Nothing can beat a massage. When I can, I make time for it."

Amy nodded then relaxed completely.

Celeste worked on Amy's back for some minutes then said in a thoughtful tone, as she worked her thumbs into the base of her spine, "I'm sure I can rewrite my brief, and add masseuse, along with lover."

Amy's eyes popped open. *Lover!*

"You're stiffening up," Celeste said. Bending, she kissed between Amy's shoulder blades. "Try to relax. Let your mind free."

Not wanting to analyze anything, Amy forced herself to relax and let her mind drift.

"How does that feel?" Celeste asked after a few minutes.

"Good," Amy responded drowsily.

"Just good," Celeste said seductively. "Are you sure?"

Feeling Celeste's breasts press into her back. Amy replied, "Wonderful."

Celeste kissed along Amy's shoulders. "I would like to sleep with you."

Amy's body tingled at the idea. But if what had happened earlier was a sign of what was to come, she didn't think she could cope. This whole thing was still too new. Looking over her shoulder, she stuttered, "I…I…don't want to do…for us to have…anymore tonight!"

"No." Kissing Amy's cheek, Celeste replied reassuringly. "Not to make love. Just share a bed, to hold you."

Still shocked by what happened earlier and too tired to think coherently Amy clumsily replied, "I don't think that's a good idea. Sleeping together is…a…an intimacy I want to keep for Josh."

Celeste stiffened then quickly moved off the bed.

Amy rolled over to face her.

Her eyes darkening, Celeste glared at Amy. "A simple no would have done, Amy."

Amy's heart gripped convulsively, she whispered, "I'm sorry."

Her apology fell on the closing door of the connecting room.

Amy rolled over. Closing her eyes, she listened as the key turned in the door.

Chapter 32

Amy couldn't concentrate. All morning she had been swamped by reminders of the night before. Wherever she went, it was inescapable. An hour before she had to leave waiting in line at a toy store when the woman in front of her with dark, shoulder-length hair invoked a full screening of the previous night.

Leaving the store, Amy continued to be plagued as the most inconsequential act prompted a replay. Outside, little bits of Celeste surrounded her as many women carried similarities in their hair, their height, their shapes, their legs, their smiles, their eyes, their brows, their breasts. All indistinctive to Amy on their own, but this morning they formed a powerful collage of sexual potency.

Driven to distraction, Amy found solace in a bookstore near Fifth Avenue renowned for its architectural collection, and waited it out until it was time to meet Celeste for lunch. She just hoped that the arrangement still stood. Early this morning she had knocked on the connecting door but there was no response.

Arriving at the restaurant Amy was surprised when Celeste introduced Susan, a friend who also worked for MSF. Susan, apparently, was joining them for lunch.

At just over five foot, Susan was slim and pretty with short brown hair, big green eyes and, as Amy was about to find out, an enormous personality.

During lunch Susan told Celeste that she wouldn't be going on another assignment. "I've always found it easy when I get home after a mission, but this time it's different." She sighed. "I won't be going back." She shrugged. "I'm burned out."

"Have you talked to anyone about this?" Celeste said, touching her friend's arm.

"Yeah, I've gone through the usual channels," Susan replied, nodding. "But it's not working." She clasped Celeste's hand and smiled. "It's time for me to move on." Turning her attention to

Amy, she said, "Do you know anything about Médecins sans Frontières?"

Swallowing her food, Amy shook her head; she wiped her mouth with her napkin. "Not that much."

"Ah," Susan responded, then straightened her shoulders. "Well, I might not be able to tell you the true meaning of life, but as far as I'm concerned," she tapped the table, "it is the simple things that give life meaning." She looked at Amy. "What do you think are most people's goals?"

Blindsided, Amy shrugged. "I don't know."

"It's chiefly a desire for happiness." Susan leaned forward. "Now, it might not be in everyone's power to be happy, but it's in everyone's power to be good."

Confused, Amy raised her eyebrows at Celeste.

Celeste winked at her.

"Okay," Amy responded slowly.

"And that's why people work for organizations like MSF," Susan said. She sipped her wine. "At first I found it really difficult to adapt to some of the horrific sights you see." She looked at Celeste. "You know what I'm talking about."

Celeste nodded.

"But somewhere along the line you deal with it. You deal with the violence, the disease, the starvation, the death…"

Celeste rolled her eyes and listened for another half hour as Susan told Amy what their lives had been like over the last several years, but it was only when Susan mentioned four-year-old-Daniel and his baby sister, from Sierra Leone, that Celeste contributed to the conversation.

Celeste hadn't told Susan or anyone that the reason she was home was to set the wheels in motion to adopt Daniel and his sister. She hadn't told her because the adoption process was a long haul with no guarantees, and Susan, although a good friend, was not known for holding her tongue. It was better to keep everything under wraps until she was sure.

"So, what are your plans, Celeste?" Susan asked curiously.

Denial

"I've just started working at Memorial Hospital in Sarasota. I haven't set any definite plans, yet." Celeste glanced at Amy. "It all depends on how certain things work out."

"What!" Susan exclaimed. "You're not considering dumping the gorgeous Dr. Laura Selby are you? According to Ritchie, she's pining desperately for you."

Celeste swallowed hard when Amy's face darkened. She looked at Susan and said softly, "As I said, I haven't made any plans yet."

Stunned, Amy's body tensed. Feeling anger sweep through her she stood. "Excuse me; I need to use the restroom."

In the restroom Amy splashed water on her face and whispered, "Jesus. This woman is a complete stranger!" She gripped the sink. "Who else does she have stashed away?" She looked at her reflection. "It doesn't matter," she told herself. "What you have with her is a short-term arrangement with no emotional involvement. It's better that someone else is in her life; makes it less complicated for you."

Returning to the table Amy heard Susan chastise Celeste. "You are such a dark horse, Celeste," she said. "Don't keep Laura hanging too long. She might be crazy about you, but she's nobody's fool."

Celeste looked at Susan. "Let's talk about something else."

Susan shrugged. "Okay, but you know Ritchie would willingly die for a lick of her cherry."

Celeste laughed. "Wouldn't you be a little put out if he were licking any cherry other than yours?"

Stunned, Amy listened as Susan released the most incredible high-pitched laugh.

Susan said in a hushed tone, "Actually, I have a little confession." She leaned in. "We are here for two reasons." She looked from Celeste to Amy. "First, Ritchie's meeting my folks. And second, we're here to buy an engagement ring." She clapped her hands. "We're getting married!"

Amy's face paled when Susan laughed again. *Good God, this woman's like a performing seal on helium.*

"Can you believe it?"

Celeste shrugged then congratulated Susan.

The lunch, and Susan's long story about the lead-up to Ritchie's proposal, seemed to drag on for hours. After shredding her napkin, then everything else possible, Amy had had enough. "Do you mind if we get the bill?" she asked Celeste wearily.

Celeste nodded.

Amy caught the eye of a passing waiter.

As they prepared to leave, Celeste invited Susan to the art exhibition they were attending that afternoon.

Amy's heart sank. She managed to nod reassuringly when Susan whispered, "Is that okay?"

They caught the subway to Brooklyn. Sitting on the train, Amy tried to work up some enthusiasm for the show. Once there, she wandered off on her own for quiet contemplation. The gallery was spacious, but it seemed that wherever she stood she could hear Susan's laughter.

Eventually, Amy accepted that the only thing she could concentrate on was Celeste, and her temperature rose when she looked at her. She wore a crisp, fashionably cut, light blue suit. The jacket had slick lapels and flap pockets. She wore it buttoned with a hint of cleavage; it fit perfectly. Her trousers were long, lean and minimum, and her shoes low-heeled. Amy had imagined her this morning, delivering her lecture to an entranced audience.

Amy sucked on her bottom lip. She loved the way Celeste's hair was caught up at the back, fixed with two small intertwining latticed chopsticks. The style lent elegance to her look, and length to her neck. With a long dark fringe falling seductively over her face, she thought Celeste was a complete knockout.

Susan smiled as she passed Amy, heading for the restroom. Amy's stomach knotted when Celeste approached her.

Celeste stopped in front of Amy and stroked her arm. Her fingers ventured upward and dangerously close to Amy's breast. She whispered, her mouth coming close to Amy's, "Are you enjoying the exhibition?"

"Yes," Amy croaked. Unconsciously, she licked her lips in anticipation.

"There's a problem with the restroom," Susan said, returning.

Amy swallowed in relief. Her knees weakened when she realized that she would have kissed Celeste openly if she had wanted. She shook her head slightly and wondered what the hell kind of person she was turning into.

Chapter 33

That evening, lying in bed, alone and exhausted, Amy wondered why the day had gone so wrong. She pushed and pulled her pillows into shape, then pulling the covers around her, went over the day's events.

†

Standing outside the gallery, filled with a sense of excitement when Susan said she had to go meet Ritchie, her libido roared to life. Amy looked at Celeste and entertained the thought that, if they hurried, they might just have time to get back to the hotel and make love before attending the show that evening.

"I have an idea," Susan said to them. "Why don't Ritchie and I come to the show with you tonight?"

"Eh…yes…Susan. Of course," Celeste said.

In disbelief, Amy managed to quash a sudden urge to stomp her foot in frustration.

"Is that okay with you, Amy," Susan asked.

Amy smiled graciously. "Of course, Susan," she replied, hiding her annoyance. "Both of you should join us."

Smiling, Susan hurriedly pulled her cell phone out of her purse, and hugging Celeste, then Amy, told them that Ritchie would be thrilled.

Amy didn't know whether to laugh or cry. All she knew was that her need for Celeste was in overdrive and she couldn't do a thing about it. Rubbing her brow, she listened to Susan prattle on about how much Ritchie would love to catch up with Celeste and how much he loved the theater.

Eventually, to Amy's relief, Susan pressed digits on her phone then turned and walked away from them.

Watching her, Amy realized that Susan hadn't stopped talking in hours. *She must be on crack cocaine to be as hyper as that!* Amy folded her arms. She looked at Celeste and felt her temper rise dangerously close to the surface. She couldn't believe she was going to have to spend another minute with Susan never mind a whole evening, and God only knows what Ritchie was going to be like.

"I'm sorry. It was too awkward to say no," Celeste said.

Looking down at her shoes, Amy decided to play it cool. She shrugged.

"Are you okay with them joining us?" Celeste asked.

No, goddamit! "It's not a problem," Amy said.

Celeste gave Amy a look.

Amy blushed, knowing Celeste knew she wasn't being honest.

"Well, I guess it's good it's not the two of us tonight," Celeste said. She reached out to stroke Amy's face then dropped her hand. "That would be far too intimate. *And*, intimacy is not part of the arrangement. Is it?"

Amy didn't respond. Instead, she watched Susan waving madly for their attention.

Celeste nodded when Susan gave them the thumbs-up.

Dreading the next few hours, Amy closed her eyes.

Turning her back on Susan and positioning herself in front of Amy, Celeste said quietly, "Saddle your broomstick, Amy. Tonight, you're in for one helluva ride!"

Amy stared at Celeste. This might not have been a deliberate act of sabotage, but it clearly suited the brunette who was obviously still hurting from her comments last night. She frowned and thought two can play this game.

Checking over Celeste's shoulder, Amy could see Susan was still on her cell phone. Too annoyed to worry about the passing crowd, she lifted her hand and stroked Celeste's cheek, then ran it down her throat and over the lapel of her jacket. She moved her hand back up then down Celeste's throat until she reached the gentle swell of her breasts and, for the first time that day, feeling calm, she smiled flirtatiously.

Pleased, Amy watched Celeste's pupils dilate and her skin color deepen. "Oh, I don't think it'll be all that bad," she replied throatily as she ran a finger over Celeste's bottom lip.

Celeste's eyes widened.

Amy moved closer to Celeste. Lifting her head she whispered in her ear, "You'll just owe me," she said then bit her earlobe.

Celeste yelped.

Amy tilted her head and batted her eyelashes innocently, then fixed a smile for Susan who was rushing toward them.

†

That night, unbelievably, things got worse. There was no doubt Susan and Ritchie were a double act. Ritchie, if it were possible, chatted even more than his girlfriend. After the introductions, the couple spent most of their time squabbling for airtime.

Amy didn't utter more than a few words the whole evening.

At the show Ritchie positioned himself next to her and, to Amy's frustration, revealed little bits of the story line during the performance. After the show, she couldn't believe it when Celeste invited the couple back to the hotel for a nightcap. It was after midnight when they left.

Alone, they rode the elevator in silence. When it stopped at their floor, Celeste got out first and walked briskly ahead. Amy followed a few steps behind.

Feeling shell-shocked, Amy rested her head against the door of her room. Suddenly aware Celeste was speaking she lifted her tired head. Apologizing, she asked Celeste to repeat what she had just said.

"I have a headache. I think it's best that we get some rest," Celeste repeated. Sliding her key in the door, she added, "It's been a busy weekend, and I have a few errands to run before we leave tomorrow afternoon."

Surprised, Amy watched Celeste unlock her door quickly and enter without a backward glance.

†

Throwing off the covers, Amy tried to stop thinking about what had happened. She forced herself to clear her mind and focus on getting some sleep. After a few minutes, like a wayward child, she kicked her legs out. Regardless of how angry she was with Celeste right now, if she walked into the room…into her bed…she would forgive her anything.

Staring at the connecting door, Amy willed Celeste to walk through. Several times she got out of bed and made her way to the door only to lose her nerve and turn back.

†

Unable to sleep, Celeste tossed in her bed. Restless, she thought over the events of the day. Meeting Susan was unexpected and had brought a reminder of the life she had before Amy consumed it. Tonight, she had needed some distance from the blonde. If she was truthful, she was still smarting from the comment from the previous night.

Unwilling to explore why she was feeling so put out Celeste closed her eyes. She groaned when Laura flashed into her mind. She hated this part. Every time she got involved, which was rare, the relationship seemed to move faster than she ever wanted it to. She hadn't thought about Laura that much since coming home, but this morning when she checked her e-mail there was one from her, detailing that she would be traveling from Sudan to attend a conference in Boston next month and wanted to spend time together.

Celeste felt ashamed. She knew Laura didn't understand her cooling off. Although she hadn't said as much, she could tell by her e-mail that she was hurting.

Since her marriage ended Celeste had intentionally never been seriously involved. She had hoped the time apart would cool things between them, but now realized that Laura was in much deeper than she had thought. She needed to make it clear that it was over, and soon.

Trying to settle, Celeste punched her pillows into shape. Throwing her head on them she forced her eyes closed. Immediately, an image of Amy lying next door, naked, flashed. No matter how she tried to change it, the image was always of Amy, naked and enticing.

Determined that she wasn't going anywhere tonight, Celeste clenched her jaw and pulled the covers around her. But, after what felt like hours, she turned and looked at the clock, it had barely moved. Her determination crumbled.

Unable to stay in bed any longer, Celeste threw back the covers and headed for the connecting door. There was some natural light filtering through when she opened it. Her eyes adjusting, she swallowed when she saw Amy lying on her back with the covers off, naked and asleep.

Groaning inwardly, Celeste told herself that if she had any willpower she would turn and leave. Needing some sleep she justified, as she slipped through the door, she would just lay beside Amy.

Slipping into the empty side of the bed, Celeste lay still. She thought about turning her back but somehow couldn't. Instead, she closed her eyes and let Amy's breathing lull her to sleep.

Within minutes, Celeste's eyes flew open when, still asleep, Amy's hand rested on her inner thigh. Groaning at the razor-sharp heat the light touch generated Celeste felt the fight leave her. Sitting up, she slipped her T-shirt off.

Slowly, Amy opened her eyes and whispered, "Celeste?"

Celeste smiled. She loved the sultry quality of Amy's voice. The seductive huskiness and Scottish burr. She lightly kissed Amy's lips. "Hi," she said.

Still sleepy, Amy whispered, "My stomach flipped just then when you kissed me." Looking at Celeste she said in surprise, "I've never had that before." Amy held eye contact for a long moment. "I missed you."

Catching her breath, Celeste's stomach clenched.

"Why didn't you tell me about Laura," Amy asked.

Denial

Celeste sighed. "I didn't tell you because it's nothing."
"Do you have feelings for her?"
Celeste whispered. "Some." She frowned. "But not enough."
"Have you had many lovers?" Amy asked. "Women lovers I mean?"
"A few."
"Felice?"
Celeste nodded.
"Where did she fit in?"
"My first."
"Oh," Amy said. "That explains a lot."
"What?"
"Your openness that night."
"The night in your apartment?"
"Uh-huh."
"I didn't mean for it to happen."
Amy nodded. "I know. Neither did I."
Celeste stroked Amy's face.
"Is that really why you stayed away for so long?" Amy asked.
"I should have come home earlier."
"But you didn't, because you thought this might happen?"
Celeste nodded. "But I hoped it wouldn't."
"What are we doing?" Amy asked. "You're involved. I'm married, and we're doing this." She shook her head. "What does that make us?"
"Confused," Celeste offered. Smiling slightly, she kissed the tip of Amy's nose.
Amy laughed. "Okay, agreed," she said, looking at Celeste. "Confused is definitely where I'm at."
"But I know now that, when it comes to you, I'm not confused," Celeste said, looking at Amy intently.
Amy frowned. "But when it comes to you, I am."
Celeste pressed a finger against Amy's lips when she formed another question.
Amy raised her eyebrows and looked at Celeste inquiringly.

Wanting to change the subject Celeste said, "I think Susan and Ritchie really like you."

Slowly, Amy removed Celeste's finger from her lips. "No kidding. Why did you want to spend so much time with them?" she asked, frowning.

"It wasn't deliberate, Amy. It was really good to see her, and out in the field Susan is a great antidote to the grim day-to-day situations we face. I genuinely have a soft spot for her."

"But she laughs like a hyena, for God's sake," Amy said, her face showing annoyance and amusement at the same time.

"I know," Celeste replied. "But the qualities that you might find…unappealing are the same qualities that often get many of our team through the day." She brushed her fingers over Amy's chest. "Susan is larger than life, and I love her for that."

"I guess so." Amy said.

Celeste smiled at Amy's petulant lip. She did feel slightly guilty that Amy had struggled through the evening. She had built a friendship with the couple separately, but meeting them as a duo for the first time would drive anyone crazy.

"Is it enough to accept that the chance of it happening again is highly unlikely?"

Amy looked at Celeste. A strange, almost wistful, expression crossed her face. She nodded.

"Did you enjoy the exhibition today?"

Amy shrugged. "I couldn't really focus."

Celeste nodded. She knew Amy struggled to focus at the gallery. The few times that the artwork had absorbed her Celeste watched her, adoring what she saw. She recalled Amy's outfit: a light cashmere V-neck sweater that showed the swell of her breasts beautifully. With her washed-out jeans and her hair down, Amy carried that look of sophisticated casualness that only artisans and the city chic get away with.

Celeste whispered, "At the gallery, you looked beautiful."

Surprise, then pleasure, filled Amy as she looked at Celeste.

"More than once I had to stop myself from wrapping my arms around you. I loved it when a piece of work intrigued you,"

Celeste said, brushing her lips over Amy's. "Do you know you have a little habit when something catches your attention?"

"No," Amy said. "What do I do?"

"Well, you tuck your hair behind your ears, fold your arms and tilt your head, just so." Celeste tilted her own head to show Amy. "Then you'd catch your bottom lip as you fully absorb the canvas."

Amy looked at Celeste. Eyelids heavy, she whispered, "Kiss me."

Amy uttered a groan of pleasure when Celeste's naked body moved on top of hers and her knees urged her thighs apart. She eagerly opened and spread them wide, wrapping her legs around Celeste, giving her complete access.

The feel of Amy was exquisite. Celeste wanted to savor this—being here, caught, watching this beautiful woman give herself freely. Looking deeply into her eyes she felt a deep connection. Taking Amy's hands she brought them to the edge of the bed. Pinning her down and keeping eye contact, she pushed her hips into her.

Amy gasped and tried to capture Celeste's mouth. But each time Celeste teasingly pulled away. Eventually, she let out a low moan of frustration. "Stop teasing, Celeste. I need you to kiss me really, really badly!"

When Celeste didn't answer, Amy struggled to break free of her grip but Celeste held her. Enjoying her struggles, she continued to pull away each time Amy tried to kiss her.

"Kiss me, Celeste...*please*."

"Not yet."

Celeste's eyebrows rose when she felt Amy's wetness begin to cover her lower abdomen. She whispered seductively, "You're a hungry little tiger, aren't you?"

Amy growled, then whispered, "Hungry isn't the word I have in mind. Try craving." Her eyes narrowed. "I'm craving you. I need a fix. I *need* you, Celeste." Groaning, Amy's head fell back. Her lashes fluttered closed. She finished, almost unwillingly, "I need you."

For the second time, Celeste's stomach clenched.

Frustrated, Amy pleaded, "Please...I need to taste you." Her hips surged. "I've needed you like this all day."

Wanting to cherish the feel of Amy trembling underneath her, Celeste slowly put her lips to Amy's and lightly kissed her.

Impatient, Amy pushed her tongue into Celeste's mouth. Groaning, Celeste kissed her deeply.

Moaning, Amy's hips undulated eagerly.

Not wanting Amy to come quickly, Celeste stilled and broke the kiss.

Amy groaned into Celeste's throat. "Don't stop."

"Shhh."

Amy's head dropped back, closing her eyes, a sigh escaped.

Celeste watched Amy, adoring her. She waited for Amy's breathing to quiet, for her body to still before catching her lips again.

Gently, Celeste began thrusting her hips as she explored Amy's mouth fully.

Amy pulled her mouth away. "Bite...me," she said, gasping between words.

No longer able to resist, Celeste placed a hand between Amy's thighs and touched her clit. She kissed down her neck, and at the base, bit hard.

Amy bucked underneath, heels digging into the bed. Crying out, she shuddered long and hard as she climaxed.

Celeste couldn't help but be amazed at how quickly Amy reached orgasm and how intense they tended to be. Breathing heavily, she slowed her movements as Amy stilled. The strength of Amy's orgasm filled her with a sense of elation. She loved the feeling of being here, in bed, with the woman she adored. It felt as if this was her rightful place.

Celeste didn't want it to be over so soon but she couldn't hold off any longer. Urgently, she placed Amy's hand between her thighs and, closing her eyes, moved against her.

Feeling the first twinges of her orgasm, Celeste opened her eyes to look at Amy. A strong image of Josh making love to Amy pierced her. A shock wave hit her when she realized that this is how incredible Josh must feel. As her mind grappled with the thought a new emotion ran through her, one of raw naked resentment.

Celeste's stomach churned as jealousy rode through her body just as her orgasm pushed through. She had no choice but to ride with it. Afterward, breathing heavily, she collapsed on top of Amy.

Chapter 34

Amy struggled to release her trapped hand. Wrapping her arms around Celeste, she smiled, surprised by how much she loved the feel of Celeste on top of her and loved the film of hard-earned sweat between them. "God, that was incredible," she said, nuzzling her neck.

Listening to Celeste gulp for air, Amy's groin clenched as she replayed Celeste building to orgasm. "That was amazing," she said, stroking Celeste's hair, unable to believe how quickly her own desire was building again. After a moment, Amy frowned. Sensing something was wrong, she asked, "Are you okay?"

Lifting her head, Celeste frowned. "I…"

To Amy's complete surprise, Celeste began to cry. Shocked, she put her arms around her comfortingly and held her tight.

Stroking Celeste's hair until she quieted, Amy lifted her face and kissed her gently. "Sleep with me," she said tenderly. "I want to hold you tonight."

Nodding, Celeste slid off Amy and lay on her back.

Turning on her side, Amy wondered why she was so upset. Reaching out to stroke Celeste's cheek, fascinated, she watched her take control of her emotions.

Eventually, Amy whispered, "When was the last time you cried?"

Wiping the tears, Celeste laughed, and sounding slightly self-conscious, answered, "When I first started with MSF, I cried all the time." She smiled weakly. "I used to cry out of frustration, in anger, in empathy at the situations people, often with no control, found themselves in, but the last time," she said looking at Amy, "was with you."

Amy kissed Celeste tenderly. "Why did you join MSF?"

Celeste looked at Amy. "I wanted to help." She turned her head and fell silent.

Amy whispered, "Look at me."

Celeste looked at Amy.

"Tell me."

"I joined MSF because when I was eight years old I watched some TV documentary on international relief." She looked at Amy. "It was as if a light went on in my head and I thought, that's it, that's what I want to do."

Amy smiled when Celeste laughed. "That year, I plagued my parents for a doctor's uniform, a hospital playset and everything medical, but, like all kids, soon something else caught my attention and I hung up the stethoscope, so to speak."

Celeste turned to face Amy.

Amy smiled, enjoying Celeste confiding in her. "But you went to medical school?"

"Yeah," Celeste revealed. "I guess the seed was sown. It wasn't until I left med school, intending to work that..." She stopped talking and focused on Amy's lips. Cupping her face, she rubbed her thumb seductively over Amy's bottom lip.

Not wanting to get sidetracked, and knowing that Celeste didn't talk about herself much, Amy grasped her hand, *"And..."*

"And," Celeste answered, amusement flicking across her eyes, "when I graduated a friend gave me a book on the founder of Médecins sans Frontières and when I read this incredible story, I remembered that was why I went to med school in the first place."

Amy smiled at her. "As simple as that?" she whispered. "No big complicated story?"

Looking at Amy, Celeste whispered, "Yes." She kissed her. "As simple as that."

Amy smoothed Celeste's hair from her face. "I cry at the drop of a hat," she shared. "Even more since I had the boys."

Celeste placed a hand where she had bitten Amy earlier and, stroking the faint marks, asked, "Have you always needed that to bring you to orgasm?"

Surprised by the question, Amy drew in her breath. Aware that they were being open, she made the decision to answer her.

"No," she replied. "I have never needed that…before …before…you."

Celeste hesitated then asked, "Why do you like it now?"

Amy looked at her. "I like a lot of things I didn't know I liked."

"Why that?"

Amy gave it some thought. "I think I like it because the first night it added something." She eyed Celeste. "I'm not into pain or anything like that, you know."

Celeste laughed. "I know. That's not what I'm asking." She ran her fingers along Amy's neck and shoulder. "Added something. What?"

Amy's pulse quickened and her stomach tensed. "It added something to my orgasm."

"Do you ask Josh to do it?"

Amy's eyebrows rose in surprise.

"Does he?" Celeste asked, eyeing her intently.

Amy hesitated. "No."

"Why?"

Amy stared at her.

Celeste repeated, "Why?"

Unsure where this line of questioning was going, Amy replied slowly, "Because I don't want him to."

Amy noted relief flicker across Celeste's features.

"Why do you think that is?"

Amy shrugged and hesitated. *Should we be discussing this? Hadn't we agreed that this was a no-go area? Hadn't we agreed that we wouldn't talk about Josh, never mind how we made love?*

Amy cringed at the thought of discussing how she and Josh made love. The reality of who Celeste was, in relation to Josh, was always lurking around in her mind. It's bad enough what you're doing, her inner voice muttered. Don't start comparing notes!

Amy closed her eyes, wanting to be honest with Celeste but knowing she couldn't.

Celeste cupped Amy's breast lightly and began kissing her throat.

Denial

Opening her eyes, Amy moaned. She was being driven to distraction by this woman. She was feeling hot, *very* hot. To her surprise, she really had to fight the urge to place Celeste's hand between her thighs.

Celeste asked again, "Why?"

Unwilling to give a detailed response, Amy muttered, "Josh and I...it... Well...it's just different."

Celeste pushed. "Why is it different?"

"Celeste, I can't talk to you about that." Her jaw clenched. "I need you to touch me."

"Talk to me."

Amy fought with her internal voice, which was cautioning her to say nothing. Worried that Celeste might leave, and the need for her to stay too strong, she stuttered, "Celeste...I...Josh and I...we've...I've never felt..." She sighed and ignoring the warning bells in her head said, "I've never been this..." She didn't know what to say. Blanking her mind, she let the words form. "I've never been this sexual with him, with anyone." Her brows rose. "It seems I have no control over my body when it comes to you."

Amy's internal voice choked with her disclosure.

A look of satisfaction flickered across Celeste's eyes. Reaching out, she stroked Amy's face. "Tell me what it feels like."

Amy whispered, "Why don't I show you?"

Celeste kissed Amy deeply then replied stubbornly, "Tell me."

"Och." Annoyed, Amy balled the bedsheet in her hands.

Celeste rose on her elbow and, propping her head on her hand, drew her thigh over Amy. Deliberately, she made a show of pressing her breasts into her as she stroked up and down Amy's trembling stomach.

Eyes smoldering, Celeste waited for a response.

Annoyed, Amy huffed. "You're enjoying this," she said, kicking her feet out.

Amy knew that Celeste was using her power over her. Her internal chatter turned up the volume and told her to back away, to stop the conversation, stick to the arrangement, avoid the emotional detail; otherwise, closure would be difficult. She opened her mouth to tell Celeste that she'd had enough and wanted to sleep, but instead she whispered, "I'll tell you, if you'll touch me."

Amy's inner voice sighed.

Celeste ran her fingers lightly down Amy's hips down her leg and up the inside of her thighs.

Instantly, Amy opened her legs to allow her access.

Celeste stroked Amy's clit lightly, teasingly.

Amy groaned.

Celeste's hand stilled. With her head resting on her palm, she leaned her face close to Amy. "Tell me," she whispered.

"For God's sake, stop this!"

Amy was close to losing her temper, but Celeste insisted. "Tell me."

Amy wanted to scream with frustration, but instead uttered, "The first time with you it should have hurt, but it didn't." She reached for Celeste's breast. Stroking her nipple, she muttered, "It seemed so…"

Celeste groaned. Her breath caught when Amy pinched her nipple. "No, Amy," she said, pushing her hand away. "No distractions. Answer the question."

Ignoring her, Amy continued to cup and stroke her breast.

Celeste slid her fingers inside Amy.

Amy's hand abruptly stilled. She drew her leg up when a jolt passed through her. Moving her hand to grasp the bedsheet, she closed her eyes and pumped her hips.

Celeste slid out of Amy and began stroking her clit, slowly, lightly.

Amy's eyes fluttered open. She focused on Celeste.

Celeste purred. "You were saying?"

Amy murmured, "Uhmmm…it seemed to heighten my orgasm." Letting go of the bedsheet, Amy pulled Celeste to her until their lips touched and she whispered, "And make it more—" She abruptly stopped speaking when her groin clenched.

Celeste's hand stilled.

Denial

Amy groaned. "Powerful," she finished then sighed. "Uggghhh." Forcing herself to speak she pleaded, "Please, Celeste. Go inside me again." She kissed her hungrily.

Celeste pulled her mouth away. "Not until you tell me," she replied, dancing her fingers lightly around Amy's clit.

"Uhmmm," Amy said quickly. "Highly aroused," she whispered against Celeste's mouth. "My orgasms are powerful with you. Aagghh." Celeste's teasing was unbearable. She begged, "Inside me, please. *Please*, Celeste."

"Tell me more."

Amy didn't want to talk anymore.

Celeste's hand stilled.

In frustration, Amy covered Celeste's hand with her own. Desperate to keep the momentum, she pressed both their hands into her clit. She stared at Celeste and with her voice deadly serious, said, "Please, Celeste…this is torture."

Celeste moved Amy's hand away then rubbed her thumb lightly over her clit, keeping her on the edge.

Amy's hips rose high with each slight touch.

Celeste asked, "Why do you think there is a such as strong attraction between us?"

Amy didn't respond.

Celeste stilled her hand.

Amy continued to move her hips.

Celeste asked again, "Why?"

Amy stopped moving and, looking directly into Celeste's eyes, said in anger, "Celeste, I really don't know. All I know is that right now I need you."

Celeste groaned heavily. She stretched out and pressed her full length into her. With her fingers, she opened Amy up and slid inside. Sliding down she anchored Amy's thigh between hers, then took a nipple in her mouth and bit it lightly.

"Celeste I—"

Amy's words were cut short when Celeste pressed into her. She groaned heavily when Celeste flicked her nipple back and forth with her tongue. "Oh God."

Celeste gasped when Amy pushed her thigh into her, rubbing it deliberately against her clit. Groaning, she made her way up and kissed Amy deeply, her tongue thrusting into her mouth. Eventually, the kiss slowed and stopped. Their eyes locked. Breathing each other's air, Celeste rode Amy's thigh as she thrust into her.

"Oh God..." Amy arched against Celeste.

Celeste could barely catch her breath. Keeping eye contact, she moved against Amy; sweat formed between them.

"Ohhh." Amy's hands tightened painfully in Celeste's hair.

Overcome by the sensation of feeling Amy's internal muscles contract, Celeste groaned into Amy's mouth and told her how much she loved being inside her.

Amy pulled on Celeste's hip, pushing her thigh into her hard. She whispered, "Come with me."

Celeste's eyes shuttered down. Amy's words drove her over the edge. She threw her head back. Their movements frantic, they cried out, bodies arched, they came hard.

Slowly, Celeste kissed Amy's throat and lips. She kissed her gently until she calmed.

"I want to touch you," Amy said. Breathing deeply, she slid Celeste's hand from inside her. Moving onto her side, she pressed Celeste flat on her back, then quickly buried her fingers deep inside her.

Surprised by the maneuver, Celeste moaned.

Holding her gaze, Amy slowly moved inside Celeste.

Celeste's eyes widened when Amy slid down her. She moaned when hot, wet lips sucked on her clit.

After a few minutes, Amy kissed Celeste's thighs gently. Looking up at her, she whispered, "Are you ready?"

Celeste groaned and tried to focus. "Yes..."

"Not yet," Amy said. "Don't move your hips until I tell you."

With difficulty, Celeste stilled her hips.

Amy reached up and cupped Celeste's breast. "You have the most beautiful breasts," she said, pulling on a nipple and pinching it.

Denial

Celeste moaned and thrust her hips forward.

Amy stopped touching her. "Don't move until I tell you."

Celeste's breath caught. Her muscles trembling inside, she whispered, "I'm not sure how long I can hold on."

"Not yet," Amy replied. Thrusting gently, she explored as she kissed her way up to Celeste's throat.

"Amy, baby... Please," Celeste whispered with quiet desperation.

"Don't move," Amy said, her voice low and charged with sensuality.

Completely surprised by Amy's actions, Celeste surrendered entirely.

Amy changed pace from slow to fast then back again. She bit Celeste lightly on her stomach, her shoulder, her side; the gentler the thrust, the gentler the bite; the deeper the thrust, the harder the bite. Some were created to leave their mark, but all were deliriously hot designed to take Celeste to the edge then tear her back.

Celeste tried to hold on but couldn't, her voice rose. "Now...I need to come *now*... Please." Celeste convulsed forward, then shuddered. "Please."

"Not yet."

"*Please!*" Celeste said, her voice ragged. She reached for her clit.

Amy whispered, "Touch. But don't move your hips."

Celeste's mouth opened and she sucked on her bottom lip as her groin tensed sweetly in gratification.

Amy positioned herself between Celeste's legs. "I want to watch you," she said, running her hands slowly up and down Celeste's inner thighs.

Groaning, Celeste's eyelids closed.

"Look at me."

Slowly opening her eyes, Celeste focused on Amy.

"Don't move your hips," Amy instructed. "Touch yourself slowly."

Nodding, Celeste swallowed visibly then moaned repeatedly as she tried to follow Amy's instructions. Eventually, unable to stand the intensity, she said, in a strangled voice, *"Now,* Amy!"

Smiling wickedly, Amy slid her fingers deep inside Celeste. "Not so easy, is it?"

Leaning over Celeste and holding her gaze, Amy thrust inside her.

Blood pounded in Celeste's ears.

"Tell me what it feels like?"

Celeste tried to focus on Amy but was forced to close her eyes. *Sweet revenge!* Certain she would pass out, Celeste groaned. She couldn't stand it; a rush of excitement so strong she could barely draw breath consumed her.

Amy increased her speed. "Come for me," she said huskily.

Celeste cried out. She stretched out taut as Amy thrust into her. Within seconds, she released a long, wonderfully slow, strangling guttural cry, as her orgasm swept through her.

Breathing raggedly, it was a few moments before Celeste slowly opened her eyes.

Looking at Celeste hungrily, Amy moved on top of her. Gripping Celeste's left hand she pushed it between her own thighs. "Now, Celeste," she said urgently. *"Now!"*

Amy kissed Celeste passionately. Their teeth gnashed together with the intensity of the kiss.

Celeste ran her fingers over Amy's clit and stroked it. She groaned when Amy, shuddering, thrust her hips forward and instantly came.

Exhausted, a deep laugh of pleasure escaped Celeste when Amy slumped on top of her. Tenderly, she wrapped her arms around her.

Eventually, Amy slipped off Celeste and moved to her side. Throwing a leg over Celeste's lean thigh she muttered as she positioned her head comfortably on Celeste's breast, "Don't move." She yawned. "I want to sleep with you like this."

Celeste smiled when Amy mumbled sleepily, "You're insatiable."

Denial

Kissing her head, Celeste responded affectionately, "You too."

Amy chuckled. "So it seems."

Celeste listened to Amy's breathing even out. She felt fully awake. More awake than she had ever been. Tonight, everything had shifted for her and she had needed answers. The image of Josh making love to Amy had created a tidal wave of emotions inside her. Cuddling Amy, she touched the light perspiration on her back and felt a protectiveness that she had never experienced.

Celeste bit her lip pensively, understanding that she wanted more than the physical; she wanted the emotional feedback. She looked down at Amy's sleeping face and quashed an urge to wake her and ask what she felt about what was happening between them. She wanted her to talk about what it meant to her.

Celeste fought the urge to wake Amy and tell her that she was scared of losing what she didn't have, that she didn't want it to end, that the thought of it tore her apart.

Exhaling, Celeste finally acknowledged that she was deeply in love with Amy. Holding Amy tightly, terror swept through her when she realized that she could never have her, not only had Amy made it clear that there was no future for them, but Celeste could never ask for anything more than what they had. Anything more would be impossible as openly loving Amy would tear her family apart.

Chapter 35

Amy pulled out a weed and, lifting her head, listened. She turned down the radio and waited to hear the doorbell ring again. It was Sunday morning and some months since her trip to New York. Frowning, she looked at her watch. It couldn't be Josh, he had just left with the boys to watch a baseball game. It couldn't be Maggie, she and Sean had dropped by about twenty minutes ago to take the dogs to the dog park on Venice Beach. The only person she was expecting was her mother. Irene had arranged to drop off some plant cuttings late in the afternoon, but it wouldn't have surprised Amy if she decided to come by early.

Thinking she was wrong, Amy turned the radio volume up again and continued to dig knowing that if it was Irene, she would know to come to the backyard.

Picking up again on the faint but definite sound of the doorbell, Amy heaved a sigh of frustration and got up to answer it. Making her way through the kitchen she headed for the front door.

The doorbell rang again and Amy hurried to answer it. Opening the door she saw that it was Celeste. Without a word she turned around and headed back out to the garden.

Returning to her spot, Amy got on her knees to weed.

"Amy, we need to talk."

Amy stopped digging. "Oh really, Celeste?" she replied, color creeping in her cheeks. "We need to talk about what exactly?"

Celeste moved closer. "We need to talk about last night."

Amy sat back on her heels. "Okay, let's talk!" she said. "Who should we talk about first? Let's see, Laura?" She shook her head. "Oh, that's right, you've dumped her, haven't you. Maybe we should talk about your *new* girlfriend, Robin? Or maybe your other shag, *me*, your brother's wife!" She stood up.

"God, I don't know what to admire more: your audacity or your stamina!"

Celeste lifted her hands then dropped them. "She's not my girlfriend," she replied, moving to stand in front of Amy.

"Are you sure about that, Celeste?" Amy asked, peeling off her gloves. Scrunching them, she threw them into the refuse bag. "Because from where I was sitting last night I could have sworn she was."

Amy looked at Celeste. She gritted her teeth. It was driving her crazy, the thought of Celeste with someone else.

"Do you have *any* idea the dangerous position I've put myself in over the last four months?" Amy said. Her stomach churned as images of Celeste touching Robin Fernandez flashed through her mind. "Celeste, what is wrong with you? We are having a fucking affair, and I'm trying to keep my sanity together by keeping hold of the darkest secret I have ever had. And you come waltzing into the restaurant last night with your bit of fluff and sit with us and let her drool all over you!" Amy threw up her arms. "What am I supposed think? That it's a joke? That it's all a bit of fun to you?" She stared at Celeste and memories of the previous night flooded in.

†

Last night Amy and Josh had dined out in a newly opened restaurant in South Venice. Josh had arranged for a work colleague and his wife, who were new in town, to dine with them. When they arrived at the restaurant they were seated on a large sofa made of antelope skin. Amy liked the look and feel of it, and mentally positioned it in various rooms in the house. They hadn't been in the restaurant for more than five minutes before Josh became agitated and decided to call their guests. He was a real stickler for good timekeeping.

While he called Amy sipped her gin and tonic and perused the menu on her knee.

Josh hung up the phone and slid close to Amy, putting his arm around the back of the sofa and pulling her into him. "They took a wrong turn," he said. "They'll be here any minute." He kissed her lightly. "Have I told you how beautiful you look this evening?"

Amy smiled and nodded. She had bought a new outfit—a tight-fitting, low-cut, cream dress and new shoes, with three-inch heels. She had bought them when she was out shopping with Maggie earlier that week. She had dithered whether or not to buy the dress, as it was more risqué than what she usually wore, but Maggie had encouraged her.

Getting ready, Amy was pleased that she had bought it. Ever since her return from New York she was increasingly feeling adventurous and the outfit reflected that. When Josh saw her in the dress, it had taken all her powers of persuasion to get him out the door.

Josh murmured, "Do you know how fantastic you look in that dress? I can't wait to get you home tonight," he said and kissed her.

"Hi."

Amy broke the kiss and looked up. The color drained from her face. It was Celeste.

Josh, resting his hand on Amy's thigh, grinned up at his sister. "Hi Cel," he replied in surprise. "You got reservations here too?"

Celeste looked at Josh's hand, then directly at Amy. "Yes," she answered, eyes ablaze.

Josh looked around. "That's great," he replied, trying to catch the eye of the maître d'. "We're waiting for another couple but we can easily organize for you to join us. He caught the maître d's eye and gestured to him. "Who are you with?"

Amy stared at Celeste in shock, unable to believe she was standing over them. She took in a sharp breath when a beautiful, dark-headed woman approached. Standing next to Celeste, she linked her arm through hers.

"Robin," Celeste said, "I would like you to meet my brother, Josh, and his wife, Amy."

†

Denial

"Amy?"

"What?" Amy replied. She picked up her garden tools then looked at Celeste. "Is she your lover?"

"No," Celeste replied.

Amy looked at Celeste for a moment, and sounding unconvinced asked, "Maybe not. But you're not denying that you've slept with her?"

Celeste didn't respond.

Amy angrily tried to push past her, but Celeste grabbed her arms and held her tight.

Amy looked at her. "When?" She tried to pull away. "It doesn't matter. I don't want to know."

Celeste held her. She opened her mouth, about to explain when Amy broke in, "Don't bother answering," she said angrily. "There's probably a string of us," she said accusingly. "How could you, Celeste? For God's sake, isn't it complicated enough?"

Celeste shook Amy gently, aware that the pressure of hiding their relationship over the last few months was more than getting to her. "Listen to me. There is nothing going on with her or anyone." She desperately wanted to tell Amy that her night with Robin was a mistake. "Amy, it was one night. It was a—"

Amy pulled out of her arms and slapped Celeste hard across the face.

Staring at Amy, Celeste moved her jaw back and forth, unable to believe that in less than twenty-four hours she had received two of those.

Since the trip to the Keys Robin had telephoned a few times but Celeste had made it abundantly clear she wasn't interested in pursuing anything other than a friendship.

Robin had originally arranged to spend this weekend with Alex, but Alex had bowed out with a lame excuse leaving Celeste with no choice but to entertain her.

When Robin arrived yesterday morning, Celeste picked her up from her hotel and they spent the day shopping. She had to admit she did enjoy Robin's company; the air always seemed charged with energy around her, and she had attitude—swinging her hips when she walked as if she had a game plan for every step.

Celeste couldn't help but admire the woman; she knew exactly who she was and where she was going.

As it turned out, Robin had expensive tastes and throughout the day Celeste watched her swipe her credit card until it was threadbare. More than once Robin offered to buy her an expensive gift, and regardless of how often she refused, Robin, it seemed, was only ever used to getting her own way. She insisted to such a point that Celeste's mood darkened and she cut their shopping spree short.

When Celeste dropped Robin off at her hotel, she refused her not-so-subtle advances to join her for a drink in her room. Instead, she arranged to pick her up later that evening.

At the restaurant, during the meal, Josh had asked how they knew each other. Celeste explained that Robin was a friend of Alex's and she was playing host as he was out of town.

To Celeste's astonishment, Robin let out a deep throaty laugh, and clasping her hand, looked at Josh, then directly at Amy, and almost purred. "Yes," she said, winking at Amy. "It's just as well, because, you know the old adage: two's company and three's a crowd."

Not amused, Celeste quickly removed her hand and said coldly, before changing the subject, "I don't think that applies here."

From then on the rest of the evening seemed to unfold like a nightmare. It wasn't so much what Robin was saying—her innuendos were cleverly disguised—but it was the subtleness of her challenging looks at Amy that caused Celeste concern.

Josh, thankfully, didn't appear to pick up on anything. For most of the evening he chatted to his colleague and his wife, who were also software engineers, about some new prototype about to be released.

When she could, Celeste cut the evening short.

Once in the car, Robin, to Celeste's surprise, seemed content to sit quietly.

Denial

When they pulled up outside her hotel, Celeste reached over Robin opened the passenger door and quietly said, "Out."

Robin looked at Celeste intently for a moment before slapping her hard across the face.

Shocked, Celeste put her hand to her face. Looking confused, she asked, "Why?"

"That, my friend, is from your brother, for fucking his wife."

Celeste rubbed her cheek. "How did you know?"

Robin grimaced. "Well," she replied. "Let's say it's the fact that your little plaything seethed the entire evening?" She half smiled. "And the night we spent together you called me Amy." She laughed when Celeste's eyes widened. "Oh don't worry, your brother, the fool, doesn't have any idea, yet, that you two are lovesick puppies. But it won't take him long to figure it out if you don't show a little more discretion and learn to hide it better."

Robin leaned across the seat. Bringing her face close to Celeste's, she whispered, "I really, really like you, Celeste. When you tire of her, give me a call. There is a real spark between us."

Robin kissed Celeste softly on the mouth then got out of the car.

Moving her jaw, Celeste watched Robin swing her hips for all she was worth.

†

Shaken out of her memory by Amy trying to pull out of her arms, Celeste refused to let her go.

Amy leaned in and nipped Celeste's bottom lip, hard.

Celeste yelped but kept Amy close. "I was confused and drunk, Amy. It was a mistake."

"When?"

"It doesn't matter."

"*When?*" Amy insisted as she tried to pull out of Celeste's arms.

"Before New York," Celeste replied, holding Amy tight. "Before we agreed."

Relief filled Celeste when she felt Amy relax a little.

"She's Alex's friend. She would have been with him this weekend had he been here."

Amy stilled.

"There's nothing between us."

"Is that so," Amy said, eyeing Celeste. "Something tells me that she wouldn't agree with you on that one."

"There's nothing."

"She wants you."

"But I don't want her."

Amy looked at Celeste. Her eyes closed briefly and she whispered, "Maybe you don't want her…right now." She shook head. "Why am I torturing myself?" she said, sounding confused. "It doesn't matter."

"Yes, it does." Celeste placed her hands on either side of Amy's head. "Listen to me, it matters. You matter. Believe me, there has been no one else." Celeste brought Amy's mouth to her and kissed her. Immediately, she felt the fight leave Amy.

They kissed intensely.

As if needing to restake her claim, Amy pulled Celeste's top out of her shorts and ran her hand urgently up and down her back before cupping her breasts.

Celeste groaned when Amy said, "Inside. Now!"

†

Surprised that the front door was open, Irene entered the house carrying plant cuttings for Amy. She made her way through the house to the garden, stopping in the kitchen to put the cuttings on the work surface.

About to shout out hello, Irene was surprised when she looked out the patio doors and saw Amy and Celeste in the backyard, arguing. Frowning, she watched.

Irene couldn't hear what they were saying, but she could tell that it was an intense argument. She watched her daughter peel off her garden gloves and yell something at Celeste.

Denial

Unsure what to do Irene watched them continue to argue, until, unable to believe her eyes, she saw Amy slap Celeste hard across the face. Irene started toward the door only to stop when Celeste pulled Amy into her arms. She moved again when Amy tried to pull away but Celeste held her tight, and she let out a gasp when Celeste kissed Amy. Stunned, her hand flew to her mouth when her daughter kissed Celeste with a hunger that astounded her.

Swiftly, Irene turned her back on them and left the house. She got into her car and sat for a moment trying to gather her thoughts. *Her baby girl. My God*, she thought in shock, *Amy with Celeste!*

Irene rested her head on the steering wheel. She had always thought that Amy and Josh were an extremely happy couple and never once thought there was a problem with their marriage. To see Amy kiss Celeste like *that* completely floored her. *Why?* she thought, *why has this happened, and how long has it been going on?*

Feeling a sense of dread wash through her, Irene couldn't believe her daughter and Celeste were... She couldn't bring herself to put a name to it. Needing time to think she started the car and drove to the beach.

Watching waves crash against the rocks Irene decided she needed to find out what was going on. The best place to start, she thought, was with Celeste. She knew, after speaking to Camille, that she was working this evening. Whether Celeste liked it or not, Irene decided she was going to pay her a visit.

†

After a few pleasantries with Celeste, Irene got right to the point. "This morning I saw you and Amy together." She hesitated. "You kissed."

Celeste sat back in her chair. When told she had a visitor, the last person she expected to see was Irene.

Irene continued, "To say I was shocked would be an understatement. I've always thought Josh and Amy were happy.

It never entered my head that she needed something outside her marriage with a man, never mind," she stopped, looked at Celeste and added gently, "a woman."

Feeling extremely uncomfortable, Celeste lifted her coffee cup and drank from it.

Looking solemn, Irene asked, "What's going on Celeste?"

Gathering her thoughts, Celeste continued to drink her coffee.

Irene waited.

Celeste knew she owed Irene some kind of explanation and decided to be frank. "We're involved."

Irene sat back. "When? *Why?*"

Celeste wished she could spare Irene this. Over the last few months Amy had confided about her past, about how difficult it was not having her mother in her life. She knew they were building a relationship and was only too aware how much Amy loved getting to know her younger sisters.

"We've been together for a few months," Celeste replied. "Why? Well, we've been," she paused when Irene's face paled, "we've been attracted to each other from the beginning."

"I didn't even know you were gay," Irene said. Her eyes narrowed. "How did this happen?"

"Irene, this has not been easy for either of us. If I told you how hard we tried to fight it…" Celeste looked at Irene intently. "I haven't been home in four years, mostly in order to try to put some distance between us. But, when I came back, it…well…" Celeste struggled, not wanting to explain too fully. "We couldn't stop it."

"Four years ago?" Irene said astonished. "And *now?*"

Celeste frowned. She looked at her pager when it buzzed. "It seemed simple. A brief affair would burn it out." She stood. "I need to go."

Irene grabbed Celeste's arm and asked, "And for you, Celeste. Has it burned itself out for you?"

Surprised by the softness in Irene's tone, Celeste looked at the older woman.

Irene sighed then asked with a note of sincerity, "Are you in love with Amy?"

Celeste meant to shake her head and say no, but instead she nodded. She said slowly in recognition of the truth, "Yes…yes, I've been in love with Amy for a very long time."

Irene looked at her intently. "And Amy?"

"I don't know how she feels."

"Does she know how you feel?"

Celeste looked at Irene quizzically.

"Have you told her?"

"No," Celeste replied. "And she doesn't want to know." She picked up her empty coffee cup and crumpled it. "We agreed this would happen for a brief time only. Amy has it planned out. Soon it will be over." She looked down at Irene and exhaled deeply. "I know you must think that I am an appalling person. Josh is my brother. Believe me, Irene, I had no choice. I love Amy and I…couldn't fight it any longer."

"I understand, Celeste," Irene said, looking at her with a pained expression. "I understand only too well. I still carry the scars from decisions I've made." Still holding Celeste's arm, she asked, "But if you knew you felt this way why didn't you continue to stay away? Why come back?"

Celeste's eyebrows drew together. "I couldn't stay away forever. I have plans. And," she hesitated, "when I came back, I had convinced myself that it had passed. I didn't recognize that it was love."

"What are you going to do now?"

Celeste's voice broke slightly and raw pain flashed across her eyes when she replied quietly, "What else, but stick to the arrangement."

Turning, Celeste walked away from Irene.

Chapter 36

It was early evening and Amy was running late. She had promised Maggie that she would quit early. Her cousin was taking the twins camping this weekend and the boys were barely able to contain their excitement at the idea of camping.

Amy felt a twinge of guilt. Josh was in Seattle for a few weeks. Although her workload was heavy the reality was that her client wouldn't be in town until next week. Unable to resist the opportunity to spend a few days with Celeste she had let her cousin think that she needed to work this weekend.

Standing at her car, Amy searched through her bag for her car keys. She scratched her head; she could have sworn that she had picked them up from the office. Emptying the contents out on the ground she searched through the pile.

A hand tapped her shoulder.

Losing her balance, Amy toppled. Sprawled against the car she looked up to see her mother.

"For God's sake, Irene," Amy said. "You almost gave me a heart attack. What are you doing here?"

"Amy, we need to talk," Irene replied, helping Amy up.

Looking down, Amy saw all her things scattered around her feet. Sighing, she bent down to gather them up. Packing her shoulder bag hurriedly she promised herself that she was going to stop using bags that could easily hide small countries. Collecting the last item, she asked. "Is everything okay? There's nothing wrong with Bruce or the girls is there?"

"No. Everyone is okay," Irene hesitated. "It's about you and Celeste, actually."

Standing slowly, Amy stared wide-eyed at her mother.

Blood pounding in her ears, her mind worked frantically. *Oh my God, she knows! How does she know? What does she know? Who else knows?*

Denial

"The park is close by. Let's find a quiet spot there and talk," Irene said gently.

Stunned, Amy followed her mother as she headed quickly toward the park.

After they settled on a park bench Irene, always a straight talker, explained how she knew. Amy sat quietly and listened. Unable to make eye contact she looked straight ahead. Color periodically stained then drained from her face as Irene explained what she witnessed in Amy's backyard.

Head bowed, Amy felt ashamed. Her jaw dropped fully when her mother told her that she had met with Celeste.

Not ready to talk to Irene about Celeste, Amy asked her mother for the first time, "What happened between you and dad?"

Irene's jaw slackened in surprise. She realized that her daughter had never really asked her about her marriage. Why now, she wasn't sure. "Amy, we were young, so very young. I was only fifteen when I fell pregnant with you, and I was only sixteen when we married. I was a wee lassie. I didn't know my own mind. What child does at that age?" She shook her head. "There was an extreme amount of pressure put on me to marry." Irene ran her fingers through Amy's hair. "Don't get me wrong, Amy. Your dad was a good man. Not much older than me and he stood by me the whole time."

Irene looked at Amy and felt a surge of pride that they had produced such a beautiful daughter. "The one good thing to come from our marriage was you, jellybean." She reached out and touched Amy's chin. "But like all childhood crushes, it quickly passed. I wasn't in love with him, Amy. And as time passed, I loved your dad more as a friend."

Frowning, Amy turned away.

"Please believe me, Amy," Irene continued. "I tried. I tried really hard." She grabbed Amy's hand and held it tightly. "For a while, I convinced myself that I did. But when I met Bruce, it was right; our being together was right. I couldn't have continued to stay and lie. I was thirty years old. Only thirty years old," Irene said, her eyes wide. "Just a year older than you are now, with a fourteen-year-old child. I was too young to sacrifice my happiness and I hoped against hope that, because you were a teenager, you would have had some acceptance."

Irene looked up to the sky. "But your dad was a stubborn man and he put ideas in your head." She looked at Amy and added fiercely, "The wrong ideas that turned you against me. And no matter how hard I tried, I couldn't convince you otherwise." Her eyes pleaded. "Jellybean, please understand that even if Bruce hadn't come along, I couldn't have kept up the pretense. Although I tried to convince myself, I knew that the only reason I had stayed so long was for you."

Tears formed in Amy's eyes. Irene choked back her own. Removing a hankie from her pocket, she wiped away the tears that were falling from her daughter's eyes and asked softly, "Are you in love with her?"

Amy lowered her head and whispered, "No."

"It's not a crime to fall in love, Amy," Irene said tenderly. She squeezed her hand. "Baby, you must go with your heart. People who have lived their lives will understand why. The point for you is that everything has changed. You can't keep what you have with Josh. If you do, you are being less than honest with him, your children, and yourself. At least give him the chance to meet someone who truly loves him."

Amy's eyes widened. She looked at Irene in surprise, then shock. She said stubbornly, "But I do truly love him and he loves me. I can't leave him. Do you have any idea the devastation you caused?" Her eyes narrowed. "You ruined our lives," she said, anger edging her tone. "You left me and dad. Your family. Everything. For what?"

Amy stopped when she saw Irene become upset. "Look Irene," she said, her tone softening. "I know that you're happy, and believe me, I'm happy for you. But you have to understand, I watched dad change. You were the only one for him and you turned your back on him. He never recovered after you left, you know."

Irene knew that she shouldn't be shocked at Amy's outburst. It was no surprise to her that Amy still carried a lot of anger.

Even now, regret still burned inside about the divorce and how it devastated Amy.

Even though Mark was dead, Irene still found it difficult to forgive him for poisoning Amy's mind against her. She shook her head. "But think about it. Your dad was in his early thirties when we divorced. He was a young, good-looking guy, with a good business head. He was an engineer with a successful business. He could easily have found love. But he chose not to. He was angry, Amy. Angry that I had the audacity to leave him for someone else—"

"You brought shame to his door."

Irene drew back in surprise. The harshness of those words, she realized as she shivered slightly, was straight from her own father's lips. She steeled herself and continued, "I fell in love, Amy, and there is no shame in that. The only thing that I regret is that I lost you." She moved closer. "Amy, listen to me, Mark's heart wasn't in our relationship. He knew that there had never been real passion between us. We were friends and he knew it."

"But that was enough for him," Amy replied angrily.

"I know." Irene sighed. She wondered how she could reach Amy. "But you're a grown woman now. And," she hesitated, "you now know the difference."

Amy looked at her sharply.

"Settling wasn't for me, and it shouldn't be for you."

Confusion crossed Amy's face. "I like my life." She bowed her head. "I liked what I had with Josh." She lifted her head to look at Irene. "And we had more than a friendship! There was nothing wrong with our relationship."

Irene was sure that Amy was unaware that she had switched tenses. "If you're so happy in your relationship, then why are you having an affair?"

Amy flinched and looked away. "I know what we're doing isn't right." She gave Irene a sideways look and added wryly, "What an understatement." She looked at her feet. "But I can't stop it." She lifted her chin. "Because...because..." she shook her head, then whispered, defeated, "God, I don't even know why anymore." Amy laughed. "How ironic, don't you think, that the old adage is true? Like mother, like daughter. Here I am about to discuss my adulterous affair with my adulterous mother!"

Irene had come too far to allow Amy to push her away. "Does Maggie know?"

Amy sighed. "No. she doesn't."

"So, I take it that you haven't spoken to anyone about this?"

"No." Amy frowned. "No one."

Irene moved closer. "Amy, you desperately need to talk," she said. "You are so like your father—always bottling things up." She smiled. "When you were a wee girl you used to go and hide yourself away. I used to have to hunt the house high and low to find you, and then I would have to bribe you out of your cubbyhole with sweets." Irene chuckled. "Jellybeans would always entice you out of anywhere."

Amy smiled. "They still do."

Irene laughed. She looked at her daughter. *You were my pride and joy. You still are.* "Amy, I'm here to help you. Talk to me."

Amy's next question made Irene reel.

"Why did you let me go?"

Irene gasped. Amy had never looked so defeated. Suddenly overwhelmed with sadness, and knowing that it had taken a lot of courage to ask, Irene closed her eyes for a moment. "I never wanted to leave you," she replied. "I love you. You are my wee girl and I'll always love you. When I was pregnant with you, I was so scared," she confided. "I didn't have a clue what was happening to me. My dad was so ashamed of me when he found out. Well, you know why. A Presbyterian minister and an underage pregnant daughter are not a match made in heaven." Irene laughed then shook her head. "Teenage pregnancies were something that he preached about from the pulpit."

Irene sighed and thought back to that time. Her father was never the same with her and the loss of his love still hurt. "I married your dad to please him. I got married to please everyone," she admitted. "And because I was scared." She tightened her grip on Amy's hand. "The day I turned sixteen my dad married us." She looked at Amy and said, in way of explanation, "I honestly didn't have a clue what was happening. It was only the moment that I held you," she reached out and smoothed Amy's hair from her face, "that I knew everything would be okay."

Irene looked at her daughter pensively and thought back to when Amy found out about Bruce. Amy built a barrier that kept her out, and even though they had been extremely close, she was never able to breech that barrier, no matter how hard she tried.

"When Bruce came along I tried so hard to make you see that it hadn't anything to do with you." Irene's face filled with sadness. "But Mark was terrified that I would try to take you away, so he went to great lengths to ensure that you were going nowhere."

Amy looked at her mother, and with a heavy heart, accepted that what she said was true. Even after her affair had become public knowledge and Bruce had returned to the States when his contract ended, Irene stayed, even though he insisted she go with him. She stayed even when Amy's grandparents rejected her, stayed when her friends rejected her. She remembered her trying desperately hard. Amy realized that Irene stayed until she rejected her.

Irene was right, Amy realized. Her father was terrified that she intended to take her away. Amy remembered the many times that he would quietly talk about Irene's betrayal and how, when Amy married, she would never be capable of doing such a thing.

Irene pulled Amy into her arms and hugged her. "I'm here for you, jellybean. And you never know, maybe your adulterous mother can be good for at least one thing," she said, kissing Amy's head, "listening to you."

She's right. I desperately need to talk.

Moving out of her mother's arms, Amy drew a breath. After a moment she looked at Irene, and eyes wide, explained that apart from a few teenage crushes she had never even thought about being with a woman.

"You're not attracted to women normally?"

"No." Amy looked at her mother. "But, I must have been. You can't just suddenly switch, can you?"

Irene shook her head. "I don't know, but I don't think attraction is necessarily always based on what gender you are. Sometimes, it simply comes down to what the other person makes you feel. She looked at Amy. "I guess the real question is, what does Celeste make you feel?"

"I don't know," Amy answered. "At first I thought it might have something to do with Josh." She looked at Irene. "You know, something to do with the strong resemblance. But now," she bit her bottom lip, "I know it has nothing to do with him. It's her. I'm attracted to her." Amy looked at her hands. "Something happened before the wedding."

"What?"

Amy hung her head. "I didn't want it to happen, you know."

"What?"

"I can't explain it." Amy rubbed her forehead. "Not so that you would understand. God, even I still don't understand it."

Amy stared into space.

"Amy?"

"I just couldn't stop myself." Amy closed her eyes. "I couldn't resist her." She looked at her mother. "Somehow when we began this, I thought it would fade." Her hands clenched. "I desperately wanted it to fade."

"I'm not sure if that was a good game plan."

"No, it wasn't" Amy half-smiled. "I thought because she hadn't been around for four years, I would be able to put it behind me and get on with my life." Determination crossed her eyes. "And that's exactly what I intend to do. I'll get back on track."

"What do you mean?"

"I mean, it has to end. After this, I'll put it behind me, like I did before."

"Celeste is in love with you, Amy."

Amy looked at her mother. "She said that?"

"Yes," Irene said and then smiled. "Very much so."

"She actually said she loved me?"

"Amy, why else do you think you'd put yourselves through this?"

Surprised and not knowing what to think, Amy tried to absorb her mother's words.

"I'm beginning to think that you don't know how you truly feel," Irene said tentatively. "Celeste loves you, Amy. After seeing you together and with what you've said just now, I'm in no doubt that you feel the same way." Irene closed her eyes and sighed. "But, you can't be with the both of them. If you stay with Josh, then your life might not be empty, but you will be denying yourself the most important thing in life."

Amy looked at her mother. "What?"

"Being with someone you love, jellybean."

Amy shook her head. "But I don't intend to be with them both. I intend to be with Josh."

"Maybe I'm to blame for you seeking security and comfort from a man so similar to your father." Irene looked away and brushed a tear from her eye.

Blindsided, Amy raised her eyebrows in surprise. She didn't think that Josh was anything like her dad. "What do you mean?"

"Josh is dependable," Irene revealed. "Amy, he's the type of man that you can always rely on. He's solid. He makes you feel safe, just like your father."

Shock crossed Amy's face.

"In my experience, life has a strange way of showing you what is real," her mother continued. "When you make a decision to settle for second place, it bites you on the bum and reminds you that it isn't going to be that easy." She looked at Amy for a moment. "I can't say anything other than I know that Josh will survive, the children will survive."

Amy looked at her mother and words of reinforcement spilled from her lips about how much she loved Josh and the children.

Irene sighed. "You are so like your father," she said. "You've got that steely determination in your eyes. Amy, I'm pleading with you to realize that you can't stay in a marriage when it's clear you're in love with someone else." She added slowly, "You can't stay because you have some sense that you are righting a wrong. It was me who left your father. Not you!"

Amy shook her head. "I'm staying because I love Josh. I'm staying because it's the right thing to do. I could never leave Josh for Celeste, never."

Irene was frustrated. Amy wasn't prepared to accept that she had put herself at terrible risk to be with Celeste. She pushed. "Do you love her?"

Amy didn't respond.

Determined, Irene repeated, "Do you love her?"

Amy looked at her and said as if the suggestion was absurd. "No! All that's between Celeste and I is…" Her words dried up. She looked at Irene. "I…There's…"

Irene watched Amy struggle to form the words.

Amy stopped and took a deep breath. "There's…" She dried up again.

"I…"

Irene wanted to tell her about love. That instead of fencing you in it sets you free. She wanted to tell her that it was like giving birth to a life, but instead of you feeding it, it feeds you. But, instead, she said, "Let your heart speak, Amy."

Amy's shoulders slumped. "I can't stop thinking about her. I can't eat. I can't sleep. I can't seem to function very well unless she's around me." She straightened and looked away. "It doesn't matter, I've no intention of breaking up my family."

"But Amy, if you accept that you love her," Irene said, frustration creeping into her voice, "then you can't stay with Josh just because of the boys."

"I don't accept anything!" Amy replied angrily. "And of course I can stay in anything as long as my family stays together! Look," she said, moving her hands and feet, "I'm not in a ball and chain. I'm happy!"

"Amy," Irene said. "People who are happy do not have affairs."

Apparently unable to argue with the simple truth, Amy looked at her mother intently. "I'll get over Celeste and things will be all right, eventually. They'll sort themselves out."

Irene was reminded of the fourteen-year-old, frightened child she left behind. It was clear that Amy was frightened now.

Denial

Irene moved closer and taking her child in her arms, whispered, "I'm here for you." She hugged her tightly. "I'll always be here for you."

Chapter 37

It was Friday night and Amy was excited. This morning she had helped Maggie pack the Jeep for their camping trip. Maggie's parting words were that she was glad that Amy wasn't coming as this trip would give her a chance to check out what kind of father material Sean was. She laughed and then added that if her boyfriend could handle Amy's two for a weekend, then he could handle anything. She had hugged Amy and told her not to work too hard.

Amy felt guilty as she waved goodbye. Maggie thought her entire weekend would be taken up by work. But her guilt didn't last; she was too excited about spending time with Celeste. Throughout the last four months they had only managed to snatch a few hours with each other here and there. This would be their first weekend since New York.

Josh had called from Seattle during a break from a round of afternoon meetings. He was keyed up. The company he was working for had decided to pull out of software development and had offered him and a few of his colleagues the opportunity of a management buyout. This round of meetings was designed to whip up investor interest. This was his big break.

The doorbell rang. Straightening her top, Amy looked in the mirror to check that she looked okay. Feeling the familiar tightness in her stomach, she ran downstairs. Not wanting to appear too keen she stopped at the bottom step, gathered herself, and then made her way slowly to the front door. When she opened it Celeste was standing there wearing dark jeans and a low-cut, cerise, sleeveless top.

Eyes wide, Amy followed Celeste's long legs up over her waist only to halt at her protruding nipples, which, braless, stood out. Amy's stomach knotted when she registered that Celeste's hair was down. Celeste had a tendency to wear her hair up. A few

Denial

months ago Amy told her that she liked it down and, ever since, Celeste had worn her hair down when she was with her.

"Hi," Amy said. Giving Celeste an impatient smile she hurried her into the house.

Celeste barely had time to close the door behind her and put down her weekend bag, along with some grocery bags, before Amy pushed her up against the wall.

Amy hadn't seen Celeste the entire week. Desperately wanting to taste that teasing mouth, she kissed her hard. Celeste responded with the same ardor and kissed her deeply.

Loosening Amy's hair Celeste let it spill over her fingers before running her hands over Amy's black cashmere top, searching out the swell of her breasts.

Amy groaned when Celeste touched her, and too impatient for niceties, said huskily, "I want you." Pressing Celeste into the wall, she whispered, "God, how I want you."

"Not here," Celeste murmured between kisses.

Amy looked at her and, nodding, took Celeste's hand and led her to the guest bedroom.

Once there, Celeste kissed Amy everywhere. Undressing her she registered that Amy's movements were slowing and began to work faster at removing her clothes. Celeste had, over the last few months, seen Amy like this a few times. She had discovered, to her great pleasure that Amy only became languorous when she needed to come quickly.

Lying on the bed with her eyes half-closed, Amy murmured, "Hurry."

Heart pounding at the sight of Amy's naked body, Celeste hastily undressed. Groaning, she threw a thigh over Amy's hip and lowering herself positioned her clit over Amy's.

Groaning loudly, Amy's eyes lost focus then closed.

Celeste pressed into Amy. This was a relatively new position they had found. "Amy look at me," she whispered.

Amy slowly opened her eyes, and reaching up, cupped Celeste's breasts. Celeste smiled knowingly. The blonde was fascinated with her breasts and whenever they made love, to

Celeste's amusement, she gave them her full attention. She particularly liked to knead them when coming.

Pressing down, Celeste groaned. She loved this, adored the sensation of sensitive wet flesh against sensitive wet flesh. She wasn't surprised anymore by how quickly she was ready to come. Often, just touching Amy was enough to make her ready. Her breathing shallow, Celeste slid back and forth. Her eyes rolled back when Amy moaned loudly. Breathing heavily, she watched as Amy built to orgasm.

Gasping, Amy whispered, "I missed you." She stroked Celeste's nipple. "I couldn't think of anything else since I woke up this morning," her breathing deepened, "but being with you like this."

Celeste listened as Amy told her how much she needed her, needed this. She adored her love chat. Amy often mentioned how it took her by surprise, her need to vocalize her desire for Celeste during their lovemaking.

Watching Amy Celeste smiled, knowing that over the last few months Amy was discovering much about herself.

The fire built inside her and Celeste let out a low moan. Needing release, she pressed into Amy and brought them both to orgasm.

Slowly, Celeste slipped off Amy and lay next to her. Stretching out she sighed luxuriously, then pulled Amy to her and hugged her tightly.

Amy laughed and, cupping Celeste's face, whispered, "I have some fresh food and a few appetizers laid out in the kitchen for us, you know."

Celeste raised her eyebrows. "Well, I don't know about you," she teased, "but I've worked up an appetite." She let Amy go and leapt out of bed. Standing, she held out her hand. "Let's go eat, I'm famished."

Amy looked Celeste over. "Later," she said seductively. Sitting up, she pulled Celeste to her. "We'll eat later. Right now," she whispered as she kissed Celeste's shoulder, "I'm hungry for something else."

Denial

It was much later before Celeste convinced Amy to leave the bed.

†

The next day Celeste and Amy spent the morning in bed, chatting and making love. By late afternoon Amy insisted that Celeste model for her. She had, over the last few months, talked Celeste into allowing her to sketch her in various positions.

Smiling, Celeste stretched out, only too happy to indulge Amy's every whim.

Eventually, in the early evening, Celeste coaxed Amy out of bed and out for a stroll.

Outside, the beach was quiet and the evening sky was bright blue with no clouds.

"Have you spoken to your mom?" Celeste asked as they walked along the beach.

Amy looked at her and, folding her arms, replied, "Yes. But I'm not ready to talk about it."

Celeste nodded.

They walked along the beach for a while. "Susan called me yesterday."

Removing her flip-flops, Amy held them in one hand. "How is she?" she asked as they walked.

"She's fine," Celeste replied, taking Amy's free hand. "They've set a date."

"Oh," Amy said in surprise. Looking around she pulled her hand away then placed a flip-flop in each. Suddenly taking a great interest in the water pooling around her feet with each step, she asked, "When?"

Celeste stopped walking.

Amy stopped beside her and, not looking at her, flicked wet sand with her toe.

Trying to hide her irritation, Celeste kept her voice even, "The beach is empty."

"I'm sorry," Amy responded, trailing her toe along the sand. Not looking at Celeste, she added, "I can't."

After a moment, Celeste sighed and nodded. "I know." She walked on.

Amy quickly followed. "When are they getting married?"

"In a few months," Celeste replied. "But Ritchie isn't happy, because the date coincides with the rugby world cup."

"He likes rugby?" Amy asked in surprise.

"Yes."

"I never got a chance to tell him I'm a rugby fan." Amy chuckled. "I think we were still working through his teenage angst that night." She looked at Celeste and grinned. "Maybe he was saving that little nugget for the next session…I mean…eh…the next time we met."

Celeste laughed, and not able to resist, pulled Amy to her. "Felt like a therapy session did it?"

Amy smiled and nodded. "A bit." She looked at Celeste. "He can really talk, you know." She winked. "I mean, really talk!"

Celeste leaned her forehead against Amy's and teased, "It's a tough world out there, kiddo."

"Yeah, yeah," Amy replied. Casting her eyes around, she pulled out of Celeste's arms and walked on. "Did I tell you that Maggie's thinking about proposing to Sean?"

"No!" Celeste answered, walking alongside. No longer surprised that Amy confided in her, she asked, "I bet you told her that you thought it was too soon?"

Amy stopped walking and stared at Celeste, her mouth hung open slightly. "Am I that transparent?" she managed eventually.

"I hate to break it to you," Celeste said as she reached out and smoothed windswept hair from Amy's face. "But when it comes to those sorts of things you're a bit old-fashioned."

"Hell, no way am I old-fashioned."

"Really?" Celeste raised an eyebrow challengingly. "I bet you told her to give it a year. Settle in. See what he's like first."

Amy's eyes widened. "How do you know that?"

"I bet you even went as far as to say that the reason she should wait a year was because she was impulsive by nature and she should listen to the voice of reason. Your reason."

"I…Well…I didn't say that exactly. Not in so many words." Amy scowled. "How did you know?"

Celeste laughed then winked at Amy, before walking on.

"I didn't say it like that," Amy said, catching up. "I just asked why she was in such a rush."

"You didn't tell her to wait?"

"Okay," Amy said. "Okay. Maybe, I did say she should wait," she squeezed her thumb and forefinger together, "a wee bit." She pulled on Celeste's arm for her to stop. "What's wrong with a little patience," she asked. She threw out her arms. "Why is everybody in such a rush?" She stared at Celeste. "For all we know, he might be a complete fruitcake."

"What? And Maggie isn't?" Celeste asked as laughter danced across her eyes. "Admit it, Amy. You don't want her to rush."

"Why aren't you being supportive," Amy huffed then folded her arms.

"Because," Celeste replied as she reached out and rubbed Amy's arms, "Maggie could line a runway with the number of lovers she's had. She's been in the dating game for a long, long time." She pulled Amy to her. "She knows better than anyone what the real thing is when it comes along." *Just like I do, and just like you would, if you opened your eyes.*

At that moment Celeste desperately wanted to kiss Amy but knew she would literally pass out if she tried. Increasingly, over the last few months, Amy was wary of them being seen together in public and worried often about how tactile they were. It amused Celeste that no matter how on guard Amy was, she was unable to hide the hunger in her eyes when they were together. Celeste knew that sometimes the intensity of that hunger frightened Amy.

"So, you think she shouldn't wait?" Amy asked.

The need to kiss her was strong. Celeste sighed. "Let her do what she wants," she replied. "Maggie's a big girl."

"Josh doesn't think she should rush either."

To stop herself from kissing Amy, Celeste stretched. To her amusement, whenever they debated, when Amy was pushed into a corner, she would occasionally defend her point of view by saying that Josh thought that way also.

"Why doesn't that surprise me?" Celeste replied then walked on.

"You think we're wrong?" Amy asked, walking alongside.

"Not necessarily, but I think Maggie knows her own mind."

After a moment, Amy placed her hand on Celeste's elbow. Celeste watched uncertainty show in Amy's eyes. She caught her bottom lip and bit it lightly.

Smiling reassuringly, Celeste took Amy's arm and folded it through hers.

"Do you think I should encourage her?" Amy asked.

Celeste walked on, in contemplation. "I think you should give Maggie whatever support she asks for."

Amy looked at Celeste then nodding, said, "Maybe you're right."

Celeste smiled at her. "Trust her, Amy."

Amy smiled back. "Okay."

Holding Amy's arm tightly, Celeste headed for a quiet bay she knew. When they arrived, she rested against sheltered rocks and pulled Amy to her. Sliding down the rock, she wrapped her arms around Amy. They settled to watch the herons and egrets stalk the beach.

"I love this place," Amy said. "This is a magical place to watch the world go by." She looked over her shoulder and, eyes glowing, said, "It's especially beautiful today."

Celeste nodded. Amy smiled then snuggled in.

Hidden by the rock, they watched a dog and its owner run past. Amy whispered, "Do you know that I didn't know the inside joke about Bud?" Wide-eyed, she turned her head to look at Celeste. "Nobody told me that the family dog was a 'talker.'"

Celeste snuggled her head into Amy's neck and buried her laughter.

"Just after I moved here I went for a walk along the beach at your folks and he tagged along. I didn't know that when he wanted to play he would show me by gnashing his teeth and growling." Amy tried pushing Celeste out of her neck. "Most dogs just drop the ball and wag their tails."

Laughing, Celeste buried her head further into Amy's neck.

"*And,*" Amy said as she pushed Celeste gently from the crook of her neck. "Nobody told me," she bracketed her fingers, "that the more excited he got, the louder he 'talked,' and the more teeth he displayed." She chuckled. "So, when he dropped the ball in front of me and I picked it up to throw it he started gnashing his teeth like a deranged loony!"

Celeste laughed so hard her body was shaking and she had tears in her eyes.

Amy laughed. "I didn't know that it was his act. I didn't know that he was saying, 'Yeah, yeah, lady. C'mon, hurry up and throw the ball.' Instead, I translated it as 'move and I'll kill you.' So, I didn't move." She grabbed Celeste's hand and brought it close to her heart. "I thought my heart might beat out of my chest. I stood frozen with my arm in the air for ages until Bud got fed up and wandered off."

Eventually, controlling her laugher, Celeste cupped Amy's cheek. "I can't believe that nobody told you." She tenderly kissed one cheek, then the other, before staring deeply into her eyes. "God, I adore you."

Chapter 38

That evening Celeste insisted on cooking for Amy. This was a pleasure often denied them. Their times together tended to be too short, and only sometimes would Amy indulge Celeste and allow her to cook for her.

"Sit," Celeste said when Amy entered the kitchen. She pointed to a kitchen stool at the breakfast bar next to where she was cooking. She poured a glass of red wine. "I'm cooking for you tonight," she told Amy, handing her a glass.

"Don't you want me to help?"

Celeste smiled. "I want you to sit there and talk to me."

"Just talk?" Amy asked, seductively "Not touch?"

Celeste lifted her eyebrows. "For now."

Amy stuck out her bottom lip.

"Put that away," Celeste said, eyes dancing. "Don't you want to know what's cooking?"

"Yes," Amy replied, then sipped her wine.

"Tonight, I'm going to whip up an extravaganza of risotto and nuggets of langoustine tails, followed by a to-die-for chocolate dessert."

Amy's eyes opened wide. "I don't have anything like that here."

"I know," Celeste replied, opening the fridge. "I brought the stuff I need with me."

"Oh," Amy responded. A look of pleasure crossed her face as she sipped her wine. "I wish I could cook," she said, watching Celeste. "I can barely boil an egg." She sucked on her bottom lip for a moment. "Maybe, I should stop being a takeaway queen and sign up for a cookery class."

"Maybe," Celeste replied as she stirred the risotto. "Doesn't Maggie do most of the cooking?"

"Yeah, but she's not much better than me." Amy smiled. "And fortunately the kids don't have much taste, so they don't

Denial

notice how bad our cooking is." She laughed. "We don't have to force feed them just yet."

"I thought Josh cooked?"

"He does, but he's not much better than me either. The chicken he cooked the other night was so tough it asked me if I wanted to fight."

Celeste laughed. "You might not be able to cook, but you are one helluva artist." She looked at Amy. "How's the painting coming along?"

Amy swallowed a mouthful of wine and then licking her lips put the glass down. "Well," she replied, tucking her hair behind her ears. "I bought a six-foot canvas."

"Why?" Celeste asked as she focused on the risotto she was stirring.

"Because, I want to give you something as a parting—"

Celeste looked up sharply and not wanting to hear it said, "Don't." Her eyes pleaded. "Please, not tonight."

Amy looked at the brunette then nodded. She picked up her glass and twirled the wine for a while. "I got it because I want to paint you naked."

Celeste stopped stirring the risotto. "You're joking?"

Amy shook her head and pointed at the risotto. "Keep stirring."

"I'm flattered," Celeste said as she stirred. "But really?" She stopped stirring and stared at Amy in disbelief. "Are you crazy?"

"Of course not," Amy replied then laughed.

"Don't you think that it would be seriously wrong for you to have a painting of me draped over something," she looked down at herself, "naked?"

"The bed," Amy responded with a mischievous glint in her eyes.

"What?" Celeste asked, in confusion.

"I want to paint you buck naked, stretched out on the bed." The tip of Amy's tongue slid out and touched her top lip. "I'd paint you lying there, with no inhibition, disheveled from our lovemaking, heavy-eyed, full-breasted…sated."

Celeste stared at Amy then blew out air before shaking her top, allowing some cold air to circulate.

Amy laughed. "Feeling the heat?"

"Yes," Celeste replied. Walking around the breakfast bar, she took Amy in her arms, and kissed her passionately.

"Isn't risotto tricky to cook?" Amy mumbled against Celeste's lips.

"Mmmm," Celeste answered, letting Amy go.

Celeste returned to the stove and stirred the risotto before throwing in the langoustines. "I love the idea of you painting me." She looked at Amy as she worked. "But it's dangerous."

"I know. But, I want to." Amy looked at Celeste for a few moments. "You're a painter's dream, you know. You're a beautiful, sassy, sexy Goddess."

Celeste stared at Amy, then looked at her wineglass. "It's only one glass you've had so far, right?"

Amy laughed and held up her glass. "So far." Sipping her wine, she gave Celeste a sultry look. "Let's play our game," she said. "I thought up some more things I like."

"More?" Celeste's lips twitched. "Okay."

"You first."

Celeste looked around then held up the wooden spoon. "I like kitchen utensils."

"That's lame, Celeste!"

Celeste laughed. "I know, but I'm not in the zone yet." She eyed Amy playfully. "Anyway, just go with the flow."

"Okay," Amy replied, wiggling her eyebrows.

Celeste smiled. "I like…uhmmm…sleeping out, under the stars, in the desert, in a sleeping bag, with the wind howling around me."

Amy gave Celeste a cheeky grin. "I like sunrises, then I like to sleep late."

"I like sundowns," Celeste responded, grinning. "I like seeing the sun set over different horizons."

"Hmmm," Amy replied. Over the lip of her wineglass she eyed Celeste. Sipping some wine, she put the glass down and circled the rim with her finger. "On your own, Ms. Cameron?"

Denial

Their eyes locking, Celeste replied as she stirred. "Maybe."

Amy smiled, then caught her bottom lip and thought for a moment. "I like making hot drinks on cold nights."

"I like taking cold swims on hot nights."

Amy picked up her glass. "On your own Ms. Cameron?"

"Maybe," Celeste responded, then smiled fully.

Amy eyed Celeste for a moment. Then raising her eyebrows said provocatively, "I like making love with a brunette who has a body to die for."

Surprised, Celeste sucked in air and held it for a moment. "Isn't it my mind you're supposed to adore?" she asked eventually.

Amy smiled seductively.

"Jeez, Amy, and here I was thinking that all this time it was my conversation that titillated you."

Amy reached for her.

Celeste pulled away and growled playfully. "Amy, if you want to eat tonight you'd better stop teasing me, or I'll switch this off and we'll finish," she pointed to the door, "in bed."

Sitting back, Amy put her hand to her mouth and pretended to zip it. She picked up her wineglass. "Not another word."

Celeste lifted the spoon to Amy's mouth. "Taste."

Amy's eyes widened with pleasure as she chewed. "Mmmm. It's delicious."

"Let's eat," Celeste said. She switched off the stove and served up their meal.

"I'm starved," Amy said as they sat at the kitchen table. She picked up her fork and tucked into her dish.

Celeste sat next to Amy, and not wanting the evening to end, closed her eyes and tried to savor the moment.

Amy slowly stopped chewing. "What's wrong?"

"Nothing," Celeste replied, opening her eyes.

"Then eat." Amy picked up her glass and took a mouthful of wine.

Celeste nodded. Shaking out her napkin she dropped it on her lap.

"This is amazing," Amy said. "You really are a fabulous cook."

Enjoying the compliment, Celeste smiled. "Thank you." She picked up her fork and began to eat.

"I dug out my guitar, just like you asked," Amy said.

Celeste smiled. "Would you play it for me tonight?"

"Hmmm," Amy said as she chewed. She swallowed then asked mischievously, "What do I get in return?"

Celeste looked at her challengingly. "I might reciprocate and play violin for you next time at mom and dad's."

"What?" Amy said, holding her fork midway to her mouth. "You play violin?"

Chewing, Celeste nodded.

"God, I can't believe you sometimes," Amy said, lowering the fork. "Why haven't you told me?" she asked. "I can't believe that in all the discussions we've had about music you've never mentioned to me once that you play violin."

"Amy," Celeste said with a note of exasperation. "I've never mentioned it because, until recently, I hadn't played since high school. Anyway, it all came down to Sophie digging the violins we played as kids out of the attic."

"Oh," Amy replied. "So, it was Sophie who encouraged you then?"

"Yes," Celeste said, smiling. "But, now I'm beginning to regret it because my folks want us to play whenever I drop by."

Amy laughed. "Sophie's trying to get on their good side?"

"Hmmm," Celeste replied as she chewed her food. "She's hoping that all her late night exploits will be forgiven."

"Why did you marry Nick?"

Surprised at the change of subject, Celeste paused then put her fork down and wiped her mouth with her napkin. "I didn't know you were curious about that."

"You hold back a lot," Amy replied, picking up her wineglass.

Celeste looked at her. "Not when I'm with you."

"But, there are things that you never discuss."

"Whatever you want to know, I'll tell you."

Amy swirled the wine in her glass for a while.

Celeste encouraged, "Amy, what do you want to know?"

"I'd like to know things like why you got married," Amy replied. "And why you decided to come home now." She looked at Celeste. "I've been trying hard not to ask you these questions but," her eyes widened, "I can't help it, I want to know everything." She studied her glass. "I want to know everything about you."

Celeste sighed inwardly. She was aware that over the last few months Amy had tried to hold a part of her back, mostly by not exploring Celeste's personal life too deeply. Although their discussions were extensive, Celeste had gone with the flow, never forcing anything, always allowing the direction of their conversations to shape naturally.

Celeste looked at Amy. How could she tell her that she didn't often let people in? How could she even begin to explain that every moment, of every day, she wanted her, craved her, in fact? How could she tell Amy the core things about why she married, that she chose to return now because she was hoping to adopt, without first telling her the thing she knew Amy didn't want to hear—that she loved her.

Amy looked at her. "Why did you marry?"

"I married Nick because I fell in love with him," Celeste answered, looking at Amy. "Or, I thought I was in love with him." She sipped her wine. "When I was a teenager, I was painfully shy."

"Yes, Josh said as much." Amy nodded. "And I can see it sometimes."

"Nick somehow understood that and he helped me overcome it, to some degree. His personality was big enough for the two of us." Celeste swirled the wine in her glass. "You would have liked him. He was easy company, full of fun, and I didn't have to try too hard when I was around him."

"Why marry? Why not just go out with him?"

"If I'm truthful, I think I just needed to let loose." Celeste smiled. "And he was the first real taste of freedom I had." She drank more wine, then sat back. "Between training and studying,

I hadn't time to really let go." She stared off. "And Nick was captivating; full of life, impulsive. Everything about him seemed fast-paced, chaotic, all about chasing the moment. Whereas everything in my life was planned. Everything was based around my swimming. What time I got up, how many days I trained, how many training sessions I had in a day, for how long. What I would eat, when I would sleep, when I would study." She looked at Amy, the corners of her mouth quirked. "The list is long."

Amy reached for her wineglass then sat back. "He was the opposite to everything that you were at the time?"

Understanding that Amy wanted to know, Celeste nodded. "I liked him. I liked his passion."

"And when he asked you to marry him?"

"I just went with it," Celeste said. "Swimming was over." She touched her right shoulder. "And it was the nature of how we were together, to just go with things." She smiled when Amy's eyebrows lifted.

"Where is he now?"

Celeste looked away. "I don't know. We lost contact." She shrugged. "We were kids. His parents were divorced and moved out of state just before we met." She looked at Amy. "That probably goes a long way to explaining why he was desperate to marry. He needed something solid and secure in his life. He was an only child with no close ties."

"Apart from you?"

Celeste didn't answer.

"What would you do if he came back?"

Celeste eyed Amy curiously. "Why?"

"Just wondering," Amy replied. "You wouldn't be tempted to," she hesitated, "reconcile?"

Recognizing a note of jealously, Celeste hid her smile and toyed with teasing Amy. She opened her mouth then caught the serious look in Amy's eyes. "No," she said as she eyed her appreciatively. "I know what I like now. My tastes have matured."

Amy looked at Celeste. "Is that so?"

Denial

"Yes," Celeste replied softly. "That's definitely so." Taking Amy's hand in hers, she added, "Eat."

†

That evening, lying in bed with Amy, feeling filled and content, Celeste sighed. She had, amongst the small gifts that she had brought and given Amy over the weekend, a final surprise. Most of the gifts were things that she couldn't resist buying when they inspired thoughts of Amy, which were constant these days, but this one was special.

Celeste got up and left the room, returning with a package. Sitting, she handed it to Amy.

Sitting up eagerly, Amy took the shoe-sized package. Looking at it, she turned it around in her hands a few times. She smiled excitedly and shook it. Hearing it rattle, she asked, "What is it?"

Thankful it wasn't fragile, Celeste tried to hide her enthusiasm. "Open it."

Sitting straight, Amy tucked her legs underneath her.

Celeste moved closer. She caught her breath when Amy tucked her hair behind her ears and gave the package her full attention. She loved Amy's little idiosyncrasies. Like the way she tucked her hair behind her ears when she needed to focus, or rubbed her forehead whenever she was about to say something serious. She particularly loved the way she said 'of course,' whenever she was caught off guard, but the one that made her knees weak, always, was when making a decision, Amy often caught her bottom lip in contemplation.

Reaching out, Celeste smoothed Amy's tousled hair then let her fingers trail down to her full breasts, before drawing a finger slowly around and over the nearest nipple.

"Now, new rule," Amy said, removing Celeste's hand. "When you bring gifts, you've got to wait."

Unwrapping her package, Amy smiled widely when Celeste huffed at her.

Opening the box, Amy's mouth hung open. She dropped the bundle as if it had burnt her fingers. Looking at Celeste in bewilderment, she blushed deeply. Staring at the contents of the box, then at Celeste, she stuttered, "You've…you've got to be joking, right?"

Amy stabbed at the strap lightly with her finger. Repulsed but curious at the same time she picked it up and said as if she was holding something macabre, "I've never actually seen one of these in the flesh so to speak."

Intrigued, Celeste watched Amy.

Holding it high, Amy stretched out a strap and said in amazement as she studied it, "It's very real looking isn't it?" Her expression changed quickly from amazement to alarm. Raising her eyebrows, a touch of panic tinged her tone, "You don't honestly expect me to wear this thing, do you?"

Celeste had bought it earlier that week. It had been on her mind for many months, since that night in New York, in fact. Amused, she stretched out on the bed. "I think that I was expecting to wear it."

Amy looked at her "What!" she said in astonishment. "I can't take *that!*" Her eyes widened. "Jesus, Celeste, that thing is huge! Much bigger than…" Her voice trailed off. A deep color suffused her face. She stared at Celeste then nervously threw the object on the bed and said with some alarm, "The thought of using something like that has never even entered my head." She leaned over to where she had thrown it and pushed it off the bed.

Seeing she was upset, Celeste reached out and pulled Amy down on top of her. Feeling the tension in her body, she wrapped her arms around and held her tight.

Amy let Celeste hold her. Angrily, she thought about the strap-on and a familiar sense of confusion began to build up inside her. *What is she trying to do? Push me to my limit!* She closed her eyes. Here they were, two women together, making love, finding pleasure, absolute and unbelievable pleasure with each other.

Pleasure that she should be having with Josh, Amy thought guiltily. She tried to ignore her inner voice when it told her that it was much more than physical.

Since her talk with Irene, Amy hadn't stopped thinking about what it all meant. Focusing on Celeste, she said gravely, "I don't think we'll be using that. I mean what has gotten into you!" She pushed away from Celeste and sat up. "I mean why would you want to wear...a...a...*dildo!* I don't understand!" She threw her hands in the air and moved off the bed. "Isn't what we have good enough?"

Reaching out, Celeste grabbed Amy's arm. "Shhh." She pulled her into her arms. "It's okay. It's okay."

Eyes wide, Amy asked, "Why, Celeste? Why?"

"Because," Celeste replied as she held her, "I want to know what it feels like to share this part of you. I want to watch you move underneath me and be inside you."

Frowning, Amy said in growing confusion, "You have been inside me! I don't need that." She pointed to the empty space on the bed. "I just need you."

Stroking Amy's face, Celeste rubbed her nose against her. "I want it," she said. "I promise you, it will be a very sensual experience." She kissed Amy gently. "Can you trust me?"

Amy's frown deepened. She said nothing but her stomach flipped at Celeste's plea. Celeste was intoxicating and Amy knew if she pushed she wouldn't have the willpower to resist any of her demands.

Celeste kissed her deeply then whispered, "Trust me, Amy."

Catching her bottom lip, Amy thought about how this was the one area that was exclusive to Josh, and how he had something that up until now Celeste could never give her. Amy realized, stupidly, that she had believed that somehow she would never be able to compare them.

Now there is nothing, no matter how flimsy, that I can keep for him alone. Amy rubbed her forehead as she looked at Celeste.

Looking for an answer, Celeste raised an eyebrow then did the one thing that Amy could never resist. She whispered, "Please."

Amy bit her bottom lip then sighing in defeat nodded.

Celeste climbed off the bed where Amy had pushed 'it' off, and slipped it on.

Amy watched with fascination and had to stifle a laugh at how ridiculous Celeste looked. She raised her eyebrows in surprise when the brunette opened a small bottle and watched in shock as she applied lubricant.

What the hell have I let myself in for? Amy thought, her mouth hanging open.

"It comes with it," Celeste said, her eyes twinkling as she applied the lubricant liberally. She snapped her mouth shut when Celeste approached, unable to believe that she was actually going to let her put that thing anywhere near her.

When Celeste slipped onto the bed and lay down, Amy looked at her. *If it is a floorshow she wants, then a floorshow is exactly what she's going to get!*

Sitting up, Amy straddled Celeste and suppressed her laughter when she looked up at her in surprise.

Amy looked down at Celeste. It was rare that she was immediately ready for entry, usually she needed some foreplay, and even though Celeste had used lubricant, Amy knew the girth of the thing between her thighs was certainly something she wasn't used to. Lifting her hips, she positioned herself over Celeste's new toy and held it.

Celeste caught her breath. A look of astonishment, then pleasure, crossed her face.

Amy stopped. She looked down at the woman beneath her. The incongruity of Celeste's breasts and the thing between her legs made her feel strange. "This is weird," she said, pulling back a little.

Celeste rested her hands on Amy's thighs and stroked them. "A good weird? she asked her eyes full of desire.

Amy looked at Celeste. A deep need gripped her. "Yes," she replied huskily. "A good weird."

"Amy I—"

"Hush," Amy said. Looking into Celeste's eyes, she lowered herself slowly. Closing her eyes she let out a loud groan, half in pain and half in pleasure, as she slowly pushed past the band of muscles. Opening her eyes, Amy looked down. She had taken it all. Eyes widening, she looked at Celeste. Neither moved.

Celeste seemed too terrified to even breathe. Eventually, she uttered, "Oh God, Amy."

Feeling completely filled, Amy's nipples tightened until they ached. She whispered, "Touch my breasts."

Celeste moved her hands to Amy's breasts and closed over them. She almost purred as she stroked them.

Amy groaned and rocked her hips gently. Lifting high, she let Celeste see her toy enter her a few times, as she slid up then down it slowly. Letting her insides adjust, Amy became aware of the ridges and nubs as they caressed her inner walls.

Placing her hands on Amy's hips, Celeste whispered, "I love this. I love—"

Amy groaned loudly, losing Celeste's words as she slid all the way down.

Celeste moaned and moved her hips up and down. Their eyes locked. Amy felt the power of her actions. With each slow teasing movement, Celeste's eyes grew darker and more intense. Her face flushed, she gasped for air each time Amy raised up then pushed down.

To Amy's delight, every time she moaned Celeste's eyelids drooped and her head fell back. Amy's eyes sparkled when Celeste's jaw worked back and forth. Smiling wickedly, she ran her hands up and down Celeste's stomach, loving the way the muscles underneath her skin trembled, the way they tensed up then relaxed to the movement of their hips.

Breathing hard, Celeste pulled Amy's hips close to her for some anchorage then thrust with complete abandon.

Flushed with excitement at Celeste's loss of control, Amy laughed and whispered, "Slow down."

Breathless, Celeste's eyes focused. Smiling, she sucked in air. "You on top of me like this. It's…overwhelming."

Amy bent over and teased Celeste with her breasts.

"Oh God," Celeste uttered, then caught Amy's left nipple, and sucking it into her mouth, thrust her hips fast.

"Celeste," Amy said, trying not to laugh. "Try not to peak before the show starts."

Celeste stopped sucking and pulled her mouth away. She looked at Amy, her color deepened. "Okay." She inhaled deeply and, reaching up, captured Amy's right nipple in her mouth.

Adoring the way that Celeste sucked her breast, Amy started to grind. She smiled when Celeste let go of her nipple, her breathing too rapid and shallow to continue.

Amy cupped Celeste's breasts.

Raising her head, Celeste looked at Amy. Eyes intent, she gripped Amy's hips and flipped her over.

Amy gasped in surprise.

Resting her weight fully on Amy, Celeste hunched her hips and slid deeply inside her.

Feeling an intense contraction, Amy cried out.

Groaning, Celeste pumped her hips.

Completely filled, Amy looked up at the beautiful, sexy, sultry woman above her, and feeling her breasts press into her with each thrust, moaned.

Looking at Amy, Celeste swallowed then whispered, "I want you so much." She pressed her head into Amy's neck and muffled, "So, so much."

"Oh God," Amy whispered. She spread her legs wide then hooked her ankles around Celeste's thighs. The grinding rhythm Celeste took up and the deep penetration was something Amy was unused to. "Oh, Celeste," she said in a half sob. "Don't stop."

Sweat formed between them. Amy cried out when Celeste drilled down, her pace increasing deeper, faster.

"Yes," Amy hissed. Her orgasm building, her head falling back, she began to shake. Arching, her nails digging deep into Celeste's flesh, Amy came.

Celeste groaned. Her crotch and stomach soaked with Amy's juice, wildness overtook her. Sliding against the hot, slick sweat between them, she thrust into Amy as her own orgasm climbed. The friction from the base of the dildo and the excitement of being inside the blonde was more than she could ever have imagined. A deep guttural animal cry broke free from her lips as she came.

Pressing into Amy, Celeste's body convulsed. Breathing hard, she slowly climbed down, twitching involuntarily as the last of her orgasm left her. Exhausted, she buried her face in Amy's neck and whispered, "I'm glad you trusted me."

Amy swallowed, then muttered, "It just seems to get better and better."

Celeste started to withdraw, but Amy wrapped her arms around her. "Stay."

Celeste looked at her questioningly.

"It's comfortable," Amy reassured and held her tightly. "Stay. I'll tell you when it's not."

Celeste felt a bittersweet void fill her. This weekend marked the end; their time was up. Resting her full weight on Amy she stared into her turquoise-blue eyes. All she wanted to do was tell her that she was in her blood, a part of her. She wanted to hold on to her, stay connected, stay in her warmth. Stay inside. But the choice wasn't hers. Amy, she knew, regardless of what happened between them, intended to let her go.

Celeste looked at Amy and took a deep breath. Tears spilled from her eyes. "Amy," her voice broke, "I—"

"You're making a habit of this," Amy said teasingly. Leaning up, she gently caught all of Celeste's tears before kissing her fully on the mouth.

Celeste pulled her mouth away. "I need you to know..." she looked at Amy through wet lashes, "...I love you."

Without breaking eye contact, Amy cupped Celeste's cheeks and stroked them. Eyes wide and tears brimming, she exhaled then buried her head into Celeste's shoulder and sobbed.

Cradling Amy as she wept, Celeste stroked her hair. Completely disarmed by Amy's loss of control, she shifted on to her side and pulled Amy with her. Wrapping her arms around her, she held her tight.

Tears spilling over, Celeste closed her eyes, finally accepting that it was over.

Chapter 39

Amy woke and smiled when she registered that she was in Celeste's arms. Slipping away, she carefully reached out to the bedside cabinet for a drink of water. She looked at the bedside clock; it was just after eleven in the morning. Feeling languid, she stretched out carefully, delighted that she had slept so well and so long.

Amy smiled when her stomach quietly grumbled. She thought that she would make pancakes this morning—pancakes with syrup, sweet and filling. She turned around to face Celeste and, because she was lightly snoring, pinched her nose until she stopped. She then ran a hand down the length of her, enjoying touching her as she slept.

Moving down the bed, Amy smiled. Although hungry, she had no intention of rushing out of bed. She put her hand on Celeste's hip and placed her chin on it, then carefully ran her other hand up and over Celeste's breast. She slid her finger over her nipple and rubbed it lightly until erect.

Idly, Amy stroked Celeste and thought about the night before. After they had made love, wanting to prolong the night, they bathed together, then made love until exhaustion overtook them.

Listening to Celeste breathe, Amy circled her belly button with her finger then followed the outline of her tattoo. Breathing in the soft scent of her body, Amy's artistic eye followed the tattoo's intricacy. She drew a finger along the detail and wondered why Celeste had gotten the tattoo, and if she had gotten it in some exotic place. She thought about how Celeste's life was so much of an unknown to her. Leaning in, she listened to the steady heartbeat and acknowledged that in all her life she had never felt this right.

Amy's face tightened when she recalled the moment, last night, when Celeste said that she loved her. That moment was exceptionally painful. She was left with no choice but to face the absolute truth and dismiss it at the same time. It had taken every bit of self-control not to tell Celeste the same. Instead, she sobbed in her arms, wanting to tell her but knowing she couldn't.

It was impossible. Somehow, Amy forced all the emotions circling inside down deep. This, she reconciled, was what they had agreed on. This, she acknowledged, was the end.

Not wanting to think about it, Amy grinned when Celeste opened her eyes slowly and smiled at her.

"Morning gorgeous," Amy whispered.

"Morning," Celeste replied. Pulling Amy into her arms she kissed her.

Amy welcomed the long, luxurious kiss. Eventually, she pulled back and smiled. "Tell me about your tattoo."

Celeste arched an eyebrow in surprise.

"I like its intricacy and the circular design. Where did you get it?"

About to answer, Celeste was interrupted. "Did you get it in some tribal village?" Amy said, touching Celeste's stomach. "Maybe during one of your field assignments?" she asked. "Or was it when you were on holiday visiting some remote location?"

Celeste let out a hearty laugh.

Pulling Amy close, Celeste hugged her. "Sorry to break your illusion," she said, kissing Amy's forehead, "but I got it in a tattoo parlor in Paris."

Amy pulled back and smiled. "What? No Maori tribesman in New Zealand carefully decorating you in tribal honor?" she asked in a teasing tone. "No Amazonian women decorating you as part of their initiation ceremony?"

Amy grinned when Celeste laughed hard.

"My, my," Celeste teased. "What a vivid imagination you have, little girl." She kissed Amy on the lips. "Nope, it was none of the above," she answered playfully. "I got it on my first introduction to tequila!" Celeste grinned at Amy's disappointment. "When I was eighteen I was out with a few girlfriends and we passed a tattoo parlor. We all decided to get a tattoo." She looked at Amy. "This," she said drawing an elegant finger around the tattoo, "was agony."

Amy laughed.

Celeste winked. "I threw up. Right there in the parlor. I even managed to pass out. But," she fluttered her dark eyelashes, "the tattooist insisted on finishing the job. After all," she said, looking down at her stomach, "it was, according to him, a work of art!"

Tracing the outline of the Celtic design, Amy said approvingly, "He did a great job. In fact, I really like it." She kissed it then moving up, snuggled closer. She whispered seductively as her hands began to roam, "And do you know where else I really—"

The doorbell rang.

Amy froze. Holding her breath, her eyes widening in surprise, she looked at Celeste. They listened for further sounds. After a few minutes, the doorbell rang again. Raising her eyebrows, Celeste looked at Amy. "Are you expecting anyone?"

Amy shook her head and frowned when the doorbell rang a third time. Taking a few deep breaths, she tried to fight off her growing panic.

"You'd better answer it."

Amy nodded and rolled out of bed. Standing, she was thankful that Maggie had taken the dogs with her; otherwise, they would have barked the house down.

Throwing on her robe, Amy mumbled, "Can you get dressed." She quickly left the room. At the door, she lifted her hair and ran her fingers through it. Pulling the belt of her robe tight she braced herself, hoping that she could easily explain why Celeste was here.

Opening the door Amy drew in her breath, shocked to see two county sheriff deputies.

They flashed quick smiles and the balding male officer asked, "Mrs. Cameron? Mrs. Amy Cameron?"

Amy's stomach heaved as she answered, "Yes. Yes, I'm Amy Cameron."

She glanced over her shoulder when she heard footsteps and looked to see Celeste, fully dressed.

Denial

"I'm Officer Jenkins and this is Officer Daley." The younger, female officer said. "Can we come in, Mrs. Cameron?"

"Of course." Stepping aside, Amy allowed them entry.

Standing in the hallway the officers shuffled their feet a little. Aware that Amy was staring at them, Celeste said, "Please, follow me." Turning, she led the way.

Once the officers were seated in the lounge, Celeste sat beside Amy and across from them.

Officer Daley took a deep breath and said quietly, "Mrs. Cameron, I'm afraid we have to share some bad news with you. This morning at eight thirty, there was an accident."

Amy covered her face and whispered, "Oh my God. Something's happened to Josh."

The officer looked at Celeste before reading from his notepad. "An eighteen-wheel truck crashed into a Jeep Grand Cherokee Laredo registered to," he checked his notes, "you and Mr. Josh Cameron." He quickly finished, "I'm sorry to tell you that all the people inside the vehicle were killed instantly."

Instinctively, Celeste pulled Amy closer to her and placed her arm protectively around her shoulders.

Amy dropped her hands from her face and, stared dumbfounded at the male officer before whispering, "No." Shaking her head incredulously, eyes wide, she looked at Celeste. "No. Tell him no way, Celeste. Tell him that those Jeeps are designed to withstand all sorts of things," she pleaded. "Tell him, Celeste. Tell him that Jeep has air bags, side impact bars, rollover resistance. It has everything."

Celeste felt Amy's body start to shake, fully aware that adrenaline had kicked in and was now pumping through it.

Amy's hands thumped down on the sofa and standing, she stared at the officers. "Tell them," she said hoarsely. "Tell them now, Celeste."

Celeste looked up at Amy, wanting desperately to comfort her, but whatever safety features the Jeep had it would have had no resistance to a truck that size hitting it.

Opening her mouth to offer comfort, Celeste closed it when Amy rushed to Officer Daley and, falling to her knees grasped his hand with both of hers. Imploringly, she asked, "Who? Who has been killed?"

With old eyes, Officer Daley looked down at Amy.

Amy repeated, "Tell me! Who? Who has been killed?"

Looking at Amy, pain mixed with deep sympathy crossed his face. He sighed and shook his head. Slowly, he lifted his notebook and read from it. "The driver of the vehicle, Margaret Forsythe, and the passengers, Sean MacDonald, Christopher, and Ryan Cameron."

Amy gaped at him and watched his mouth move in slow motion. His voice seemed distorted and extraordinarily loud. Her hands flew to her ears. She tried to cover them to block out the sound, but she couldn't. Instead, she was forced to listen in horror as his voice boomed out names that were anonymous to him; but to her, those names were the lifeblood that pumped through her veins, the very reason for her existence.

When his mouth closed, the whole world crashed in on Amy. Sounds and smells surrounded her. Everything seemed to pulse with frightening clarity.

Amy squeezed her eyes shut, and doubling over, gasped in agony when an unseen fist punched through her chest and ripped her heart out.

When she fell forward, Celeste shot up and moved quickly. Dropping to her knees, she wrapped her arms around Amy.

Surprised at the contact, Amy's eyes flew open. Straightening, she looked down at her chest expecting to see a gaping hole, but to her surprise there was nothing. For a fraction of a second, calm steeled her spine. Her mouth opened and a disembodied voice asked, "How? How did it happen?"

Officer Daley's voice full of remorse, said gently, "The Jeep was hit as it crossed an intersection. "The truck was speeding, went through a stop sign and," he paused, "hit the Jeep." He cleared his throat. "The driver allegedly was using a cell phone at the time and claims that he didn't see the sign."

Reaching out he squeezed Amy's shoulder. "I'm so sorry, Mrs. Cameron."

Denial

A surge of panic coursed through Amy. She put her hand to her mouth, sure that she was going to vomit.

Vaguely aware of Celeste holding her tightly, Amy removed her hand and looked up at the officer. Needing absolute verification, she asked, as her body shook violently, "Are you sure they've been...killed?" She pushed forcibly out of Celeste's arms, stood shakily, and added desperately, "They might not have been in the Jeep. It could have been stolen." She looked pleadingly at the officers. "How do you know for sure?" Her voice cracked. "How do you know they were in that Jeep?"

Officer Jenkins stood. Shaking and desperately trying to fight back tears, she approached Amy. "Mrs. Cameron, I think you should sit down."

Amy grasped the younger woman's arms and, shaking her firmly, said, "How do you know? How can you be sure?"

Officer Daley looked at Celeste and both moved toward Amy. Gently they removed her grip from the young woman. Leading Amy to the sofa, Celeste sat next to her and pulled her tightly to her.

Amy looked at the officers and croaked, "How can you be sure?"

Officer Daley sighed and a look of weariness crossed his eyes and then sympathy filled them, as if knowing that what he said next was about to destroy her world.

"Miss Forsythe had photo identification of herself and the two..." he hesitated then cleared his throat, "the two boys. The other passenger, Mr. MacDonald, also carried identification." He hesitated again and looked to Celeste before saying as gently as the words would allow, "But, obviously, we still require formal identification."

Amy looked at the strangers and wanted to scream but she only managed to croak, "No. No. *No!*" Then an animal sound of pain and loss echoed around the room. Amy was so startled it took a moment for her to realize that the sound was coming from her own throat.

Celeste grasped her tightly. "Amy," she said, her voice carrying a note of despair. "Amy," she repeated.

This can't be happening, Amy thought in horror. "No," she cried out in agony. They can't be dead she tried to shout. They can't have been killed. She tried to ask Celeste why, but all the words lodged in her throat and blackness enveloped her.

Chapter 40

Amy listened to the sound of dirt falling on the boxes, the wooden boxes that her whole life was buried in. She was aware of Josh holding her, grasping her arms and leaning her against him. She wanted to laugh and tell him that it wasn't her that needed protecting. Didn't he know? Didn't he know she had sold him out? Sold out the people who mattered?

Amy looked from the open grave and watched the weeping faces standing over it. She listened with indifference to the priest conclude his graveside prayer. The reassuring smile she gave the mourners when their hands grasped for hers never once reached her eyes.

It wasn't any surprise to Amy that Celeste wasn't one of them. Since the accident, she had ignored the one presence that made the harsh unremitting reality of her world acute. Her guilt would not allow her to recognize Celeste, other than through perfunctory courtesy. But even here, even now, she sensed her. Somehow, without looking, she knew exactly where she was and she couldn't stand it.

Amy smiled at the priest when he held her hand and offered words of comfort. She was Presbyterian, more by birthright than practice, but Josh was Catholic. Not practicing, but he wanted a Catholic burial, and who was she to refuse him? She just wanted it over. He wanted a wake; she wanted to die. He wanted to be there for her; she wanted to be left alone.

To the outside world Amy knew she appeared too still, too detached, but inside she raged—a rage that was nothing like when her father died. This rage was incomprehensible, an inferno burning inside her.

Another mourner grasped her hand and Amy wondered why none of her anger showed. Why the feeling of wanting to slice her life away, rip it into shreds, burn it, and stomp on it didn't show through. She smiled unseeing as the last mourner dropped her hand and moved away.

Josh wrapped his arms around her. Aware of his increasing concern, Amy put her head on his shoulder. He placed his chin on her head and rubbed her back. Since the accident she had barely shown any signs of grief.

Amy knew that it wasn't only her behavior that was frightening Josh, but the distance she was putting between them. Unlike Josh, she had cried little. Not because she hadn't wanted to, but because she couldn't. Not yet. Not until everything was over she told herself.

As Josh hugged her tightly Amy was aware that even at his most vulnerable, he was trying to be strong for her. He was in hell. His world, like hers, was shattered. Encased in his arms she felt nothing for him, other than a searing sense of disloyalty.

"You gave a wonderful reading," Josh whispered.

In a desperate bid to force her to communicate her feelings, Josh had asked her to say something at the mass, give a reading. At first Amy was surprised, although she didn't show it because she had stopped showing anything. The idea of standing up in front of people and paying homage was something she would never have considered, but from the moment Josh mentioned it her mind fixated on it. The dramatist in Maggie would have loved nothing more than a heartfelt eulogy, but the true reason was that Amy would be able to express her love. It would allow her to talk about her family as if they were still here. Give her that chance to engage with them, explore them, and feel them around her without question.

This morning Amy had stood in front of a sea of familiar faces and opened a well-thumbed book of poetry that Maggie had loved since a teenager. She quoted a verse that Maggie often used then spoke words that she hadn't written or rehearsed.

Amy didn't speak for Josh, she couldn't; her time with Celeste had robbed her of that right. She could only speak of what had been hers, outright and without compromise. She could only speak about her love for Maggie, her children and her brief time with Sean.

Denial

In a strong voice, Amy regaled their lives and, to her surprise, her words brought the mourners, weeping helplessly and hopelessly, to their knees.

When she finished Amy briefly closed her eyes. A surprise emotion swept through her, a feeling of pride. She had given Maggie and her children their due. When she closed the book she caressed the cover for a moment, acknowledging that she was also closing the book on her life.

Enough, Amy decided at that moment, was enough.

Chapter 41

On duty at the hospital Celeste was paged to a small waiting room reserved for patients' families. Looking through the window she saw Josh crumpled in a chair. Outside the door, she turned to the nurse. "Thank you, Christine." She touched her arm. "It's good that you brought him here."

"No problem, Celeste," Christine replied. She looked through the window. "He's in pretty bad shape. I hope everything's okay."

Celeste nodded and opened the door.

Josh stood and rushed to her. He grabbed her in a bone-crushing hug.

"Josh, what is it?" Celeste asked, hugging him back.

"She's gone," he replied, his voice catching.

"Amy?"

Josh nodded and let her go.

"Where?"

He ran a hand through his tousled hair. "She's gone."

"Where?" Celeste repeated. Frowning, she cleared her throat to loosen the tremor that was building there. "Where has she gone?"

"She's gone," Josh said, throwing out his arms. "She's taken her passport." He staggered to a chair. "She's gone." He slumped into it and looked at her disbelievingly. "There was only a note, telling me it was over."

Celeste's heart started to pound. "Josh," she said, approaching him. "Maybe, she's just taken some time out."

"Fuck, Celeste!" Josh yelled, wringing his hands. "You've seen her over the last few months. You know what she's been like." He smacked his fist into his hand. "I can't reach her. She won't talk to me. She can barely look at me." Defeated, he placed his head in his hands. "It's as if she can't bear to be near me."

Denial

Celeste watched her brother. She felt waves of panic come from him. "She's in shock, Josh," she said, sitting beside him.

Since the accident Amy had refused any contact with Celeste, couldn't bear to be near her. Even the rare times that they had been in the same place she would leave the moment Celeste entered. Swallowing the pain, Celeste placed a reassuring hand on her brother's arm. "It just takes time," she said, pulling him into her arms for a hug.

Josh jerked out of her arms and stood. He moved close to the large window. Rubbing his heavy stubble he stared out across the parking lot for a while. "I brought a counselor to her a few weeks ago." He thudded his head lightly against the glass. "I didn't tell her. I just had him visit the house." He closed his bleary eyes. "She insisted that he leave." He lifted his head. "She went crazy." He turned and looked at Celeste, his eyes swam with tears. "I mean, really crazy." He shook his head. "She smashed the entire kitchen up."

Josh clenched his fists then ran them over his face and through his hair. He blew out a heavy sigh. "In all the time that I've known her she's hardly raised her voice." His eyes grew wide and tears formed. "You know," he said, "I don't think I've ever seen anger like that in my life."

Josh closed his eyes and fat tears fell.

Panic coursed through Celeste. Since the accident Amy barely communicated with anyone. "Josh," she said, careful to ensure that her tone was even, "we can't lose sight of the fact that Amy might just have taken some time out. I'm sure," she said, trying to hide her uncertainty, "we'll hear from her soon enough."

Josh shook his head. "I got a call from George this morning." He looked at Celeste. "You know, Amy's boss."

Celeste nodded.

"He was upset. He told me that Amy had contacted him." Josh sighed heavily. "She told him that she didn't want the job." An incredulous look crossed his face. "She loves that job. I mean really loves it."

"Did she give him an explanation?" Celeste said. Hands trembling, she pushed them into her whites, fully aware that Amy had only just returned to work.

Josh nodded. "She told him that it wasn't what she wanted to do anymore." He looked at Celeste helplessly. "But that's all she's ever wanted to do."

Celeste looked at him in surprise. A memory of the morning of the accident flooded in. She recalled Amy slumped in her arms when she was told of the deaths. Celeste had gathered her up and held her tightly.

Over the years Celeste had seen many deaths and always without doubt the most difficult were the loss of children. That morning, she, more than anyone, understood the agonies that Amy was about to endure.

As the weeks and months passed, Celeste had tried to talk to Amy but she refused, eventually refusing to even look at her. Although she never spoke the words Celeste knew Amy was crippled with guilt, somehow believing that the deaths were recompense for their affair.

Standing Celeste said, "We'll find her."

"It's not that easy," Josh replied, shaking his head.

"C'mon, Josh," Celeste said, trying to rally him. "You're the IT guy. Surely tracking someone down in the twenty-first century has to be fairly easy," she said, frowning.

"No, you don't understand." He shook his head. "When I did my thesis, I worked for a few months with Interpol." He paused when Celeste looked confused. "It was when I lived in Scotland." Josh paused again and stared out the window.

Celeste encouraged. "And?"

Josh looked at her for a long moment, the pain evident in his eyes. "And, I helped set up an Internet-based tool for missing and unidentified people to make it easier for investigators and forensics to cross-reference. He snorted slightly. "It was at the beginning of our relationship." He looked at Celeste, his tired eyes wide. "I wanted to impress her. I told her everything." He slapped a hand on his forehead then rapped his knuckles on either

Denial

side of his head. "I can't believe I told her all the different ways a person can manufacture their own disappearance."

Celeste felt her heart spasm. Unable to believe what Josh was saying she asked, "What are you telling me?"

Frustration marked Josh's face. "I'm saying that I shared the whole fucking thing with her." He paced the room. "God, she knows better than anyone how easy it is to disappear!"

"But surely we can put a," Celeste searched for the word, "trace on her?"

"Do you know how many people go missing each year in the States alone, Celeste?" Josh said, throwing his hands in the air. "Tens of thousands, and that's people with no resources and no inside knowledge."

Celeste shook her head. "But surely we can contact someone? Do something?"

"It's not that easy," Josh said. He stopped in front of her. "I contacted the sheriff's office and missing persons. They did everything by the book, but as far as they are concerned she's a grown woman with no criminal record, who, given the circumstances, has probably gone back to her native country." He hugged himself. "It's been noted and filed."

"There must be something we can do. Don't you have any contacts at Interpol?"

Josh shook his head. "Celeste, I was an intern. I didn't even have clearance to get into Interpol. I worked for a third-party company developing the software. I was a small cog in a big wheel."

"Don't you have even one contact from then?" Celeste asked, her whole body trembling now.

Josh shook his head. "The company I worked for went bust."

Celeste looked at him in disbelief.

"It's not unusual for software companies to go bust."

"There's no one you can contact?" Celeste asked incredulously.

Josh slumped in the chair. His palms covered his face. "Like I said, I was an intern."

"What about you?" he asked. "What about MSF? Can they find missing people?"

Celeste shook her head slowly. "It's not what they do."

Josh dropped his hands and sat up. Shoulders slumped, he asked, "What am I going to do, Celeste?"

Celeste stared at Josh, suddenly aware that they were helpless to do anything.

"What if she never comes back," he asked then started to cry. "What if I never see her again?"

Chapter 42

Four years later...

Celeste leaned against the wall, unable to believe her eyes. Watching Amy leave the hospital she studied her closely. *God, she looks so thin and so pale.*

Celeste thought back to the way that Amy completely shut down after the boys' and Maggie's deaths. Within months she had cleared out her own personal accounts, leaving in her wake a brief note addressed to Josh explaining that their marriage was over. Four years ago, she simply had disappeared.

Celeste watched Amy leave the hospital entrance in her crisp blue nurse's uniform and stand for a moment to put a sweater on. She looked at her watch. It was after six. Amy had just finished her shift. Looking up into the early evening, clear July sky, Celeste briefly wondered why Amy needed a sweater; there was still heat in the sun.

Watching Amy, she remembered when she disappeared. Josh had informed his bewildered family that Amy's father had left her money. With that, he said, it would have been relatively easy for her to organize her own disappearance. For years, the Cameron family desperately tried to make contact with Amy, checking with all sorts of agencies in the hope of tracking her down. Nothing worked. They had never found her, until now.

Celeste's heart leapt into her mouth when Amy came closer. She noted her appearance. Her hair was tied back in a ponytail but needed tidying. Amy's hair had always looked magnificent, but, as she approached, Celeste noticed how lackluster it was. Amy, she realized, looked washed out.

A few weeks ago Irene had contacted Celeste to let her know that she had a permanent address for Amy. Irene had, over the last four years, occasionally received short letters from Amy, letting her know she was okay. It hadn't been long into Amy's disappearance before they stopped trying to trace her correspondence. It only ever led to a dead-end.

When Irene received a recent letter she immediately called Celeste to discuss what they were going to do. It never ceased to surprise her, that over the years, Irene had never judged or doubted Celeste's feelings for her daughter. Celeste reasoned it was because Irene had been in a similar situation once.

With the permanent address came a clear warning that Irene was not to pass the address on to anyone. If she did, Amy said she would relocate and all future contact would be broken off permanently. Regardless of the warning there was no doubt in Irene's mind that contact needed to be made, and that Celeste would be the one to make it.

Celeste stiffened as Amy walked swiftly in her direction. She still couldn't quite believe that Amy had trained to be a nurse, obviously hoping in some way to follow in Maggie's footsteps. She watched with disbelief when Amy was stopped by a fellow nurse, who offered her a cigarette and Amy accepted. The blonde had never smoked in her life. After a few moments, the two nurses parted, and stubbing her cigarette out, Amy walked toward Celeste.

Celeste almost let her walk past, suddenly worried about Amy's reaction to seeing her. But she needed this. She needed to make contact. She hadn't come this far and waited for so long to let it go.

Reaching out, Celeste placed her hand on Amy's arm and said, "Hello, Amy."

Amy started. She looked at the hand holding her arm and then the face. For a moment, it was clear she had no idea who Celeste was. Then she whispered, "Celeste?"

Celeste smiled and nodded. "Amy," she said with relief. "It's wonderful to see you."

Amy's jaw dropped open. "What are you doing here?" she asked, frowning in evident confusion.

What else? Celeste wanted to say, but to find you!

Not wanting to scare Amy, Celeste tried to be nonchalant. "I'm on vacation," she offered. "I'm traveling through. Irene gave me your contact details, and I thought it would be nice to see you." Celeste dropped her hand when Amy stiffened. "Why don't we find a café," she said gently. "It would be nice to catch up."

In evident shock, Amy nodded mutely.

Completely disarmed at seeing Celeste, Amy walked with her down the street in awkward silence. She was surprised and seriously annoyed that her mother had given Celeste her details despite clearly being told her not to pass them on to anyone. Her inner voice reminded her that she should have kept things as they were. It told her that she should have followed her instinct not to send Irene her permanent address.

At the café, Celeste suggested that Amy take a seat while she ordered coffee. Amy took a table close by and watched Celeste walk to the counter unable to believe that she was here, in Glasgow.

Looking around, Amy watched people openly appraise Celeste. She could see that, even in jeans and a simple black V-neck sweater, she still managed to stand out in the crowd. Celeste, Amy observed, was tanned and her hair was down. She grudgingly admitted that Celeste was as beautiful as ever.

Amy knew she looked bedraggled. Today was such a busy day that she hadn't had time to stop to even fix her hair. She was tired and knew she looked it. All those extra shifts, covering for the holiday period, had taken their toll. She was knackered, but she didn't mind not going on vacation. She didn't feel comfortable sitting out in the sun, particularly now with her scars.

Unclasping her hair, Amy pulled it tight then re-clasped it and felt slightly more respectable.

Waiting for Celeste, Amy looked at her hands and realized how pale they were; she could easily see blue veins. She was thankful that the scars on her hands were more translucent now.

As Celeste approached, Amy put her pale, scarred hands in her lap.

Celeste placed the tray on the table. She had bought a black coffee for her and a white coffee for Amy and two muffins—a blueberry and a chocolate one.

The blueberry was Amy's favorite and as Celeste slid the coffee and blueberry muffin over to her, her stomach rumbled. She hadn't eaten anything since breakfast.

Thanking Celeste, Amy took a sip from her coffee before biting into her muffin. She chewed slowly, wondering what to say. She was still in shock; seeing Celeste was just so unexpected.

The café was a favorite for many of the nursing staff when they clocked off work. Neil and Sandra, two of Amy's colleagues, entered. Neil looked around and catching sight of Amy quickly approached and asked if he could join them.

Amy opened her mouth to answer just as Neil plunked himself next to Celeste. He proceeded to tell Amy about his day. Joining them with two coffees, Sandra sat next to Amy.

Amy introduced her colleagues.

Neil focused completely on Celeste, asking where she came from and what she did then followed her answers with a barrage of questions.

After answering several questions, Celeste raised her eyebrows and looked to Amy for help.

Usually Amy enjoyed Neil's company, and since they had finished nursing college together he had become a good friend, but there was no denying he was incredibly vain. He obsessed about his body-builder's physique and worked out more than necessary. She liked him well enough because, when he wasn't obsessing about his looks, he was good fun.

Amused, Amy and Sandra watched Celeste squirm as Neil made his moves. Amy could tell he was completely bowled over by Celeste and was working hard to capture her interest. To her further amusement, within minutes, he produced every contactable number and address in the known universe, just in case Celeste needed a tour of city.

Sandra eventually interrupted. "Are you old friends?"

Blushing, Amy glanced at Celeste before answering, "Yes. You could say that."

Neil immediately asked, "How did you two meet?"

There was an awkward silence. Amy didn't want to go into that part of her past.

Neil looked at Celeste. "She's always been so mysterious about her past," he said, sounding miffed.

Celeste immediately responded, "Amy used to…date my brother."

Neil looked at Amy and grunted. "Huh," he said. "So you're not a lezzie after all!"

Amy almost choked on her muffin.

Shocked silence fell across the table. Neil looked at Sandra, then Amy. "No offense, Amy."

Wiping the crumbs from her mouth, Amy blushed.

Sandra visibly cringed.

Neil turned to Celeste. "You know," he said, waving a finger between Sandra and himself. "We've known Amy for a couple of years, but she's never been out on a date." He gazed at Amy as if she was an alien. *"Never!"* he said. He looked at Sandra. "Isn't that right?"

Flabbergasted, Sandra's mouth hung open.

Neil looked at Amy and said carefully, "You don't…bat for the other side, do you?"

Sandra stood up. "Neil," she said, her voice rising alarmingly. "The only bat you'll be getting is across that big mouth of yours if you keep this crap up." Given her small demeanor, at just over five foot, with surprising strength she hauled Neil off the seat.

Neil lurched up.

"My apologies Celeste, but we'd better get going," Sandra said. "It's closing time at the zoo. So, I better hurry up and get him home."

Dragging Neil out, Sandra called, "See you tomorrow Amy, and, Celeste, nice meeting you. Hope you have a good time while you're here." She stopped at the door and asked Neil, "Want to grunt your goodbyes?"

Neil shouted, "Call me," to Celeste as Sandra pushed him out of the café door.

Amused, Amy and Celeste watched through the window as she gave Neil a dressing down.

Amy looked at Celeste and burst out laughing.

Celeste laughed with Amy, relieved that Neil the Neanderthal had served one good purpose—he had broken the ice between them.

For the next hour they chatted, avoiding any intimate conversation. Amy talked about nursing and some of her patients, and Celeste talked about being a doctor. Eventually the conversation lulled.

Celeste decided to tell Amy that she wasn't here alone, that she had brought her two adopted children with her. Amy looked at her in surprise. Celeste produced some photographs and explained. "A few years ago I adopted Daniel."

Amy looked at the photographs. "I remember your friend Susan talking about him. Wasn't he the wee boy that you took to in Sierra Leone?"

Surprised that Amy remembered, Celeste nodded. "Daniel's mother died of AIDS and they were orphaned."

There was a long moment of silence then Amy asked, "Why?"

Celeste wasn't sure if Amy was asking why she adopted or why she hadn't mentioned this during their time together. She decided to go for the first and easiest explanation.

"The options for kids in that kind of environment are grim, and since they only had elderly grandparents as supporting family I made the decision to adopt them, with their grandparents blessing, of course."

Celeste showed Amy more photographs and explained carefully that she hadn't told anyone at the time because the adoption process was extremely long with no guarantees.

Amy showed no emotion, but asked, "What are the children like?"

Painfully aware of Amy's loss and that she needed to tread carefully, Celeste cautiously told Amy about them.

Denial

When she stopped talking, Celeste watched Amy study the photographs. Swallowing, she thought, I have missed you so much.

Amy put the photographs down. She looked at her watch and said, in surprise, "It's nine o'clock."

Worried that Amy wanted to leave, Celeste asked, "Would you like to meet them?"

Amy picked up a photograph, one with Celeste and the children. She looked at it for a long moment. Celeste watched conflict cross her face. "Just once, Amy," she said tenderly. "Alex is here and he would love to see you."

Amy's face softened. "How is he?"

"Oh, he's great. The kids love him, and he's been in a relationship for a few years now. He's here with his partner, Colin."

Celeste watched curiosity flit through Amy's eyes.

Amy looked at her for a long moment. "Okay," she replied finally.

Delighted, Celeste let out the breath she hadn't realized she'd been holding. They both agreed that she would visit the following day at noon. After they parted, Celeste spent a restless night wondering if she would ever see Amy again.

Chapter 43

After her first visit to meet the children, Amy found it hard to resist them, particularly the little girl, Naomi, whom she got on with immediately. Daniel, although slightly hesitant, was as warm as Naomi.

When Celeste asked her to meet the children that night in the café, Amy had thought, No, it ends here. But when she looked at Celeste's tense face the will to refuse disappeared. Just this once, she had thought. Surely, that can't do any harm.

Amy admired Celeste for taking on such a big responsibility and she couldn't hide her curiosity about the children, and once she discovered that Alex was here, she knew she just had to see him.

As it turned out, one visit stretched into several as Amy found the children irresistible. After her training, Amy had chosen to work in a children's ward, and although she had grown attached to many of the children, being around healthy, boisterous kids was a good antidote to some of stresses of dealing with sick children.

Amy also liked Alex's boyfriend, Colin. He was taller than Alex, six-foot-four with dark, wavy hair. He was a sports teacher with a crooked nose from playing sports. Amy was surprised by how extremely funny and warm he was, and quite unintentionally took his good humor to heart, finding his and Alex's company extremely enjoyable.

Amy had developed a strong relationship with Alex, Colin, and the children over the last three weeks, but kept Celeste at a distance. This weekend, though, the children had asked her to go camping with them to Loch Lomond.

†

Denial

"The burgers will be ready soon," Alex shouted to Colin who wanted to know when they would eat. Attending the barbecue, Alex was in the middle of preparing lunch. "Just get on with your job and get the tents up."

It was a hot day and Amy was busy trying to get a wriggling Naomi into a swimsuit. Succeeding, she picked her up and hugged her. Celeste, standing beside them, teased Naomi with ice cream.

Alex watched them for a few moments then looked around him. He had fallen in love with Scotland. He loved the rugged landscape and the warmth of the people. Somehow, on their trip to this loch, he thought they would see Nessie, but Amy told him that Nessie resided in Loch Ness, in Inverness, more than an hour and a bit drive away.

Buttering the buns, Alex smiled. He liked the way Amy said an hour and a bit, instead of the precise time. In fact, he liked the whole Scottish way of doing things, which tended to be relaxed and informal. But, he thought, opening a carton of orange juice, there seemed to be a plethora of lochs in Scotland. Why he had got it into his head there was only one, he didn't know.

Alex's reverie was broken when he heard a couple of jet boats whiz by. He growled. He hated those things with a passion. They were noisy, pollutants to the natural habitat, and with their spinning rotors, chopped up anything that came within reach. He continued to lightly growl until they disappeared, leaving them to the quite solitude of the small beach they had found.

Alex smiled when Celeste splodged Naomi's nose with ice cream and laughed when Naomi fell into a fit of giggles. He laughed even harder when Celeste did the same to Amy's nose. The look of shock on Amy's face sent Naomi into further kinks of laughter.

Dodging Amy's playful swipe, Celeste moved out of the way then innocently licked her ice cream.

Alex's heart twisted, Celeste and Amy looked so natural, so right together. He smiled thinking about how caught up Colin had become with the whole situation. Although Colin was aware of Celeste and Amy's history, over the years he had tried to encourage Celeste to date. No matter how often Alex explained the situation, Colin just volleyed with a simple explanation that he didn't like her being on her own. Since meeting Amy and seeing how much they fit together, Colin was now desperate for a happy ending. He wanted them together.

"I'm starved. When are the burgers going to be ready?"

Alex looked at Colin. "Almost done, sweetie," he replied lovingly.

"God, Amy is really attractive, isn't she?" Colin said. "The more I get to know her, the more attractive she's becoming."

Alex smiled. He looked over at Amy and noted the changes in her. Since meeting up a few weeks ago, her mood seemed much lighter and she laughed more often. She also looked healthier. There was color to her face. Her hair seemed more luscious. Her natural beauty was shining through.

"Did you see the look on her face when Naomi told her that we were going camping?"

Alex nodded and said quietly, "Her kids were killed on a camping trip."

"I know that!" Colin replied. "I thought she was going to pass out. She almost jumped at the offer to come when Celeste asked her."

Alex picked up the orange juice. It was very clear to him that Amy was a tortured soul. He poured juice into plastic cups.

"They look so right together, don't they?"

Alex nodded. When Celeste told him she had taken a leave of absence and would he and Colin like to go with her to Europe, he had been keen—until she told him the true reason. He had tried to talk her out of it, thinking there was no way that Amy would want to see them. Colin, the eternal romantic, agreed with Celeste and here they were.

To Alex's surprise and great pleasure, they seemed to be making inroads with Amy. Colin and the children had made her promise to quit smoking, and because she doted on the children, it had been over a week since her last cigarette.

Alex felt a sudden twinge of disquiet. Those inroads though, so far, hadn't extended to Celeste. For the last few weeks, Amy

Denial

had given little attention to Celeste. What he could do about it, he didn't know. He did know that Amy had been to hell and back and, at this moment in time, he was just glad that she was accepting their company.

"Yes," Alex responded, coming out of his reverie. "They do look right together." Filling a few buns with burgers he tried to hide his disquiet. "They look every inch the happy family."

"Talking about family, and not that I know Amy," Colin said, reaching for a bun. "But don't you think it's weird that she's never asked about Celeste's family. I mean she knows that Josh is in a relationship, yet she doesn't seem even a little curious about it." Biting into the bun and chewing, he added with a mouth full of food, "She must see that Celeste is completely and utterly crazy about her?"

Alex frowned. He was also concerned that Amy was avoiding any intimate conversation. Over the weeks he had noticed that she never mentioned Maggie or the twins, or asked about the Cameron family. Never once had she asked about Josh or his new life. Josh and his partner of three years had an eighteen-month-old baby girl with one on the way.

The first time that Naomi mentioned Uncle Josh, Denise, and the baby, Alex's mouth gaped open but Amy didn't react. From then on, any time Naomi or Daniel mentioned them Amy never once queried.

Alex looked at his partner. "Colin, she knows full well about Josh from Irene, I'm sure. She certainly knows how Celeste feels, but it's obvious she's not ready to deal with anything yet. *And,"* he said seriously, "we can't push her. When she's ready to talk, she will." Colin opened his mouth, but Alex gave him a look. "She'll talk when she's ready." He stuffed another bun into Colin's hand. "Okay?"

"Okay," Colin replied as he looked at Alex's frowning face. "I know you're right." Colin said, adding ketchup to his burger. "Maybe when we're in Greece next week, she'll open up."

Colin had never been outside of the States and next week, as part of their two-month trip, they were going to Greece to sail the Ionian Sea. Amy had refused to come with them. So, Colin took the indirect route and coached the children. Fortunately, Alex thought as he smiled to himself, the little gremlins wore her down until she agreed.

Serving up lunch, Alex hoped the sailing trip would relax Amy enough to let down her guard with Celeste. He smiled at his partner. "Colin, she's been gone for a long time and we don't know much about it. I don't think it's going to be the happy ending that you think it is."

"Look, I'm an optimistic guy."

"You're also someone who doesn't understand what Amy's been through." He looked at Colin. "Don't push it."

Colin winked at Alex before biting into his second burger.

†

Normally vacation time from the hospital required at least a few weeks' notice, but since she had never taken any time off and Sandra was her Staff Nurse, Amy arranged leave for the sailing trip easily.

On Saturday, they flew to Corfu and set sail in the afternoon. The Jeanneau yacht Celeste had chartered was luxurious.

From the first day, Amy wore long sleeve shirts and linen trousers. She hoped that everyone would think it was because she was so pale and unused to the intense heat of the sun. On the second day, Colin snapped her out of her absorption of watching Celeste plot the next day's course on the chart. "Why aren't you sunbathing?" he asked, sitting next to her.

Amy hesitated. When they had been at Loch Lomond for the weekend she had covered up there too, but the weather hadn't been warm enough to raise concern. Now, the sun was searing and it was obviously too hot for the clothes she was wearing. Amy hadn't known how to address the reason and was surprised that she hadn't explained earlier. She hadn't expected to be as self-conscious as she was. Knowing that Celeste was close by and would hear, she took a deep breath. "A few years ago, I was in a fire. I was burned."

Denial

Celeste's head flew up at the word burned. Fear flitted across her eyes and her stomach clenched. She felt sick at the thought of Amy being hurt. She held her breath and listened. That day in the café, she had seen scars on Amy's hand, but they were just a few and didn't seem serious.

Celeste put down her charts and approached Amy. "Show me."

Amy hesitated. "I—"

She touched Amy's cheek. "Show me, please."

Self-consciously, Amy unbuttoned her shirt and dropped it.

Celeste caught her breath and Colin covered his mouth, stifling a gasp. The shirt hung around Amy's waist with only a bra to cover her. Celeste could see that the scarring was bad. It was mostly based on her right side and ran from her shoulder down her side, covering part of her chest and stomach, only stopping at her hip. Celeste whispered, "Turn around."

Amy did as she requested.

Her back, across its entire length, was scarred. Some parts were thick with white, gnarled skin. Celeste asked quietly, sadly, "Your legs?"

Amy turned back to face them. "Not touched in the fire, but my thighs are marked from skin grafts."

Celeste placed her hand on Amy's hip. "What happened?"

"Wrong place." Amy pulled her shirt up. "Wrong time."

"Tell me."

Amy looked at Celeste. "I stayed at a hostel in the outback of Australia," she said, buttoning her shirt. "The building was mostly wood and caught fire. It was an accident waiting to happen; the place was poorly built. I only intended to stay there a few days." She smiled faintly. "A few travelers were moving on, so there was a farewell night with lots of cocktails."

Amy folded her arms protectively. "I don't really remember much other than it was some crazy themed night and someone gave me a Hawaiian-style shirt to wear." She raised her eyebrows. "The cocktails were potent and I got drunk pretty quickly, then fell asleep."

"The shirt, I take it," Colin asked, "was highly flammable?"

Amy nodded.

"How did you get away?"

"It was shouting that woke me up. When I tried to escape, my shirt caught fire. It wasn't fully buttoned," she reported, matter-of-factly. "And I managed to get some of it off." She pointed to her side. "Most of the damage was on my side and my back."

Celeste looked at Amy and swallowed hard. All that pain, she thought. Lifting her hand she ran her fingers lightly from Amy's shoulder down to her hip, slowly feeling the contours of the scar tissue through the shirt. She looked into Amy's eyes and whispered, "I'm sorry, Amy. I'm sorry I wasn't there for you."

Pulling away, Amy frowned and said, rather self-consciously, "Don't be silly. There was nothing anyone could have done. It was an accident." She looked away. "Like so many things in life."

Reaching out, Colin pulled Amy into him for a hug.

A wave of jealousy washed over Celeste. So*meday, I will be there for you. Someday, I will be able to hold you in my arms and comfort you.* Watching them, Celeste only hoped that the day would come soon.

†

A week into the vacation they arrived in Paxos, the smallest of the Ionian Islands located just south of Corfu, where they spent the day swimming and snorkeling. Eventually, they anchored at the picturesque Port of Gios and stopped at a *taverna* for a lengthy evening meal. After a few hours they returned to the yacht and settled the children in their berths before settling themselves for the rest of the evening.

Amy sipped her orange juice as Colin dealt the cards for poker. "Why don't you drink alcohol?" Colin asked, picking up his glass of Ouzo and lemon.

Amy looked up. From experience she knew that Ouzo was potent, especially on top of other alcohol. Colin had drunk quite a lot of wine at dinner. Raising her eyebrows, she realized that

Colin was now on his third glass. She smiled at him, certain that both Celeste and Alex were also desperate to find out about the last four years.

Feeling the tension build Amy decided to be open. "When I left Sarasota everything, probably for the next year, was and still is a blur." She pointed to Colin's glass as the reason why. She didn't tell them how seriously she hadn't cared whether she lived or died.

"When you left, where did you go?" Celeste asked.

"I intended to go on a journey," Amy replied, looking from her hand to Celeste. "I wanted to visit some of the cities that my dad wanted us to see."

Amy lowered her eyes when a look of tenderness crossed Celeste's face.

What Amy didn't tell them was that she didn't manage more than a few cities because she hooked up with a group of travelers and spent too many nights in bars and strange places trying to block out her pain. When the fire happened, she was hospitalized. It was there, drying out and recovering from her injuries, that the full realization and subsequent terror that her children and Maggie were never coming back hit her full force.

For months, Amy barely communicated. As time slipped by watching the nurses go about their duties and daily routines began to soothe her, made her feel that Maggie was close by. It was there she met Sandra, who was working her way across Australia. As fellow Glaswegians, Sandra worked hard to bring Amy around. As their friendship grew Amy never shared her past with Sandra. She couldn't, it was balled up and buried deep inside her. All Sandra knew was that she was a fellow traveler, caught up in a dreadful accident.

Colin burped. "Did you get to see the cities you wanted?"

Amy half-smiled. "Some."

Celeste looked at Amy intently. "What made you study nursing?"

Amy looked at Celeste. "It was when I was in hospital that I knew what I wanted to do. I decided to become a nurse."

"Why?" Alex asked.

Amy sighed, because she really didn't want to discuss this, she kept her answer brief. "I wanted to give something back." *I could give something back to the boys and to Maggie.* "And by being a nurse, I could be of some use." She smiled. "Fortunately, I was accepted into second year at nursing school and the rest, as they say, is history."

Studying her cards, Celeste asked, "Does Irene know about your burns?"

Amy looked at her for a moment. "No. No one knows."

"Traveling, never to arrive," Alex whispered almost to himself. "Amy, no one could find you," he said, putting his cards down. "How did you just vanish without a trace?"

"Believe me, it's not that difficult," Amy said, looking at her cards intently.

Colin reached over and clasped Amy's hand. "'Unbelievable," he said his voice catching. "You lost your children, your best friend, your marriage and Celeste. You suffered those horrific burns. Alone." He hiccupped then slurred, "It's like some fucking Greek tragedy."

There was stunned silence.

Alex stood up and grabbed Colin's arm. "I think you've had too much to drink." He pulled Colin up. "I'm sorry, Amy, for his insensitivity."

Colin staggered when Alex pulled him toward their cabin, lurching behind him. He called out before disappearing behind a firmly closed door, "I'm sorry, Amy. No offense was meant, honey."

Celeste looked at Amy apprehensively, waiting for a reaction.

Amy shrugged. "What?" she said to a surprised Celeste. "He didn't mean to offend me." She stood. "C'mon, let's get an early night. We've got a busy day tomorrow."

†

Denial

It was nearing the end of their vacation. Alex sat with Celeste on the deck of the yacht. "It's the end of July and the accident happened in November. It'll be almost five—"

"I know, Alex," Celeste interrupted. She watched Amy and Colin play with the children in the water. "Let's not go there today, huh."

Alex nodded. "Those burns," he said, picking up a bottle of sunscreen. "God, I can't believe she went through all that on her own."

Swinging her long legs off the edge of the deck, Celeste whispered, "Don't, Alex." Pulling her knees in she hugged them. "Please, I can't bear the thought of her going through that on her own."

Applying the lotion to his arms, Alex stopped and said in surprise, "You've seen much worse than that."

"I know," Celeste said. "But it's not just the burns, Alex. It's the associated trauma that goes with injuries like hers that is often the problem." Celeste fell silent.

"Go on," Alex said, snapping the cap on the sunscreen bottle closed.

"The burns are treatable," Celeste said, pressing her chin into her knees. "It's the psychological impact that's extremely difficult. Severe depression is common."

"At least the burns aren't debilitating and she can cover them up easily enough."

Celeste lifted her chin. "But she was at the lowest point in her life, and to suffer that alone given her loss." She shook her head and whispered, "Why didn't she tell someone?"

"She didn't tell anyone, honey," Alex said, rubbing the lotion between his toes, "because the girl believes she deserves them. They're her punishment."

The children shouted for them to watch them being thrown into the water by Colin and Amy, for the umpteenth time. Waving, Alex frowned. "Since the accident there has been little happiness in her life. I think she's been determined not to let it back in."

"Alex," Celeste said, hugging her legs. "I want to be with her so much that I can't even begin to describe it." She closed her eyes. "When I saw the scars I wanted to taste them." She opened her eyes and looked at him. "Does that sound strange?" she asked, sounding genuinely confused.

Alex raised his brows. "Touching her wasn't enough," he said tenderly. "You wanted to taste it so that you could absorb her pain."

Celeste arched an eyebrow. "I think I'm losing the plot."

Alex waved a hand. "Oh, don't worry about it." He smiled. "It's commonplace in literature. You know, needing to absorb the pain." He teased. "It's written in the rules."

Celeste smiled briefly. Resting her chin on her knees she gazed at Amy. "I want her in my life, Alex," she said. "So badly, that sometimes I can't breathe because I panic at the thought of losing her again." She drew in a deep breath then exhaled slowly. "I want to find out where she's been and what she's been doing for the last few years." She looked at him. "I want to know everything, every detail, regardless of how small."

"I know." Alex sighed. "But I don't think it's a good idea to push."

Celeste nodded. "For the last few weeks I've never been happier." She looked at Amy. "She means everything to me. But I'm scared that if I show any emotion she'll run." She closed her eyes. "And I'm terrified that I'll never be able to break down those barriers."

"I know," Alex said, moving closer to her. "But, for now, you'll have to be careful or there is a real chance that Amy might bolt. She's been to hell and back," he said, touching her arm. "She's dealing with a lot of emotional baggage. Right now, she needs her friends around her. She needs to be cared for and nurtured. Things will turn out good, for sure, Celeste. I can feel it. Just give it some time, all it needs is time."

"I hope so, Alex," Celeste said. "God, I hope so, because I can't lose her again."

Chapter 44

Celeste, Amy, and the children were at the airport, seeing off Alex and Colin who were heading for Italy before returning home. Celeste and the children were due to fly back home the following Saturday. Their time, Celeste thought regretfully, was up. She was due back at work and the kids at school.

Alex hugged Amy. "It's been wonderful seeing you," he said. "And I want you to promise that you'll come back to the States for Christmas. You must." He hugged her tightly. "I'm determined not to accept anything other than yes for an answer. And if I have to," he warned, "I'll catch a flight all the way over here and drag your sorry ass back. And that's a promise." Smiling, he looked at her. "Seriously, Amy, stay in touch." He hugged her one more time. "Okay!"

Celeste watched Amy smile at Alex but say nothing. Since they had arrived Amy had spent a lot of her free time with them. Just a few pleading cries, Celeste happily acknowledged, from the children was enough to make her concede every time.

With several more rounds of hugs and kisses, and a few more subtle threats from Alex, then Colin, for Amy to visit, they eventually waved them through the departure gate.

"What do you want to do today?" Celeste asked Amy as they left the airport.

"Well," Amy responded, then smiled at Naomi when she took her hand. "I really need to do some house stuff." She looked at Celeste. "What do you think about visiting some scrap yards," she asked. "I want to get a dining table made from railway sleepers. Do you think the kids would like that?"

Celeste smiled. "Yes."

Amy nodded. "Good."

That afternoon, to Celeste's delight, the kids seemed to enjoy traipsing around scrap yards, particularly Daniel. Amy was good for him, Celeste thought. She spent a lot of time encouraging him to sketch, encouraging his artistic side.

As they looked around the yard Amy told her that this was familiar territory. When she was at college she did a sculpting and welding course and, over the years, had spent many afternoons scouring these yards looking for things to use. At the third scrap yard, she found wood in good enough condition and ordered it to be cut to size and delivered to an ironmonger for fitting.

Celeste watched Amy make arrangements with the site owner and wondered if she missed being an architect, missed the creative element. She has such talent, she thought, as she watched Daniel stand next to Amy and listen intently as the man spoke in his broad Glaswegian dialect.

Celeste smiled. She could see by the look on Daniel's face that he didn't understand a word the guy was saying, but it was clear that he was determined to stand by Amy, and every time she nodded, he nodded too. *He has such talent. Help me Amy. Help me nurture his talent.*

By the time they were ready to go home, it was early evening and time for food. The children decided that they would go back to Amy's apartment, rent a movie and order takeout.

†

Celeste woke with a start when a foot thudded into the side of her ribs and a hand smacked her face. She realized she was in the middle of the sofa, squashed between Daniel and Naomi. Gently, she extricated herself. Smiling, she tried to remember at what point in the movie she had fallen asleep.

Standing, Celeste looked at Amy who was stretched out on the floor. She knelt down next to her and gently woke her up.

Sitting up, Amy rubbed her eyes then yawned and stretched. She looked over at the sleeping children. "I think it's probably best that you all stay here tonight."

"Are you sure?" Celeste asked uncertainly.

Denial

Amy nodded and whispered, "Just give me a few moments to make up the bed in the spare room."

"Do you need a hand?" Celeste whispered back.

Smiling gently, Amy whispered, "If you like."

Celeste nodded eagerly.

After the bed was made they carried the children through, stripped them to their underwear, tucked them in and kissed them goodnight. Thankfully, neither stirred.

Amy closed the bedroom door behind her and Celeste's stomach twisted when she grinned and winked at her.

"That was easy," Amy said, before turning and walking down the hall. "I think that the bed is too wee for everyone to sleep in?" She asked over her shoulder, "Do you mind sleeping on the couch?"

"No," Celeste replied, following her.

Pointing to her bedroom, Amy told her, "There's a spare duvet in the top cupboard in my bedroom. I'll get a sheet from the linen cupboard, if you'll get the duvet."

Entering Amy's bedroom Celeste's nostrils flared when the blonde's lingering scent hit her. The apartment that she lived in was in an old tenement block with high ceilings; Glasgow was famous for them. Locating the cupboard Celeste reached up to the handle. She stretched her full length but couldn't reach. Looking around for something to stand on she noticed how sparse the room was.

When Celeste had first visited Amy she was surprised that the apartment had nothing more than basic amenities, so basic, Amy bought a TV and media player when the kids couldn't hide their horror that she didn't have either.

When she first entered this apartment, Celeste had hoped to see some artwork adorning the walls. Amy's home in South Venice was filled with it, filled with color and life, but this apartment carried none of that color or that creativity.

A deep sadness filled Celeste as she looked around and realized that Amy probably hadn't touched a canvas in years. Standing in the room, she hoped that somehow Daniel would be able to bridge the gap and encourage her to paint again.

Noticing a wicker chair near the window Celeste pulled it over to the cupboard to stand on. Trying to balance her weight on the wobbly chair she reached for the handle. Grasping it, she pulled on it. The door creaked as it opened and, feeling pleased, she grinned—just as her foot shot through the center of the chair. Falling to the ground she hit the floor with a thud.

"What happened?" Amy asked, moving into the room hurriedly.

Celeste looked at the chair, then at Amy. *Isn't it obvious?* she thought, but to make amends said, "I think I've ruined your chair. She grimaced as she tried to nudge her foot loose. "I used it to get to the cupboard."

"Let me help," Amy said and gently helped Celeste remove her foot. "I'll help you onto the bed."

Standing, Celeste leaned on Amy and hobbled to the edge of the bed. Sitting, she removed her left shoe and sock. Leaning forward, she gently touched the area around her ankle. "It's only a slight twist," she said, moving it from side to side.

"Good," Amy replied, sounding relieved.

Straightening, Celeste pointed to the cupboard. "How do you normally get up there?"

Amy looked at the cupboard. "Some eejit who owned the flat before me must have moved the original handles and now they're too high. So I use a ladder when I need to get up there."

Celeste raised her eyebrows in consternation and wondered where the hell the ladder was now.

"Somehow," Amy said, lips twitching. "I thought you would've been tall enough to reach." Looking at Celeste's foot, she added drolly, "But obviously not." She moved to the door. "Let me bind that for you. Do you want some painkillers?"

Celeste nodded, and feeling slightly queasy lay down. After a few minutes, Amy returned and handed her a glass of water with two painkillers. "I checked on the kids, they didn't hear a thing," she said. "They're sound asleep."

"Good," Celeste replied. Accepting the painkillers she placed them in her mouth and looked up at Amy, then closed her eyes. All day she had been intensely aware of her. The need to have some physical contact with her was growing. She called on all her resolve not to do anything that would threaten the harmony that had been with them all day.

Sitting up, Celeste sipped some water. Chinking the ice in the glass, she lay back down and rubbed it against her forehead. She inhaled deeply when Amy gently stretched out her leg.

Resting Celeste's leg between her thighs, Amy slid up the leg of her jeans before carefully positioning the crepe bandage over her toes.

Amy's touch was unnerving. Celeste swallowed hard. Biting her bottom lip she pressed the glass against her forehead, all too aware that, right now, being around this woman was beginning to drive her absolutely crazy. Since her arrival in Scotland she had struggled every day to hide her feelings, but today it had been particularly hard. Today there seemed to be a special connection between them.

"You'll feel just a little pressure as I move it up your leg," Amy advised.

Celeste nodded and closing her eyes, groaned in dismay when Amy's feathery touch made her groin clench.

Halting, Amy asked, "Are you okay?"

Celeste squeaked, "Yes." Her eyes flew open and she quickly cleared her throat. "Yes," she replied more firmly this time. "I'm great, thanks." She coughed lightly. "I've just got a tickle at the back of my throat."

Raising her eyebrows, Amy looked at her as she finished. "All done."

Not moving, Celeste looked up at her.

"Are you okay?" Amy asked, leaning over her.

"Yes," Celeste responded. Desperate for Amy not to find out the truth, she added quickly, "I'm just feeling a little shaky, that's all."

Standing, Amy looked at her closely. "You do look a bit pale." Frowning, she asked, "Did you hit your head?"

Heart hammering, Celeste shook her head.

Amy looked at Celeste for a moment. "C'mon," she said, taking the glass from her. "Let's get you into bed. I think it's best that you have the bed. I'll sleep on the couch."

In no mood to argue, Celeste nodded and allowed Amy to remove her other shoe, then sock, before lifting her legs from the floor onto the bed.

Removing pajamas from a drawer Amy said, "Celeste, take your jeans off."

Celeste's eyes widened. She didn't want to get undressed.

Holding the pajamas, Amy looked at her and frowned. "What's wrong?"

"Uhmm...Nothing." *It'll appear stupid to make a fuss,* Celeste thought. She unbuckled her belt and popped open the buttons. She tried to pull her jeans off quickly but was slowed by her injured foot. Grimacing, she looked up in surprise when Amy took over, pulling her jeans down and gently off. This was the last thing she expected. Fighting the urge to pull Amy into her arms, she covered her face with her hands.

"Sorry," Amy said quietly. "I should have let you take them off yourself. Automatic reaction, I'm afraid. Blame it on my nurse training," she handed Celeste her pajamas. "You should manage to get into these all right."

Feeling sick, Celeste turned on her side and folded into a fetal position.

Concerned, Amy leaned over her and placed a hand on her forehead, it was cold and clammy. She looked at Celeste. "Are you sure you didn't hit your head when you fell?"

Celeste didn't answer.

"Can you turn on your back?" Amy asked. Frowning, she watched Celeste hesitate. "Please," she added, beginning to worry.

Celeste took a deep breath, and nodding, lay on her back.

Worried, Amy looked into Celeste's eyes and checked her pupils. Satisfied, she looked at her. *This is dangerous. She's fine. Just get up and get the hell out of here!* Removing her hand, Amy croaked, "You seem to be fine."

Denial

Amy looked at Celeste and her heart clenched. Lying there, she looked so exposed, with evident desire and longing shining in her eyes. Amy's gut tightened and a surprising twist of desire knotted through it. The whole moment took on a surreal quality. Unable to resist, she reached out and gently stroked Celeste's face.

Swallowing hard, Celeste caught Amy's hand and whispered, "Amy...I..." hesitating, she licked her lips and then looked at her pleadingly.

Amy tried to move but Celeste's hands rose up and caught her arms tightly. She pulled her down and rolled them over. Lying on top of her, breathing heavily, Celeste rested her head gently on hers.

Amy closed her eyes, flushed and breathless she clenched the bedspread, acknowledging with much surprise that she was aroused. It had been years since she felt like this. Opening her eyes, Celeste lifted her head and Amy watched, with a growing mixture of alarm and curiosity an array of emotions flicker over her face—desire, uncertainty, fear.

Celeste captured Amy's mouth, kissing her openly, hotly, deeply, her lips exploring.

Instinctively responding to the kiss, desire flooded Amy. She had forgotten the exquisite taste of her mouth. She tried to think straight, tried to tell herself that this was wrong, that she should stop, pull away, but she couldn't. To her shame an incredible surge of excitement shot through her, just like the rush of hormones on that first night. As always, she had little control over her physical response to Celeste. Her body was hungry.

Amy's head began to spin when a deep moan from Celeste vibrated through her. An unexpected emotion filled her, a feeling of returning to a warm, familiar, much-loved place. The heat grew between her thighs. *How long has it been?* Not since they were last together, she realized.

Eventually, Celeste slowed the deep, intense kiss and gently brushed her lips over Amy's. Eyes glowing, she looked at her.

Captivated, Amy reached up and outlined Celeste's mouth with her finger. In response, Celeste allowed more of her weight to settle on her. She kissed her again working her tongue deep into her mouth.

Amy moaned in response and, unable to stop herself, slid an index finger down Celeste's T-shirt over the swell of her breast to the erect nipple she knew she would find. She cupped it, and kneading it gently, closed her eyes and remembered how much she adored the sensual feel of Celeste.

Amy moaned with pleasure when Celeste ground her hips into her. A yearning rose from a deep void. Right now, Amy knew with certainty she needed Celeste. Right now, she needed to taste her, to touch her skin, feel her warmth. *Right now*, having Celeste close was all that mattered.

Amy's hands moved quickly under Celeste's top then urgently over her back, exploring it. She gasped when Celeste arched and moaned.

Heart pounding, Amy needed to touch more. She pulled Celeste's T-shirt up and unclipped her bra then slid it and the T-shirt free. She placed both hands on Celeste's breasts, adoring the weight in her palms. She groaned then closed her eyes, only opening them when Celeste moaned deeply.

Amy shuddered, her excitement intensifying incalculably. Leaning forward, she strained to nip the soft skin at the base of Celeste's neck before trailing down and capturing a nipple, hungrily sucking on it. Desperate to feel more flesh she ran her hands down Celeste's back and inside her briefs before pulling her grinding hips into hers. She let Celeste's generous breast fill her mouth.

Her arousal at fever pitch, Amy wanted to touch, to grope, to shred and destroy anything between them. Feeling starved, she desperately wanted to touch every inch. Working her right hand around she dipped her fingers between Celeste's thighs. When Celeste bucked, Amy used her tongue, tasting and sucking everywhere she could. Each time Celeste pressed into her she groaned. Her own clit pulsing, then aching as it pulsed.

Amy ran a hand up Celeste's back, clawing at it. She was gripped by a desperate need to taste her. No, more than taste her,

Denial

she needed to be inside her. She needed to consume her. Amy pushed Celeste's briefs down and murmured, "Off."

Helping Celeste, Amy pushed them over her knees and off. She looked into Celeste's hazel-green eyes then slid down the bed. She stopped between her thighs and whispered, "I want to taste you." Amy felt Celeste stiffen, but unable to stop herself she pulled impatiently at her thighs to open them further. Celeste didn't move. "Please."

Celeste drew in a deep breath before straddling Amy's face. She positioned herself above her mouth then, exhaling sharply, looked into her eyes before lowering herself.

Amy stopped breathing when she caught sight of the beauty above her. Her stomach taut and firm, her full breasts swaying slightly as she lowered herself trustingly down onto her mouth.

Her heart beating fiercely, Amy exhaled then filled her lungs with the scent of Celeste's deep arousal. Stretching her neck, she pushed out her tongue, spread it wide, flat, and ran it between the folds of Celeste's slick lips. Slowly, she licked up the entire length of her; tasting her. *Delicious*, her mind cried out as she remembered how much she loved the taste of Celeste.

"Lower. You need to be lower."

Breathing heavily, Celeste spread her legs wide and lowered herself further onto Amy's mouth. Wanting to expose her fully, Amy reached up and pulled Celeste open. Unable to control her craving she licked ferociously, flattening her tongue to lick up, shaping it to a point then twirling her clit before sucking it fully into her mouth. With her fingers, she slid into Celeste, driving in and out, moving deeper and deeper, further and further, all the while sucking Celeste's clit.

Moaning repeatedly, Celeste placed her hands on Amy's head. Holding it in position she rotated then ground her hips. She pulled back slightly when Amy's teeth grated against her then moaned, pressing harder and faster until, holding Amy head's tightly, she cried out, climaxing. Her muscles clenched around Amy's fingers and she shuddered for a long while before eventually stilling.

Feeling weak, Celeste moved off Amy. Breathing heavily, she lay beside her and tried to capture her mouth.

Amy wouldn't let her. She pushed Celeste away. "No," she rasped. "I…I…need…to…breathe," she gasped, then sucked in air until her breathing evened out. After a few moments, she clutched blindly for Celeste's hand and whispered, "Now…Celeste."

Aware that Amy wasn't in control Celeste knew they shouldn't be doing this. Amy had made it abundantly clear that she didn't want physical contact. Watching her Celeste knew there would be regrets and recriminations, but the pleasure of being here was beyond anything she had experienced in a long time. The pleasure of being here drove out all her doubts. She wanted nothing more than to taste this woman.

Celeste's stomach flipped. Quickly sitting on her knees, she unzipped Amy's jeans and pulled them and her underwear hastily off, along with the rest of her clothing. Positioning herself between Amy's legs she barely noticed the scarring as she spread her thighs wide. She took a moment, unable to believe that she was here with the woman she adored, doing exactly what she had dreamed about for the longest time.

Celeste had waited so long for this moment; she wanted to savor it. Slowly, she spread Amy's thighs. Slowly, she touched her clit with her fingers, feeling its slickness.

Amy shuddered. "Hurry, Celeste."

Leaning in, Celeste slid her tongue lightly over Amy's clit. She groaned and pushed her tongue into her. Closing her eyes, she let it rest inside Amy. Let it absorb the heat; absorb her. If she could've, she would push all the way into her, be inside of her; be where she belonged.

When Amy moaned impatiently Celeste pulled her tongue out and opened her mouth fully to cover as much of Amy as possible. Swallowing, she consumed her. She repeated this several times before sucking Amy's clit hard.

Amy gasped. Moaning, she bunched the sheets in her hands and cried out until her orgasm hit.

Denial

Celeste felt the waves of an immense orgasm rush through Amy, making her shake violently. When Amy went limp, Celeste smiled when a satisfied moan fell from Amy's lips, but she wasn't finished, she had a thirst to quench.

Dazed, Amy lay on the bed as a euphoric feeling of release swept through her. For years she had never felt like this because, quite simply, until now, she thought she was dead inside.

Her natural high receding fast, the reality of what she was doing seeped in. Amy took a few deep breaths. She felt conflict. Her chest constricted, guilt filled her. *You know you shouldn't be doing this,* her inner voice boomed. *You made a deal. You promised your dead cousin and your dead children that you would never allow this to happen again.*

Abruptly, Amy's eyes rolled back. She gasped when Celeste bit gently on her clit, stretching it out, the tip of her tongue flicking it back and forth, increasing speed each time.

Amy felt trapped. Her body refused to do anything but respond to Celeste's touch. Guilt was beginning to tear at her. She stiffened when Celeste's fingers entered her and her tongue licked her adoringly. Her back arched when Celeste pushed her fingers in further and teased her clit gently with her teeth, then sucked the tip.

Amy gulped in air and sheer desire pushed all thoughts away. Gripping the sheets she, as in the past during these moments, told Celeste things she never intended to: that she needed her, needed this. That she wanted nothing more than for her to be inside her. Then it slammed into her, her orgasm throwing her into a series of spasms until, eventually spent, she slowly came down.

Hips stilling, Amy covered her face with her hands.

"Amy?" she heard Celeste say with concern.

A sharp pain of loss clamped around Amy's heart and the dam that she thought had dried up long ago broke. Folding her arms over her face, she started to cry for her boys, for Maggie, for Sean, for her father, for the pups. She cried for every one of them.

When the boys died Amy thought that she had failed them, failed Maggie, failed everyone. She had lied, connived, and deceived to feed her habit, feed her need for Celeste. Since the day they were killed she had never allowed herself to think what being with Celeste this way was like or how Celeste made her feel. If it ever entered her head, the thoughts were always pushed aside by a tidal wave of guilt.

Amy curled into a tight ball.

Celeste moved up the bed. Placing her hands lightly on her shoulders she turned Amy and cradled her in her arms. "Shhh," she whispered soothingly. "It's going to be okay. I promise you," she said comfortingly. "It's going to be okay."

Amy continued to cry. She cried inconsolably. Unable to believe that after all her promises, she had let this happen.

Chapter 45

Celeste closed the children's bedroom door, pleased that they were sound asleep. Hobbling to the kitchen, she looked through Amy's cupboards until she found some alcohol. Shifting a few bottles of wine aside she found a bottle of single malt whiskey. Locating a glass she broke the seal and poured a sizeable measure. Leaning heavily against the counter, she swallowed a large amount then swallowed more, not thinking until the glass was drained.

Celeste sat wearily on a kitchen chair. She placed her head in her hands. The warmth in her stomach quickly emptied, leaving a chasm when she thought about how inconsolable Amy had been. She shook her head. No matter how hard she had tried she couldn't hush Amy. She had cried, until exhausted, she fell asleep.

Celeste sighed and ran her hands through her hair knowing that if they were to have anything together it needed to come from Amy. Tonight, she realized, would only have pushed her further away.

†

Opening the kitchen door, Amy saw Celeste sitting at the table. She squinted; the kitchen was bright with early morning sunshine. She pulled out a chair and sat across from her.

Sipping coffee, Celeste looked at her.

They sat in silence.

Amy remembered how Celeste rarely broke the silence. The pull of Celeste's seductiveness was strong and unexpected. She noted that her dark hair hung freely around her shoulders; her eyes were luminous and her lips…she cut her thoughts short. She didn't want to think about how good Celeste looked. Her stomach twisted and color rose in her cheeks. She briefly closed her eyes.

Last night, their lovemaking had released an avalanche of pent-up desire and her body wasn't about to let her forget it or think that it was satisfied.

Amy looked down at her hands; already they were shaking with fresh need. For years, she hadn't felt even a twinge of desire, but now her senses were being assaulted, reawakened.

Tucking her hair behind her ears Amy opened her hands expressively. It was time to be honest. "I care about you, Celeste."

Celeste's eyebrows rose in surprise.

"I always have; and maybe if things had been different, maybe if I had met you first instead of Josh, I probably would never have married him knowing how explosive things were with you." She hesitated and unable to deny it after last night, amended, "are with you." She stopped and inhaled deeply. "But I didn't meet you first. I met Josh and I married him and we had," her voice cracked, "two beautiful children." The pain rang deep. "And now, they're gone. Everything has gone."

Celeste bowed her head.

Amy gathered herself. "Celeste, I blame myself for it all." She shook her head. "I know if I hadn't been so wrapped up with you that I probably wouldn't have let Maggie take the children away. Maybe," she paused then added with a faint note of hope, "maybe we would have organized something else. Maggie and I did everything together. Maybe Maggie wouldn't have gone camping?"

Amy sat reflectively for a moment then sighed. "The bottom line is if Maggie had known that I hadn't been busy that weekend she would have insisted that I tag along." She said nothing for a few moments. "Every day I regret it," her voice grew huskier. "That I wasn't with them."

"Oh, Amy," Celeste said with a note of despair.

"Celeste, I shouldn't be alive today; but I am," Amy explained. "I shouldn't have survived that fire, but I did." She opened her hands as if everything was suddenly clear. "I feel as if I'm being punished, Celeste," she said with conviction. "I'm being punished for doing something that was wrong."

Denial

Celeste shook her head.

Amy clasped her hands together. "When Irene left my dad he was devastated." Her hands tightened. "He never really recovered from her leaving." Her knuckles whitened. "He made me promise over and over that I would never be like her. Never betray my family."

Celeste closed her eyes briefly.

"But that's exactly what I did! Even though I knew the devastation it would cause if we were found out." Amy rolled her eyes in disbelief. "I still took that chance. I hoodwinked everyone into believing that I was a model wife and mom, a good all-rounder. But the reality was quite different."

Celeste looked at Amy intently.

Amy stared off into the distance. "I often think about why Maggie never picked up on what we were doing. But now I realize that she would never have believed that I was capable of deceiving her like that." She looked at Celeste. "She would never have believed that her precious little cousin could be such a slut."

"Amy," Celeste said, her tone full of compassion.

"I know what has just happened, but I can't ever, *ever* let that happen again." Amy looked at her pleadingly. "If I do, it is betraying Maggie and the children."

Celeste paled.

Amy's voice grew huskier. "It would be like saying everything we did was somehow all right."

"I understand why, after the accident," Celeste paused, struggling for words, "why you couldn't bear to be near me." She bowed her head. "But you didn't need to run. You still have family." She lifted her head and looked at Amy. "You have people who love and care very deeply for you."

"How could I let them be there for me?" Amy said, her tone accusing. "How could I pretend? How could I be the loving supporting wife to Josh? I had betrayed him. He had no idea what I had done. He didn't know who I was. I didn't know who I was. How could I be there for him when it was my fault? How could I grieve with him when it was me who caused his grief?"

Celeste reached out to touch her.

Amy flinched and pulled away. "I'm dead inside, Celeste," she said, her eyes pleading with her to understand. "Don't you see that?"

Celeste frowned and withdrew her hand. "Amy, you're not dead inside. What you're experiencing may cause you to feel that way," she said. "It's symptomatic, due to an unremitting sense of guilt." She looked at Amy. "But I can assure you, Amy, you're not dead inside. I've seen it many times over the years and I—"

"Don't patronize me," Amy interrupted, her eyes sparking fire. "Don't you dare try to explain away how I feel with words! Don't sit there and put on your doctor's hat and box me in with jargon!" She repeated Celeste's words with disdain, "Symptomatic...unremitting sense of guilt..." She stared at her. "You might find it comforting, but they're just empty, cheap words to me." Leaning forward, her eyes narrowing, she tried to hold her temper as she said in a precise tone, "Don't *ever* think your words could ever, ever describe how I feel."

Celeste's years of training should have allowed her to sit and listen, to offer Amy support and comfort, to remain detached, but she couldn't, this was too personal. She wanted to ask Amy about last night. She wanted to tell her it wasn't just about the physical, it was about the connection they had. The connection that had existed from the moment they met. The connection that was still as strong, even after everything. She wanted to say what about the fact that she loved her, had never stopped loving her every second of every hour of every day? She wanted to shout through her pain, *WHAT ABOUT THAT?*

Instead, Celeste said, "What about last night?"

"Don't you understand?" Amy replied coldly. "Don't you get it, Celeste? You are a reminder."

Celeste regarded her intently, disappointment etching her face.

"Every time I look at you," Amy's voice grew unsteady, "I'm reminded of what I've done."

Celeste lowered her head, the pain of Amy's words made her want to throw up. She exhaled slowly. From the moment of the accident Amy had blocked out the world, closed down. Nobody could reach her, least of all Celeste. It had been so difficult. Finally, the words she dreaded hearing, the words she had expected since the day of the accident, those words were finally spoken.

Amy said softly, "I'm sorry, Celeste. I don't want to hurt you, but I need you to promise me that you'll let me go, that you'll go back to your own life. Bring up those beautiful children. Move on, meet someone else."

Celeste inhaled deeply. *Meet someone else!* She almost laughed. *If it was as simple as that don't you think I would be with someone else? I don't understand it either, Amy, but my heart doesn't seem to think there is anyone else!*

Celeste couldn't draw a line here in this empty apartment. She knew that regardless of what the terms of their relationship were, she could never give up on her.

"Nothing will happen unless you want it to," Celeste whispered. "Amy, I promise."

The kitchen door opened and Naomi, rubbing her eyes, wandered in. She gave them both a sleepy smile before climbing up onto Amy's lap. Heavy-eyed, she looked at Amy and then the cereal box on the breakfast bar. "I'm hungry."

Celeste's entire body shook with relief. Naomi could not have timed it better. She watched Amy cuddle Naomi to her.

"Believe me, Amy. I cannot walk away from you. Nothing will jeopardize our friendship again. The children love you. I..." she hesitated..."we need you."

Naomi, picking up that something was wrong, cuddled into Amy and wrapped her arms around her. Sounding more than a little scared, she said, "Don't go away, Meme."

Amy smiled down at Naomi. It amused her that this little girl called her Meme. Acutely aware that she was tiny for her age, Amy looked adoringly into the beautiful ebony face. Naomi had been a premature baby who survived against strong odds. She had Celeste to thank for that. According to Alex, her survival was due to Celeste taking such a personal interest and ensuring that this precious little bundle received the best medical care.

Amy held Naomi protectively then kissed her forehead lovingly. She had never met a child that smiled and laughed so much. Looking at Celeste she noted the strain on her face. Amy's heart wrenched. She should tell her no, that after last night, friendship was out of the question. She should tell Naomi that yes, she would have to go away.

Amy opened her mouth and tried to push out words. She looked down at Naomi and tried to push out words of regret, but she couldn't. Instead, her mouth dried up and no words left her lips.

Naomi repeated, "Don't go, Meme."

Amy hugged Naomi close and kissed her head. "No, baby," she said devotedly. "Meme isn't going anywhere. She will always be here for you, sweetie."

Celeste mouthed the words, thank you, and pushed back her chair. "Why don't I fix us all something to eat?"

Amy gave her a weak smile. "No, let me," she responded. "You should rest your foot."

Amy kissed Naomi's head again then let the little girl slip off her lap. Standing, her inner voice chastised, *When will you ever learn?*

Chapter 46

Celeste put the receiver down.

"What time does Amy's flight get in?" Colin asked, handing her a glass of juice.

Celeste looked at her watch. "There's a delay, it'll be around midnight."

Alex patted Celeste's shoulder. "Excited that she'll be here for Christmas?"

Celeste nodded. Since coming home they had kept in regular contact with Naomi and Daniel calling Amy every week. Celeste realized that she had come to rely on those calls as reassurance that Amy was okay.

After she and the children returned in August the kids had excitedly filled their grandparents in on their vacation. It had taken Celeste all her powers of persuasion to stop her parents, particularly her mother, from making contact with Amy.

After many discussions, her parents eventually agreed not to rush and to leave contact until Amy was ready. Josh was a different matter. Celeste had no idea how he would react. Fortunately, she had a little breathing space; Josh's company was growing fast and he had recently relocated his head office to New York. Moving and setting up a home meant that she hadn't spent any time with him since their return.

It also meant that, because he was busy, the kids had not had the opportunity to speak with him. To Celeste's relief she had only spoken to him on the phone briefly a few times and the conversations tended to be about the difficulties of the move.

Celeste was acutely aware that since the accident and Amy's leaving a part of Josh left too. The loss and years without contact with Amy had taken their toll. Even though he had a new life his easy manner and relaxed attitude had been replaced with a more somber, serious side.

Alex sat down. "So, the kids finally wore Amy down and convinced her to stay with you?"

Snapping out of her reverie, Celeste looked at him. "You know Irene, she's always doing some renovation to the house. Fortunately, it's major this time. There's barely room to swing a cat."

Alex smiled. "Amy stood no chance with Irene and the kids pushing for her to stay here."

Celeste smiled faintly and nodded.

"We just need to make sure that we're careful around her." Alex looked at Celeste. "I mean very careful this time."

Colin slugged his beer. "This is ridiculous," he said. "When are we going to get her out of this denial mode? The best thing for her to do is to meet up with the family and Josh. How else is she going to get on with her life if she doesn't have closure?"

Alex raised his eyebrows at Celeste. "Colin, calm down," he said. "As well you know, there are too many painful memories for her here. God only knows how she would react to seeing Josh with his two kids."

"Fuck me. This is driving me crazy," Colin said. Eyes wide, he pointed his beer bottle at Celeste. "We all know she wants you. That's a given. But," he said, throwing a hand in the air, "she needs help to move on. Seeing Josh and his kids is exactly what she needs to help her."

Celeste pulled out a chair and sat.

"I, for one, am not happy to sit back and do nothing. Jeez," Colin said, looking at Celeste. "You lesbians kill me, you know. It's all or nothing for you gals. You have U-Hauls turning up at your front door because the girl you met the night before is moving in with you, along with her strap-on and her cat. Or, if you refuse to let her in because you're sensible enough to realize you just met her the night before, then you get your very own personal stalker who takes root, watches your every move, and it's adios to happiness and hello spinsterhood." Colin frantically shook his leg. "'Cause you can't shake the bitch off. Yup," he said, looking at them, "it's all drama, drama, drama with you lesbians."

Denial

Celeste raised her eyebrows in amused confusion and looked at Alex.

"Boy, do you need a lesbian education," Alex said then sighed. "Honey, you ever heard of the word cliché? I think you've been watching far too much late night cable TV."

Colin coughed. "Hmm. Yes...well, what I'm saying is that Amy needs to build a bridge and get over it. You're the one, sweetie, and she should be damned pleased at that."

Colin held up his hands as they both began to protest. "Hey, I'm not saying it's easy, but she's got a spark, you know. There's still a lot of living in that gal. But as long as you two treat her like she's an emotional cripple she'll never move on!"

Colin looked at Celeste's shocked face. "Celeste, listen to me, I'm a teacher. I teach kids that are fat, slow, unmotivated, who have parents that have learned their parenting skills on the back of a cereal box. There are lots of kids out there who have shit lives. Some of them you can't help and, as painful as it is, you have to accept that. But there are ones that you can help, even though the odds are against them, because you can see that spark. That no matter how tough life is, they're going to come right back at you." Colin stretched out his hands and puffed up his chest. "I've turned a lot of those kids around and into goddamn great athletes who take pride in themselves."

"Your point?" Alex asked, interrupting.

"The point is that I can smell potential within a hundred yards. And what you two don't see is that she has potential." He looked at them in exasperation. "Because, like I said, you two are too busy treating her like an emotional cripple."

Both Alex and Celeste shook their heads.

"Celeste, this isn't an unrequited love situation," Colin said. "If it was, I wouldn't be long in telling you to drop this thing with Amy and to stop wasting your time and energy searching for the unobtainable." He lifted a finger. "Believe it or not," he said, "too many people search for the unattainable as a way to avoid real intimacy with someone available and suitable. But with you two," he pointed a finger at Celeste, "there is great energy. And you, Celeste, need to believe that she loves you." He slapped his hand on the table. "That she loves your kids. You need to believe that you're her family now, and you need to push her and help her see that."

"Colin, you don't understand," Celeste said, her color deepening and anger flitting across her face.

Colin said in a placating tone, "Look, don't you see? Most people who have gone through what she has don't come back from the edge. I mean, she's been out there, on her own, with no one to offer her support. And when I talked to Sandra she didn't even know about Amy's past."

Celeste groaned.

Alex looked at Colin in horror. "Don't tell me you told Sandra?"

Colin looked at each of them and shrugged.

Celeste paled. Appalled that he could have broken such a confidence she said in growing anger, "Don't you think that if Amy wanted her to know she would have told her?"

Holding his position, Colin shook his head. "No," he replied. "I don't think she ever had any intention of telling Sandra."

Colin lifted his hand when Celeste slammed her glass of juice down on the table. "Celeste," he appeased. "Sandra is Amy's friend. And it looks like her only good friend over the last few years." He quickly added when Celeste scraped her chair back, "Sandra loves her. She has a right to know in order to be there for her."

About to stand, Colin put his hand on Celeste's shoulder to stop her. "Listen to me first, Celeste. I couldn't have survived losing my children and my best friend. My marriage breaking down and," he looked at Alex lovingly, "losing my lover. I'm not that strong."

"Regardless, Colin—"

"Please," Colin interrupted. "Listen to me."

Hesitating, Celeste nodded then sat back on the chair.

Colin continued. "The key point I'm trying to make is that given all that she has survived. And," he looked from her to Alex, then back, "what you don't see is that she's come back stronger. She's become a nurse for fuck sake. One of the hardest, most

Denial

committed professions there is. And she chose it. She's a fighter and neither of you two is prepared to see it."

Colin had Celeste's attention. He placed a hand briefly on Celeste's upper chest. "Now I know there is a fighter in here that's waiting for the opportunity to win Amy over. But it ain't gonna happen if you keep buying into the fact that she doesn't need you." He raised his eyebrows for emphasis. "She does." He sat back. "And maybe all she needs is a little reminding."

Celeste sighed and, trying not to lose her temper, explained in an even tone. "Colin, Amy blames me." She stopped and thought, *no, she blames us.* Old pain broke through her voice. "She believes that if she hadn't been so preoccupied with us then the variables would have changed and their deaths would not have happened."

"But does she really blame you?" Colin queried. He leaned forward. "I think if she did she wouldn't have you anywhere near her." He paused to slug from his beer bottle. "Celeste, she isn't out there with some other guy, gal, whatever. She isn't remarried. She isn't dating. Hasn't had anyone close to her for years and suddenly she's hanging out with you all the time."

"Your point?" Alex asked, frowning.

"*The point…*is that since you've made contact, she's kept you close."

Surprised that his words were having an effect on her, Celeste looked at him and feeling slightly uncertain said, "It's because of the children."

Colin leaned back in his chair and drank more beer. "Personally," he said, wiping his mouth with the back of his hand, "I don't buy it. She deals with kids every day of her life. And, okay, your kids are sweet and I love them, but if she really didn't want you in her life then kids or no kids she'd have no qualms in cutting you loose." He moved back into her space. "Celeste, she is used to being on her own. She doesn't need you to support her. She needs you around because she loves you."

Sitting back obviously satisfied that he had Celeste's full attention, Colin smiled sagely. "Now, I don't believe she truly blames you. She loves you. You have to make her believe that what you had, and what you now have, is real." He leaned forward and looked into Celeste's eyes. "You love her deeply. You've never loved anyone else this way. That's not wrong, Celeste. It's not wrong to love your soul mate."

Celeste stopped herself from rolling her eyes. Colin had a propensity to be overdramatic.

"He might be right, Celeste."

Celeste looked at Alex in surprise.

"We have to make her see," Alex continued. "But, she's frightened, probably scared to death. Everything that she has touched has been taken away from her. I don't think it's only about her loss. I think she believes that she is being punished."

Celeste frowned and thought back to the conversation she'd had with Amy at her kitchen table a few hours after they had made love. She had said how she believed she was being punished. Maybe he's right, Celeste thought, maybe she's terrified to let anyone close to her in case something happens. Then she thought, No, she's made it clear she blames me. She shook her head. This is crazy, she told herself, unable to believe that their point of view was beginning to carry some plausibility.

"You have to begin to see how strong she is, Celeste," Colin said, his hand going round the back of her chair. "How much of a fighter she is. See her potential. See what she can become, and make her believe in you. You can do it, Celeste. I know you can." He sat back and looked at Alex. "When Alex and I were with you both in Scotland you couldn't miss how deeply in love she is with you."

Alex nodded. "He's right, Celeste."

Evidently pleased that Alex was backing him, Colin laughed. "I mean, for fuck sake, the temperature shot through the roof whenever you two got together. There were enough lesbian pheromones to give even an avowed homo like me a buzz."

Celeste looked at him and, feeling a sudden glimmer of hope, thought, maybe he's right.

Colin watched Celeste, pleased that at last he was getting through to her. Over the last few weeks he had been working hard to get Amy here. He smiled at Celeste, then got up and opened the fridge for another beer. He grinned, aware that his hard work was paying off. Popping open the bottle he recalled his conversation with Irene a few weeks ago.

†

"I can't believe it."

Colin placed his coffee cup on the table. "Irene, I know." He could tell she was in shock.

"Burnt so badly she needed skin grafts!" Irene lurched forward, grasping her stomach. "It's my fault," she uttered, tears spilling from her eyes. "If I hadn't left her when I did, so young and vulnerable, she would never have gone through this the way she has." Tears streaming down her face. "She would have wanted her family with her. But all the things that matter to her have been taken away," she said, shaking her head.

Colin took Irene's hand.

Irene wiped at the tears spilling from her eyes. "I'm so glad you told me. I'm sure she's still furious with me for giving Celeste her contact details." She reached for a tissue. "She didn't tell me as much, but I'm sure she only gave me the address because of her little sisters." She looked at Colin. "She wants them to know who she is." She wiped the tears from her eyes and blew her nose. "Maggie, her cousin, meant so much to her, you see." She looked at him, fresh tears brewing. "Maggie was always there for Amy. She was more like her big sister, and I think Amy wants the girls to know that they have a big sister. That she'll be there for them if they need her."

Colin picked up their cups, and poured some more coffee.

"Why didn't Celeste tell me?"

Colin sat down and placed Irene's cup in front of her. "You know Celeste," he said then drank from his cup. "She's not one to break a confidence." He looked at Irene and winked. "But I am." He lifted a finger. "But, only when it's necessary." Colin reached for her hand. "I didn't have the heart to tell Celeste, but when I spoke to Amy last she was dropping heavy hints that she might not be coming over. She was gearing up to work straight through the holidays." He clasped her hand. "I think she was preparing to cancel."

"Oh God," Irene said, sighing heavily. "She doesn't want me to visit her." She looked at Colin. "She blames it on the job." She took in a deep breath. "She keeps telling me to wait until she gets a clear run, until she gets a few weeks off." Irene threw up her arms. "I believed her." She shook her head. "That bloody job. She seems to be working all sorts of funny hours and shifts." Irene looked bleakly at him. "Oh Colin, she so needs to be here." She closed her eyes briefly. "I was hoping that, with her coming here, she would find closure."

"Yup, she won't find closure over there, that's for sure," Colin replied, patting Irene's arm. "She needs us now and that's what's important. We have to work together on this. Amy and Celeste belong together. But Amy needs us to help her see that."

Irene nodded.

Colin drank some more coffee. "Her home is here, Irene, not thousands of miles away, working too hard, alone. You know she'll keep you at arm's length, pretend that everything is okay and say that she has to work all sorts of shifts." He pulled his chair closer. "But, really, she's working herself into the ground." He looked at Irene. "She'll never have closure as long as she stays away."

"Yes," Irene said, sounding stronger. "So, what we need to do is start being a lot more proactive about getting Amy here," she said with a sparkle in her eyes, "And make sure that Amy spends as much time with Celeste as possible."

Colin winked. "Exactly."

†

"What time do you want us to take the kids?" Alex asked Celeste.

"Whenever you're ready."

"Is Irene going with you to the airport," Alex asked.

"No," Celeste said, standing. "Bruce called to say that Irene has some sort of bug. She's laid up in bed."

Colin nodded. "C'mon, Alex," he said. "Let's get the kids organized."

Chapter 47

Celeste waved to Amy when she came through the international gates at the airport. Amy looked pale and thin. Celeste sighed heavily, annoyed that Amy continued to neglect herself so badly.

Amy smiled when she saw Celeste and hugged her quickly. "Thanks for picking me up."

"And how were the flights?"

"The stopover at Amsterdam was hellish," Amy said as they headed out of the airport. "I wasn't sure if the flights were going to be canceled because of the snow."

Celeste nodded and they walked in silence to the parking lot.

"How are the kids," Amy asked as they reached the car.

"Good," Celeste said then smiled. "They can't wait to see you, but because your flight was due in so late they're staying with Colin and Alex tonight. You'll see them in the morning."

Amy got into Celeste's BMW and buckled up. "Thanks for putting me up."

Celeste smiled. "I'm glad Irene eventually convinced you not to stay in a hotel."

Amy laughed. "I think Irene would have physically dragged me out and dumped me at your place, even if I had."

Amy unclipped her seat belt and, removing her coat, said, "I forgot how hot it is in December. It's absolutely freezing in Glasgow."

Amy rebuckled her seat belt, sat back and looked out the window. She looked at the changes that had taken place over the years. New buildings had appeared and although there were many changes, the familiar route soothed her. She stretched out her legs and laid her head against the headrest then looked at Celeste. She stared at Celeste's hands and how strong they looked as they gripped the steering wheel. Amy let her eyes follow Celeste's arms to her face where she studied her profile. As always, her

Denial

eyes were drawn to the fullness of Celeste's lips and then her scar. Amy fought the urge to touch the small scar. She was always stunned by the perfect symmetry of Celeste's face and how her scar, instead of detracting, seemed to add additional depth to her looks. Turning her thoughts sharply away from how Celeste looked, she asked, "How are you?"

"Fine," Celeste responded. "I'm glad you came." She glanced at Amy. "Even though Irene threatened to bring the entire family, and everyone else she could find, over to Scotland if you didn't. I'm still glad you came." She kept her eyes focused on the road. "The kids have missed you."

"How are they?"

Celeste smiled broadly. "Naomi hasn't stopped talking about you. She is so excited at the thought of seeing you, and Daniel has been painting frantically. He has received merits for his artwork and wants to show you his portfolio."

Amy, feeling suddenly lighthearted, laughed and said teasingly, "Oh, a portfolio. My how very impressive." She smiled and closing her eyes said, "We might have a budding artist on our hands yet."

†

Celeste shook Amy gently awake. "Amy, we're here." She drew in a sharp breath as she slowly came around; Amy took her hand in hers and stroked it gently.

Aware that Amy was still sleepy and unaware of her actions, Celeste's stomach twisted. The urge to pull Amy into her arms was overwhelming so she gently pulled her hand away, and needing some air, opened the car door.

Amy sat up and yawned. "Are we here already?"

"Yes," Celeste replied, getting out of the car. "I think you should try to get more rest."

Amy got out of the car and stretched. "Yes." She nodded. "I'm really tired." She looked around expectantly. "I can't wait to see the kids."

Celeste got Amy's luggage out of the car and, turning toward Amy, smiled. "You'll see them soon enough."

Celeste's heart almost melted when Amy smiled back. She closed her eyes briefly and wondered how she was going to cope with the idea of never being physically close to this woman again.

†

Celeste drove Amy over to visit her mother the next day. Pulling up outside the house, Amy got out of the car and looked around, noting with surprise that the place really did look like a demolition site. She smiled to herself knowing that Irene was a huge do-it-yourselfer and was forever making modifications.

Standing at the door, Amy was attacked by a strong wave of guilt. She hadn't seen Irene in years and that was unfair to her mother; it made her think about how much she had missed out on her little sisters' growing up. That was the main reason she had given her mother her permanent address so she could be involved in her sisters' lives.

Bruce opened the front door and gave Amy an almighty hug before taking her directly up to Irene's bedroom.

Apprehensively, Amy entered the room and approached a sleeping Irene. She gently shook her awake.

As soon as Irene's eyes opened she started to cry, sobbing "My baby," through her tears. "Thank God, you're here at last."

Celeste watched the extremely emotional reunion unfold for a while before excusing herself and going to find Bruce.

Since Amy left there was no doubt in Celeste's mind that Irene struggled. Often, she would phone Celeste or come round for dinner or a chat and the conversation inevitably turned to Amy. Irene desperately missed her.

As the morning rolled on, Bruce and Celeste eventually interrupted and encouraged Irene to get some rest. "Although, she looks strong," Bruce said, looking at his wife tenderly, "she's very weak. This bug has knocked her out."

Denial

Nodding, Amy leaned over Irene and kissed her mother's cheek. "You're going to be okay, Mum." She looked into Irene's eyes for a long moment. "I've missed you."

Irene's jaw slackened, and holding Amy's hand tightly, sobbed.

The joy that crossed Irene's face when Amy called her 'Mum' brought a smile to Celeste's face.

Before leaving, Amy tried to talk Irene into letting her stay, insisting that she needed her. Irene shook her head, adamant that Amy stay with Celeste and visit her every day if she wanted. She told her firmly that Bruce would be more than able to look after her. She wanted Amy to spend time with Celeste's children.

"Please, jellybean. The girls are away until the end of the week on a trip," Irene said, her voice just above a whisper. "I would rather you visit every day."

Amy looked at her mother for a long moment. "Okay," she said finally then kissed her goodbye. "I'll see you tomorrow."

Celeste and Amy made their way downstairs where they spent some time with Bruce.

It was only after giving a list of instructions, Celeste noted with some amusement, that Amy seemed confident that Bruce would be able to look after Irene well.

†

Driving back to Celeste's house Amy thought about Josh. She had known for some time about his two children. She laughed inwardly. *Two children out of wedlock. How un-Josh like.* She smiled wistfully, realizing that even though he had a whole new life he was still married to her. There was no reason for them to be married, she thought. It was time they cut the strings. It was time they divorced.

Looking out the car window she wondered what Josh looked like now. She looked at Celeste and thought how little she had changed. He probably looked just the same. She caught her breath when her thoughts turned to Ryan and Christopher. They would be over eight years old now. She wondered what his children looked like. Her stomach lurched at the strangeness of thinking that Josh's children weren't hers.

Amy watched Celeste's hands for a while then asked, "How's Josh?"

Celeste gripped the steering wheel tightly.

"He's good," she said. "He's had a few ups and downs with the software company." She paused. "For a while it looked like it wasn't going to make it. They had serious problems with software bugs and the release date kept changing." She glanced at Amy. "The company almost went under. But, fortunately, they found some new investors. So, right now, he's sitting pretty." She glanced at her again. "He lives in New York."

Amy closed her eyes briefly, glad that she was genuinely pleased for Josh. Pleased that his business didn't go under and that he'd made it. He worked hard. He deserved it. New York, she thought.

Amy was fully aware that underneath Josh's easygoing manner there hid the heart of an ambitious entrepreneur. Familiar guilt filled her. Guilt she always felt whenever she thought of him, guilt that, even though he was suffering, she had left him. "Does he know I'm here?" she asked, somehow already knowing the answer. If he did, he would stop at nothing from seeing her.

"No."

"What are his children like?" Amy asked. But again, she knew the answer. During their visit, often out of earshot of Celeste and the boys, Naomi talked freely about all of her family—including Josh and his children. Naomi had whispered to her one day that her mommy had asked her and Daniel not talk about Josh and his family to Amy. Innocently, Naomi had explained that she wasn't to tell her too much about them so she didn't spoil Amy's surprise when she visited them.

Poor Celeste, she has tried so hard to protect me from the truth that Josh has moved on.

"Simone, she's a character," Celeste said carefully. She glanced at Amy. "Looks just like Josh and she has him wrapped around her little finger. She's almost two." She smiled. "And

Rachel, she's feisty like her mother. She's just a few months old and, like her father, she's always hungry."

"How did they meet?"

"They," Celeste hesitated, "they worked together. She's a software engineer."

Celeste searched Amy's face.

"Don't worry," Amy said, understanding that Celeste was concerned. "I understand Josh was never the type to be on his own for long." Amy couldn't help but smile. "What's his…partner's name?" Again, she knew the answer.

Celeste held her breath then exhaled slowly. "Denise," Amy whispered, "Denise." She said, "Josh, Denise, Simone, and Rachel."

Celeste threw her a look filled with deep concern. "Are you okay?"

"Yes," Amy replied. She sighed heavily. "It's him and the girls." She looked at Celeste. "Funny isn't it?" she said. "When we were together it was just me and the boys." She looked out of the window. "I think he should know I'm here."

Chapter 48

"Hi, Mom, Grand-mère is here."

"Is she?" Celeste said, putting her bag down. She reached for Daniel and pulled him into hug. "How are you?"

Daniel hugged her back then smiled and said excitedly, "Good. I've done lots more paintings today, and I want Amy to see them. Do you know when she'll be back?"

"I don't, sweetheart. She has a lot to do," Celeste said. "Where's your grand-mère?"

"She is in the kitchen," he replied, disappearing through the front door. "I'm going outside for a while."

Celeste entered the kitchen. She greeted Kate, the kids' nanny and swinging Naomi into her arms gave her a big kiss. With Naomi in her arms, Celeste went to her mother.

Camille was sitting at the kitchen table.

"Hi Mom, how's things?"

Camille stood up. "Kate, would you mind taking Naomi outside for a little time?"

Kate nodded. There was apprehension on her face as she looked from Camille to Celeste.

Celeste smiled reassuringly. Kate was a great help. She had been with Celeste for a few years now and while she was initially employed to help with the children they had quickly become good friends.

Celeste frowned and let Naomi slide out of her arms.

Kate shooed her outside.

Confused, Celeste said, "Mom, what's—"

"Shhh!" Camille interrupted and, holding up her hand, watched Kate and Naomi leave.

Closing her mouth, Celeste stared at her mother.

After a few moments Camille asked in French, "Why did you not tell me that Amy is here?" Then waving her finger back

Denial

and forth in reprimand, said, "It is not nice that she is here and you did not tell me."

Camille often reverted to her native tongue when she was around her daughter.

Celeste squared her shoulders. She should have known it wouldn't be long before the drums started beating. Concerned that everyone now knew she responded. "How did you know?"

Camille clicked her tongue. "I spoke to Kate yesterday." She tapped her nose with her index finger. She smiled cleverly. "I sensed she was not telling me everything." She shrugged. "And when I called back I spoke to Naomi and she told me." She tapped her foot. "Thank God it is not in the nature of a child to mislead."

Relieved, Celeste asked, "So, no one else knows?"

Camille clicked her tongue again. "*Non.*"

"Look Mom," Celeste said, suddenly weary. "I'm sorry I didn't tell you but that decision lies with Amy."

In typical French fashion, Camille expressed her disbelief by pulling down the skin under her right eye with her index finger. "My eye!" she said in annoyance.

Celeste held out her hands in frustration. "It's true. It's up to Amy whether she wants to contact you or not."

"*Chéri,*" Camille responded, looking at her daughter as if she'd been beamed down from another planet. "I am not going to bite her. If anything, you know I have missed her terribly and to find out she is *here* and that you may not have told me." She lifted her hands in the air. "Well, I know you are my child, but I shall never understand how your mind works."

Celeste looked at her mother. "Like I said, I didn't want to pressure Amy. The decision was and is hers." She turned her back on Camille and poured coffee into a mug. Keeping her back to her mother, she sipped it.

Camille approached Celeste and standing next to her looked at the counter. Ignoring the coffee mugs she removed a china cup from the shelf.

"When did Amy arrive?" she asked, pouring coffee into her cup.

"Two days ago."

"Where is she?" Camille asked, searching the shelf.

"I think she's at Irene's."

Clicking her tongue, Camille sounded aggrieved when she found what she was looking for. "Why do you insist on having sugar granules when you know that I like only sugar cubes?"

Celeste could not be bothered with indulging her mother's persnickety French traits. She said in English, "They're both sugar, Mom!"

Spooning the sugar into her cup, Camille tutted then sighed. "Mmmm…I suppose I shall just have to wait then. Maybe it is not a bad thing that she is not here. It will give you and I time to talk." She looked at Celeste and, sounding serious, added, "And we do need to talk, very much."

What about? Celeste thought with dread.

Camille had always been a rock for Celeste. She supported Celeste during her divorce and during the adoption process, and was a great help with the children. She was never one to criticize and only ever gave advice when asked. But Celeste sensed by the inflection in her mother's voice that things were about to change.

"Celeste, why is Amy here?"

Celeste's heart thudded. She took her time answering. "She's here to spend Christmas with her family."

"No. I mean, why is Amy staying here with you and not with Irene?"

"What do you mean?"

Camille breathed out slowly, obviously gathering courage. "What I mean, *chéri*, is that I know."

Celeste drank her coffee, then asked, "You know what?"

"Celeste, I have, possibly to my detriment, allowed you to hide your feelings for too many years without talking." She clicked her tongue. "Everything should be out in the open. It is healthier then, no?"

Celeste didn't respond.

Camille sat down and motioned for her daughter to join her. Celeste pulled out a chair and sat across from her mother.

Denial

"I know that you care for Amy. In fact, much more than care for her."

Celeste choked on her coffee. Spraying out of her mouth it splattered across the table.

Camille got out of her chair quickly and moved to Celeste. She rubbed her back as if winding a newborn, then reached for a cloth to clean the table.

"What are you talking about?" Celeste exclaimed in a raspy voice.

"You know exactly what I am talking about," Camille said. She stopped cleaning the table. "I am talking about you, my darling, being madly in love with Amy for some years now."

Astonished, Celeste stared at her mother.

"Call it mother's intuition," Camille said then shrugged. "I saw how you were around her." She waved her hand nonchalantly. "You can also blame your sister. When she has a few glasses of wine she likes to talk about how forlorn her sister is." Her voice mimicked Sophie's and she said in English, "Lost and in love with another." She looked at Celeste. "You know how dramatic she can be. It did not take much guesswork to understand whom she was talking about."

Celeste groaned and closed her eyes briefly. *Fuck! I'm going to kill Sophie!*

Camille picked up Celeste's mug and her cup and refilled them. She returned and sat down.

Celeste waited patiently for Camille to continue, knowing that Sophie was only dramatic because she had inherited that part of their mother's nature.

"To be frank, before the accident I was not fully aware of it. I saw that you had a strong interest in her. But I did not realize that it was of a...shall we say...romantic nature!"

Watching her daughter, Camille lifted her cup and slowly drank from it.

Celeste cringed. Blushing heavily, she wanted the ground to open and swallow her up. She looked at her mother, aware that she had a liberal attitude, which up until this very moment, she had enjoyed.

Camille put her cup down. "As far as I knew you had never shown any interest in women. And…well…you were married!"

Celeste, face deep crimson, decided at that moment that she really was going to kill Sophie. "Mother," she said abruptly, "where are you going with this?"

"Does Amy know how you feel?"

Celeste looked at her hands and was thankful that she had never confided too much in Sophie. She sat in silence, simply dumbstruck. She had no idea what to say.

"*Chéri*," Camille said. "You are my child. I have watched over you all your life. And there has always been a certain amount of remoteness that surrounds you." She shrugged and waved her hand dismissively. "Which I have never truly understood, but in the last few months, since you have made contact with Amy, I have never seen you so happy…so contented." Camille reached out and clasped her daughter's hand. "What I want is the truth, Celeste. I want to understand what is going on so that I can help you. Help Amy. Help us all." Pain edged her tone as she grasped Celeste's hand tightly. "The loss of the children has left a hole that has never been filled in my heart."

"Mom, where are you going with this?" Celeste asked gently this time.

Camille looked at her daughter for a moment. "Where I am going with this, Celeste, is that it was only after the accident happened and when Amy left that I fully understood your feelings for her." She patted Celeste's hand. "And I watched you go through your pain alone. I hope you understand I had to give what I had to Josh. Even though I knew that your pain was great also." Camille tightened her grip. "And somehow, as time slipped by, I was never able to tell you that I knew. Never able to take you in my arms and comfort you. But now I understand that I was not ready." She sighed. "In my day two women together were almost unheard of. But now," she shrugged, "times have changed. It is now the era of the individual."

Camille sat back and sipped her coffee. "Of course, I do not truly understand the satisfaction that women can have together," she said, her mouth turning down. "I think it would be

Denial

so…so…unfulfilling." She looked at Celeste. "But, I suppose that is because I like men, no."

Celeste rolled her eyes. This is impossible.

Obviously aware of Celeste's growing impatience, Camille said quickly, "*Chéri*, the point is that I want to know what is happening between you and Amy." Camille let go of Celeste's hand. "I want to help, that is all."

All her life Celeste had put her intellect before emotion, except with Amy. In all other areas she had balance. Now, her life was becoming more surreal by the minute. Her own mother was sitting here telling her that this was the era of the individual and, as such, she accepted that her daughter was in love with her son's wife.

Celeste couldn't handle it. Needing some distance, she stood. Lifting her mug she moved toward the kitchen sink. Sighing, she placed it in the sink and turned to Camille. She had no choice but to take an honest tack with her mother.

"Mom, it's true, I do love Amy." Anticipating her question, she held up her hand. "I've probably loved her since the first day I met her." Answering the question she knew would follow she added, "And no. I don't know why."

Celeste smiled faintly when Camille closed her mouth slowly.

Looking at her daughter intently Camille asked, "Have there been other…women?"

Aware that Camille was trying to understand, Celeste let her in. "Yes."

Looking confused, Camille asked, "But you were married?" She shook her head. "Are you bisexual or gay?"

Celeste rolled her eyes again. She didn't know if she had the strength for this. "Uhmmm…yes, I was married. But I had never been in love, truly in love, until I met Amy."

"Does Amy know?"

Celeste didn't answer.

Camille folded her arms and asked, "So, now that I know you are no longer bisexual should I refer to you as gay or lesbian?" She waved her hand. "I can never understand what the difference is."

Celeste growled. Impatience brewing in her face she said carefully, "Mom, I don't think that's relevant right now. Do you?"

Camille said soothingly, "No darling, of course not." She straightened. "You never answered my question."

Celeste frowned.

"Does Amy know?"

Celeste looked at her mother and realized that she may be kooky but she was as sharp as a tack. "Yes, Amy knows. But, before you start," she held up her hand again, "she doesn't want a relationship," she said, deciding the best way to handle this was to keep it simple and let her mother think that it was unrequited love.

Camille visibly relaxed. Celeste suddenly realized that her mother had probably carried the suspicion that Celeste and Amy had had an affair, and no matter how sympathetic her mother wanted to be that reality would have been distasteful to her.

Wanting to end the conversation, Celeste turned around and washed her mug. She watched the water run through her fingers and wondered if what she felt for Amy would ever be allowed to be like the water: clear, pure, and healthy.

It all seemed so complicated; how could Celeste explain that what she felt for Amy was unfettered and uncomplicated and always had been. She realized that what she felt for Amy had never wavered. Like the water running through her fingers it was a constant stream that flowed without doubt. Being with Amy had never felt anything but right.

Celeste turned to her mother and felt a wave of love. *How unique you are,* she thought. *Here you are, trying to accept that your daughter loves not only a woman, but the woman who is still married to your son and who gave birth to your grandchildren, the same grandchildren that you now miss desperately.*

Celeste wondered how truly crazy this entire situation must seem to her. She had newfound respect for her mother. Going to Camille, she hugged her. "Mom, I love you, and I appreciate you making this effort." She looked at her. "But right now I am finding my own feet, and I would appreciate if you don't say anything to anyone, especially Amy. It has taken a lot for her to be here and she has her own demons to face. I think she should be allowed to focus on what she needs to do, which is to find some closure. Okay?"

Camille smiled then nodded. Standing, she followed Celeste outside.

Tonight, Kate and her husband Sam were taking Celeste's children out with their own two kids.

Celeste hadn't spent any time alone with Amy. She had swapped shifts this evening to remedy that. Amy was due to return to Glasgow soon after Christmas and Celeste needed time with her.

Celeste sighed, aware that by the look on her mother's face that wouldn't be happening anytime soon. Camille, she knew, was going nowhere. Needing to release some of the tension that was building within her Celeste kissed the kids goodbye and told her mom she was going for a swim.

Celeste quickly changed into a bikini and headed for the water. Swimming out she felt the tension leave her. She loved the feel of the water; it soothed her like nothing else could. She thought back to when she and Nick bought the house, just after they married. When they divorced, it was part of her settlement.

Back then it was ramshackle and Nick didn't want anything to do with it. Fortunately, her father happily carried out the extensive renovation. At the time she was too restless to enjoy the finished property. Back then, she had desperately needed to get away and explore the world, but now the house and its location on Lido Beach were just perfect for her and, in particular, her children.

Celeste wondered fleetingly how differently Amy would have designed the house had they bought it together. Pulled up short by her thoughts, she stopped swimming.

Looking around Celeste was surprised that she couldn't see the shoreline. She'd been so deep in thought she had swam much farther than she intended. Words of warning from her old swimming coach flashed in her mind—it's always the strongest swimmers who drown first he often told her. As a young swimmer she had never truly understood what he meant but now, as she resisted swimming on, she knew that it was a swimmer's overconfidence in their ability that eventually brought them down. Turning, she swam back toward the shore.

Drawing closer Celeste saw Amy and Camille out on the deck. Her pulse thrummed in her ears. Even though she was confident of her mother's discretion she still felt a strong sense of disquiet now that Camille knew some of the truth.

Celeste swam the remaining distance quickly, then walked slowly back to the house.

†

Camille was delighted that Amy seemed so genuinely happy to see her. She could not believe the change in her. Camille had always thought of Amy as a child, even though she knew her to be a woman. She had always looked much younger than her years. But now, the person who sat before her was a woman of her years, and all the more beautiful with it.

Camille smiled, feeling such relief that Amy was here. She had missed her so much and thought of her every day. When Amy had chosen to go she had left a brief note for Josh, which, as it turned out, said nothing of importance other than she would not be back. Although shocked that Amy had gone, somehow, in her heart it did not surprise her. Camille understood that her daughter-in-law was broken. The loss of the children and her dear cousin, Maggie, had taken everything from her, and with nothing left, it appeared that the people around her were no longer enough.

Every day Camille prayed that Amy would return, and now, here she was. She reached over and patted Amy's hand. Amy looked at her, smiled and covered her hand with her own.

Camille looked at the hand that held hers and noticed small scars. She stroked Amy's hand reassuringly and tried to hide the sadness that filled her as she realized that this woman would never be the same young woman she once knew.

They sat in silence watching as Celeste approached. Camille looked at Celeste, taking pride in the fact that her daughter was not only very beautiful, but looked in excellent physical shape. A lot of that is down to her parents' good genes, Camille decided. Celeste's father was so handsome.

Camille was caught off guard when she saw Amy's face flush and a pulse begin to throb violently in her neck as Celeste approached them.

It took Camille seconds to realize that it was her daughter who was having this effect on Amy. To her surprise, instead of feeling upset she was delighted to find she was filled with a sense of relief. Sitting back Camille thought, I may be getting old, but regardless, I can still recognize that look when I see it. She watched Amy. Well, well. So, it is not all one-way after all.

Camille watched as her daughter approached and, patting Amy's hand, prayed that this young woman would find it in her heart to trust Celeste. She closed her eyes briefly and vowed silently: I promise you this, Amy, your love could not be in better hands.

Chapter 49

Feeling the heat, Alex took off his jacket and made his way along the beach. He smiled when he saw Amy sitting on a blanket with a picnic basket. His smile quickly faded when he realized they had hardly spent any time together since she'd arrived.

Walking closer, Alex saw Celeste and Colin in the water with the kids.

He looked at Amy and noted with surprise that she had a sketchpad.

Walking toward Amy Alex thought how truly stunning she was. Her yellow hair was loose around her shoulders. She was tanned and looking healthy. She wore a loose-fitting white linen shirt and linen shorts. Looking at her, Alex could clearly see why Celeste was so in love with her. He grinned, knowing that Amy hadn't painted in many years and was surprised and delighted to see her sketching now. This is a good sign, he thought, quickening his step.

Alex looked out to Celeste. He frowned. Celeste, in his mind, was becoming more withdrawn. Although she was trying to hide it he was aware that Amy being here was causing her tremendous strain. It was time for that wake-up call, he thought.

Approaching Amy, Alex watched her. He followed her eyes; she was watching Celeste and the kids intently. So intently that she didn't notice him nearing. He stopped and followed her gaze, noting that she was watching Celeste mostly. She wants her, he thought. She wants her and Colin's right, we need to help her see it.

"Hi," Alex said and sat down on the blanket.

Amy looked at him in surprise then pulled the sketchpad to her chest. "Hi."

Alex looked out to the water. "Don't you think Celeste is looking thinner?"

Amy looked at Celeste then shrugged.

Alex's hackles rose. Hating that she was so dismissive, he closed his eyes briefly aware he was about to step into the unknown. "She isn't coping."

Amy placed her sketchpad facedown.

Alex looked at the blonde surprised that she didn't ask him what he meant. Putting tact aside, he forged ahead. "Amy, she needs you and it's obvious you want her."

Amy didn't appear surprised by his frankness. She leaned back on her elbows, looked at him and then slowly turned her gaze to Celeste.

"Since you left she hasn't had anyone in her life, Amy. Not a single person." Alex looked out to Celeste. "She just couldn't." He paused. "After you left, at first I thought she would go insane." He shook his head, remembering. "I mean, I really did. She lost focus and direction," he said, looking at her intently. "Did you know she tried to find you?"

Amy looked at him and shook her head.

Alex frowned. There was no emotion in Amy's eyes. "Celeste begged Irene to tell her where you were." He pursed his lips before adding, "Well, you know yourself she didn't know anything." He ran a hand through his hair. "Amy, I know she hasn't told you, but the only thing that kept her going was the kids." Wanting some response he asked, "Do you understand what I'm saying. Losing you almost destroyed her. She loves you desperately. Always has."

Amy sat up and Alex took her hands. "It was never a game for her, Amy." He exhaled, and feeling like he was taking his life in his hands, added, "You can't keep punishing her for the loss of Maggie and the boys."

Amy flinched.

"She had no control over any of it," Alex added earnestly. "All she wanted to do was be with you, love you. Surely, you realize that. She needs you, as you need her. Look at them, Amy." He looked out. "We are your family."

Amy visibly choked and pulled her hands from Alex's. "Are you quite finished?"

Alex's stomach churned. Something was seriously wrong. "Are you?"

He nodded.

Amy locked eyes with him. He looked into her clear turquoise-blue eyes and his heart began to pound.

"If that's how you want to play it, Alex," Amy said coldly. "Then that's okay by me." She didn't hesitate. "Yes, Alex, I do blame her." She looked at Celeste. "I blame her for the affair."

Alex's brow broke out in sweat. Knowing it was risky ground but not wanting Celeste to take all the blame, he asked quietly, "Do you think you could have stopped it?"

Amy's eyebrows rose. "Probably not," she said with a note of resignation. "Not back then." She ran her hands through her hair. "You were there, Alex. You saw how addicted I was to Celeste. You saw how much control she had over me."

Alex cringed at the word control. Wanting to push the conversation away from the harsh word he asked the question he had been waiting years to ask. "Do you love her?"

Amy straightened. She looked at him, cocking her head to one side. "Love!" she said mockingly. "What exactly do you think that love is going to do, Alex? Change everything?" Her eyes gleamed with a coldness he had never seen before. "That suddenly all is forgiven? That we'll skip off and live as one big happy family?"

Alex looked at her, surprised at the sharpness of her tone.

"Well, it won't," Amy said with finality. "Do you want to know the truth?" Not waiting for his response she answered in a low tone as she looked at Celeste. "I am infested with her."

Alex drew in a sharp breath.

She looked at him then leaned her face to within inches of his. "Do you know what that feels like, Alex?" she asked bitterly. "To crave someone you want to hate?"

Stunned, Alex dropped his head into his hands. This wasn't turning out how he had planned it at all. He turned her words over in his head: *infested...hate.*

Amy leaned back. "Even now," she said, "even after everything, the pull is still as strong. Sometimes it is so

Denial

overwhelming," she added softly, her voice belying the anger that stoked her eyes, "that all I want to do is to tear her to shreds so I can breathe."

Looking at her Alex watched her metaphorically remove the pin from the grenade and launch it, blowing Celeste and everything he had hoped for out of the water.

Feeling tired Alex shook his head, realizing that he was delusional—more romantic than realist. Being an English Lit teacher he decided, as he dug his hands into the baking hot sand, had curbed his view of the world. He said brokenly, "You really are punishing her, aren't you?"

Amy stared at him as he shook his head. "You're punishing her by staying close to her." He added slowly. "Denying her."

Amy stared at him coldly, her face emotionless.

He leaned in. "God, Amy," he said. "You really know what you're doing. Don't you? Fuck, how I wish you could see that her love for you isn't ugly. She wasn't having a dirty little affair with you just for her own entertainment." Alex looked at her, his eyes filling up with tears. "You know she adores Josh." He thrust his hand out and pointing to the ocean, said angrily, "She's the one who hasn't breathed in years because of you. Because of what *you've* made her feel—love, passion, obsession, whatever the fuck it is that you two have. All those things arrived with you, Amy. *With you!*" Wanting her to take some responsibility, Alex wiped the tears from his eyes. "The reason you two came together was simply through love, Amy. Doesn't that mean anything to you?"

Amy reached out and held his arm tightly. "So what, Alex," she said. "People fall in love all the time." There was bitterness in her tone. "But most people make the choice to bury it and move on if it involves tearing their own family apart."

Alex knew he was losing ground. "You can't continue to punish her for loving you," he said in frustration. "Their death was an accident and you need to see that. You must see that she loves you with everything she has." Tears fell, as he pleaded, "You must see that what you're doing is destroying her."

Alex's jaw loosened when Amy turned to look at Celeste, "Oh, I know it is, Alex," she said chillingly. "But it's her choice."

Alex shook his head in disbelief. His mind filled with all the pivotal, but doomed, love affairs in the world of literature. He thought about the thin line between love and hate. His face paled as he realized that Amy might have crossed it.

Amy shifted. "Alex, I told her in Glasgow that I couldn't give her anything anymore. But she used the children." She stood. "Don't you get it, Alex?" She looked at him as if he were thick. "She's always had a choice. But she gave me none. I had a family. I was married to her brother, *her brother*, for God's sake, and I didn't want to have an affair with her. She left me with no choice." She turned her head and looking at Celeste said accusingly, "But she had a choice. I asked her to let me go and she refused and she still refuses."

Alex knew the one thing that Amy was denying was that their affair was inevitable, the attraction between them too strong. But everything had gone horribly wrong. Somehow, he had expected that if he spoke to Amy and was honest she would see the truth. He looked at her with disbelief and realized how seriously they had underestimated her anger and resentment.

Amy touched his arm. "Alex," she said gently. "I'm sorry. I know it isn't what you want to hear. I know you want a fairytale ending, but you're not going to get one. I don't want to blame her but being here has made me realize that I do." She stood and walked from Alex toward the house.

Alex stared after Amy. Reaching over, he flipped over her sketchpad. Startled, he blinked a few times. The hair rose on the back of his neck as he looked down at a grotesque caricature of Celeste.

†

Watching Alex from the window, Amy poured some water into a glass. How dare he? How dare he think he could give a pep talk and then everything would be okay? What did he expect?

She thought. That I would flounce into Celeste's arms after his little speech?

Looking out the window Amy watched Colin approach Alex. She drank some water and watched Alex's hands gesticulate when Colin took the sketchpad from him and looked at it. She caught her breath when Celeste approached them. She watched Colin slowly give her the pad.

Celeste never once lifted her eyes from the sketchpad while Alex spoke to her. When he finished she straightened. Her arms falling to her sides she moved slowly toward the house.

Amy placed her glass carefully on the kitchen work surface. She turned to face the door.

Celeste entered and stood across from Amy. Her movements slow, she put the sketchpad down on the table.

After a few moments Celeste spoke. "I had hoped being here would allow you to find some closure; would allow us to, somehow, put the past behind us. Allow us to build something together. A friendship? A relationship? It didn't matter what it was. I would have accepted anything. Any morsel you were prepared to give." Celeste smiled derisively. "It seems very naive of me, doesn't it?" she said, searching Amy's face. "Naive to hope that loving you would be enough?"

Amy stared transfixed at Celeste but said nothing. She focused on Celeste's lips, drinking in their fullness. Her pulse quickened. The sexual tension that had been building since they had made love a few months ago thrust forward as it had that day she sat on the deck watching Celeste emerge from the ocean. Again, it forged into one moment of absolute need.

Amy closed her eyes briefly in despair when a pool of desire flooded her. She turned to look out of the window and carefully monitored her breathing.

"That night in your apartment when we first made love, it was so unexpected," Celeste said, bending her head. "Believe me, I prayed, Amy. I desperately wanted not to want you. But whatever happened that night, you touched me. You made me feel things that no one ever had."

They stood in silence.

Celeste eventually spoke. "Because you were marrying Josh, and..." she hesitated, "and because you were carrying his child...children, I kept away. Hoping what I felt for you would pass. That it was some weird infatuation. But when I came home, the feelings intensified. They were so intense; so new, so uncontrollable. At the beginning I was genuinely confused. I actually believed that if we got together the infatuation would burn itself out."

"How naive!" Celeste looked at Amy. "The night I knew I loved you," she offered gently, "was when we were in New York. I held you in my arms and watched you sleep. I had never felt so frightened. I was thirty-three years old. I had seen atrocities that could unhinge the mind. But nothing had prepared me for what I felt for you. My heart, body, mind, everything was yours," she whispered. Her eyes darkened. "I am yours, Amy. And because of that I hope you understand that the choice has never been mine."

Celeste pulled Amy close and rested her forehead on hers for a moment before kissing her.

Amy's mouth instinctively opened and Celeste kissed her fully. The kiss carried none of the tension and anger between them.

Celeste kissed Amy for a long time, eventually taking it to a light, sweet, lingering kiss. Letting her go, she moved away.

Amy swayed at the loss.

"I'll give you time to pack and say goodbye to the children." Sadness filled her voice. "I would like it if you occasionally contacted them. But," she shrugged heavily, "it's up to you."

Celeste looked at Amy for a moment longer, misery pouring from her eyes.

Amy closed her eyes and turned away from her.

After a few moments Amy heard a car start. *At last! You've got what you wanted. Now quickly say goodbye and leave.*

But Amy didn't move. Instead, she watched the children play and gently stroked her lips, still wet from Celeste's kiss. She bowed her head realizing that even with everything she had been through, at this moment, she had never felt so alone.

Chapter 50

It had been weeks since Amy had come home. Since her return she had been unable to shake the cocoon of emptiness that surrounded her the moment she had parted from Celeste. Somehow, she had expected to feel a great sense of relief. But instead, to her surprise, everything she had successfully buried for the last few years was being pushed to the surface to such an extent that she was now unable to settle into a routine.

Following the first week of her return, on a whim, Amy had bought canvases, paintbrushes, and oils, and over the last few weeks, when she wasn't at work, she spent her time painting.

Amy stood back and looked at the painting that was half finished. "It's not my usual work," she muttered, before turning full circle to look at all the other canvases. She eyed them. Lifting her T-shirt she scratched her side and felt her ribs. She fingered each one, aware that she was neglecting herself, but she couldn't help it, she reconciled. Whatever time she had to spare, she needed it to paint.

Amy's stomach grumbled. Rubbing it she told herself that as soon as she got this out of her system she'd pay attention to herself and get right back on track, but her stomach rumbled loudly this time and Amy realized she couldn't wait; she needed to eat. She left the living room and walked down the hallway; it was dark. Recently, she liked it that way.

Entering the kitchen with a flourish, Amy threw open the fridge door and bending down, inspected it. To her disappointment the fridge was bare apart from a half-empty carton of congealed Chinese food. She smelled it, grimaced, then threw it in the bin. Her internal voice rankled, *You need to get your act together and get some shopping done.*

Over the last month Amy had been unable to work up any enthusiasm for shopping. Whenever she felt hungry she ate at the local café or at the hospital canteen. This was her weekend off and looking in the fridge she tried to remember the last time she'd eaten. She straightened and thought hard. Was it Saturday? She scratched her head and thought. No. It was Friday. I had a bowl of soup at the café on Friday.

Amy cringed when she realized that today was Sunday. She looked at her watch; surprised that it was ten in the evening. She hadn't eaten properly in more than three days.

"You must remember to eat," she told herself. "Otherwise, everyone will think you're losing the plot and—"

Amy stopped and listened. The phone was ringing. Expecting the call to be from her mother she slowly closed the fridge door and headed toward the living room. Before answering, she wondered how quickly she could get Irene off the phone and get back to work.

"Hello," she answered distractedly.

When she heard Daniel's voice Amy's focused sharply. He was excited, explaining he had won an art competition. Amy smiled as she listened. She had desperately missed the children.

After a few minutes she heard Naomi's voice grow louder. She was impatient to speak to her. After some wrangling, Daniel passed the phone to Naomi. Grinning, Amy took a seat and chatted with Naomi about what the little girl had been doing. She smiled when Naomi told her that her favorite pastime now was horse riding, and that she had recently lost her front tooth and had gotten *five* whole dollars under her pillow when the tooth fairy visited. Now she couldn't wait to lose all of her teeth, if that meant she would get five whole dollars every time.

Eventually, after much persuasion, Naomi passed the phone to Colin. "Hi, Amy," he said as he shooed the kids out into the backyard. "We've got them because Celeste is working late tonight." He hesitated. "They've been at me to let them call you, and since Danny won the art competition it's been the zillionth time, at least, that they've asked this week alone." He muttered in a low voice, "They miss you badly, you know."

Amy could tell he was anxious. He hadn't stopped for breath.

Denial

"And, well, you know, with kids it's too hard to explain what's really happening. I hope you don't mind. But I promise it'll be just this one time."

Amy's throat constricted and she coughed to clear it. "No," she replied. "Of course I don't mind." She paused. "How are you?"

"Oh, I'm fine. You know, everything's fine." His voice held a tinge of pride. "Alex has got a travel bug and wants us to go to Australia. He's convinced that my horizons need broadened." He laughed.

Amy smiled. To her surprise, she asked, "How's Celeste?"

Colin breathed in sharply. "Well," he answered after a moment. "I'd like to say she's fine but she's not. She's really struggling." Frustration crept into his tone. "Oh, look man...I don't know if it matters now. Does it?" He didn't wait for her to respond. "You've made it pretty clear where you stand. And anyway I called for the kids' sake."

Amy's heart sank. She could hear the tension in his voice. She was sorry their friendship had ended this way.

Colin said quickly, "I gotta go, Amy. The kids are calling me out back." He hesitated then lowered his voice, "But if you really want to know, I've never seen her look so bad." To Amy's surprise he sounded almost wistful. "I have always admired Celeste for her strength." He laughed a little. "You know she's that type with the quiet but strong demeanor. But since you've been gone, she's agitated. She's thin...too thin." He breathed. "She's not herself. She can't eat, she can't sleep because she's missing you. She needs you. But," he added so harshly that Amy could almost see him squaring his shoulders, "you know that, Amy. Don't you?" He finished coldly. "You've always known that, haven't you?"

Amy's jaw dropped.

He whispered into the receiver, "Huh, don't you?" His tone softened. "I wish I could knock some sense into you, Amy. I want to wake you up. You love her. You don't hate her. But your anger and resentment is affecting not only you but all of us. And to be honest, it has for a long time now." He sighed heavily. "Too long."

Surprised, Amy struggled, but couldn't find anything to say.

"Do you know what the cruel part is, Amy?" Colin asked. "It's that you've allowed her to take all the blame. You need to stop blaming her and wake up to the real world, take some of the responsibility on board yourself. It takes two to tango, sweetie."

Amy still hadn't uttered a word.

She heard anger in his tone. "Don't make me believe you're a lost cause, Amy."

Again, she said nothing.

Colin sighed. "Good luck with your life, Amy. If you continue like this you'll need it."

Amy heard a click, then the dial tone. She stared at the phone, stunned. Her stomach churned as his words replayed in her mind. The familiar anxiety she had been experiencing since she returned rose a notch. Tired and very upset she slouched and sat for a long time with the phone in her hand. Eventually, she put it down and standing, approached her painting. She stood for a moment, staring at it, before picking up the paintbrush and working on the canvas.

†

Amy looked at her watch. It was seven in the morning and she hadn't stopped since the phone call last night. She let out a frustrated sigh realizing that she had less than one hour to get showered and ready for work. She put down her paintbrush and looked at her hands; they were covered in paint. She pulled at her T-shirt and looked at it; it was soaked in paint. Amy moved quickly toward the bathroom. Partway there, she started feeling lightheaded. She stopped to lean against the wall. She thought about sitting down but knew that if she did she wouldn't have the energy to get back up. She pressed her head against the wall, aware she was reaching her limit.

After a few minutes, she made it. Weak, she undressed before opening the glass door to turn on the shower. Standing under the cold blast of water, shivering, she waited for the water to heat up. Once the water warmed, she bent forward and put some turpentine on a cloth. Following a ritual that she had been carrying out every workday since she started painting again she began to remove the paint from her arms before scrubbing the rest of her body.

Methodically, Amy removed all traces of paint. She had gotten into the habit of painting barefoot in Sarasota and preferred to paint barefoot even though it was winter here.

Working on her feet, which were blocks of ice, and too weak to stand, Amy was forced to sit in the bathtub to finish the job.

After she finished dressing for work Amy sniffed the air. Although the turpentine she used was odorless, she always ensured there was absolutely no evidence of a smell with spray deodorant and perfume.

Her stomach grumbled loudly and Amy decided as she put her coat on that she would stop off and order some hot broth and hot bread rolls at Denny's. At the front door she bent down to collect the post. It was the usual mail, which recently she hadn't even bothered opening.

Amy picked up the bundle and put it with the other mail on the dresser in the hall. A large manila envelope, postmarked from Sarasota, caught her attention. Her heart thudded. Opening it she carefully pulled out its contents. She read the note attached to the sheet of paper.

Hi Amy,
Danny is desperate for you to see his work. Hope you like it.
Drop a note to let us know how you are and what you think.
Hope you're well.
Love,
Alex

Amy held a copy of Daniel's painting. It was his home on Lido Beach. She looked at it. His painting was beautiful. There was a huge yellow sun on the rise and big black birds flying across the sky. There were sand dunes that didn't belong, but at his age it was a good sign of a fertile imagination. The colors were vibrant.

Amy smiled, acknowledging that he had a real talent. She felt a lump in her throat and squeezed it to relieve the tightness forming. She touched her cheek, expecting tears, but there were none. Surprised, she wiped her hand across her cheekbone just to check before carefully sliding the sheet back in the envelope.

On my next day off, I'll get it framed.

Chapter 51

Arriving at work carrying her hot soup and hot, buttered rolls Amy pushed open the heavy door that led into the children's ward with her shoulder and entered the nurses' room. She smiled when she saw Sandra, who was back for the first time since taking six weeks of unpaid leave to backpack across Indonesia.

Sandra gasped when she saw Amy, unable to believe the transformation. Amy looked terribly thin, her hair tied back in a tight bun, her skin pale with dark circles under her eyes. She looked ghastly. Sandra was surprised. Since Celeste and the children's visit during the summer, Amy had put on some weight, had looked in good shape and the picture of health. In fact, Sandra had met Celeste and the children many times during their stay and loved the fact that they were such a good influence on her friend.

Amy hugged Sandra. "Thought you might need this," she said, handing her a cup of hot soup. "It's bloody freezing outside."

Accepting the soup Sandra said, half-jokingly, "You look like hell. You haven't missed me that much have you?"

Putting down the cup, Amy smiled and shrugged out of her coat, then took off her gloves and scarf.

Sandra gawked at her friend, shocked at how loose her uniform was.

Sitting down Amy peeled the lid off her cup and shoved her nose into the steaming smell of the delicious soup. She opened up a bag with the hot buttered rolls and passed one to Sandra.

Transfixed, Sandra watched Amy dunk the roll into her cup and catch the soggy bread in her mouth. Amy moaned and her eyes rolled back. She dunked again and gave the task of eating her full attention. She finished her roll quickly.

Sandra pushed her bread roll toward Amy, offering it to her. "Are you sure?"

"Yes," Sandra replied. "I had something to eat this morning." She tried to hide her concern with a smile.

Amy smiled back and took Sandra's bread roll and dunked it into her soup.

Sandra watched, aware by the looks of her that Amy hadn't eaten a proper meal in a while. She queried gently, "What have you been up to?"

Amy chewed and swallowed. "You know me, busy, busy, busy."

Yes, Amy, Sandra thought. By the looks of it you've been too bloody busy, busy, busy!

Concern showed on Sandra's face as she watched Amy eat. With sudden insight she thought, sadly, *you haven't been coping since you got back from Florida, have you?* She felt a stab of guilt that she hadn't been there for Amy. Taking her friend's hand and deciding to keep it light she said jokingly, "I hope busy, busy, busy involved shagging all weekend because you look absolutely knackered."

Amy grinned. "If I said yes would that put a hold on you nagging me?"

"It would certainly explain why you look like you haven't slept in a week," she said affectionately. But unable to hide her concern, added, "Amy, you really do look like shit. Has this anything to do with Celeste or the children?"

Lifting her cup to her mouth, Amy paused for a second before draining it. Putting the empty cup down she stood and reached out, touching Sandra's cheek. Completely ignoring her question she said, "I'm glad you're back." Then turning she headed out the room to begin her shift.

Sandra frowned. Concerned and wanting to know what the hell was going on she said, "Amy, I'm—"

As she turned to look at Sandra Amy hit the edge of the table near the door. Tumbling forward, she fell to the ground.

Sandra rushed to her. "How are you feeling, honey?" she asked, taking her hand and helping her up.

Amy nodded dazedly. "Fine," she replied, grimacing as she held her side. "I'm winded, that's all."

Denial

Sandra helped her over to the nearest chair. "Amy, I think you should go home. You look shattered."

Amy looked at her in surprise.

"I'll arrange for a taxi, and I'll stop by and check on you tonight. Okay? No arguments. I'm not taking no for an answer," she said forcefully. "You're going."

Sandra picked up the phone and dialed a local taxi number. Waiting for the call to be answered she looked at Amy and said in a worried tone, "You really do look absolutely exhausted."

Organizing the taxi, Sandra put down the phone and looked at her watch; she really needed to get back to work. She had been off the ward for far too long already.

Sandra sat next to Amy. "Amy, you're exhausted," she said. "You need to rest. Why don't you take the next couple of days off? We'll cope. It seems pretty quiet and if there's any change I promise I'll get your bony arse in here, pronto." She took Amy's hands into her own. "Honey, by the look of you it's evident that you've been pushing yourself far too hard. Neil mentioned to me on the phone that you were working all sorts of weird and wonderful shifts. You need to stop that. You can't be here twenty-four seven. You'll burn yourself out if you keep this up!"

Amy looked at her.

Sandra looked into Amy's eyes and whispered with shock, "That's what you're trying to do, isn't it?" She gave her an incredulous look then said with determination, "But no more, because Sandra's back to make sure you're okay. Okay?"

Amy smiled faintly.

Sandra stood up. "Go home and rest. I'll drop by and see you tonight after I've finished my shift." She pulled Amy up and helped her into her coat, wrapping her scarf around her as if she were a child.

Picking up her gloves Amy murmured, "You're right. I'm tired. I need some rest."

Relieved Amy had come to her senses Sandra gave her a hug before walking her out of the ward.

†

Sandra parked her car, grabbed the Chinese food and the bottle of wine she had bought, and headed toward Amy's apartment. Stomping her feet to shift the snow from her shoes, she buzzed for entry. Over the last few years she had taken to dropping by Amy's apartment at least a couple of times a month for some Chinese food, a bottle of wine and some gossip. Amy never drank so Sandra usually had the bottle and stayed over. She knew Amy wasn't into going out so it tended to be a girls night in.

When Celeste, the children, and the boys were here, Sandra had stopped by often. She really enjoyed their company and picked up pretty quickly that there was a something between Amy and the gorgeous brunette.

When Colin and Alex were here Sandra had bonded with Colin straightaway. During an evening out with Colin he filled her in on everything she needed to know, including the affair with Celeste and the accident. She hadn't been surprised that Amy had a history. It was evident when she treated her in hospital in Australia that Amy had a past by the very fact that she never spoke about it.

Sandra's heart went out to her friend. She had always felt a sense of protection over her for some reason. When Colin told her the full story she had actually cried like a baby right there in the pub. Colin too, albeit the couple of bottles of wine they had might have contributed to a large part of their public display.

Desperate to get into the heat, Sandra buzzed Amy's apartment again. She shivered and thought about how exhausted her friend looked this morning. *What the hell happened over there in Sarasota that's driving her to work herself to sheer exhaustion?* Even though Amy had never confided in her about her past, other than cursory information, Sandra decided that tonight, whether Amy liked it or not, they were going to have a serious talk.

Shivering, Sandra buzzed again. She had phoned Amy once today but there had been no answer; she hoped the blonde was catching up on some much-needed shuteye. During her trip,

Denial

Sandra had phoned Amy lots of times and always got reassurance over the phone that she was fine. Sandra rolled her eyes and thought if only she'd known.

Pulling the lapels of her coat closer Sandra frowned, remembering that before she left for her vacation she had specifically asked Neil to look after Amy. She had even spoken to him several times during her vacation. Never once had he cracked a light that something was up. Sandra shook her head and thought she shouldn't be surprised that the twit had never noticed the state Amy was in. He only ever paid attention to what he could get his leg over, and recently he'd been dating a girl with a pulse, which meant that he had the attention span of a gnat. Sandra made a mental note to put him on permanent night shift for the next month.

Impatiently, she buzzed several times and sighed with relief when Amy eventually buzzed her in. Shivering, Sandra made her way up the stairs. She sighed, pleased that her shift was over. The first day back was always a killer. She smiled when she saw Amy had left the door ajar. Pushing it fully open she walked straight in.

Sandra stood for a moment, surprised that the hallway was dark. There were no lights on, apart from the living room. Calling out Amy's name she followed the light and entered the room.

Sandra stood stock-still. Her mouth fell open and only her eyes moved, absorbing her surroundings. The place was a mess. There was paint everywhere; over all the furniture, up the walls, on the curtains, even on the ceiling.

Sandra blinked a few times then noticed Amy in the corner. She stared at her and waited for some sort of explanation. She blinked, suddenly aware that Amy was standing in front of a painting with a paint-splattered sweater on.

Sandra let out her breath and watched it evaporate in the cold air registering with shock that the temperature in here was cold. She frowned and looked around.

Not wanting to let Amy know Colin had blabbed her whole life story Sandra stammered, "I...I didn't know you painted, Amy..." Her words fell away when she realized the room was dank and depressing, not the bright room she was used to. She caught her breath when she noticed that all of Amy's paintings were unremittingly dark. There was no life in any of them. They appeared to be variations of the same theme—all filled with women holding their heads and screaming, all crying out in pain. Some of the paintings had just one woman and others had women squashed against each other morphing into one.

The blood drained from Sandra's face when she realized she was surrounded by what seemed like hundreds of silent voices screaming out in pain. Horror crossed her face as she looked around the room; it was littered with canvases. Some stacked on top of each other. Others leaned against walls. All were painted with detail, and all put aside obviously never to be looked at again.

Sandra dropped the Chinese food and the bottle of wine. The wine clanged when it hit the wooden floor. Clasping her hands to her chest she looked agog at the faces, screaming their pain and agony. She covered her ears positive she could hear them. Her eyes stopped at Amy. She was standing with a paintbrush in her hand, staring at her.

Sandra dropped her hands and walking quickly toward Amy, pulled her out of the room with her. Breathless, she leaned heavily against the closed door. Goose bumps ran up and down the length of her. She shook and then shivered.

"Bloody hell, Amy," Sandra said, reaching blindly for the light switch. "It's a psychiatrist's playground in there. No offense, honey. But your paintings are gruesome." She sighed with relief when she found the switch. She flicked it up and down a few times.

"Don't bother," Amy replied quietly. "I took all the lightbulbs out."

Sandra squeezed open the door of the living room just enough to allow some light to filter out. She looked at Amy but couldn't see her properly. After seeing those screaming faces she didn't need to ask why she had taken the lightbulbs out. She asked slowly, "Amy, have you put them somewhere?"

Denial

Amy nodded. "Yes. They're all in the living room, in a paper bag."

Sandra shivered and thought that there was no way she was going back in there. "Amy, listen to me," she said, holding her friend's arms. "This all adds up to one thing!"

"What?"

"Honey, you are having one serious, fucking meltdown!" She pushed Amy forward. "Right, get your coat. We're getting the hell out of here!"

Chapter 52

Nerves hit Amy's stomach as she prepared her uniform for work. She reassured herself as she hung it up that everyone felt like this when they had time off. When Sandra had hustled her out of her apartment that night a few weeks ago she had insisted that Amy stay with her. It didn't take Sandra long to get information out of Amy. She was shocked when she realized that Amy had been locked up in her apartment, painting frantically, each night the same thing over and over again.

Amy tried to explain to Sandra that she had only been exorcising her demons and it should be looked on as nothing more than a cathartic experience. But it was only on returning to her apartment and looking around that Amy was left in no doubt that, for a period, she had lost it completely.

Amy was shocked to see, not only the volume of paintings she had produced, but also what they depicted. Somehow, she hadn't understood how dark and oppressive her exhibition truly was. What had really taken her by surprise was the actual state of the apartment. She was shocked when she saw handprints over practically everything; every piece of furniture was ruined.

Amy shivered as she thought back to that night when Sandra had showed up. She grimaced as she remembered the look of horror on her face. It was only then that she fully saw what she had been painting. That was five weeks ago and for the last two, Amy, Sandra, and Neil had gutted her apartment and completely redecorated it. It had been hard work, but as Amy looked around her newly decorated pad, it was well worth it.

For the second time Amy owed much of her recovery to Sandra. In Australia, she was a great friend. When Sandra thought she was ready she had revealed to Amy that Colin had told her about her past. Unsurprisingly, Amy found Sandra an easy confidant and their conversations went a long way toward healing her. Now, more than ever, Amy was appreciative of

Denial

Sandra's friendship. In some ways, Sandra reminded her so much of Maggie and she drew great comfort from that.

A few well-chosen colors and some new furniture made the apartment look terrific. Amy had to admit they had done a grand job.

The phone rang.

Amy picked it up. "Hello."

It was Irene. Amy settled into the sofa, knowing this wouldn't be a short call.

Over the phone Amy reassured her mother that everything was fine. Irene intended to visit with the girls in a few weeks. Amy told her that everything was ready, and there was nothing she needed.

Still Irene asked, "Are you sure you don't need anything?"

Amy smiled and replied affectionately, "Look Mum, what part of *no* don't you understand? Everything is ready for you and the girls. The flat has been given a complete makeover. Now relax, will you."

Amy eventually got Irene off the phone with a promise that she would call her the next day.

†

Amy woke with a start. She felt for her watch and realized with surprise that she wasn't wearing it. She rubbed her forehead and tried to think where it was then drew in a sharp breath when she realized she wasn't in bed. Sitting up, she looked around in bewilderment then realized she was on a beach. She gasped when she noticed Celeste close by, lying on her side.

Amy stretched out her hand but wasn't close enough to touch her. She leaned on her elbow and reached out again, but still, she wasn't close enough to touch. She called to Celeste several times, but she didn't respond. Eventually she stood up and went to her, bending down she gently shook her, but Celeste wouldn't stir.

Concerned, Amy shook her hard, but Celeste didn't wake.

There was the sound of children's laughter. Amy stood up and shaded her eyes. Looking out toward the ocean she could see

Daniel and Naomi in the water, playing. She noted with surprise that there was a giant yellow sun in the sky, and feeling strangely lighthearted, she smiled when a flock of big, black birds flew by.

Amy looked around her. The sky and the ocean seemed different somehow. She couldn't believe the colors. Everything was so vibrant, so familiar. Like, she struggled to remember, like one of her paintings. No, she thought. It's like the print that Alex sent of Daniel's painting.

Looking around, Amy was aware of how surreal things seemed and how sharply focused they were at the same time. She looked down. "Celeste, please wake up. You need to see this." She looked around. "It's paradise!"

Amy repeated Celeste's name, louder this time. She bent down and shook her again, but still Celeste wouldn't wake. She looked up sharply; the children's laughter was getting louder as if they were coming closer.

Amy stood and looked out but the children hadn't moved. She shaded her eyes and watched them play. Even though everything felt strange, she smiled. Somehow, this felt right. After a moment, she frowned and rubbed her forehead trying to remember how she got here. A movement from the side of her vision caught her attention—a figure was moving toward them.

Amazed that even from a distance she could clearly make out the shape of a person, Amy frowned and thought it should be a complete blur. She chewed her bottom lip, unable to understand. Her attention fixed on the shape moving toward her. Intrigued, she studied it. The shape was tall and the walk familiar.

Wanting a better look, Amy moved forward a few steps. Her heartbeat quickened as the figure moved closer. She turned her head and looked at Celeste. She was still sleeping. She looked back at the figure and caught her breath.

Amy exhaled heavily before whispering, "No. It can't be! It's impossible!"

The figure progressed toward her with a steady pace. Impatient, Amy moved toward it fast, needing to get close so she could see more clearly who it was.

Denial

Knowing this couldn't be real and unable to believe her own eyes, Amy uttered, "It can't be? It can't. It can't be...*Maggie?*"

Amy broke into a run, quickly closing the distance between them. Without a thought she fell into Maggie's arms. Unable to believe it was truly her Amy kissed her face all over as tears streamed down her own. She hugged her cousin and, needing to be convinced, cried out, "It's you, isn't it?" She grabbed Maggie's arms firmly. "It is you, isn't it?" She laughed wildly. "It's definitely you!" She looked at Maggie incredulously. "I can feel you!" She ran her hands up and down the redhead's arms in wonderment. "You're skin and bone!" she said excitedly. "I can definitely feel you."

Amy looked at her with elation. "You're real, aren't you?" she said as she hugged Maggie and laughed heartily. "You're so real." She held her tight. "You're so very, very real! I've missed you so much, Maggie. I can't believe you're here!"

Maggie kissed her back. "I've missed you too, jellybean," she replied gently.

For the next few minutes they danced around hugging and kissing each other.

Eventually Maggie stopped but still held Amy in her arms.

Amy was grinning so wide she thought her face might split. She looked at her cousin and her heart missed a beat. She looked around, hoping against hope.

"Maggie," Amy hesitated and looked around once more. Almost too frightened to ask, she uttered, "Are they here with you?" She gripped Maggie's arms and said in growing excitement, "I mean...the boys. Are the boys here with you?"

Maggie smiled and nodded. "Yes, jellybean, they're here."

Amy's legs went weak. She leaned into Maggie. "Where?" She looked frantically around her. "Where are they, Maggie?"

"They're over the sand dunes, Amy," Maggie said, pointing westward.

Unable to believe that she was minutes away from seeing her sons, Amy excitedly grabbed Maggie's hands and pulled her toward the dunes. "Let's go, Maggie," she said feverishly. "Let's go and get them."

Maggie pulled Amy back into her arms and smiled. "No need," she replied comfortingly. "They're safe."

Confused, Amy pulled out of her cousin's arms and looked at her. Beginning to feel uneasy she said, "I want to see them, Maggie." Then firming her voice, insisted, "I want to go to see them now, Maggie!"

Maggie, still smiling, moved closer and stroking Amy's face said softly, "Jellybean, you can't."

Amy's stomach heaved, she sobbed. "Please, Maggie. Please."

The redhead pulled Amy back into her arms. Unable to hold back Amy sobbed hard. Maggie held her tight and cooed, "Let it all out, jellybean."

Amy cried inconsolably.

Eventually she looked at Maggie. "I miss you so much." She closed her eyes. "I miss the boys so, so much." Tears flowed. "I'm so sorry I didn't go with you that weekend."

Maggie lifted Amy's chin smiled at her then kissed her forehead. "It's all right, jellybean. It's all right." She shushed Amy as she protested.

Hurting, and not wanting to hear Maggie's words, Amy pulled out of her arms. "Please, Maggie, come with me to get the boys."

Maggie shook her head. "No."

Amy stared at her, then stomped her foot into the sand and insisted that she see her boys.

Maggie was unrelenting. Amy tried again. She begged the redhead to take her to see them.

"No," Maggie said, shaking her head.

Amy looked at Maggie with pleading eyes, then hanging her head moved off toward the sand dunes, leaving her cousin behind. She walked slowly but soon excitement overtook her at the thought of seeing her boys. She started to run but quickly realized that no matter how much ground she covered she wasn't nearing the dunes. Feeling the heat, she slowed to a jog then slowed to a walk. Eventually, exhausted, she stopped and stared at the dunes. She was no closer. It seemed the more she moved toward them, the more they moved away.

Maggie shimmered in front of her.

In shock, Amy staggered back. She looked back to where Maggie should have been no more than a blip on the horizon. She stared at her cousin and stuttered, "How…how did you do that?"

Maggie moved closer and taking her cousin into her arms let out a real belly laugh. Obviously loving that she had surprised Amy she eventually managed to say, "It's good isn't it?" She laughed hard.

The shock left Amy and was quickly replaced with laughter. She had forgotten how much of a tease Maggie was. She joined her when the redhead let out another raucous laugh.

Amy was laughing hard when Maggie looked past her. She stopped laughing. She looked at Amy and said in a serious tone, "Jellybean, there's no need to worry. They're fine. I'm looking after the boys." She tenderly swept sticky hair from Amy's forehead, "Just as I've always done. Just as I always did with you."

"I miss you."

"I know," Maggie said, rubbing Amy's arms. "Amy, everything happens for a reason, great love as well as great loss. They happen to test the limits of our souls." She smiled at Amy. "Without these tests, life would be a straight, flat road; safe, dull, and completely and utterly pointless."

Blinking, Amy looked at Maggie with confusion.

Maggie looked over Amy's shoulder. "Now listen to me," she said anxiously. "You need to focus on what I'm saying." She looked at Amy. "She will need you. Go to—"

Buzzzzzzzzzzzzzzzzzzzzzzzzzzzzzzzzz

Amy woke with a start. Heart pounding she sat up and dazedly looked around her. Reaching over she hit her alarm. "Dream," she told herself as she wiped a hand over her sweating face. "A dream," she reassured, running her hands through her hair. Eyes wide, she breathed in and out until she calmed.

Waves of crippling sadness washed over Amy when she finally understood it was just a dream.

Chapter 53

"Glad your first day's over?" Sandra asked as she tucked into Chinese takeout.

Amy nodded.

Sandra chewed on her food. "It always takes me a few days to get back into the swing of things."

"Thanks for your concern, but I'm fine, Sandra," Amy said, putting down her fork, she lifted her glass of juice.

Sandra nodded. "I know."

They ate in silence.

"What's on your mind?" Sandra asked, scooping a forkful of noodles into her mouth.

Amy looked at her friend and shook her head. "Nothing, I'm just tired."

"Amy," Sandra responded. "I know you."

Amy smiled. "I know."

Sandra wrapped some more noodles around her fork. "Are you going to tell me?"

Amy sighed. "I had a dream last night, that's all. And it's on my mind."

"What kind of dream?"

"Vivid," Amy replied. Losing her appetite she got up and moved toward the garbage can.

"And?"

Amy flipped the lid and emptied her plate. "*And*," she answered, moving around the kitchen. "I don't know." She put her plate in the dishwasher. "I don't really know what it was about." She shook her head. "But Maggie was there and it felt real. She felt real."

"Maybe it was," Sandra replied, pushing her plate aside.

"What?"

"What did Maggie say?"

"I'm not sure," Amy said, shaking her head.

Denial

"Think."

"Why are you so interested?" Amy asked, frowning.

"Because sometimes these things can be really important."

Amy shrugged. "It was a dream, that's all."

"Was there anyone else there?" Sandra asked, picking up her beer bottle.

Amy raised her eyebrows. It never ceased to amaze her how sharp Sandra was. "Celeste," she replied, throwing the empty containers in the bin. "Celeste and the boys were there."

"They say dreams that appear so vivid, that seem real, happen so that we can be communicated with—"

"Don't," Amy said. "Whatever you have to say I don't want to hear it."

Sandra took a deep breath then exhaled. "When I was married I lost a baby."

Startled, Amy looked at her friend. "You never told me."

"Skeletons in closets have a habit of staying there, Amy," Sandra replied, shrugging. "Anyway, you knew about the marriage."

"I knew you were married, but that's about it."

"What is there to know? He was an arse who left me for another woman. End of story."

Amy returned to her seat and took Sandra's hand. "What happened?"

Sandra looked at their hands. "She died when she was a few months old."

Amy's grip tightened. "I'm so sorry."

Sandra nodded. "Her name was Mia," she said the pain shining bright in her eyes. "After my Gran."

"Why didn't you tell me?"

Sandra's eyes widened. "Do you really need me to tell you why?"

"Okay, point taken." Amy smiled. "We're even. No more secrets."

"Agreed." Sandra sipped her beer. "The bastard left me when I was pregnant. Eight months to be exact."

Amy closed her eyes briefly.

"I blamed him at first." Sandra sighed. "Then I blamed myself."

Amy reached out and stroked her friend's face. "I'm here for you. Tell me."

"I don't know what to tell you," Sandra replied. "One minute she was healthy, next minute she had heart problems." Tears brimmed then fell from her eyes. "Congenital cardiovascular malformations." She sniffed. "Her wee heart gave out. They didn't pick it up. There was nothing they could do." She wiped her face with the corner of her sleeve and sniffed again. "There was nothing I could do."

Amy moved out of her chair and hugged Sandra.

"I blamed myself. Thought it was because of the split," Sandra said, holding Amy tightly. "But, in retrospect, I totally focused on not getting stressed in anyway during the pregnancy." Sandra looked at Amy. "I can't really blame him. I was in a marriage that should never have happened and I was glad to be rid of him, to be honest." She smiled through her tears. "I've already told you he was an arse?"

"Aye." Tears falling, Amy laughed. "I think you've mentioned that already."

Sandra let Amy go. She rubbed her wet nose. "Amy, I'm dripping all over the place, any chance of a tissue?"

Sniffing, Amy nodded. "I need one too." She got up and brought back a box of tissues. She passed Sandra a handful.

Sandra looked at the bundle. "Crikey, my nose isn't that big!"

"No?" Amy teased. "Let me know when you're going to blow. I'll take cover."

Sandra laughed. "Any chance of a cup of tea," she asked. "To finish off the night."

"No problem." Amy replied. She put the kettle on.

"Anyway, the whole point of me telling you this is that I had a dream," Sandra said. "Just like yours. It was vivid. So vivid that every detail has stayed with me." She looked off into the distance then shivered slightly.

Denial

Putting the cups out Amy noticed that her hands were shaking. Sandra must have noticed too because she got out of her chair and came to her. Taking Amy's trembling hands in hers she gave them a reassuring squeeze before moving over to the fridge.

"When my Gran died I was in my mid-twenties," Sandra said, taking out the milk. "She brought me up, you know."

"What happened to your folks," Amy asked with concern.

"Nothing really," Sandra replied. "Nothing that dramatic, anyway." She shrugged. "I'm the product of a teenage pregnancy; a one-night-stand."

Amy looked at Sandra.

"I never knew who my dad was, and my mum," Sandra said, shaking her head, "she was too young to cope. My gran fell into the role of looking after me." An affectionate look crossed Sandra's face "She was a great old biddy, brilliant to the end."

Amy filled the teapot with hot water.

"In my dream," Sandra said, taking the milk top off the carton. "Gran was standing with her arms out to me, wanting me to pass Mia to her but I didn't want to. I was crying really hard." She looked at Amy. "You know, that way when you cry so hard you can't get your breath."

Pouring tea into the cups, Amy nodded.

"But she kept smiling and telling me it was okay." Sandra passed Amy the milk. "That she would look after her and that I wasn't to worry. That she would look after my baby, like she had me."

Amy stirred the milk into the cups and not looking at Sandra said, "Maggie told me the same."

Nodding, Sandra came close to Amy. "Did she?" she encouraged.

Amy nodded. "What does it mean?"

Sandra picked up a steaming cup. "I don't know." She paused. "It could mean everything. It could mean nothing." She blew into the cup. "I'm not very religious, but maybe it's not all over when you die. Maybe there's something more." She looked at Amy. "All I know is that we don't have all the answers. On a bad day, I get a lot of comfort knowing that maybe Mia is being looked after by someone I love."

Amy picked up her cup.

Sandra sipped her tea. "What did Maggie say?"

Amy tensed. Her voice choked up a little. "That she had the boys."

"Good," Sandra said. "What did she say about Celeste?"

Amy looked at her in surprise. "She...I..." She shook her head. "Nothing."

"Tell me. We agreed. No more secrets."

Amy inhaled and, evading the question, replied, "Celeste was beside me on the beach."

"What was she doing?"

"Nothing." Amy shrugged. "She was lying on the sand and I couldn't wake her. And then Maggie appeared." She shook her head in frustration. "It felt so real."

"What did Maggie want?"

Amy sipped her tea, then replied, "I don't know."

Sandra wrapped her fingers around the cup. "Yes, you do."

Amy drew in her breath. "She told me that the boys were safe."

"What else?"

"Sandra." Amy sighed in frustration. "It was a dream!"

Sandra sipped her tea. Raising her eyebrows, she said, "Humor me. What did she say about Celeste?"

Staring into her cup, Amy replied, "I'm not sure."

"Yes, you are."

Unsure of where this was going, Amy looked at Sandra.

"What do you think she was trying to tell you?"

"I don't know." Amy closed her eyes briefly. "I wish it hadn't happened. It sharpens everything. Makes me realize how much I miss them."

"I know."

"Why does it have to be so hard?"

"It's not that it's hard, Amy. It's painful." Sandra looked at Amy intently. "It's time," she added. "You're struggling because

Denial

you already know what to do. Otherwise, you wouldn't be in so much pain."

"It's almost unbearable sometimes," Amy said, letting Sandra in.

Sandra nodded. "What did she say about Celeste?"

Amy's mouth firmed and she shook her head.

Sandra looked at Amy for a long moment. "I married for all the wrong reasons, you know, Amy," she said. "He was fifteen years older than me." She looked into her cup. "He was ready to settle. But I was literally just out of the pram when we got together." She smiled wryly. "He liked his women young."

Amy looked surprised.

Pain showed on Sandra's face. She looked out the window.

Amy waited.

"I'd been brought up by my gran," Sandra said eventually. "She loved me to pieces but didn't have two pennies to rub together." Sandra closed her eyes. "When I was young, I wanted it all. I dreamed about having a big house, fancy car, luxury holidays, and the white picket fence. I wanted all of it. So, I made a promise to myself that I was going to get it, but I didn't know how." She opened her eyes and focused on Amy. "Until Stuart came along."

A shiver ran down Amy's spine. She had never seen Sandra's eyes so cold.

"Gran didn't want me to marry him. She knew the truth, you see. She knew I didn't love him and that it was the financial security I was after. She knew even before I did." Her eyes widened. "All I could see were gifts and treats, nothing else. I couldn't see past the money." She breathed in deeply. "And he was difficult, in all the ways that a selfish person can be difficult."

Intrigued, Amy sipped her tea.

"Everything that could go wrong, did!" Sandra's eyes glittered. "No matter what I did, it wasn't enough." She looked down. "And within a year, it was me that wasn't enough. He took lovers, and God, did he have an appetite for women." She shook her head in disbelief. "But I didn't leave, I stayed. Got used to the money you see." She looked at Amy. "And he knew it. He knew he had me. He knew he'd bought me. So, he did what he liked and I pretended not to see it."

Wide-eyed, Amy stared at Sandra, unable to reconcile the woman she was describing as her friend.

Sandra smiled and shrugged. "I was twenty-three and had just finished my nurse training when we married. You're optimistic at that age," she said, raising her eyebrows. "Your identity is still being defined. But by thirty," she frowned, "I felt as if I'd lived a lifetime."

Amy looked at Sandra, sympathy filling her eyes.

"That's why I travel, Amy. After I lost Mia," she said, "it helps me reconnect with what's important. My gran always wanted to travel. She worked hard all her life. Like all women did at that time. But she talked of traveling." Sandra's eyes darkened. "If her life hadn't been so dictated by the times she would have visited every place on the map." She smiled weakly. "But, in her time, it was unheard of. Then, a working-class girl couldn't contemplate more than a trip to the local beach." She shook her head. "Gran brought up six kids. Worked hard all her life, and in the end I thought she died with nothing to show for it."

Amy touched Sandra's arm and squeezed it.

Sandra shook her head. "Worked with nothing to show for it, what an idiot I was then." She half smiled. "It wasn't until I lost Mia and was sitting in a big, empty, old house, alone, that I saw what my life truly was. I was pretending." She rubbed her forehead. "I thought I had the perfect life. Lived in the right area, had the right friends, went on the right holidays. Even when my gran died, I didn't see it." She shook her head. "Only after Mia, did I realize that it was me who had nothing to show." She looked at Amy. "He owned everything, even me."

Sandra moved to the kitchen sink.

"Gran used to tell me that life was messy and that I wasn't to fall into the trap of trying to build a perfect world around me. But I ignored her," she said, washing her cup. "I can hear her words now, telling me to find perspective, get out there, find life. That the whole point of living is not to box yourself in with things that

Denial

don't matter or try to make too much sense of it. Just live it." She shook her head. "God, I miss her."

Sandra looked at Amy. "The reason I'm telling you this is that my gran didn't have choices, Amy." Her eyes widened. "We're lucky. We live in a time where our lives aren't dictated too much. We don't have to stay on the road with no interruptions, no deviations, no loose ends. We have the freedom to do things that we want to, change direction; live our lives as we choose." She frowned. "Do you understand?"

Amy nodded. "It's one revelation after another tonight."

"I know. But you get the gist?" she replied. "You have the choice."

"I get it," Amy said, biting her bottom lip.

Sandra dried her cup. "Getting out of my everyday life helps me get a better perspective because sometimes after a shift I'm so tired that I fall asleep the moment I sit down. And it's not unusual for me to wake up and still have my coat on." She looked at Amy. "It's an empty existence." She put her cup away. "I don't want that to be what my life's about, and I don't want that to be your life either."

Amy could sense the air changing. She folded her arms protectively.

Sandra breathed in deeply. "I'm thirty-eight years old, and since my marriage I've never met someone that I want to be with more than casually." She smiled. "In fact, that applies to my ex as well." She frowned. "I've never found someone I care enough about to want to know what they think of my opinions, my ideas, the way I look, my friends. I've never found someone who can get to the heart of me," she looked at Amy, "that consumes me, makes me unable to function properly without them."

Amy shivered. She could feel it coming. She could feel the shift, the cracks starting to appear around her.

Sandra watched Amy. She waited for a moment.

Amy could almost hear the question.

Sandra asked quietly, tenderly, "What does it feel like, Amy?"

Not wanting her world to shatter, Amy looked at Sandra. "Don't," she replied, her face paling.

"What does it feel like, Amy, to be madly, crazily in love?" Sandra asked. Face filled with compassion, she approached.

"I don't know," Amy whispered.

"Yes, you do," Sandra replied. "You're crazy about Celeste." She gently touched Amy's arms and whispered, "It's something that you'll have to come to terms with, because, the truth is, you will never outrun it."

Amy breathed in deeply.

"Tell me," Sandra said gently. "Tell me, Amy. I'm here for you." She looked at her. "Tell me what it feels like."

Amy bit her bottom lip. "I know you think this will help if I talk about it. But, I can't go there, Sandra."

"You can't outrun it, Amy."

Amy looked at her friend for a long time then replied, "Watch me."

†

Amy woke up. Surprised she looked around. She couldn't believe it. She was back on the beach. Right where she was before.

"Maggie?" Amy said feeling dazed.

Maggie replied anxiously, "Amy, listen to me, there's very little time. She needs you."

Confused, Amy frowned. She looked at her cousin.

Maggie's fingers dug into her arms. She spoke slowly and deliberately. "It's real, Amy. Believe me, it's very real." Maggie put pressure on Amy's arm and turned her around. She pointed toward the sand dunes.

Amy was surprised to see Celeste and the children walking toward the dunes. They were quickly gaining distance. She squinted her eyes; Celeste seemed to be fading in and out.

Maggie whispered into her ear, "You have to go to her."

Confused, Amy turned her head to look at Maggie, but Maggie shoved her.

Denial

Amy fell to her knees.

"Sorry," Maggie said, helping Amy up. "Too much oomph."

Maggie brushed Amy down then shoved her, gently this time. "Trust me, Amy." She looked past her and said with some urgency before pushing her again. "Trust your instinct."

"What's wrong?"

Maggie pushed Amy forward.

"Maggie, tell me."

"Go."

Amy looked up toward Celeste and concern rushed through her. She ran hesitantly forward, but kept glancing over her shoulder to Maggie.

Maggie waved her arms, frantic for her to hurry.

Amy started to jog, and although her cousin was soon a distance away, her voice rang out clearly, "Hurry."

A wave of panic washed over Amy and, not looking back, she broke into a full run and tried to catch up with Celeste and the children. She shouted for them to wait, but they were speeding up. As they sped up, she slowed down. With alarm, Amy realized that with each step she was sinking into the sand deeper and deeper and no matter how hard she shouted neither Celeste nor the children turned around. She tried to move faster, but her legs felt like leaden weights. With horror, she looked down and realized she was stuck and sinking fast.

†

Amy woke up. Blind panic shot through her. She bolted out of the bed and ran through her entire apartment. Throwing on every light, she searched. Eventually, she stopped and yelled in bewilderment, "What am I doing? There's nobody here."

Standing alone in her living room, Amy tried to catch her breath. Her knees buckling she dropped to the floor. Leaning forward on all fours she tried to calm herself, but couldn't. Instinctively, she got to her feet and reached for the phone. She called Celeste.

"Allo."

Surprised, Amy said, "Camille? Camille, it's Amy."
"Oh, Amy!"
"Camille, where is Celeste?" Amy asked urgently.
Camille sobbed. "Amy, there has been a terrible accident."

Chapter 54

In the final hour of her flight, in the cramped, confined toilet, Amy wiped her mouth. She had just thrown up. After the call with Camille, to her relief, Alex called within minutes to say he had booked her the first available flight out.

Amy rinsed her mouth then wiped it again. She leaned her head heavily against the mirror and thought about the accident that Celeste had been involved in while out swimming. The dream from earlier burned in her mind. It wasn't a dream, she finally reconciled as she lifted her head from the mirror. Somehow, it had been Maggie telling her to get to Celeste.

Amy pushed away the niggling of her internal voice telling her she might be too late. She closed her eyes and all she could see was the image of Celeste fading in and out. Unable to hold her fear in any longer, she whispered, "Please don't let it mean goodbye. If it really was you, Maggie, then I'm begging you, don't let me be too late."

Tears flowed freely. Wiping them away Amy thought how ironic life would be if Celeste were taken from her now. She thought about the what-ifs and wondered if she would have married Josh if Celeste had stayed. For the first time Amy faced the truth. Closing her eyes, she accepted that she wouldn't have married him. If Celeste had stayed she would have been unable to ignore the truth that she was deeply in love with her. She looked at her reflection and finally accepted that she would never outrun her love for Celeste.

Pressing her head to the mirror, Amy released a deep sob. The thought of losing Celeste unbearable she gulped in some air. She lifted her head when the door rattled. It was the air steward asking her to take a seat. The plane was due to land.

†

Spotting Colin just as he noticed her Amy hurried toward him. He looked drawn. She stopped in front of him. "How is she?"

Colin hugged her. "She's still in surgery."

Amy sank into him, relieved that he was here and that Celeste was still fighting.

Colin hugged her tight. "I'm so glad you're here, Amy. So glad you're here."

"Hurry, Colin," Amy whispered. "I need to be with her."

They made their way to his car.

Onboard the plane Amy had been allowed to make a few in-flight calls, but now Colin was giving her more details of Celeste's injuries. "Ultimately, she's seriously battered with several broken bones," he said, getting into the car.

Feeling increasingly uneasy, Amy bit her bottom lip pensively. "But they've been operating for hours?"

Colin glanced at Amy. "She's back in surgery," he said quietly. "There's internal bleeding."

Amy's head sank into the headrest. She knew how serious it was to stop internal bleeding. She uttered, her voice croaking, "What happened exactly?"

"I don't know much more than what I've already told you."

Amy looked at Colin. "Tell me everything again."

Colin sighed and nodded. "From what I understand, Celeste went out for a swim when she was hit." He smacked the steering wheel. "Those fucking Jet Skis!" he roared. "They are the curse of the coastline. You can't move without those fucking, noisy pollutants being forced down your throat. The number of people hit this year alone, is a record high."

Colin went off on a rant.

Not listening, the color drained from Amy's face as she visualized Celeste being hit. Closing her eyes she willed her to fight.

†

Denial

When they arrived at the hospital Camille was the first to spot Amy. She ran toward her and took her in her arms.

"Amy! My darling. Thank God you are here," Camille said, hugging her hard.

Sophie and Alex followed. Wrapping their arms around her they hugged and welcomed her.

Breaking free, Amy asked, "How is she?"

Camille looked at Amy then stroked her face. "We do not know yet," she replied. "They are still operating." She smiled weakly. "But we know that she is fighting." Camille whispered, "And now you are here, she will fight even harder."

Amy smiled reassuringly and whispered, "I hope so, Camille. I hope so."

Hugging Camille, Amy made eye contact with Josh. He was standing with a small, dark-haired, very attractive woman. After a few moments, Amy moved away from Camille and approached him. During her last visit she had intended to see him, but her confrontation with Alex and Celeste meant that it didn't happen.

"Hello, Josh."

Josh eyed her cautiously. "Hello, Amy," he said, putting his arm around the woman next to him.

"Hi Amy, I'm Denise." The brunette smiled nervously as she held her hand out.

Amy looked at it. She took the hand then pulled a surprised Denise into her for a hug. "Hello, Denise," she replied. "It's really nice to meet you."

Amy heard a din behind her. She broke the embrace and turned to see her mother, followed by Bruce and Fraser carrying trays. Daniel, Naomi, and Amy's sisters were with Kate because there was no stopping her mother. She was determined to be here. Amy watched Irene commandeer the distribution of the coffee and sandwiches. She couldn't help a brief smile. Some things, she realized, just never changed. She turned to look at Josh and Denise and excusing herself, joined her mother.

☦

Amy looked at her watch for the umpteenth time. She had been here just over twenty minutes already, but it felt like an eternity.

Josh approached her. He cleared his throat and handed her a fresh cup of coffee. She took it and they stood for a while in awkward silence. Amy knew it was difficult for Josh. She had left him with so many questions. After the accident she had completely shut down on him, on life.

They spoke at the same time.

Amy smiled. "Please," she said, "what were you going to say?"

Josh cleared his throat again. "Mom told me you were coming," he said, creasing lines with his thumbnail in the cup he held. "She told me that you have been in contact with Celeste for quite a while. That you'd even come home." He looked at her intently. "Words seem inadequate right now, Amy, to describe how you showing up like this makes me feel."

Amy nodded. "I know."

"You know I kept in contact with Irene?"

Amy nodded.

"She let me know that you were okay. But, I..." Josh trailed off. Sounding deeply wounded and with more than a note of disbelief, he finished, "I can't believe that you've never contacted me." He shook his head. "Did you care at all, Amy?"

How could she explain? Amy looked at Josh, although he was trying to hide it she could see anger in the way his face was set. He looked so different. She realized that the fun-loving, jovial man she married was gone.

Waiting for an answer, Josh stared at her.

Amy knew that forming words to explain how he felt right now was too painful. She also knew he wanted to tell her that he was devastated when she ran out on him. That he was enraged that she could disregard him. Amy watched him struggle and knew that now that she was here and intending to stay, she would see that anger soon. She watched him litter his cup with lines.

"Yes, I cared."

Sounding confused Josh asked, "Why are you here?" He frowned and shook his head. "Why?"

Why am I here for Celeste and not you? Amy sighed inwardly. This was too difficult. They needed to seriously talk but here wasn't the right time for either of them.

Amy looked at him. "Josh, for now," she said, "would you accept that I'm sorry? I'm so sorry for running off the way I did. And for not being strong enough to be honest with you about what was happening to me." *Not honest enough to tell you about Celeste.*

Amy looked at Josh. *He's moved on. He's with someone else. He has two kids and however hard it's been he's gotten on with his life. He hasn't curled up and shut life out.* She realized then that she was exactly like her father. She had done the same as he did when her mother left; locked the world outside and kept grief and resentment on the boil.

Since working in a children's ward, Amy had been part of the process of helping parents come to terms with and cope with the adversities their child faced. The strength and resolve that many parents showed, and the will to fight regardless of the hardship and sometimes loss, was truly amazing. Amy needed to find that resolve. It was time she shouldered some of the responsibility. It was time for closure.

For the first time in years Amy felt the guilt lift a little. She looked over Josh's shoulder and straightened when she saw the physician approach them. Her heart began to pound.

He addressed them all. "The next forty-eight hours are critical." He held up his hand when Fraser moved forward. "And I can't give you any guarantees other than to say we are quietly optimistic."

Sophie came to Amy and put her arm around her.

Josh frowned deeply.

Something told Amy that Sophie knew. She looked at the smaller woman for a long moment then hugged her tightly, drawing strength from her.

Chapter 55

There was a big yellow sun in the early evening sky. Amy stood by the window in Celeste's hospital room, entranced. For a while she watched it before an involuntary shudder passed through her. She realized that its size and color was reminiscent of the sun in her dreams of Maggie. She turned when she heard a slight moan and moved quickly toward the bed.

Looking down at Celeste, Amy waited for a moment to make sure she was asleep before flexing her fingers and laying them gently on her chest. She smiled faintly, reassured by the strong rhythmic beat of Celeste's heart.

Even though Celeste had barely been conscious over the last few days, whenever she had a moment alone Amy would stand like this, desperately needing to reassure herself through physical contact that she was indeed going to pull through.

When Celeste stirred Amy removed her hand quickly, registering the loss of warmth.

"Amy," Celeste rasped in surprise when her eyes fluttered open.

"Hi," Amy replied. She reached for the jug of water at Celeste's bedside. "Would you like some?" she asked, trying to sound as normal as possible.

Celeste tried to nod.

Amy poured some water then placed a straw in the glass. She held it to Celeste's mouth. "Here."

Celeste managed a few sips. "Thanks," she replied, her eyes closing.

Aware of how much that small effort took Amy watched Celeste for a while.

"How long," Celeste asked weakly, opening her eyes. "How long have you been here?"

Denial

Grateful that she hadn't asked why she had come, Amy leaned in. "I got here as soon as I could," she replied. "You've barely been awake since the operation."

Amy watched Celeste's eyelids flutter shut. Over these last few days Celeste had only been vaguely aware of her surroundings.

Celeste's eyes opened and Amy was very grateful that Camille had ensured that no one would be visiting this evening.

The last few days had been extremely difficult, not only because of the seriousness of Celeste's injuries, but because Josh sought an explanation from Amy as soon as Celeste was out of danger. He wanted to know everything; where she had been all these years, and more importantly, why she had left.

Their meeting was hard. Josh pulled no punches, wanting to meet at the graveside where their sons were buried. Amy closed her eyes, remembering. It was no surprise that he had been difficult. What else could she expect? She had left the man at his lowest point. Did she really deserve anything less?

The visit to the graveside had been upsetting enough, but that day Amy could only describe Josh as hostile. He grilled her, wanting to know exactly why she was here and why the sudden interest in Celeste.

Before meeting Josh that day Amy decided that if he insisted she would tell him about Celeste. It was a risk, a dangerous one, but she knew Josh. He would push her until he got the answers he wanted. Instinctively, Amy knew that in order to give her and Celeste a chance she needed to put a stake in the ground. There was no room for deceit in their life any more, no matter what the fallout. She decided, if forced, she would say that they had met up recently and that their relationship had progressed into something more.

Josh pushed hard that day, question after question about why she disappeared. Wanting to know why she was here now. To say he reacted badly when she finally told him why she was here now would be an understatement. Josh wasn't a violent man, but sitting in the diner, she watched him battle for control.

The look of rage that crossed his face would stay with Amy forever. Every emotion showed as he stared at her for the longest time. Then, without a word, he scraped his chair back, stood and left. They hadn't spoken since.

Wanting the familiar contact she had a few moments ago, Amy reached out and gently laid a hand on top of Celeste's. She said with some relief, "I can't tell you how wonderful it is to know that you're going to be okay." A tremor ran through her hand. "I've been so worried. I—" Amy stopped when Celeste frowned. Remembering that she had agreed with Alex, to Colin's annoyance, that Celeste might not be strong enough to hear what she had to say, she finished softly. "I'm so glad you're going to get better." She tightened her grip slightly before letting go of Celeste's hand.

Amy smiled and, to stop from saying too much, clasped her hands together.

Celeste watched Amy.

After Amy arrived Colin had blocked all offers from Camille and Irene that she should stay with them, insisting she pitch up at their house with the children. Over the last few days he and Alex had squabbled incessantly about the situation. For some strange reason Amy drew comfort from their bickering. There was no doubt they loved Celeste deeply, and if anything, their debating brought out the practicalities of the situation.

Colin had decided that it would be best for Amy to move back to the States, back where she belonged. Alex would counter about the level of acceptance. Surely, the Cameron family wouldn't just roll over and welcome the new situation with open arms? And what about the fallout with Josh? But Colin would allow no obstacle in his way. Generally, after much dialogue and disagreement around the subject, the discussions would eventually settle on Celeste and Amy's future…*together*.

"Do you need anything?" Amy asked, shaking herself mentally.

Celeste shook her head.

"Do you remember what happened?"

Celeste closed her eyes briefly before focusing on Amy. "Only what I was told this morning."

Amy downplayed Celeste's injuries and tried to sound optimistic. "So you'll be pleased to know that you're missing a spleen and have a few broken bones."

Celeste smiled weakly.

"What a way to get my attention," Amy teased. "There were a few touch and go moments in the operating theater but five pints of blood and a splenectomy had you sorted."

Celeste raised an eyebrow and winced as she tried to move. "Tell that to my poor body."

Going into automatic mode Amy helped Celeste find a better position. "Being a nurse has its moments." Gently, she tucked dark strands of hair behind Celeste's ear and smiled. She added suggestively, "You get to help gorgeous damsels in distress."

Celeste looked at Amy in surprise, then said with a note of curiosity, "Is that so?" She watched through heavy lids as Amy's color heightened dramatically.

Amy caught her breath when Celeste's eyes absorbed her. Not able to hold back any longer, she whispered, "I love you."

Celeste looked at Amy. "I know," she replied tenderly.

Amy's heart almost broke open when Celeste whispered, "I've always known."

"Can you forgive me?"

Celeste looked at Amy, her hazel-green eyes clear of any troubled thoughts. "There is nothing to forgive."

Not surprised that there was no hurt ego to overcome with this woman, Amy bowed her head, aware that she should take a lesson from how quickly Celeste forgave.

"We need to talk, Amy," Celeste said, struggling to keep her eyes open. "But I can't seem to focus right now," she murmured as they closed.

Aware that Celeste was exhausted Amy reassured her, "We'll talk soon. Just go to sleep. I'll be here when you wake up."

Celeste opened her eyes quickly and, looking at Amy, asked, "Promise?"

Amy smiled indulgently. Reaching out, she took Celeste's hand and squeezed it gently. "I promise."

Celeste's eyelids drooped but like a stubborn child she fought them when they closed. "You promise you'll be here when I wake?" she asked.

"I promise, I'll always be here for you."

Epilogue

Eighteen Months later

Celeste frowned. It was her father's birthday today and they were attending his party. Daniel and Naomi had already left with Kate and her children. She yelled up the stairs. "Are you ready yet?"

No response.

Celeste easily bounded up stairs, smiling when she reached the top, pleased that all her recent hard work was paying off. Although her physician had released her several months after her accident, it had taken her until now to fully recover her physical fitness.

She opened the bedroom door and entered. Amy had changed out of her outfit and was standing in her underwear in front of the mirror gently rubbing her stomach.

Celeste's heart skipped a beat. She smiled and moved to stand behind Amy. Putting her arms around her, she pulled her close.

"No, I'm not ready!" Amy said. Her bottom lip trembled. "I can't find anything to wear because I'm massive!"

Lovingly, Celeste rubbed Amy's stomach. She looked at her in the mirror. "You're only five months pregnant. You're far from massive." She smiled at Amy's reflection and kissed the top of her head. She loved every minute of her partner's pregnancy.

Amy leaned into Celeste. She pointed to her clothes strewn about. "But can't you see? I am! I can't find anything to wear!" She lifted her eyebrows and looked at Celeste. Wanting attention, she pouted, and with the biggest blue-eyed expression she could muster said, "All my clothes are too wee!"

Smiling patiently, Celeste looked down at Amy, then at their reflection.

Amy looked at the mirror then put her hands over Celeste's, and together they rubbed her stomach.

Celeste sighed, enjoying the intimacy.

Amy tilted her head back so Celeste could kiss her.

Celeste gently pulled Amy's hair aside and kissed down her neck. Eager to feel the reassuring weight of her increasingly heavy breasts, she sneakily unclipped her bra.

"Hey," Amy protested. "I know exactly what you're up to." She tried to slap Celeste's hands away. "Not now," she said, laughing. "Celeste, we have to go. You have to help me find something to wear!"

Celeste turned Amy to face her and kissed her deeply.

Aware that it might be quite a while before they arrived at the barbecue, Amy closed her eyes and surrendered completely to Celeste.

†

No sooner had they arrived at Celeste's parents' than Camille was over patting Amy's stomach and commenting on how good she looked. Amy smiled at Camille but it was evident she was distracted. She gave Camille the briefest answers to her questions about the baby as she busily watched Fraser take food off the grill. As soon as he had finished she excused herself. "Time to feed the baby elephant," she said, patting her stomach. And before anyone could say anything, Amy made a beeline for the food.

Camille laughed and watched Amy pile food onto her plate. She looked at Celeste and asked, "Are you not feeding her enough, *chéri*?"

Celeste grinned and said with a note of astonishment, "Mom, she can hear a sweet wrapper rustle from four hundred yards. She even munches on the kids' leftovers after every evening meal." She didn't tell her mother that she was never hungrier than when they made love. "Do you know she asked me for a slice of pizza while she was having her bath this morning? It was just after nine!" Celeste elaborated, "And she hates pizza."

Denial

"So, she likes pizza now too, hmmm."

Celeste stiffened when Josh stood beside them. Although, she was beginning to tire of his innuendos she forced herself to bite back her comment. She knew how hard it was for him to come to terms with the fact that she and Amy were together. She could still hardly believe it herself. When she fully regained consciousness, which was almost a week after the accident, the first clear memory was of looking into Amy's blue eyes. She was stunned when Amy had wrapped her arms around her and for the longest time told her how much she loved and needed her in her life.

Celeste's eyes narrowed when Josh smirked, and for the first time she retaliated. "What are you trying to say, Josh, that she never used to like being with a woman either?"

Camille frowned anxiously at them, then quickly moved off toward the children, clearly intending to move them out of the way should the tension increase. Celeste understood that her mother was afraid of a confrontation but she was also aware that one was long overdue.

Josh grimaced as he looked at Amy. He eyed Celeste for a long moment before sneering and moving away.

Celeste watched him then released her breath slowly and wondered if it was just a matter of time before he blew? *Or is this it? Is this the way it's always going to be? Is this the way he wants it, so he can always carry his grievance card to play his hand whenever he decides?*

Celeste shook her head, aware that she genuinely didn't know if he would ever be able to move past this. Obviously, he had not taken the news that she and Amy were together well. He had refused, unless absolutely necessary, to have any contact with them. He only agreed to be in their company on specific occasions, such as today, to appease their parents. All other visits had to be well organized to ensure that there would be no accidental contact with either of them. Last week her mother told her, with some distress, that he was opening a new office in California and in all likelihood would relocate there.

Josh, she knew, was putting distance between them.

Celeste sipped her beer. She remembered how stunned she was when, a few days after she regained full consciousness, Amy had told her, as she sat on her hospital bed, that it was important to have closure. So, she told him that she and Celeste had recently gotten together, that they were in love and that she intended to have a relationship.

Lying on the hospital bed, Celeste could hardly believe what Amy was telling her. Holding her hand, Amy explained that she knew it was a decision they should have made together, but it felt right. And as she smoothed hair from Celeste's face she told her that their future had no room for deception.

Since Amy's announcement he had refused to speak to either of them. Celeste had desperately tried to speak to him, to explain. But he wouldn't listen. It was now at the stage where she didn't even try. He didn't want to know. She closed her eyes briefly, aware that no matter Josh's reaction and no matter how much it hurt, she couldn't deny that she was proud of Amy. Proud that she had made the decision to love her openly.

Celeste looked at her father. She had thought she would have a battle with him, but to her surprise he had accepted it. Accept was maybe too broad a term, she realized, and conceded that he was only as accepting as he was because of the hard work on Camille's part, and because he was genuinely happy to have Amy back home and safe. Fraser had always had a soft spot for Amy, and it wasn't too long after he found out about the fire she was involved in that she was able to wrap him around her finger.

Her biggest concern was that Josh's comments would affect Amy, but to her amazement nothing fazed her these days. If anything, Amy was the one reassuring her that he would come around one day. When she told Amy that she wasn't so sure he would, Amy told her gently, as she took her in her arms, that sometimes life had loose ends and that it's that very messy unresolvedness that makes it what it is; that life is a mystery to be lived, not a problem to be solved. And no matter what, they just had to keep trying.

Celeste wasn't easily won over by Amy's newfound dime-store philosophy, but she was grateful that she was so upbeat.

Aware that Amy and Sophie had been watching her interaction with Josh, Celeste smiled at them. She watched Sophie whisper something in Amy's ear.

Amy took a bite of chicken, nodded and gave Sophie a hug.

Celeste was about to join them when Denise joined her.

"Josh doesn't mean it, Celeste," she said, looking at her. "It's just hard for him. I think he can accept Amy moving on. It's just difficult that she's moved on and found happiness with you."

Celeste looked at Denise. She liked that she was such a straight talker. "Do you think he'll ever come around?"

Denise smiled. "Maybe," she said, rubbing her stomach. "Maybe I'll keep him so preoccupied with babies that he won't have time to think about anything else." She smiled broadly then whispered, "I'm pregnant."

Celeste hugged her and said quietly, "Congratulations."

After the barbecue and the gifts were opened Josh quickly organized for his family to leave. Celeste hated how uncomfortable these once routine family gatherings had become. She hated that Josh was so unhappy, but she accepted that for now that was how it was. She watched him pack the kids into the car. Denise hugged Camille and Fraser goodbye, Josh didn't. Celeste hoped he wouldn't hold a grudge against her parents for too long. She watched her brother drive away and, feeling tense, decided to take Colin up on his offer of a walk along the beach with the kids.

Alex waited for Amy to finish eating her cake before taking her hand and walking slowly with her along the beach. He looked at her. "I love the way that you are so carefree, so spontaneous, so much your old self, but so much is new."

Amy laughed. "I know."

Naomi came running toward them to show yet another seashell that she had found. Amy and Alex, in good humor, rolled their eyes at each other but gave her all the attention she wanted.

A few weeks ago, Colin had caught Naomi's imagination. He had built an elaborate world of mermaids who lived far, far away and could only be heard through seashells. Since then, Naomi had fallen in love with seashells and now had one permanently stuck to her ear, waiting patiently to hear the mermaids' call. Amy had left it up to Colin to explain when Naomi wondered why she couldn't just ring them on a cell phone. Now, waiting to hear the mermaids' call was a full-blown obsession and she and Celeste were struggling to get Naomi to stop listening even at bedtime.

Amy smiled when Naomi asked her not only to listen but also to kiss the seashell she had found. In exasperation, she bent down and pulled Naomi into her for a big hug. She looked at her. "Munchkin, why do you want me to kiss the seashells?"

Naomi looked back at her as if she only had one brain cell. "Because Uncle Colin said it's good luck."

Amused, but not wanting to kiss every seashell that Naomi came across, Amy replied, "Well, I think the best thing to do is ask Uncle Colin to kiss them himself because as you know Meme's having a baby and maybe your little sister wouldn't like it." Amy looked up at Alex in disapproval then looked at Naomi. She rubbed Naomi's nose with hers. "All the good luck I ever need I get from kissing you and Danny."

This seemed to make perfect sense to Naomi. Wriggling out of Amy's arms she ran ahead to Colin.

Amy straightened and looked at Alex. "You know your partner is a complete nutter, don't you? And this seashell thing is getting completely out of hand. She's obsessed." Amy looked at him sternly. "Colin needs to stop encouraging her before Celeste wrings his neck."

Alex laughed. He picked Amy up in his arms and twirled her around. "I'll speak to him," he said as he twirled her again. "You look stunning. More beautiful than ever. Pregnancy really suits you." He gently put her down and, touching her stomach, asked, "How's the baby?"

"She's got your appetite and damn fine you know it!"

"I know," Alex said, wide-eyed. "I'm amazed that you're so neat given the amount of food you've put into your mouth recently."

Denial

Amy laughed then shoved him. "Fortunately, she's the one getting bigger, not me. But if I end up delivering a baby rhino, you're in trouble, big guy."

They laughed then sobered when Celeste strode purposefully toward them, both understanding that Amy shouldn't really tease him as his role was strictly biological and "Uncle" status only. But, still, she liked to tease him anyway.

Grinning, Amy watched her partner approach. She remembered how surprised and delighted Celeste was, when a few months after her recovery, she first broached the subject of having a baby. Amy had laughed at her shocked face. "What?" she said. "You didn't think we would stop at two did you?"

Alex swallowed and whispered, "She looks like she means business." He hurriedly told her that he would take the children for a walk along the beach with Colin.

Nodding, Amy let go of him.

Alex went to the edge of the water and rallied the children and Colin.

With a worried frown, Celeste stopped in front of Amy and took her arm. "Naomi said the baby wasn't well."

"What?"

Celeste felt for Amy's pulse.

Enjoying the attention, Amy indulged her for a while, then laughed and tried to explain. "Look, Colin's been feeding Naomi's very fertile imagination with daft things like I need to kiss the seashells for good luck. All I said to her was that I couldn't kiss them because her wee sister might not like it."

Celeste looked annoyed. "I think it's time I had a word with Colin."

Amy smiled then teased, "Colin's in for it now, isn't he?"

Celeste nodded and continued to check Amy over before she was satisfied that everything was okay.

Amy looked around. The beach was deserted and Colin and the kids were walking ahead with Alex following behind. She sat down, laid back then looked up at Celeste. "Well. What are you waiting for? There's no one around."

Celeste's eyebrows rose at Amy's provocative play.

Impatiently Amy sat up, knowing that Celeste still found it hard to believe that she didn't mind being so openly in love. "Will you hurry up and kiss me, Celeste!" She raised a hand and warned, "Just don't touch my breasts," she said, lying back, "because if you do, you'll have to finish what you start."

She looked up at Celeste seductively.

Celeste growled playfully, then dropped to her knees. She lay down, pulled Amy on top of her and gently kissed her. Ignoring Amy's words of warning she reached for her breasts.

Amy growled.

Celeste quickly held up her hands. Laughing heartily she managed to say, "Okay, okay...let's trade."

Smiling, Amy cocked her head and looked at her inquiringly.

Celeste murmured, "If I can touch you," she pointed at Amy's breasts, "then I'll promise no more hijacking you whenever you're alone!"

Amy smiled sneakily. "That includes public places?"

"No way."

Amy nodded. "Yes way."

Celeste sighed. "Oh, c'mon honey, you're driving a hard bargain here!"

"And you're driving me up the wall. I don't know whether I'm coming or going. Whenever I'm outside I don't know when you're going to pounce." Amy raised her brow. "You're like Inspector whathisname with the karate-wielding sidekick..." Amy frowned, "whathisname. He was always ambushing his boss."

"Not for sex though." Celeste smirked. "That would make it a very different movie, wouldn't it?" She laughed and said in a ridiculous French accent, "Inspector Clouseau gets a big surprise when, ambushing him Cato prods him with some-zing more than his hands."

Amy laughed. Eyes twinkling, she kissed the tip of Celeste's nose. "What's your decision, gorgeous?"

"What the hell, let's throw in public places too," Celeste said, placing her hands on Amy's breasts.

Denial

†

Ahead, Colin was walking with the children.

Trailing behind them, Alex turned and looked back. He shaded his eyes. Enchanted, he watched and grinned when he heard Amy squeal in delight as they play tussled a little.

He thought back to that day when he had confronted her on the beach. He slowly exhaled. Thankfully, that was a lifetime ago and very much a part of their past. He raised his eyebrows when he saw them making out. Smiling, he turned and shouted to Colin to wait up.

About the Author

Jackie Kennedy

Jackie Kennedy lives in Scotland. She lives an ordinary life, doing ordinary things. Until she flips open her laptop...

Other Books from Affinity eBook Press

Till There Was You
S. Anne Gardner

Julia is a woman used to power and is not afraid to use it or impose her will to get her way. She appears to have the world but a part of her is empty and cold as a frozen tundra. Julia rides in the mornings to clear her head and to make plans for what she is about to set in motion.

Theodora, known as Teddy, is trying to put together a marriage filled with uncertainties. She felt once upon a time that she would have a great love but that has eluded her.

One morning these two women meet and from the first instance, it is explosive. The attraction is undeniable, the fears very real and the end without question will change them both forever.

*

Denial
Jackie Kennedy

Time spent in Somalia has Dr. Celeste Cameron accustomed to living and working in a war zone. Coming back home to America, she is glad to see the end of the danger or so she thinks.

Danger seems to follow Celeste and she finds danger in the shape of Amy, her twin brother's fiancée. What she feels for Amy scares her more than anything she has faced in war zones.

Amy has the same feelings, but is in denial and vows to marry Josh no matter what.

When fate brings them together again, will they give in to their mutual attraction or will they once again deny what they feel.

In Name Only
JM Dragon
Sequel to The Fix-it Girl

Can an agreement forged out of necessity actually work?

*

'55 Ford
Erin O'Reilly

Andrea McBride, the author of four books, wants to find someone to restore an old '55 Ford truck that she inherited in a real estate purchase. She will only settle for the best and finds RJ Whittaker who many proclaim to be the best restorer among millions.

*

An Affair of Love
S. Anne Gardner

From a dark past, a forbidden love, a secret comes. Among the confusion and the chaos of an unwanted reality, two women find something they neither want nor can deny.

*

Desert Heat
Dannie Marsden

For Luce Diamond, an undercover policewoman, her life is in shambles. Her longtime lover left her and an automobile accident that resulted in a child's death haunts her.

*

Taming the Wolff
Del Robertson

ONLY ONE WOMAN...
HAS THE POWER...
TO TAME THE WOLFF...

*
Private Dancer
TJ Vertigo

Reece Corbett grew up on the mean streets on New York City, abused, used and in trouble with the law.

Faith Ashford grew up wealthy, with all the creature comforts that money provides. When they meet fireworks begin.

*
Miriam and Esther
Sherry Barker

Miriam thought her life would play out in the bustling metropolis of Dallas, but after a life-changing accident, she moves to the small town of Cool Lake, Texas to get her head on straight and regain her senses.

*
McKee
A.C. Henley

Private Investigator Quinlan McKee has returned to Los Angeles after a three-year absence, only to find herself embroiled in a world of child slavery and police corruption.

*
Nocturnes
JD Glass

From acclaimed author, JD Glass, and featuring some of her most loved characters. Nocturnes is a collection of events and adventures, from the sensual dreamscape of the deepest love, to the brooding intensity of desire.

E-Books, Print, Free e-books

Visit our website for more publications available online.

www.affinityebooks.com

Published by Affinity E-Book Press NZ Ltd

Canterbury, New Zealand

Registered Company 2517228

Made in the USA
Middletown, DE
10 May 2018